Harvey Klinger, Inc.
Literary Representation
301 West 53rd St.
New York, N.Y. 10019
(212) 581-7068

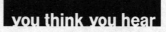

you think you hear

you think you hear

MATT O'KEEFE

thomas dunne books

st. martin's press ☙ new york

THOMAS DUNNE BOOKS.
An imprint of St. Martin's Press.

www.stmartins.com

Library of Congress Cataloging-in-Publication Data

O'Keefe, Matt.
    You think you hear / Matt O'Keefe.—1st ed.
        p. cm.
    ISBN 0-312-26903-X
    1. Popular music—Fiction. 2. Bands (Music)—
Fiction. 3. Musicians—Fiction. 4. Young men—
Fiction. I. Title.

    PS3565.K395 Y68 2001
    813'.6—dc21
                                            00-047527

First Edition: April 2001

10 9 8 7 6 5 4 3 2 1

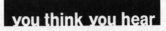
you think you hear

SOME FRIENDS OF MINE are in a pop band. When they first started out, their goal was to play a show at the Mutton and Hoover, a club that only booked hip local acts. At the time, their disdain for the Mutt's hipster quotient was balanced by their awe of it. When they finally took the stage, after six months of playing frat houses and a regular Sunday night gig at the philosophy dorm, it was with a great deal of nervousness and satisfaction.

Now they have one album, two singles, and three national tours behind them. All three national tours were conducted in a customized blue and white Ford Econoline van from the middle of the last decade. They were not the ones who customized the van. And the shows they played took place in dingy bars where the band often outnumbered the audience and received fifty dollars and a fistful of drink tickets for payment.

But they are about to make their fourth trip around the country, this time as the opening act for a famous band from England. The lights will be brighter, the stage broader, and the drinks bestowed not by the ticket but by the case. The crowds will consist of hundreds and even thousands of people, so many that my friends won't be able to remember a single face at the end of the night.

This is how it's going to be: Tim driving, Joey shotgun, Cree in the chair in the middle row, her legs draped up on the captain's table. From the back seat I will look nine feet forward to the windshield and then through it, and I will see America, parts familiar and unfamiliar, moving around me in a pattern that owes its logic to nothing more than the Rand McNally atlas in Joey's lap. I will arrive in a town and haul amp and cowbell, hawk record and T-shirt, and afterwards, I will drive while they sleep.

The Day Action Band is going on the road. I'm going with them. I'm the roadie, but I prefer you call me "Lou Farren, Tour Manager."

It is quarter past ten and Cree is not here yet. I have been waiting outside since nine-fifty, nudging my duffel bag back and forth along the pavement with my feet. Several times I have nudged the duffel bag in and out of the way of a group of truculent male college students carrying sofas into my apartment building. On their most recent pass one of these gentlemen nearly lost his footing, not because of anything I had done, and when he glared at me, I thought back at him, "Fuck you, I am about to have an *adventure.*"

We are traveling today from Newark, Delaware, to Boston, Massachusetts, site of the tour's first show and also the town of my birth. Cree is picking me up first, Joey next, and Tim last. Tim lives the farthest north but also the farthest from the freeway; I would have designed the pickup differently, but it's my first day as tour manager and I don't have the authority to make those kinds of decisions yet.

The van rumbles into view and then out of it, stopping on the other side of the undergraduate moving truck. As I bring my bags around, the van's sliding door opens from the inside and suddenly there she is. Her hair is short, black with reddish highlights, and comes to rest just above the light brown skin of her neck. She wears an untucked tan shirt with a pattern of intersecting squares and tight dark pants that flare at the ankle. Her toes poke out of a pair of thick-soled sandals, in pitiful rebellion against the coming cold. She says my name and leans down to give me a hug. When she puts her arms around my neck and presses her face against mine, I remember exactly why I have been looking forward to this trip for so long.

The van is packed already, the narrow trunk space piled high with drums and large cardboard boxes. The Day Action Band had a final preparatory practice two nights ago; they must have packed it then. I stuff my bags under the middle seat and take my place next to Cree in front. I have never been able to talk to her very easily, so on the short drive to Joey's I reach for the neutral topic of my job. I quit it yesterday. It was a dull position involving computers, alumni recordkeeping, and the elaborate ways in which I deceived my superiors into thinking I was a productive employee.

"Yeah, but you'll work there when you get back," Cree says.

"No," I say. "I told them they would never see me on the premises again." Her eyes widen, and I add, "Well, I left a note to that effect."

"Then what are you going to do?" she says.

"I haven't thought about it," I say. "I don't want to think about it."

This is a more emotional response than she was expecting, and I feel a little sorry to have given it. Nervous now, she starts chattering about their roadies from past tours. I've met all three at one time or another; like me, they are friends who were judged capable of interacting with the band in closed spaces for a long period of time. Two worked out well. The third, a woman primarily friends with Joey, caused such pervasive tension that actual physical barriers made from towels were erected inside the van.

"We don't really talk about her anymore," Cree says.

"After me," I say, "you won't be talking about any of them anymore."

"Is that right?" she says, laughing.

"That is right," I say. "You will refer to me as 'The Roadi-nator,' or perhaps, 'Lord Roadinator.' "

Cree laughs harder and reaches out to touch my arm. Only five minutes into this trip and I have already had one of my all-time great conversations with her.

When she has composed herself she sets about putting the roadies in the context of how my experience is going to differ from theirs. On this tour all the shows will be over by eleven. No lingering in dirty, smoky clubs until two-thirty in the morning and then not getting to sleep until four. In fact, no dirty, smoky clubs period. Every venue on this tour has a capacity of at least seven hundred; the largest, Wonderland in L.A., can accommo-date close to twenty-five hundred.

"All I can say is," Cree says, steering the van into Joey's drive-way, "it's about time."

Joey lives in the same house he lived in when he was a stu-dent, a two-story building a few blocks from the University of Delaware campus. His roommates are the same too; it has been surmised that they won't move out until he does. The members of the Day Action Band are local celebrities; living with one of them provides a certain notoriety and seems to be considered as good a post-collegiate occupation as anything else.

I am reaching for the latch on the screen door when Joey pushes it open from the inside. "Lou," he says. "Lou Farren." We shake hands. He and I are not great friends, but we have a routine in which we conduct our meetings with great formality.

"It's good to see you, Joey," I say, looking him in the eye. I have to tilt my chin upward to do this, as he is six feet, three inches tall. This total does not count the four-inch tufted mound of yellow curls that springs from his strangely angled head. If someone recognizes the band in public, it is usually because they have seen Joey. Since the onset of this minor fame, he has worked to accentuate his natural characteristics: the hair teased to its maximum dimension, the clothes selected to elongate and ganglify. In his acceptance of himself as a hopeless visual misfit, he has acquired a kind of crooked splendor.

"I've got some more stuff in my room," Joey says. "You can wait in the kitchen if you want."

I step inside as he disappears up a staircase to the left. One wall of the living room is dominated by a large poster of an orange car with the numerals "01" decalled on the side—the General Lee from *The Dukes of Hazzard,* caught in mid-air, Savannah dust flying. On the other wall someone has spray-painted the lines, "There's a monster in my pants / And it does a naughty dance." I hear a guitar skronking and some cymbals whishing beneath the floor, and then I reach the kitchen where two of Joey's roommates, Levin and Holmes, sit at a faintly listing table, a tall blue water pipe made of glass between them.

We've met before; they can't remember my name, but they're perfectly friendly. I sit down at the table with them to wait. Normally I'd feel compelled to take part in the conversation, but these guys are so stoned they accept my silence as merely a more subtle means of social interaction. They both work nights at Mendenhall Inn parking cars, as does the third roommate, Mitchell, who presumably is the one making the noise in the basement. Joey used to work there too, but quit a few months ago when Tim said he needed him full-time for recording. The result of this is that no one in the house has a day job and that this scene I've walked in on could probably be duplicated any day of the week. "Pardon my rudeness," Holmes says abruptly, turning from Levin and extending a book of matches. "Can I interest you in smoking some pot?" An image of Cree sitting impatiently in the van flashes through my brain, and I tell him no. I rest my arms on the table, comfortable with my decision. Holmes and Levin resume their discussion, a debate about the restrooms at Mendenhall and which one offers the finest environment in which to take a dump.

Joey walks in, holding a folder and a Magic Marker. He directs a nod to the table, a gesture that somehow acknowledges me at the same time that it expresses disgust with his roommates. I have an impulse to stand up and move away from them, but it fades before I can act on it. Stepping deliberately, Joey opens the refrigerator door and takes out a gallon of milk and a carton of orange juice. He uncaps the Magic Marker and writes a large "J" on the side of each. Then he replaces them in the refrigerator. The milk will have long since expired by the time he returns; this must be some kind of intrahouse power play.

"I thought you guys were going to rock," Joey says.

"Mitchell and some dude are down there," Levin says. He points to the floor, where the percussion and guitar noises persist.

"It sounds like that dude plays drums," Joey says. "Don't you guys need someone to play drums?"

"I don't like the way he plays," Holmes says. "He just sits on that high-hat. He doesn't groove."

"He sounds pretty good to me," Joey says. He motions to me. "Are you ready?"

"I am ready," I say.

Joey turns to Levin and Holmes and says, "Well, I'm leaving now. I'll see you in a few weeks. Don't forget to pay the phone bill if it comes while I'm gone."

"No problem, dude," Levin says.

"Have a nice time," says Holmes. They both behave as if they expect to see him later this evening. Joey snorts and then he and I head out of the kitchen.

As we walk outside Joey tells me that Levin and Holmes have been talking incessantly about starting a band.

"All day, it's 'I wanna rock, I wanna rock,' " he says. "Do they write songs? Do they practice?" He scratches hard at a place on the back of his head. "They've never even recorded their own voices."

Joey and Cree greet without much fanfare; the band has been rehearsing a lot lately and there is nothing special about this reunion. Once we are on the road to Tim's, Cree starts talking again about the particulars of this tour.

"It'll be so nice to get to bed at a reasonable hour," she says.

"I see your point." Joey says. "But really, we should be most grateful for the rider."

"I forgot about the rider!" Cree says. "Shit!"

"Shit is right," Joey says. "We're opening for rock stars now."

"Yeah, man," Cree says. "Fuck! What did we ask for?"

"What's a rider?" I say quickly. If I'm going to do this job right, I'm going to have to speak the language.

"Ah," Joey says. He reaches to get the wallet out of his back pocket. It's a difficult maneuver for someone of his height seat-belted in a moving automobile, but what's in there must be important. He gets the wallet, opens it, and pulls out a crumpled piece of paper.

"We make a list of the things we want," he says, "and then someone from the club goes out and gets them for us. Here's our list: water, Coke, beer, sandwich meats and fixins', bread, candy, mixed nuts, fruit, a regional delicacy, vodka, bourbon, cigars, and two live monkeys."

He repeats "two live monkeys" because I didn't laugh the first time.

"Vodka, bourbon, and cigars?" I say.

"We want a reputation as a hard-drinkin', hard-smokin' band," Joey says. "We want people to say, 'Look out, folks, the Day Action Band's in town. Lock up your daughters and your silverware.' "

While Cree drives us into the country north and west of Wilmington, Joey roams around the back of the van, organizing all the equipment and personal belongings, talking about what he's doing as he does it. "The goal is for four people to fit comfortably," he says. "I will use any and all necessary means to accomplish this."

"Make sure the back row is clear," Cree says. "In case I want to take a nap."

"I'm not sure that's going to be possible," Joey says.

"You do what you have to do," Cree says. "I'll understand."

The truth is there is quite a bit of space. Cree's drum kit is minimalist: snare, floor tom, bass drum, high-hat, and crash cymbal. It fits in the back of the van easily, leaving enough room for Joey's bass amp, two large boxes of T-shirts—"the merch," Joey keeps calling it—and then softer items such as pillows and sleeping bags that can be stuffed into nonlinear spaces. The bass and Tim's two guitars fit partially under the back seat, and Tim's small amp sits against the wall on the right side of the van, just behind the side door.

By the time we reach the long and winding driveway that leads up to Tim's, Joey has stowed everything but Cree's enormous red duffel bag. "I'm going to let you decide what to do with this," he tells her.

Tim lives in an old barn that was refurbished by a member of the duPont family in the late 1960s. Bay windows burst through the old slats of wood, providing vista upon vista for him to contemplate as he works out the details of his art. The three of us trudge up his steep lawn, swishing through dry leaves and tiny cracking sticks. We reach the porch and ring the bell. A noisy cat meows inside, but no one comes to the door. Finally, Joey gives it a little push and it opens.

The main room of the barn is fifty feet long, thirty feet wide, and has a ceiling twenty feet at its highest. This summer, when the Day Action Band was recording its second album here, this place was a musical wonderland: drums, guitars, amplifiers, keyboards, tables heaped with percussion, dividers used to isolate sound, microphones dangling like vines from the rafters. Tim has since put away these implements, in an effort, perhaps, to restore an aura of domesticity to his home. Somehow from this one room he has created the sensation of several rooms, each with its own specific function and feel. I find myself gravitating toward what must be the "listening zone," an arrangement of soft couches and chairs angled toward the stereo system, the whole area bathed in a dark red light. I take a step back, knowing our time here is short. The walls are decorated with giant posters of Tim's idols, Brian Wilson, Sly Stone, Lindsey Buckingham, and Prince. Since my last visit he seems to have derived a motto from their teachings and practices; it is painted in tall white letters on a board high above the fireplace: REMEMBER, IT'S NOT JUST A SONG, IT'S AN EVENT.

The sound of Tim hanging up the phone comes into the room, and then so does Tim. He is an average-looking human being, brown hair, brown eyes, medium height. He wears his standard white T-shirt and blue jeans, which he prefers to the more current rock and roll garb favored by his bandmates. I have wondered if he affects this blandness to offset the attractive force of his personality. He seems at most times to want to blunt his charisma, only letting it act unfettered at distinct moments: onstage, in certain one-on-one situations.

"Howdy," Tim says. He sets a piece of paper down on the counter beside him. From where I stand, I can make out the heading CAT INSTRUCTIONS.

"What's happening," Joey says.

"Yo," Cree says. I nod and lift my hand slightly in greeting.

"Everybody ready?" Tim says. I can tell he's excited. He adjusts the cat paper so it's even with the counter's edge.

"I think so," I say.

"Woo woo woo," Joey says. The closest to the door, he reaches down and grabs Tim's duffel bag. We stumble down the lawn, the bag bouncing against Joey's hip. There are no trees by the van so we get a rare glimpse of the glare coming off the downtown Wilmington skyscrapers, over ten miles away. Joey says that for a city of only seventy thousand people, it has an impressive skyline.

"We're going to make that skyline famous," Tim says.

"I think your mother already has!" Joey says.

"You fucker," Tim says. He moves as if to punch Joey and Joey, stepping back, trips over a root, landing on the seat of his pants. Cree doubles over laughing, her arms wrapped around her sides. For a second Joey just sits there, knees bent, looking up at us. He doesn't seem nearly as tall from this angle. Tim and I reach down to help him up while Cree continues to laugh. Soon the three of us are standing around, waiting for her to finish.

"I'm sorry," she says finally. "But that was really funny."

Tim smiles. He looks back once at his barn and then gives the hood of the van a good strong tap. "Okay," he says. "Let's tour."

Just past the Connecticut border, Cree pulls over to switch drivers. There's no discussion beforehand; she just pulls over and says, "Who's next?" I volunteer, and everyone executes a perfect clockwise rotation: Cree to the passenger seat, Joey into the middle row, Tim to the back. After I've been driving for a few minutes I notice Cree fiddling with what looks like some tinfoil in her backpack.

"What do you have there?" I say.

She takes out a bulky plate covered with foil. She holds the plate at eye level, lifts up the foil, and peers inside. Then she turns it so I can see it. It's full of Rice Krispies squares.

"Ah," I say. "You've been holding out on us. May I please have one?"

"If I let you have one, then I would have to share with everybody."

"Why can't you do that?" I say.

"Because these are for the Radials," she says. "I want them to know what a real American dessert tastes like."

"That's very hospitable of you," I say. I feel mildly irritated that she didn't make a few extra treats for Tim, Joey, and me, but I have to admire her design. This gesture could have a nice humanizing effect. Since the tour was arranged, everyone, Tim included, has been conspicuously not mentioning the possibility of intimidation. Whether this is bravado, a conscious effort not to be starstruck, or the true absence of any feeling on the matter whatsoever, I can't determine. But these treats, they could go a long way toward putting the two bands on a more even footing.

The Radials, though they play arenas in Europe, are not yet famous on this continent. A few years ago they were involved in a highly publicized battle with another of Britain's leading bands. The battle was over who was going to be Number One in England. The title is more than just a mantelpiece. The Number One Band in England becomes a sort of national commodity. If the band is anywhere from a trio to a five-piece, comparisons are made with the Beatles. In a trio, one member might be expanded to stand for both John and Paul. In a five-piece, two members might be compressed into George. The Radials are a four-piece, so during the time of this great rivalry, the British press was ready and eager to capitalize on the one-to-one relationship. Singer Brant Adman had "the poignant voice and doe-eyes of a young McCartney." "Pensive" songwriter and guitarist Peter Wren was "an iconoclast in the best spirit of John Lennon." And so on. But these comparisons never transcended their origins in the media, because the Radials lost the battle. For a band to become the Number One Band in England, they must first make it in the States.

That's not to say the Radials don't have a following here. I've seen them. They're Anglophiles, from what I can tell, and they dress mainly in black, not because it's morbid, but because it's chic. They seem to disdain the current trends in popular music and American bands in general. There are hints of androgyny and bisexuality floating around their camp. They may be upper middle class. As I said, I've only seen these fans. No one I know likes the Radials, but no one I know dislikes them either.

The Day Action Band has been making a concerted effort to turn this nullity into a positive. One of Tim's first acts upon learning that they were going to be opening for the Radials was to get permission from Joey to use band money to buy all of their albums. Joey not only approved this spending but also devoted several afternoons to researching the history of the band on the Internet; he discovered that Brant was an outstanding cricketeer in the English version of high school and that Peter has a second cousin in the House of Lords.

Cree may be most excited about the circumstances of this tour. A year ago, during a family trip to India, she was holed up in a room somewhere, watching Indian television, when a Radials video came on. The video was full of prominent close-ups of Brant, smiling and pouting, and Cree came back to America raving about this new "cutie." Even I remember her talking about it. "What was a British band doing on Indian TV?" I asked stupidly, as if I did not believe her story. "Were there subtitles?"

She became maternal. "Lou, Lou," she said, patting me on the arm, before subjecting me to a lengthy lecture involving imperialism, Rudyard Kipling, and several generations of Gandhis. "I forgot about that stuff," I kept trying to say, but the lecture persisted.

Lately Cree has been recollecting those halcyon days—"I told you he was a cutie, I told you"—with the addendum of "I hope he's as cute in real life. I bet he is."

Tim has told me he supports this affection for Brant. Although the Radials' singer is probably unattainable, it will be good for Cree to have a diversion during those long drives where boredom and tension often wage war over the human spirit. It will be good for us because she'll be on her best behavior, knowing that tantrums and bad moods are not likely to win over an older and more worldly gentleman. One thing Tim hasn't mentioned is that as a former boyfriend who left her heartbroken, he has some interest in seeing proof that her romantic faculties still exist. But I know what kind of person he is and I know that that has to be a reason too.

———

We come into the Boston area at five o'clock, but there's not much traffic going into the city. Cree, looking at the gridlock on the other side of the road, says, "I'm glad we're not going that way." Our orders are to proceed directly to the Hyatt Regency on Memorial Drive, where Colin More, the Day Action Band's manager, has set up a mini headquarters for the band. Colin is an Englishman in Los Angeles; his company, appropriately, is known as London West. He is already the manager of two soft rock groups, both with female lead singers, both with album sales in the millions. He drives a Saab with windshield wipers on its headlights.

Colin first heard the Day Action Band when his fifteen-year-old nephew gave him a copy of their first album, *That One Five Jive,* for his fortieth birthday. He didn't see any management listed in the CD jacket, so he called Sunday Driver, their record label, and spoke to Will Renshaw, label president and a former high school classmate of Tim's. He asked who was booking the band's gigs. "They are," Will said, and so Colin's next call was to Tim.

"I don't know names," he told Tim, making his pitch. "I know people."

Tim was too polite to ask him to clarify this statement but says he got this gist from it: I am skeptical of trends, I am unimpressed by fame, and I am in this business for the long haul. Also important, he was willing to work for free until the band was comfortably able to pay him his 20 percent of the gross.

Joey says that Colin is staying in a suite that costs five hundred dollars a night and contains a hot tub. We've been invited to sleep on the many couches in the living room. I tell Joey my parents are expecting me. He looks confused and then says, "That's right—you're from here."

I have memories of the Hyatt Regency. I took my junior prom date to the revolving restaurant at the top of the hotel. She was on the math team and calculated that we were rotating at a speed of five feet per minute. The view of downtown lasted twenty minutes, and the view of the bar, the dessert table, and the hallway that led down to the bathrooms lasted fifteen. The rest was just East Cambridge.

Greeting us at the door to his suite, Colin appears recently showered. His very short gray-white hair is still damp, and his shirt is tucked into his pants, but he hasn't got his belt on yet. He hugs Cree, shakes hands with Tim and Joey, and says, "Well, you must be Mr. Farren. They've spoken quite a lot about you."

"Good to meet you," I say.

"So, you're going to be traveling with the band." Then he actually says, "Jolly good show. I wish I were going with you."

"I'm looking forward to it," I say.

"Yes," he says.

He leads us around on a quick tour of the suite. There's a big TV, a kitchen, a porch looking out onto the atrium of the hotel, and giant windows with the same view of downtown that I remember from the restaurant. "We'd better be going," he says. "Soundcheck's at six-thirty."

Instinct directs Joey, Cree, and me to the back of the van, even though we reach the vehicle first and have the option to sit anywhere. Tim drives, and Colin sits next to him, and almost immediately, they turn on the radio, the modern rock station, and begin discussing what they hear. And in Tim's offhand questions—"What do you think of this one?"—and Colin's scripted responses—"A bit dodgy, isn't it?"—the implication is clear: that the Day Action Band will shake these foundations until the glass falls out of the windows, and after the glass, the computers that tabulate the Soundscans and tally the playlists, and after the computers, finally, the suits themselves, drab and same-faced, their ties flapping upward toward the escaping morning sun.

At the club Joey hops out, runs inside, and then returns. "We unload through those doors," he says, pointing. I grab a box of T-shirts and follow Cree, who is carrying the snare. A short, fat man comes charging up. "Couldn't wait for me, could you?" he says.

He goes past us. Colin, who is not carrying anything, shakes his head. We form a small pile of equipment next to the stage near a larger pile that clearly belongs to the Radials. Several men are shifting pieces of gear around on the stage; at this moment I remember that the headlining band always soundchecks first.

The fat man reappears. "As soon as they're done, get your stuff up there. Doors are at seven," he says.

"I've got some T-shirts," I say to him. "Who do I see about that?"

He says a woman's name that I don't quite catch. "She's not here yet, but I'll let you know when she gets here." The thought of this woman seems to make him feel better.

Tim and Joey come in with the bass amp. It can be carried by one strong person, but they're not taking any chances. They set the amp down, and Colin says, "I'd like to make some introductions. Come this way."

"Ooh, hold on," Cree says. "I have to get something." Joey gives Tim a look that is supposed to indicate impatience, but Tim doesn't return it. A minute later Cree walks up smiling with the plate of treats. She has removed the foil. "Okay, I'm ready now," she says.

"These look wonderful," Colin says. "May I?"

She extends the plate, and Colin takes one. "Delicious," he says. "Sweet and chewy."

We go down a corridor behind the stage. Initially I am right behind Colin, but I allow the other three to slip past me. At the end there are two rooms; the one on the left is small, and I can see the word SUPPORT written on a white piece of paper taped to the open door. Inside is a garish purple couch and a table with a sandwich spread and some sliced vegetables on it. Over the table is a wide mirror on which someone has played several games of tic tac toe in permanent ink.

The other room is much larger and noisy with people. Colin strides confidently into their midst as the band and I stay back near the door. Suddenly all the attention in the room is focused on us. It's not bawdy British pub attention, however, it's respectful royal family reserve. I regret that I never learned to curtsy. I am introduced to what seems like two dozen people, all of whose names I forget immediately, except for those I already know from magazines and MTV.

Brant has the face of someone who has spent his life thinking wistful thoughts. With brown doe eyes and tousled, sandy hair, his appeal is obvious. He has no doubt looked like this since he was six years old. Peter is skinnier and darker and edgy in a way that makes it seem as though he's about to smoke a cigarette. Gemma, the female bass player, has a pretty, round face and long brown hair parted in the middle. I imagine her at a party after a few drinks, playfully suggesting a game of strip poker that she knows no one will actually take her up on. Walter, the drummer, is painfully nondescript, except for his head of short black hair that he probably had spiked for this occasion.

Cree makes the interesting tactical decision of handing the treats over to Gemma. Looking at the plate, the bass player smiles, nods politely, points at her throat and says she'll have one after the show. Cree says, "Of course, of course, that's great, you try them later," and I can tell she feels hurt but isn't sure exactly why. For a moment she is alone at the center of the room, looking hard for someone she hasn't met yet.

I'd like to escape before these introductions turn into conversations, but it may be too late. Brant and Peter have converged on Joey, who seems only to be able to smile in return. Walter is shaking his head with too much force at something Tim has said. I've actually turned my back on the room, when I feel a hand on my shoulder. "Are you the tour manager?" a high-pitched but male voice says, compressing seven syllables into the space normally occupied by three or four. I face the man, hand extended, as if I hadn't been about to commit an act of antisocial behavior. "Yes I am," I say.

"You and I are going to be fighting then," he says, and laughs nervously. "I'm the Radials' tour manager."

I know the situation calls for a laugh, but I can't produce one. A winning smile will have to do.

"My name's Edward," he says, and I tell him mine. He is tall and thin with a long neck and a large Adam's apple. He wears wire-rimmed glasses and a leather jacket with a Motorhead patch on one of the breasts. None of it seems to go together.

"I'll have to see you about a photograph," he says.

"Photograph?"

"For your security pass. So the clubs will know you're working with us. I'll let you know when I'm ready." He says this and bobs away, to nowhere in particular. I duck out myself, ready to blame my unattended T-shirts, but no one tries to stop me. Loud laughing noise follows me as I walk off down the hall. Aside from Gemma's lack of interest in the Krispies, this initial meeting with the rock stars seems to have gone quite well.

The first thing I notice during the soundcheck is the size of the stage. Tim and Joey have to stand at least fifteen feet away from Cree and close to thirty feet away from each other. Tim won't be coming over to sing in Joey's mic tonight.

"Kick drum, hit your kick drum," calls out the soundman, and Cree responds with a steady *whack-whack-whack*. As she hits adjustments are made: the low end is removed and gradually replaced with an open-ended *smack* that seems to have its origin somewhere in deep space. Colin emerges from behind the stage and comes over to stand next to me with his arms crossed.

"The soundman is a big fan of reverb," I say.

"I think they're going to sound great in this room," Colin says.

"I'd like to hear what he does with the vocals," I say. "We don't necessarily want this to be the 'Magical Mystery Tour.' "

"No, we don't," Colin says, although clearly he has no idea what I'm talking about.

I have some experience with sound myself, having worked a handful of open mic nights and blues jams at the Mutt back in Newark. Originally there was talk of my doing the band's sound on this tour, but Tim and Colin decided that, given the high profile of the Radials and the variety of sound equipment we were likely to come across, it might be better to go with the house professionals.

"We're doing it this way for technical reasons," Tim told me. "But I trust your ears. If you hear a problem, you've got to let the guy know. Just make sure you've introduced yourself, so he doesn't think you're cutting in on his turf."

My only concern is over what level of vigilance to maintain. I did the sound for one Day Action Band show at the Mutt. Afterwards, I came up and apologized to them and many of our mutual friends. The most common reaction was: "What are you talking about? It sounded pretty good to me." The best option therefore might be to intervene only in the case of overt incompetence—a nonexistent guitar, a domineering cymbal, a tooghostly harmony section.

The fat man shows up again and directs me over to the bar, where a woman in her mid-thirties wears a tight blue dress and turns the liquor bottles so their labels face outward. "You can set up at the table down there," she says, pointing to one end of the long room. "Right between the men's and women's bathrooms." She grins. "A lot of traffic over there."

I thank her and move toward the merch boxes, which are still sitting next to the stage.

"Wait!" she says. "We take fifteen percent of the gross. Get set up, and I'll be over to count you in."

I look around for Joey, but, of course, he's up on stage. Colin wouldn't know. Is this 15 percent negotiable? Are they trying to con me because I've never done this before? What does it mean to be "counted in"?

I carry the boxes over, find the duct tape inside one of them, and commence hanging. The wall between the bathrooms is covered with used pieces of tape and the torn edges of flyers and posters, so I spend the first couple of minutes just standing on a chair and clearing some space. After that, aesthetic issues come to the fore. The shirt that promotes the new album must hang the highest, but not so high that people have to strain their necks to look at it. I decide on a peak height of about nine feet. The shirt is a handsome dark green and says THE DAY ACTION BAND in bold white lettering across the top. Underneath is a white image of the three band members, standing together and pointing at an imaginary but vast audience. And underneath that is the title of the new album, in the same bold white lettering as the band name: YOU THINK YOU HEAR. I move back from the wall and admire the shirt and the way it hangs, collar high, sleeves outstretched, wrinkles nonexistent. The other two shirts, cheap, white and light blue, designed and manufactured by the band themselves, will hang slightly lower and to either side.

On the backs of notecards I write the price of each shirt and the sizes that are available. Twelve dollars for the new shirt, seven dollars for the old ones. I also have a box of *That One Five Jive* CDs—ten dollars each—and "Wrestling" and "Lottery" seven-inches, which will be sold for three dollars, unless no one is buying them, in which case the price will be lowered to two. Fortunately for me, the tour will be over by the time *You Think You Hear* comes out. I would be worried about keeping track of all these different products, but Joey has designed a spreadsheet with multiple columns for inventory, gross, profit, and a few mystery items whose names have been abbreviated.

"Are you ready, honey?" the woman in the blue dress says. She is standing over me, her hands at her waist, inadvertently pulling the dress to its maximum tightness.

"I'm ready," I say. I step back from the merchandise and gesture as if presenting it to her. She peers at the assortment of stuff. "Oh Jesus," she says. Frowning, she removes every single

wadded-up T-shirt from both boxes and starts folding them, forming neat piles according to size and style. Then she counts them.
"I suggest you try to keep these in order," she says. "It'll be easier
on the next person that has to do it." She tells me she'll be back
at the end of the night to count me out, thus deducing how much
of each item I sold.

"You've probably had some bad luck with the honor system,"
I say, but I don't get a response.

The soundcheck ends with a full-length performance of
"Back in the Eighties," one of the standouts from the new album.
I think the song has a real chance to be a hit. It's the closest thing
Tim has ever written to an anthem, and the concept of young
love is close at hand. There's the opening staccato guitar riff, the
four dropped-in bass notes, and then the towering tom and snare
combination. I have never been so aware of how much actual
sound comes out of those huge stacks that flank the stage. The
band is enormous. It is hard to believe that this is the work of
only three people.

They are still breaking down the equipment when the doors
open. A large cluster of youth forms immediately at the front of
the stage. Some of the younger ones break off and drift up to my
table. When they see I don't have any Radials merchandise, they
depart with distracted looks on their faces.

"Looking good," Cree says. All three band members stand before me. Tim nods, but Joey has his hand on his chin.

"Maybe the shirts should be a little taller," he says. "People
should be able to see them over the crowd." I get back up on the
chair and move the shirts up six inches. Any higher, and Joey's
going to have to do it himself. I do ask him to hand me some
fresh duct tape strips, to replace the ones that come up covered
with hair and paint.

"We're going to have a quick meeting with Colin," Tim says.
"We'll come back and keep you company after we play."

I sit alone with my display for the next half hour, waiting

for the show to start. As the audience expands, the space in front of me evaporates until I am faced with an approaching wall of black clothing and slightly menacing boots. No one buys anything, but a number of people do turn around to read the lettering on the shirts. "The Day Action Band," they say to themselves, looking mystified. Then they ask me if I know who the opening act is.

I am seated during their entire set, and with the crowd pushed up against the table, I only catch a couple of glimpses of the top of Joey's hair. Of course I hear everything. The cheering when they come out is primarily the work of teenage girl voices. These are joined by male voices when Cree sings her first harmony in "Lottery." After Joey's lead vocal on "Going Country," Tim introduces the band: "And from Avondale, Pennsylvania, weighing in at one hundred ten pounds, and making sure the beat never dies, ladies and gentlemen, Cree Wakefield!" From that point on, Tim's in between song patter is interrupted by shouts of "I love you, Cree!" and "You're so beautiful!" The one-two-three punch that ends the set—"Wrestling," "Back in the Eighties," and "Outside Tokyo"—works so well in combination that I expect my table to be crushed by a slew of souvenir seeking patrons. But it isn't. There's a brief rush in which I sell a couple of the cheaper T-shirts, but then it's over. What does a truly enthusiastic crowd sound like, if not that? I have been to many concerts in venues of all sizes, and I can't seem to remember.

Twenty minutes pass. There is no sign of the Day Action Band, even though they have long since cleared their equipment from the stage. The Radials are about to go on. I have to ask a female security person to guard my merchandise while I run into the men's room. "I'll keep an eye out," she says, "but I can't be responsible . . ."

"I know, I know," I say, backing away.

I come out of the bathroom and wait ten more minutes. The Radials haven't gone on yet, but the moment is imminent. Tim walks out of the crowd.

"How did we sound?" he says.

"You can't leave me here that long," I say. "I had to piss."

He is taken aback. "Do you want to go now?" he says.

"I already went. I got her"—I point to the security woman—"to watch the stuff." Then I say, "You sounded good. There was a lot of reverb, but it was kind of nice to hear you sound so big."

"Did the crowd seem into it?" he says.

"I heard a few cheers," I say.

"I saw a lot of crossed arms," Tim says, "but some of the kids in front were moving."

The discussion is interrupted by an apocalyptic hush. The front part of the audience detects movement in the shadows behind the stage, and then a mass of noise ripples outward until it fills the room. Peter runs onto the stage, then Gemma, then Walter, and the noise increases, not in fulfillment but in anticipation. Brant is still not out there, and the noise is still increasing, and I realize there is actually quite a bit of drama in this moment. On a hidden cue the drums and bass begin, and although I don't recognize the pattern, nearly a thousand others do. Brant walks from the side of the stage over to his microphone at the center. He says a word in a low voice that no one can understand but that everyone pretends to. And then the snare hits twice, hard, and Brant jumps and yells a nonsense syllable, and by the time he's landed, the song is fully underway.

The Radials play for just over an hour. They walk off the stage one by one—Peter leaves his guitar to feed back against an amp, which it does until a guitar tech darts out and steals it away. The break between last song and encore is long, close to five minutes, but the crowd doesn't become restless, possibly because the house lights haven't come on, possibly because what kind of headlining band wouldn't play an encore. When someone does return, it's Brant, by himself, with an acoustic guitar. I didn't know he could play. He sings a song that I think must be called "Glorious." It's the last word you hear before a very pretty, climbing instrumental melody that functions in place of a chorus. At the end of the song, he holds the final note over the quieting guitar. Then the rest of the band comes in from the wings, and they play one more.

"Did you see Peter clapping?" Tim says later, as he helps me pack the merchandise back into the boxes. I am careful to preserve the shirt management provided by the lady in blue. I tell Tim I missed the clapping.

"It was after the first encore," he says. "It wasn't like he was trying to get the audience to clap with him. It was like he was clapping for Brant."

"That makes sense," I say. "Brant had just finished performing a song."

"I know," he says. "But Peter usually writes all the music. The clapping makes me think Brant wrote that one."

"Maybe he did," I say. "It was a nice song."

"I don't know," Tim says. "I just think it's interesting."

I look up and observe the departing stream of concert-goers, condensing as they approach the double set of exit doors. A single person detaches from the stream and starts walking toward us. He waves. "Do you know that guy?" Tim says, and, squinting, I realize it's Derek from high school. I can't remember his last name, but I am able to tell Tim that he once gifted me with a dime bag of marijuana after I let him cheat off me in chemistry.

Derek seems to still be in close association with the evil weed. Though it has been six years since we last saw each other, he greets me as if we had class together earlier in the day. I can't say I mind such casual reacquaintanceship. He compliments Tim on a "fantastic" performance and then invites us to a party he knows about in Brookline. I am about to tell him no, that Tim is needed back at Colin's hotel, that I have a room waiting for me at my parents' house, but Tim expresses some interest. "We'll have to check with the rest of the band," he says, and Derek says, "No problem. I'm in no hurry." He shuffles off to see if the bar will serve him another beer.

Cree declines immediately. "I'm tired," she says. "I'm going to fucking bed. But you do what you want to do." I detect hostility in her tone, but I can't see any reason for it. Perhaps cowed, Joey opts to join her.

Derek returns, beerless. We say our goodbyes and turn to walk away with him when Cree calls out, "The T stops running in forty-five minutes. How are you going to get home?"

"We'll just take the . . . ah, shit," Tim says. "You need the van, don't you?"

Cree nods without smiling. Joey says, "Yeah."

"If you guys need a ride home, I'm your man," Derek says, stepping forward. In addition to being stoned, he's also a little drunk; he puts his arm around Tim and says, "Anything for this guy." He puts his other arm around me and says, "And this guy, too."

"Okay, bye," Cree says, flat-voiced. "Have fun."

Tim answers, "We will," and we leave the two of them waiting for Colin, who is still backstage, getting in a few last minutes of schmoozing before the night is done.

Using a combination of tact and logic, I convince Derek to let me drive his car to the party. It's not even a party, more like a small gathering. When we walk in, I half expect Derek to announce something along the lines of "Rock and roll is here!" but he doesn't; he goes straight to the refrigerator and returns solemn with three beers. Within five minutes Tim is talking to a moderately attractive redhead, who, Derek tells me, is "versed in the equestrian arts." "And," he says, "she's also an accomplished flutist." Later I am in a room sitting in a circle around which a bong is being passed. The Doors are playing, and after several bong hits, I find myself struggling not to like them. One member of the circle says that the passage we're hearing now reminds him of the music for his Nintendo game, "Metroid."

"It's not just melody and harmony and bass," he says. "It has levels."

His apartment is right down the hall, and, he tells us, the game can be hooked up to his stereo speakers. We troop slowly over there to listen, but I am disappointed. There is one nice moment in the music, but it's not the moment identified by the owner of the system, and one idiot goes so far as to gush, "This is better than Tetris!" Ready to leave, I go back to the first apartment to look for Tim.

I can't find him right away. At first no one seems to be there at all; then I spot a person passed out and snoring to one side of the couch. Emboldened, I move toward one of the closed bedroom doors. I can hear low voices and classical music inside. I knock. Tim cracks the door. "What's up?" he says, smiling.

"Do you have something going on in there?" I say.

"We're listening to Karen's flute recital," he says. "If you need to leave, don't worry about it. I'll take the T back in the morning."

"I'm going to take Derek's car," I say. I haven't cleared this with Derek, but he has continued to drink, and I still have his keys. "When I drop the car off, I'll come get you."

Tim says, "I really appreciate this," with the whole of his sincerity and closes the door. As I grab my coat off a chair in the foyer, the classical music gets louder and I hear a girl's voice say, "Hey! I said not until the scherzo!"

In the morning Tim and I eat a three-dollar breakfast at a place in Washington Square called Family Restaurant. Tim reacquaints me with the myth that women who ride horses can't have orgasms.

"I spent about four hours last night trying to disprove that myth," he says.

"I'm sorry to hear that," I say.

"That's okay." He looks out the window, where two college-age women are jogging away up the street. "I ate some pussy," he says.

"You listened to some flute," I say.

"You got me, man," he says.

MY PARENTS' REQUEST THAT we eat lunch with them has been denied. Joey delivers the news, but he is supported by Tim and Cree, and, more importantly, by the tour itinerary, which I haven't seen before, and which therefore must have been provided by Colin sometime in the last eighteen hours. Tonight's show is in New York City; the soundcheck is at five, and, as Joey says, "we can't take a smooth, traffic-free arrival for granted."

This minor rejection postpones my plan to ask about the guest list. I have two friends that I'd like to invite to the show. One is Eric, my senior-year college roommate. He moved to New York a year ago and soon realized he was gay. I've spoken to him since, but I haven't seen him. The other person is Kaitlyn, a woman I dated in high school. She went to college in New York and became chronically ill and has spent the last few years concealing the facts of this illness not only from me but from her entire family. I don't know whether she'll be able to make it tonight, but I would like her to at least have the option.

Depending on the club, the band gets from ten to fifteen spots on the guest list. Two weeks down the road, when we move into the Southwest, most of these spots will go unused. But due to an abundance of family and friends, the Mid-Atlantic shows are going to be booked solid. New York will be the worst. In addition to being America's largest city, it's also home to a not inconsiderable number of record executives, many of whom Colin has already invited to the show. I am quite prepared to see my human concerns get run over by economic ones. Still, I didn't ask for any space on last night's list—my parents are in their sixties and had no interest—so I feel I have more than my usual allotment coming tonight.

We are about a third of the way through the four-hour drive, closing in on Hartford. The sky is gray and rainy; five or ten degrees colder and we'd have snow. Cree says that this pre-winter is her favorite weather, and Joey says she's only saying that because she's forgotten what the other seasons are like. He casts his vote for summer, I say spring, and after some prodding, Tim comes forth with "the first blush of fall."

"We are in complete disagreement," Joey says.

"And that's why we all get along," Cree says.

"I'm afraid it's not that simple," Joey says. "We must rochambeau to see what the best season is."

I had forgotten about this aspect of Joey. If there is an arbitrary decision to be made, he imposes order on it using the rochambeau, which, apparently, is French for "rock-paper-scissors." I have a faint memory of college, of losing a rochambeau, and of having to go out of the room and downstairs, into the presence of others, to meet the pizza man.

"There are four of us," I say. "It won't work."

"Observe," Joey says. "One, two . . ."

Tim throws rock; the rest of us throw paper.

"Sorry, fall," Joey says. "You see how it works. Again. One, two . . ."

Cree and Joey stay with paper, and I cut them with my scissors.

"Damn!" Joey says. "The old double reverse. Spring wins the day."

"A time of rebirth," Tim says. He is lying down in the back seat, obviously tired. The book he has been trying to read rests open across his chest. Shortly after we got on the road this morning, Cree asked, "Did you boys have fun last night?" Tim said,

"Yes, ma'am, we did," in a friendly patronizing tone that made no mention of his conquest. I had been waiting to relate the tale of the equestrian flautist, but something in Tim's voice told me I shouldn't mention it. Instead, I described the evening as a mediocre experience for all.

"What are the chances I could get two spots on the guest list?" I say.

Joey is the one to respond, as I thought he would be. "At this point, not good. We'll have to see who Colin wants to get in. I can't give you an answer before I know that."

"I can wait," I say.

"Who do you want to get in?" Tim says.

"Kaitlyn and Eric," I say. Tim has met Eric several times; he's never met Kaitlyn, but he's well aware of who she is.

Tim says quietly, "We'll probably be able to work something out."

This offer may not be as generous as it sounds. Kaitlyn was, and still is, a very pretty young woman. I flashed her photo many times on my freshman hall, and when we broke up over Thanksgiving, I told no one. I waited until after a long Christmas break and behaved as if it happened then. That first semester Tim often said, "Why doesn't she come visit you?" He meant it to be slightly lascivious, but my relationship with Kaitlyn was at such a strained point that I didn't hear the humor and gave instead serious answers such as "living in New York is expensive" and "she has a little bit of a thing about the bus." Perhaps I suspect Tim of too much, but maybe he just wants to get a first-hand look at a girl he thought was cute in a picture six years ago.

A line has already formed outside the club. Two enormous black men stand on either side of the main door, frowning over their crossed arms. I imagine them at home, perfecting these faces in the bathroom mirror, and then I imagine them making these faces for their friends in a bar, seeing how long they can be held before the whole table explodes in hysterical laughter. I smile at them, thinking of this, when I walk past them into the club, but their expressions hold fast.

An equally tough-looking white man in a tight black T-shirt greets us at the coat check. His name is Sean, and while his mouth and tone are hard, the things he says are innocuous: "You've got about half an hour before soundcheck," "Your backstage is downstairs," and "If there's anything I can do for you, let me know."

The three male Radials are onstage, Peter and Walter fooling quietly with their instruments while Brant sings "Fixing a Hole," a cappella. He has the first part of the melody down; after that, he trails off into tuneful mumbling.

Sean gives Joey a message that Colin and some "friends" are next door having cocktails at a sushi bar. We are to go over and meet them after we unload. I wonder privately how necessary it is for me to do this, but I don't want to offend anyone.

We find them sitting at a round table in the back of the crowded restaurant. The table was probably designed for six, but room has been made for seven. "Could we get four more chairs, please," Colin says to the host. Tonight he wears a jacket and tie, as do five of the six other people at the table. The sixth is a woman, and she looks dressed for a day at the office too.

There is a rash of handshaking and then the chairs arrive. The staff places them strategically to block the fire exit and the lanes by which patrons at surrounding tables access the bathrooms. I scoot mine up hard into the back leg of one of the executive's chairs. The man turns to me and says, "What instrument do you play?"

Repressing the urge to say, "I play the skinflute," I tell him I'm not in the band. "I'm the roadie," I say. "I drive the van and sell the T-shirts." He says, "Good for you," unsarcastically, and attempts to get involved with a conversation to his right. For the next five minutes I don't say a word. The back of someone's head blocks my view of the majority of the table, and so even eye contact is out of the question. A man with a hoarse voice talks about the last time he rode the subway. Finally I stand up. I'm not sure what I'm going to do next, but I do know that action breeds action. Cree sees me first and looks shocked, but it's Colin who speaks.

"Lou, you're leaving us," he says.

"Yes," I say. I make a regretful face. "It's time to go hang some shirts. I'm still learning some of the techniques. Well, it was nice meeting all of you." I do a sideways wave at them.

"Er, okay," Colin says. "Listen, Lou, if you're not going to be busy later, I'd like to go over a few things."

"Why don't you come by between sets?" I say. "I shouldn't be too busy at all."

Colin looks around the table and says, "I hope that's not the case." For the executives who missed the subtext he adds, "Hopefully we'll sell a lot of merchandise tonight. This being New York."

"We'll talk when the frenzy dies down," I say. "Maybe I'll see the rest of you inside." I back away, nodding, smiling, and waving, and then I turn and stride quickly out the door.

The line has doubled in size. Several teenage girls near the front are trying to banter with one of the bouncers. The man is conflicted; the girls are friendly and cute, but talking to them incurs the disdain of the other, perhaps senior, bouncer.

I need a telephone. I didn't see any that were operational inside the club, but the condition can't be citywide. Across the street is a pool hall filled with bright green fluorescent light. Men with cigarettes and dress shirts untucked from their trousers stand around the tables.

I call Kaitlyn first. After five rings the machine picks up and reports back the number I just dialed. At the beep I launch into a spiel about where the club is and what time to get there and how both of those facts might end up not mattering because she's not on the guest list yet. I hang up and reach for another quarter to call Eric and then the pay phone rings.

It's Kaitlyn, sounding like she's talking from the far end of a wind tunnel.

"I'm sick," she says. "I couldn't get to the phone."

"You made it, though," I say. "What, do you have caller ID?"

"I'm sick," she says. "You come over."

"I can't right now," I say. "I have to sell things."

"I'm sick."

"I know, baby. I'll come over when I'm done."

"When?"

"I don't know. Midnight. Twelve-thirty. Maybe sooner."

"Okay. Bye." She hangs up.

What an odd exchange. Why do I feel caught in a deja vu? My eyes scan the pool hall for the answer. They come to rest on a mound of magazines that was surely at one time an organized stack. Yes, this is how we talked as girlfriend and boyfriend. When she called me at college I would take the phone into the closet. But we've had normal conversations since then. So what does this mean? That she's regressed? That I've regressed? Maybe she's not even sick. Maybe it's a trap. Maybe she intends to pre-serve me in a chunk of amber for the next ten thousand years.

Eric says he would be "delighted to make an appearance at the Tony." He wonders if he can bring a friend. When I tell him admission is not a sure thing, he says he knows plenty of bars in the area that will keep him and his "buddy" occupied for hours and even days. He says to put them on the list if I can, and if I can't, they'll find out at the door.

Back inside the club the Radials are still soundchecking. They play one of their monotonous grooves that I am only begin-ning to learn to distinguish. The Day Action Band is nowhere to be found. Sean comes to oversee the T-shirt process and offers one of his own duct tape rolls when I can't find mine. He says go ahead, keep it, I've got more. I ask him if the Radials have T-

shirts to sell, and he says no. He makes a brief, almost embarrassed speech about how the club doesn't take a percentage of
merchandise sales and why, and then he says fixedly, "I don't
know if you want to be the T-shirt guy, but if you do, this is a
good job."

I come close to shaking my head and telling him I've been to
college. But then I remember I'm not that much of an asshole and
give him a noncommittal nod instead. Unperturbed, he continues.
He says in his twenties he was a roadie for NRBQ. He made decent money, met lots of women, traveled the world. "I say this to
you because your band reminds me of them. Not in appearance,
but in something," he says. "A friend told me to go see them last
fall, and I did. One of the best recommendations I ever got. They
were wild. They're all talented, but that Tim, he's got something
special. His muse, I don't know. I can't wait to see what he has
them doing tonight."

I tell Sean they've improved since last fall.

"That's good to hear," he says. "My point is, they're going
places, and if you stick with them, you'll go places, too. It's not
being in the band, but it's pretty close. It was worth it for me. I
just got tired. I had to settle down. And so now I'm here." He
gestures in the direction of the stage, and from the way he does
it, I can tell he means it to be positive.

"I'm just trying to enjoy myself," I say. "We'll see what happens."

A few minutes later Colin enters alone through the front of
the club. Walking rapidly, he circumnavigates the interior of the
room. His attention seems to be directed at the walls. His path
leads him to my table.

"The posters aren't here," he says. I have a pang where I wonder if the posters are my responsibility.

"Why aren't they here?" I say.

"There are two possibilities," Colin says. "Either Sunday
Driver didn't send them, or the club didn't put them up."

"What do you think it was?"

He shrugs. "The club, probably. We should have hounded them more. It's no big deal, it just would have been nice."

Then he says, "You have some friends you'd like to come tonight?"

"One, with a plus one," I say. "If the list is full, that's no problem."

"No, no," he says. "Give me a name, and I'll put them on." I feel as though I have misjudged the man. He whips out a pad of paper, asks me for a Sharpie, and then he writes Eric's name down, even making sure he's spelled the difficult Polish surname correctly. He says again that we "need to talk about some things" and indicates that he would rather do it downstairs in the dressing room.

The downstairs is a maze of rough-walled dimly lit corridors. Many of the rooms don't have doors. The Radials' dressing room, does, however, and it's shut, giving the sense that something important is taking place inside. Farther back we come to an open area marked with notebook-paper signs that say DAB. The region is populated by several random groups of college-aged people looking awkward in their coats. I recognize Joey's sister from a picture. The Day Action Band is not here, though their backpacks are tossed in a corner.

Colin walks over to a couch, conspicuously unoccupied, pulls near a battered coffee table, and says, "This will do." He still has my Sharpie, and with it, begins to make a list.

"There are a number of items which you must be responsible for, or which you must delegate responsibility for," Colin says. "I can't stress enough the importance of routine. The same people need to be doing the same things every night. Otherwise, lines get crossed, confusion results, things don't get done. Everybody gets tense, and they don't play well and this whole thing becomes a waste of time.

"First, directions." He hands me a thick wad of faxes that

have been stapled together. "This is the tour itinerary. It lists the clubs, check-in times, rudimentary directions. It has several phone numbers for each club, and it has a contact person once you get there. If there is any question on how to get there, you must call from the road. No scrambling at six P.M. in the wrong part of town . . ."

He continues in this direct manner for the next fifteen minutes, oblivious to the curious but timid people standing around us. By the end of this time he has produced a numbered but barely legible list of responsibilities often identified only by a keyword. He seems to have a decent sense of what the band members like to do. Joey is to be in charge of getting paid at the end of the night, Cree is to oversee the guest list, and Tim is supposed to be the point man on local media, radio and newspaper interviews. Aside from handling all the merchandise, my job is to make sure the band is comfortable. Colin would like me to do the bulk of the driving, to procure the buyout and research potential dinner locations, to make sure the rider is comprehensive, fresh, and delicious. The club must supply hot, clean white towels to wipe off post-concert sweat; if they don't, I must be prepared to raise a small amount of hell.

"Why don't you start there," Colin says.

"Where," I say.

"With the towels," he says. He looks around the dressing room. The components of the rider, minus the booze and two live monkeys, are spread out buffet-style against one wall. A few of the room's bolder occupants drink Fresca and nibble on celery and dip. "There are no towels in this room," he says.

I look at my watch. "They don't go on for two hours," I say, meaning the towels will lose their heat.

"You don't want to have to ask the club for anything once the doors open," Colin says, "if you can help it, and tonight, you can help it. I have some things to take care of."

He gets up and goes off down the hall, leaving me to sort

through this contradictory information. The feeling of being an errand boy, which I had been trying not to acknowledge, returns with a vengeance.

I barely see the band prior to the show. They soundcheck, disappear with Colin again, and then only Tim comes over to my table minutes before show time. It's a routine check-up: he asks after my duties and my personal well-being and promises that someone will come to keep me company after the set. As he turns to walk away, he says, "I saw some crazy shit go down tonight."

"What kind of shit?" I say.

"Inside the Radials' dressing room," he says. "I'll tell you about it later. I'll just say that Cree's a little bit bugged."

Cryptic, not usually Tim's style. But I can see Colin, Joey, and Cree standing by the entrance to the backstage area, all looking slightly anxious. The time must be near. Tim says, "Gotta go," and walks off to join them.

I turn my attention to what's happening at the coat check, less than fifteen feet to my left. I already have good feelings about the coat check; earlier, the girl behind the counter offered me a stool to sit on and I accepted it. Now a long line has formed that stretches in front of my table and beyond. Many of those in line are teenaged and college-aged women, and quite a few of these don't seem to be members of the core Radials fan base. I would describe them as conventional, fashion-conscious New Yorkers. They reach the front of the line, and then they remove their coats. The onset of "Lottery" doesn't do much to interrupt this process; whatever vocal interest there is in the Day Action Band takes place much closer to the stage. Once again the crowd prevents me from seeing the band. I kick back in my stool and start doodling in the margins of Joey's inventory sheet.

Midway through the set the executives make their entrance. I had assumed they were watching the show all along, maybe from a special balcony, complete with hors d'oeuvres and open bar, but no, they use the front door like everyone else. They

choose not to check their coats. The crowd is so dense that the
only place to stand is next to my table, and during the remainder
of the set, one man glances at me several times, unsure if he
recognizes me or not.

After they play Tim shows up as promptly as could be expected and asks if I need anything. I tell him I don't. I'd like to
hear his scandalous news, but the merchandise table is swamped
with customers, four of them, all signing or waiting to sign the
mailing list. Those waiting finger the merchandise, lifting up the
CDs and 45s and reading the information on the back with half
interest. They have no intention of buying anything. I imagine
they have put their names on a hundred mailing lists and every
day the mailman brings them a new salutation and tour schedule
from a different band. Two women who must be a couple express
concern that the mailing list won't reach them "upstate." I ask
them if they are otherwise able to receive mail; when they say
yes, I nod with forlorn significance. They retreat into the darkness, and their twin forms are replaced by those of Eric and his
friend.

"Oh my God, Lou!" Eric says. "I'm so sorry we're late. We got
caught up in something."

The friend, without looking at Eric, steps forward and introduces himself as Stephen. He seems about thirty and likely the
holder of a job in the professional world. Eric says, "Yes, this is
Stephen. He's not my boyfriend, but we have sex." He opens
his arms and gives me a big hug. "When is your band playing?"
he says.

"I'm afraid they've already come and gone," I say. I shake my
head. "They were very good. I'm sorry you missed it."

"Oh, I'm sorry too," Eric says. His eyes drift off toward Stephen; his face assumes an expression of worry. Maybe he went
too far with that having sex comment. Stephen has lifted one of
the CDs and is carefully scrutinizing the back of it. He may be
trying to pretend that Eric and I are not here, and that he is not

thirty years old and one of the older people in the rock and roll club. I'd like for him to put the CD down. No matter who it is that has the CD, a part of me can't help but feel they're going to walk away with it. I should start taping it down. Stephen leans forward and says, "Your shirt is falling down."

What is this, some kind of New York insult? "What do you mean by that?" I say.

Stephen points above my head, and I see that the "You Think You Hear" T-shirt has come untaped and is flopped over, ridiculous, illegible, and, as a marketing tool, utterly ineffective.

"Oh, thanks," I say, and climb up on the stool to fix the shirt. I wonder how long it has been in this state. No doubt the majority of the audience has been too sophisticated to mention it to me. Either that or they think that's how it's supposed to hang, casual witnesses to the birth and death of an unsuccessful trend.

Eric and Stephen have moved a few feet away, not talking to me or each other, instead gazing off in the direction of the stage, where not much is happening. I tear off a piece of duct tape, fold it over on itself, and pretty soon the CD is adhering to the table quite nicely. A lone individual, possibly an employee of college radio, is the first to attempt to pick it up. He perceives my good-natured grin as mockery and steals away to reflect on his embarrassment.

After an obvious attempt to get Stephen to come with him, Eric walks over alone and tells me that they're leaving. I tell him that I'm free until two o'clock tomorrow, and so we make plans to meet for brunch. He gets Kaitlyn's number in case something comes up. He tells me to have fun tonight and makes his eyebrows go up and down. I tell him to cut that shit out. He goes over to Stephen, and Stephen waves, and then they go past the ticket-taking bouncer and out the door, having spent about fifteen minutes inside the club.

———

At the end of the night Colin asks me if I would like to join him, the band, and some other people for drinks. If he doesn't want me to come, he's concealing it well.

"I've made plans with a friend," I say.

"Well," he says. "It was wonderful meeting you. I think you'll do a great job, and perhaps someday we'll meet again."

"That someday will come in two weeks," I say. "In Los Angeles."

"Oh, yes, I forgot," Colin says, infusing the words with a forceful laugh. He slaps himself on the coat. "Splendid. Well, until then . . ."

"Goodbye," I say, and turn, finally, to leave. Tim says, "How are you getting there?"

"The subway."

"You sure you don't want to take a cab?" he says.

"Take a cab!" Cree shouts, animating. She swells briefly with maternal instinct. "It's dangerous," she says. "People get mugged. You don't want to fool around with that."

"Do I look like someone who has any money?" I say.

Cree says "Yes," because she is no longer paying any attention to me. Two teenage boys have recognized her from inside the club and want to talk. I walk up the street to where Sean has told me the subway will be.

Kaitlyn lives on the Upper West Side, in a building at the intersection of Broadway and 110th Street. She has told me that she lives in one of the corner apartments, and before I go in, I stare up and count the floors until I locate the windows that belong to her.

There is a mirror in the lobby that makes me look several inches wider than I actually am. Near the elevator is a grid of mailboxes under partial renovation. Kaitlyn's is still intact.

I knock on her door; the lock buzzes and the door opens. Inside, the apartment is dark, except for a dim light at the end of a long hallway to my left. The hallway is so long that spatial gravity tilts my body in that direction as I stand there. I start walking. I begin to hear music, faint, but growing louder; just before the room where the light is, I realize I am hearing the "Moonlight Sonata." I am about to step over the threshold when Kaitlyn's voice says, "Wait."

I wait about five seconds.

"You can come in."

At first all I see is the bed. Queen-sized, four-poster, three-stacked mattresses, this bed was conceived in a fairy tale. A foot-high stool sits on the near side; without it, access would be impossible. Further dominion is established by the quilt, an object that could be draped across human beings during the X-ray process. A tall Halogen lamp emits a whisper of light. Two open windows on either side of the bed grant access to gale-force winds. A few papers fly around the room. Kaitlyn's long dark hair blows. She is pale. She sits up in the bed. The circles under her eyes are as dark as her hair. She wears a white gown and no bra.

"I've been waiting for you," she says.

"I know," I say. "Some people talked to me for a long time. Also, I took the local train instead of the express."

She smiles and shakes her head at my foolishness. "Come here," she says.

She leans forward to hug me. As she does I notice something odd about one of her hands. When the hug is over I reach for that hand, and she draws it back. "Let me see," I say.

"No," she says.

"Please," I say.

Kaitlyn twists a lock of her hair and puts the end of it into her mouth. She looks at many of the things in the room other than me. Her tantrum habits have not evolved much over the past ten years. But eventually she gives me her hand and, with it, the saddest expression I have ever seen.

Implanted just before the knuckles is a device made of thick, clear plastic. Two short tubes lead into it, one tinted orange, one tinted blue. The tubes each look ready to receive a needle.

"What is it for?" I say.

"You can see what it's for," she says. "Don't be impolite."

If I want a more specific answer, I'm going to have to work to get it. But I don't think that's what I'm supposed to do. So I ask questions about unimportant things. Who she has seen lately. When she was last home. How her brother Clay is liking college in Austin, Texas. I wonder whether it's okay to talk about the future, and I decide that it's probably not okay. When she asks me about myself I give a detailed account of my day and a half as tour manager, speaking with confidence and humor. But when I segue into what I might do when the tour is over, I stop suddenly, realizing that I have broached the subject of future events. There is too much not to talk about. In defeat, I ask her how she spends a typical day.

"That's a good question," she says. "I'll answer it in the living room. Can you hand me my crutches?" She points to the floor on the other side of the bed. "The wind blew them over."

The hall is about fifty feet long and it takes us three minutes to travel the length of it. Kaitlyn explains that most days are not as bad as this one. Today, she says, the joint pain and fatigue have combined as never before. But sometimes she doesn't need the crutches at all.

"I stopped using them in public when the lady picked me up," she says. "I was in the subway, about to go up the stairs, and she said, 'You poor darling, let me help you.' "

"She carried you up the stairs?" I say. "All the way? She must have been one big lady. No offense, but I don't think I could carry you up the stairs."

"Oh, she was very big," Kaitlyn says. She stretches her arms wide. She is starting to feel used to me again.

The rest of the night is very pleasant. Kaitlyn's illness precludes the possibility of sexual tension, and so our conversation proceeds as if we were two old heterosexual friends of the same gender. After a while I even forget she's not wearing a bra, and the reminder I get when she hugs me goodnight is chaste, the touch of a nun, an aunt, or a nubile second cousin.

In the morning I go down to an open market on her block and buy bagels and fruit. Kaitlyn says, "You can eat the fruit," and puts an unhalved bagel in the oven to toast. The apartment is at the corner of the building that gets the sun. From the way she moves around the kitchen I get the sense that this is going to be one of her good days. The good and bad can show up back to back, apparently, and I am not ungrateful for this, because it makes it easier to say goodbye. Before I leave to meet Eric for brunch she makes me promise to call her brother when I get to Austin. "But don't tell him that I'm sick," she says. "It's not something he needs to know right now." We hug once more, and, holding her, I think about what it used to be like to kiss her.

The meeting place is at the edge of Central Park. When I arrive Eric and Stephen are standing very close and very quiet by a plaque that tells of certain foliage. Stephen is reading the plaque, and Eric is reading Stephen's face the way a budding young poet might first read Rilke in translation. It wouldn't make a bad photograph.

The restaurant is on the other side of the park, and during the walk over, Eric keeps jumping on Stephen's back. Each time, Stephen looks startled and aggrieved, but carries Eric for a few shaky steps before setting him down. Once or twice Eric jumps on my back, and I stand there and rotate until he dismounts.

We pass a wooded region that Eric says is a popular place for anonymous gay sex, though not this time of year. I ask Stephen, joking, if he's ever been there, and Eric looks worried until Stephen says no. Stephen does say he's heard some stories, however, and these occupy us for the remainder of the walk.

I remember Eric's attempts to date various women in college, how he talked too brightly of his attractions to them, how he came home after every date seeming vaguely dispirited. There is such a happiness in him now, such a sense of rightness and possibility. I felt a version of that certainty with Kaitlyn once, but that was seven years ago, and I have often wondered if it would ever happen again. I have often wondered if it could happen again. It's one thing to love a person, but it's another entirely to get them to love you in return.

Back in the van I make a point of asking the band where they were for such a long time last night. Cree says, "What do you mean, we all stayed at different places."

I say, "No, before you played," and Cree's face darkens.

"Fuck, man," she says. "I thought we were being social."

"You could say it was social," Tim says.

"It was more social than anything I've ever seen," Joey says.

Tim says they were backstage, talking to some guests, when Brant and Peter came over to thank them for the Rice Krispies treats. "You fuckers didn't even participate in their making," Cree interjects. The three of them were invited back to the Radials' dressing room, where people dined on subs, bobbies, in fact, made of turkey, stuffing, and cranberry sauce.

"So we sat around talking about how great their rider was, blah, blah, blah—," Cree says.

Joey interrupts, "It was a kick-ass rider!"

"Anyway," Cree says, "we're just talking about their fucking food, and then, straight up, Peter says, 'Do you guys want to do some coke?' "

Behind Cree's head Tim makes a significant face.

"And I said no thank you, and Brant said, well, if you'll excuse me, and Peter said, we'll be right back, and then they went over into the corner, and all their roadies got around them, I don't know why, in case someone walked in I guess, and when they came back over they were coked up."

"Brant's face was shining like the harvest moon," Joey says.

"It was fucking gross. I wanted to scream at them."

Tim says, "I wonder if that's why Brant has so much energy onstage."

"You better not do that shit or you can play without me," Cree says. "Shit, man."

A few days before the tour began, Tim, Joey, and I purchased a bag of very nice marijuana from one of Joey's housemates. Tim told me not to mention it in front of Cree. "She gets kind of funny about drugs when we're on the road," he said. This warning made no sense to me at the time, as I had seen her stoned and been stoned with her on a number of occasions myself. But it makes sense to me now. Such a coldness, such a refusal to consider the other consciousness. I wonder what provoked this change in her moral code.

the past

TIM AND I BECAME friends on our freshman hall, two pot smokers divorced from a crowd of sanctimonious alcoholics. He might have been able to convert the rest of them but for a brutish young man who would insist to the point of violence that everyone abuse the same substance.

In those days I was somewhat more advanced than Tim. At an otherwise drunk party I commandeered the stereo with *Rumours*; when "Dreams" began with that most crisp of drum fills, Tim broke off the conversation he was having to turn to the speakers and listen. The relationship was cemented later when I dared to play the Beach Boys. I chose "Help Me Rhonda," the flawed mid-period masterpiece, for the strength and complexity of its rhythm and the wild mismatched sound of its guitar solo.

"Listen to how the guitar skitters across the surface of the music," I instructed. At the time I was writing record reviews for the school paper fraught with verbs like "tremble" and "whisper."

"My God, it's so beautiful," he said, "and so wrong." We talked about how this could be, long into the night.

Within days Tim was finding errors of his own. "Hey Jude" was marred by a tinny high-hat fifty-seven seconds in. The scissors on "Good Vibrations" were dumb, though later, when he was more familiar with the quirks of Brian Wilson, Tim reversed this decision. Even "Dreams" was faulty; Lindsey Buckingham's fingers twinged at the end of the volume swell solo. Here Tim was more forgiving. "Lindsey knew he'd never get it that close again," he said.

Still, I felt the focus was too much on the negative.

"Why are you so interested in the mistakes?" I asked him, hoping to provoke some sort of shame.

"Because those are the places where technique becomes visible," he said. "Or audible, I guess."

He bought a four-track and began to record sounds. On a Friday night in November he declared one of the two bathrooms on our hall off-limits. He persuaded a young acolyte from the radio station to sit in the doorway in a folding chair. I was the engineer, rhythm guitarist, and singer of low harmonies. The finest product of the session was a cover of Joan Jett's cover of "Crimson and Clover." Tim's falsetto had been for most of the evening thick and uncertain, but on this song it broke through with a high, thin clarity. It sounded so good to him that we sang the lyrics "Crimson and clover / Over and over" for nearly seven minutes; on the tape, toward the end, you can hear a distant dispute over bathroom rights and the noise of a metal chair clattering hard against a tile floor.

Tim spent the first part of the spring semester "unlearning" what he knew about the guitar. In high school he had played in a punk rock fusion band called Vesis, whose chief influences were King Crimson, Fugazi, and the Mahavishnu Orchestra. He carried this love of dissonance into his first days at the university; a week after arriving on campus he had organized three other guitar players, myself included, into a performance of "Frippertronics" after the stylings of Robert Fripp and his League of Crafty Guitarists. This consisted of moving in rectangular patterns up and down the neck of the instrument at even intervals. The resulting sound could be described as a synchronicity of bleeping computers, and it was about a million miles from the music that would captivate Tim in the coming months.

"The guitar can sculpt and add flourish, but it can never dominate," he said, making one of the many pronouncements that he would disown or contradict within a space of days. He borrowed a bass from a tall freaky Rush enthusiast named Joey Amonte and used it to adhere to a schedule in which he wrote three new songs a week on an instrument other than the guitar. He formed combos and disbanded them. He sang everywhere he went. He was chided by a professor for going around clapping his hands in an auditorium before class. "Why are you doing that, son?" the man asked, and Tim said, "To test the acoustics."

These activities were derailed in mid-semester when he became interested in a girl in his calculus class.

"She's beautiful," he said. "I feel like an idiot every time I talk to her." He decided one of her parents had to be foreign and speculated as to which one it was. One night he invited her over to the dorm to get high with us.

Her name was Cree, and she was small and thin, but, as Tim noted, not too thin. "I like the way she fills up her jeans," he said. Her experience with marijuana smoking was limited, and she had never used a bong at all. Tim moved next to her, and showed her how to hold the apparatus, how to find and release the shotgun. After her first unsuccessful hit, he said, "Here, put your hand on my chest and feel when I pull in and when I exhale." His body language was relentless. He always faced her, pointed his shoulders and legs toward her, touched her whenever he could. After a while she began to respond. I'm not sure when I realized I was simply watching them interact. But when Tim moved even nearer and introduced "Hot Fun in the Summertime" as his favorite song of all time, I knew I had better leave. I got up to go to the bathroom and never came back.

For someone who claimed to believe so strongly in the sanctity of love and sex, Tim provided a number of intimate details about their relationship. One image that still comes to me is that of Cree, wearing only a regular length T-shirt, standing on her bed to rehang a poster that had fallen down during their love-making. They did not go out very often; when they did, it was to Philadelphia to hear the symphony or to Tim's family house on the Chesapeake. Tim didn't have a key, but they brought blankets and food and a small radio. It was April then and still cool. Over to watch a movie, Tim and Cree recounted that weekend with a deliberateness intended more for them than for me. "You'd be surprised how much heat the body generates," Tim said. Instead of being embarrassed Cree kissed the side of his face and said, "I know, lover, I know." I said, "Well, let's start the movie"—it was *Apocalypse Now*, I think—and waited in the dark for the kissing and the painfully slow unzipping to begin. I knew they were fin-ished when Tim laughed at the line, "I love the smell of napalm in the morning," and by the time the girls came down in the helicopter they were both asleep.

By late May Tim's interest was waning. He admitted that his stamina during sex had gone from being a matter of pride to a matter for concern. He fretted about breaking Cree's heart. He said it was terrible going over to her place because he was so attracted to one of her suitemates. When he called for Cree and got Ana instead, he began to say things like, "It makes me crazy that I can never have you." You might think that a loyal friend would have gone straight to Cree with this information, but those words stirred up powerful feelings in Ana's heart. She didn't tell Cree and began sleeping with Tim.

Tim broke up with Cree at the beginning of the summer, and even though they lived only twenty miles apart, they didn't see each other again until the fall. When school resumed, Tim wanted to date Ana publicly. She and Cree were no longer room-mates, but they remained part of a large, vaguely delineated social group of which Tim and I were also members. Not wanting to disrupt this organization, Tim reluctantly worked to keep the affair private.

For a short period that semester, he became convinced that the solution was for Cree to have a new boyfriend. He would tell me how, when he and Cree were dating, she would go on and on about me, about how cute and funny I was. He was so enthusiastic that I actually began to daydream that I was the one she had wanted all along.

Somehow Tim arranged for the four of us to attend a football game together, something we wouldn't have ordinarily done. I don't know how he sold it, maybe as a reunion, maybe as a friendly reconciliation. Cree came because she wanted to prove she had recovered. After the game we drove to a neighborhood where large suburban homes were under construction. Great elaborate wooden frames had been raised, platforms had been built over the basement and first floor, and ladders and rudimentary staircases were in place. For a while we all sat on the fresh-smelling boards where the second-floor balcony was going to be and drank out of flasks and looked at the inert backhoes, the site manager's trailer, and behind that, the short row of Port-a-Pots at the base of a hill. It reminded me of high school.

Suddenly Ana said she wanted to explore. Tim said he would go with her. They got up and Cree and I heard the noise they made going down the stairs. Then there was quiet. We sat there in the quiet for what could have been half an hour. Neither of us moved. I felt like anything could happen. I knew that I didn't want her to cry, but I thought if I spoke she might. From somewhere below came a burst of giggling, followed by "Shhhhh." A board fell against another board. Footsteps landed in the grass. Now I felt like I had to talk. I made my voice strong and ironic, to acknowledge what was happening and to make it seem unimportant. I said things about the construction of the house, the football game we had just seen, what kind of night it was. I tried to generate the romance that Tim would have. Then in a horribly miscalculated gesture I said she seemed tense and asked if she wanted her shoulders rubbed. She said no.

Tim had wanted Cree to learn a musical instrument. She spoke often of her gift of rhythm—she was a good dancer, she had taken Indian classical dance, she liked to stay out all night at raves— but Tim had heard her sing along to the radio and was impressed by the harmonies she found. He still had the bass he had borrowed from Joey and presented it to Cree early in their relationship with the statement, "This is the instrument where harmony and rhythm find their natural resolution." She made a strong effort to learn to play, but the thick strings could not always be depressed by her small fingers, and the sound that emerged from the amp was earnest and thumping, but incomplete.

Away from Tim, Cree pursued her rhythmic inclinations. She bought some bongos and began jamming with two guitar players who loved to harmonize in the manner of the Indigo Girls. These two guys were notorious for their passionate expressions and literate lyrics. A student DJ created a public controversy when he played their homemade tape on his radio show and mocked it live with a studioful of his friends. When questioned about this dubious association, Cree said, "It's good practice, to take music that doesn't go on its own and try to make it go."

One night this trio, under the name Spilled Water, played a show at the Pub, a campus eatery that had begun what it called its "Thursday Night Concert Series" at the start of the scholastic year. Ads that ran in the student daily described the event as a "Pre-weekend jam," but most of the performers tended to be solo acoustic artists. Tim and I joined a number of Cree's friends in the audience, though our motive had more to do with curiosity than support. I recall that Tim asked Ana to stay home that night. The performance itself was a disaster of earnest strumming and plaintive wailing, punctuated by shouts of "Yeah, Cree!" and

"You go girl!" Cree did nothing to provoke the shouting. Her bongo playing was inaudible beneath the guitars and voices, and as for her stage presence, she simply moved her head back and forth, looking around the room with mild detachment. At one point the acoustic boys stopped singing and turned in toward her as if they expected her to sally forth with some kind of pyrotechnic solo, but she kept playing her usual rhythm, the only adjustment being that her partners were now included in that strange back and forth gaze. When this happened, Tim said, "Oh my God," and slapped his knee in disbelief. But after it was all over, he took Cree aside and told her he admired not only the way she kept time but also the way she kept her composure. From thirty feet away I could see the effect this compliment had on her, and I thought, only Tim could make a person feel like that.

Shortly after Christmas Tim broke up with Ana. This time it was not for another woman, but for music. "I love girls," he told me, "but I can't get anything done when they're around."

For a long time he refused to call it *songwriting*. The word offended him, describing as it did a process so brief and so dependent on inspiration that it was hardly a process at all. He struggled to invent alternate terminology. Justifying his plans to sit home on a Friday night, he would say, "I think I'm going to try to make a song." Other times he would allude to "putting some chords together," and once, memorably, he went in the other direction entirely and said that he was about to "add a chapter to our national songbook."

This dismissiveness was intended to mask a real obsession. Where did songs come from? Tim felt that they came from somewhere concrete. The famous story of Paul McCartney tumbling out of bed with "Yesterday" in his head aroused not suspicion but curiosity. What had Paul been listening to the night before? "A new song is an old song misremembered," Tim began to say.

He made it his mission to transform this mantra into technique. Weekend afternoons he would pick a street one block removed from frat row and walk up and down it, listening to a wide range of popular music through purely natural filters. He would put on an album of children's songs and then take a bath in the upstairs bathroom, running the water in the sink if he felt he needed the extra interference. Before he went to bed, he would set the volume on his stereo to one, which, depending on the record, was sometimes too quiet to tell what key the music was in.

And then there were the "days of silence." These were, as far as I know, unplanned, but they seemed to take place at three-week intervals. They usually involved a drive to the country, a long hike over hill and dale, and, finally, a meditative period in the quietest spot he could find. "I try to stay away from creeks and streams," he said. "Pine groves are the best." Though he would sometimes pack himself a picnic lunch, he never, ever, brought his guitar.

The songs came easily, it seemed to me. "I've got a new one," Tim would say. "Tell me what you think." And then he would play it, knowing it was good, the request for my opinion only a formality. Later, at home, I would seek to re-create from memory what I had just heard. I was always amazed at the simplicity of the work, that the chords he played were chords I knew, that the melodies could be sung just as easily in my own voice. I would think, Why, I could have written that, and cursed myself for not having done it.

As the songs accumulated, Tim began to search for a band to play them. He looked first to our immediate social group, hoping that the chemistry of friendship might extend to musicianship. But it didn't. What had been casual jam sessions became arduous auditions; I myself withdrew permanently after one desolate evening during which I was unable for four hours to provide a rhythm guitar sufficient to support Tim's lead. Next he tried the various affiliates of the radio station, but he felt their contempt for the fundamentals would hinder his efforts in the long run. Finally he approached several students in the music school. This yielded nothing beyond several diatribes on the antithetical relationship between rote learning and creativity.

The day Tim, Joey, and Cree played together for the first time, Tim and Joey were in Joey's basement fooling around with a drum and bass riff that Tim felt was too silly to turn into an actual song. He had long ago decided that Joey was not fit to be his bass player, that he lacked dedication, that he lacked belief in his own improvisational powers, but he was perfect for this sort of activity. They were pounding away on this sorry funk when Cree stopped by to drop off some biology notes that she had borrowed from one of Joey's housemates. When she could not locate anyone upstairs, she went down into the basement. She saw Tim attempting to play the drums, his arms flailing, his right leg spastically working the kick drum pedal, and she burst out laughing. Tim said to her, "You think you can do any better?" She said, "Yes, I do," and a great band was born.

They made their public debut in the basement of an off-campus residence. The event was nothing more than a keg party, but the host had ties to both the concert committee and the commission on intramural sport, so there was an uneasy balance of athlete and aesthete in the mix. They weren't called the Day Action Band then; for that one night they were known as "27 White Clay Creek" because that was the address of the party. Tim arranged it so they would play fourth out of five bands. He wanted the atmosphere to be a drunken one, to weaken the audience's critical faculties and to promote the possibility of dance. He had written a small batch of songs that he believed to be the epitome of classic rock. The slowest, he had been saying for weeks, might even produce a show of lighters.

With his history of live performance, Tim was not nervous,

but the other two were. The afternoon before, Joey took a solitary walk out to the President's Mansion, far from the heart of campus, where he "sat in the grass and looked at the trees and wondered what life lay beyond this one." Cree's preparations were less dramatic; she huddled with her housemates in their living room and debated the pros and cons of having a few drinks before the set. In the end her dedication to her art and her fear of Tim's disapproval prevailed. She played sober.

I would like to say that the show was a rocking success, but I can't, because I wasn't there. I had a long paper due the following Monday, and I begged off the evening on account of it. I said to Tim, "You guys will play many other shows," in a way that was supposed to communicate confidence and support. He was so taken aback that he didn't try to convince me otherwise. He said, "I'll hope to see you at the next one."

I stayed home that night, but I didn't write my paper. I turned on the computer and looked at the screen for a while, and then I looked at my watch and thought about how the band would not be going on for several hours and how I still had time to make it over to the party. I said to myself, "Let's try to get some work done on this paper first," but after fifteen minutes of this I sat back on my mattress and picked up my acoustic guitar and began to play. Soon I made adjustments. I closed the door to avoid noise from an incoming roommate, and I turned out the lights, so all I could see were the blank white monitor on one side of the room and the faint urban glow coming through the window on the other. The open window was above my bed, and my pillow and my bare feet were cold, but I thought these distractions might improve the quality of my music. I played and sang softly, wistful, beautiful melodies over driven arpeggios, my voice a falsetto more pure than Tim's. I became obsessed with the idea of how to make the world my backing band. I couldn't help it. I heard my voice and I heard the guitar but I also heard a million other sounds through the open window and beneath the floor and

above the ceiling and some even in the room. I heard a motorcycle three blocks away start up and drive off, the sound zooming
around the interior of the courtyard where it had been parked. I
heard the indeterminate conversation of two adult women trying
to talk over a loud TV. I heard my refrigerator come on, my ankles
brushing against the sheet, my breath as it expanded inside my
throat. I heard the quiet of night itself, a sound so subtle and
complex that I could not begin to distinguish its components. I
wanted to put all of this on record. And as I lay there, closing in
on the horizon of my own subconscious, I began to see how it
could be done. When I woke up, it was quarter past twelve, too
late to make it to the party, too late to do anything but go to sleep.
I went to the bathroom, turned off the computer, and got back in
the bed.

Monday I blew off my classes and didn't make it to campus
until late afternoon. The paper was due at five. I had spent the
morning writing it, but I might as well have spent the morning
taking drugs. I felt dazed and weird, like something important
would be lost to me forever unless I could remember what it was.
When several of my classmates and I converged on our professor's door at 4:58 I returned their triumphant grins, I too raised
my wristwatch in conquest, but I knew the satisfaction that
awaited them—in the form of sleep, dope, sex, television, or alcohol, or all of them combined—would not be waiting for me
when I returned home. On my way back to my apartment, I met
Cree, wearing overalls and walking the other way with her arms
through both straps of her backpack.

"You look fucked up!" she said. She laughed at me and at
herself and then she said, "I mean, you look really tired." She
seemed insanely happy.

"I am really tired," I said. "I've done a lot of work today."

Cree took an appraising walk around me, paying special attention to my head.

"Your hair is sticking out," she said. "In back. It looks really funny, like a clown's hair. Hold on, I'll fix it." She reached up and patted down the back of my head. She had to lean forward and stand on her tiptoes to do it, and I wondered whether those were her breasts I felt pressing against my shoulderblades. I started to feel more like a man who has just completed a fifteen-page paper.

Then Cree said, "The show went really well."

"The show?" I said. I had not thought about it all day.

"Well, it went really well until the cops came. We played four and a half songs."

"The cops," I said. "Were you that loud?"

"No," she said. "There was a fight. It was fucking crazy. These guys started fighting with bottles. Tim said to keep playing, so we did."

"Was there any blood?" I said.

"No. They didn't actually fight with the bottles, they just waved them at each other. But they were going to, until the cops showed up."

"How did you play?" I asked. This was the one question I wanted an answer to, although I wasn't aware of it until I said it.

"People really liked us," she said. She named several of her friends and housemates and talked about how they stood in front and danced and called out all their names and pretended to moon over Tim. But then she said people they didn't know were coming up afterwards—"After the cops came?" I broke in, skeptical—and saying things such as, "You're the best party band I've ever seen," and "If you had a video on MTV, I would sit home all day and wait for it to come on."

Trying to be funny, I said, "Were these compliments directed at the band, or were they directed at you?" I thought this could be taken as a little bit of a compliment itself, but Cree did not react well. The insane happiness was replaced by tolerant friendliness.

"I think they were talking about the band," she said. "The

guys seemed really sincere. It was cool. One of them was a drummer. He said I played behind the beat. He said he wished he could do that." She put her hands on her hips and looked at me.

"Tim likes drummers who play behind the beat," was all I could think of to say.

"I know," she said, still looking at me. We said our goodbyes, and I walked home fast, lurching almost as I tried to imagine what I would have thought if I had been in the audience.

I made it to their next show, three weeks later. It was at the Pub, the sight of Cree's Spilled Water debacle. Many thought it was odd that Tim chose this venue for his band's first appearance in a public space, that it had something to do with irony or kitsch or a postmodern reverse snobbery. Those closer to him cited his uncritical need to improve the band through every avenue possible. I always thought he did it for Cree, as atonement for the indignities he had forced her to endure, both onstage and inside her heart.

At quarter to seven the Pub staff turned off the college basketball game that had been on and cleared away a couple of tables at the end of the room near the fireplace. A student with engineering qualifications rigged up three microphones and coughed deeply into each one. Tim and Joey set up their amps and guitars, and then the whole band brought in the drums. I remember it took them a long time to get the drums set up, that they had to huddle and confer about how the kick drum pedal ought to be put together. As they fussed, the crowd grew and grew. By the seven-thirty start time, there were close to seventy-five people in the Pub, only some of whom I knew or recognized as being friends of the band. From what I had heard, the Thursday Night Concert Series tended to clear out more customers than it attracted; this fine turnout had to be a record.

Finally, all that remained was for Tim to tune his guitar. He turned his back to the crowd and raised the headstock until it was next to his ear. Cree made an exasperated "Aren't we ready yet?" face and began talking to her friends in the front row. Joey kept his eyes on the neck of his bass, but every so often he would look up and treat the room to an awkward smile. Then Tim hit a loud, correctly-tuned chord, turned back around, and spoke into the microphone.

"Ladies and gentlemen," he said, debonair but sincere, "this is our first show as the Day Action Band. We hope you like us."

The first song I heard them play was called "I Rock Harder." They don't play it anymore; in fact, it was dropped from the lineup within a matter of months, replaced with something better, more characteristic, no doubt. But for its time it was a great song. The groove was minimalist, the guitar ringing a two-note chord, the bass thumping a repeating figure underneath, the drums unsteady but charging, always charging. Tim sang "Indie rock / Can suck my cock," his voice nearly breaking over the high note on the word "my," and immediately Joey and Cree came back with "Sha na na na, na na na na na, na."

The crowd recoiled from the revolution contained in the opening lyric, but the music brought them back. The singing was loud, clear, and unaffected. The chorus rose high above the verse, stopping just short of anthem. I suddenly understood what Tim meant about the relationship between new songs and old songs. I knew I had never heard this song before, but I felt like Tim had cobbled it from my memory as well as his own. And how they performed it. The blankness I remembered on Cree's face from the Spilled Water show was gone, replaced by a joyous restraint. She sped up the tempo coming into the second verse and Tim slowed her down with a slightly questioning eyebrow and then a gentle nod. Her look of worry changed to a smile and I felt everyone around me smile with her. Less than a minute later, Tim stepped over to Joey's mic so they could sing the last chorus together. They leaned in their heads and hollered with all the strength in their throats. The song ended. I thought it was the greatest thing I had ever seen. It was as if Tim had decided exactly what kind of spell he wanted to cast.

There were a dozen shows over the next few months. I attended each one, always wondering when they were going to start seeming routine. In March the band was approached by the philosophers of Sconefield, who wanted a house band for their outdoor Sunday afternoon tea party. Tim was delighted, because it was these people who should have been most affronted by the message of "I Rock Harder." He began to broaden his notion of the Day Action Band's appeal. "I want everyone to like us," he said. "Little kids, old people, parents in their forties, drug addicts, Christians . . . everyone. Not just college kids who stand in front with their arms crossed."

That summer Joey did not go back to Houston. Cree too opted to stay in Newark, and while Tim did technically live with his parents, he spent most of his nights on a couch in Joey's basement, where they had set up their practice space. I took a job at a plastic factory in nearby southern New Jersey. I worked twelve-hour shifts, some days, some nights, driving a forklift truck around a warehouse and reading week-old newspapers in the breakroom. When I wasn't at work I was asleep.

I knew Tim had been recording, but I didn't know where he was in the process. When I did see him, he would always make reference to being busy; he had developed an affinity for the phrase "I've got a lot on my plate right now." Joey and Cree were also using new lingo; Joey spoke of "laying down some basic tracks," and Cree, instead of employing some variant of the verb "to sing," now said she was nervous about her upcoming "vocal." Still, they never gave any indication of when they thought they would be finished. In my mind it was a matter of months, rather than weeks or days.

The week before school resumed Tim called and asked if I would like to come over and listen to some tunes. Although it had been a while since we had done this, I assumed he meant we would smoke some pot, put on something profound such as *Rubber Soul* or the *Smile* sessions, and discuss. He didn't say anything to the contrary.

Upon my arrival, we did in fact smoke some pot, but quite a bit more than usual. Tim kept repacking the bong and handing it to me, as if it had always been our practice to get stoned with such deliberate overkill. Soon I was having concerns about my center of gravity and its shifting location. Tim rose suddenly from the bed where he was sitting and said, "Would you like to hear some music now?"

I said music would be welcome. I expected him to spend a few minutes poking around among his records and CDs, I expected eventually he would offer me a choice and I expected it would take an additional few minutes to finally make that choice, but no, Tim went straight over to the receiver, picked up a cassette sitting on the shelf next to it, and popped it into the tape deck.

I knew what it had to be. A hiss came over the speakers, and Tim sat back down on the edge of the bed, leaning forward with his forearms on his thighs. There was a tightening in my head that I now realize was a kind of mental bracing. I looked at the bong on the bedside table and wished it were possible to recant the hits I had taken. The sound began all at once.

It was wonderful. It was all I could think, "This is wonderful," over and over. The thought was in the center of my head, and it stayed there, pulsing, flashing away my deconstructive powers every time they rose up to dissect. Tim had taken a bundle of instruments and voices and words and made them into one sound. There were no places of compromise, no places that required mental compensation to be understood. Notes were colors and chords were sunsets, and the drums were huge structures, frames for skyscrapers, and down low the bass was as warm and constant as a heartbeat. When Tim sang he was the person I wanted to be. And when Cree sang she was the person I wanted to be with. She sang a song called "Drag City Baby." It was about a girl asking her lover to come to the city. The music was lilting, a promise of hope bravely overlooking all the forces that might conspire to break it. Cree's voice was clear and simple and beautiful. I could hear in it how badly she wanted to fall in love. The song ended, and the hiss filled the speakers again. Tim and I continued to sit with our heads down as the tape rolled on. Suddenly a voice louder than God's spoke, in a foreign language, counting, perhaps, and Tim jumped up, yelled "Fuck!" and hit the button that turned off the entire stereo.

"Sorry," he apologized. "I dubbed it over one of my high school Spanish tapes. It's kind of a bummer to have it end like that." His tone changed, and he said, not looking at me directly, "I was pretty into it for a while there. What did you think?"

"It's good," I said. "You walked the walk and now you're talking the talk." I kept my voice level. I told Tim what sounds intrigued me and asked him how he achieved them. At first, his answers were as technical and specific as my questions. But after a time came such an outpouring of relief, a confession of anxieties I didn't even know he had. "I've wanted to do this as long as I've ever wanted to do anything," he said. "But I didn't want to do it and find out I was no good at it, so I kept putting it off, you know?" I nodded, and he continued: "But now I know I can do it. It feels so good. I know what my life's work is going to be."

I nodded again, with something that wanted to be empathy, but wasn't. Tim continued to talk, to describe the incremental triumphs of the recording process, the joys of watching Joey and Cree mature as musicians, the satisfaction of a project completed to the best of his ability. I couldn't really listen anymore, because a terrible dark feeling was growing inside me. On the short drive home, thinking about the last weekend of shift work that lay ahead, I realized what it was. I began to breathe so heavily that I had to pull the car into a gas station that had closed for the night. What I realized was this: that my life might be significant only for its relationship to Tim's. I knew then that it was not a darkness inside me, but the world itself growing smaller, until it consisted of me, what I could see around me, and nothing beyond that.

THE PARENTS ARE COMING TONIGHT. While the Davises have been regular concert attendees since the early days, the Wakefields have never seen their daughter perform. Most of this has to do with Cree and her longstanding belief that her conservative Indian mother will suffer a meltdown if faced with the right combination of smoke, noise, and the sight of her baby behind a drum kit.

Tim, who once spent a fair amount of time at the Wakefield household, thinks Cree is overreacting. He's never pressed her on the issue but has said of her mother, "Hey, she married a white guy."

Tim's parents are making an event of the evening. They and two other couples are meeting for cocktails at four and then driving up in the Davis minivan at about five-thirty. My guess is Mrs. Davis will be the one driving. They're going to stop by the club and then go to dinner while the band soundchecks.

I ask Cree if her parents will be joining them.

"No, no, no," she says. "They're going to wait in the lobby."

"The lobby?" Joey says from the driver's seat.

"I'm going to say they're crew," she says.

"You should say they're our food tasters," Joey says. "Tell them that people keep trying to poison our mixed nuts."

"Why would anyone want to poison us?" Cree says.

"For introducing immoral rhythms to the national atmosphere," Joey says. "A small sect of Christian crusaders is mounting an offensive against lust and profanity. Part of their program involves the eradication of the downbeat, of which we are the last true advocates. We must be protected from their tyranny."

"Okay, Joey," Cree says. "If anyone asks, that's what I'm going to tell them."

We cross the Delaware River into Pennsylvania. We are about forty-five minutes outside of Philly. Remembering last night's conversation with Colin, I decide it's time to delegate some authority.

"We need to get the guest list settled," I say. "Cree, Colin says you're in charge of that."

"Oh," she says. She looks puzzled. "Sure."

"He said you like to take care of it."

"I wonder why he said that," she says. "I don't mind. How much space do we have?"

Tim looks up from his book and says, "You did the list on the last two tours." Cree doesn't say anything.

I rifle through the itinerary until I come to the information. "Twelve spots," I say.

For a couple of minutes she writes names down on a pad. Then she says to herself, several times, "Fuck!"

"What is it?" I say.

"I'm going to have to make some decisions," she says. I look over at the pad. "Who are all these people?" I say.

"Just people," she says. She starts crossing out names. Then she stops and asks Joey who he wants on the list. He names two of his housemates and a girl with whom he had a brief, unconsummated affair. Tim's parents and their friends have already bought tickets, but Tim has a few other assorted people to whom he's promised admittance. Cree dutifully notes these. She doesn't ask me who I want to get in, but that's okay because I don't have anyone. She goes back to crossing out names and writing new ones in. At one point I look over and see that numbers have been

put next to certain names. Her parents are one and two, and I
realize that she's doing a ranking.

"You'd better be careful that that doesn't fall into the wrong
hands," I say.

"It's so hard," she says. "I want all these people to see."

"Can't they just buy a ticket at the door?" I say.

"It's not the same," she says.

"It's not possible," Tim breaks in. "The show is sold out.
They're all sold out for the rest of the tour."

"Didn't you hear Colin talking about that last night?" Joey says.

"No," Cree says.

" 'Glorious' is climbing the charts," Joey says. "Modern rock
stations are adding it left and right."

"Wow," Cree says. "Fuck. That's crazy."

Tim says a hit single means we can expect to see a mix of Radials' faithful and teenyboppers at the upcoming shows. "We're
going to take our appeal to a new demographic," he says. "The
teens of the top forty."

"The girls of the Big Ten," Joey says, and this is probably
closer to what Tim actually has in mind.

Edward stands in the lobby of the club talking to a bedraggled
white-haired man. Last night I asked Edward if he was ready to
take my picture, and he reacted as though I was making an al-
lusion to something pornographic. Then he realized I was talking
about the pass, and said, "Oh, yes. We'll get around to it. The
pass you have now is getting the job done, yes?"

The pass I have now is generic. There's a colorful exploding
star with the word RADIALS in the middle of it and then the word
CREW across the bottom. Tim, Joey, and Cree all have their pictures on theirs; today in the van they held them up in a row and
made comparisons. I'm not going to mention it to Edward tonight.
I don't want him to think I have a fetish.

"Lou, hello!" he shouts across the lobby. He says "hello" so fast it's like a hiccough. He waves me over.

"Lou, this is Bob. He's going to be selling T-shirts for the Radials."

Bob is some kind of old hipster. He looks sixty, but I have the premonition that I am going to learn that he is much younger, maybe twenty years younger, and that this information, whenever I receive it, is going to surprise me.

He says, "Nice to meet you," in a dumb, dopey voice.

Edward says, "Well, I'll leave you two to sort things out."

Bob pushes his T-shirt box along the floor over to the wall the club has designated for merchandise. The wall is broad enough for two, but only half of it is well-lit.

"Do you mind if I take this half?" I say, and Bob says, "I don't care, that's fine." I have a moment in which I feel actual triumph for having defended the interests of my band. Soon I feel petty. Bob has never hung shirts before. The shoulders are bunched in, obscuring the design with folds and wrinkles. He also doesn't hang them high enough.

He looks at the wall and scratches his head. "These shirts don't say 'Radials' anywhere."

"No, you're right," I say. "I guess you're just supposed to know it's the band from the picture."

The picture is of a sports car driving toward you. Brant's at the wheel on the left side of the frame—it takes me a minute to figure out why—and Peter sits shotgun. Gemma and Walter sit in the back with their heads pressed together so you can see them between the bucket seats. They all wear sunglasses, except for Peter, who dangles his out the window. The artwork is pretty crude—if you're not already familiar with the band, you're not going to know who they are.

"I wouldn't buy it," Bob says. "But I'm gonna sell it!" He laughs in a har-de-har way. He starts making piles of shirts in a semicircle around him. He has his work cut out for him. While there's only one design, it comes in four colors and three sizes.

When a customer asks for a "blue, medium," Bob is going to want to be able to find it right away.

Edward comes back a few minutes later. He doesn't seem to notice Bob's shabby T-shirt arrangement. He hands me a little stack of laminated backstage passes. "Someone's mummy is coming tonight?" he says.

"Several mummies," I say.

"Well, I'll tell the boys to be on their best behavior," he says, departing again. I wonder if he thinks of the band as "boys." Maybe he's talking about the crew. The only females in the entire ensemble are Gemma and another woman about her age whose function I haven't yet discerned.

Through the window of the club I see Tim's parents walk up to the ticket booth.

I have a revelation about Bob and the role he can play in my life.

"Can you watch my stuff?" I say. "There's some people I need to talk to."

"Sure," he says. "No problem."

Michael Davis enters the club as if he owns it but hasn't been by to visit in years. His wife and the two couples follow him like an entourage. He walks through the lobby to the entrance of the concert area and there pauses under the archway. The empty room stretches out for over a hundred feet before it hits the stage. The floor is black and uneven. Underneath the lights Peter croons alone into his microphone, but only the monitors are on so the sound is faint.

Mr. Davis sees me and walks over.

"And you call this rock and roll?" he says.

"Frankly, sir, I don't know what you call it," I say. I have always had trouble responding to his sarcasm.

"I'd like you to meet these people," he says. "You already know my wife, but here we have a couple of physicians, Thomas and Deborah Powell—they're going to be buying us all dinner tonight, and then we have the Overtons, Susan and Dennis. I don't know what they do, so I think they're going to buy dessert."

"And what are you going to pay for, Michael?" says Thomas Powell.

"Parking," Mr. Davis says. "And when you see how much it costs, you're going to thank me, buddy."

"Look," I say, trying out some banter, "perhaps you'd like to see your son now."

"Yes, I think we would," says Tim's mother.

"Let me furnish you with these," I say. I hand out the back-stage passes. Mr. Davis makes a comment that I don't catch but draws a fair amount of laughter.

I lead them across the wide floor to an opening at the side of the stage. Mr. Davis nods and says thank you to the club security person as we go past. We go up several flights of stairs and then make a right at the top. Joey and Cree sit on a couch with pencils, pads, and a Boggle game between them. I turn to the adults and put my finger to my lips.

"Where's Tim?" Mrs. Davis whispers.

"I don't know," I say. "I'll look for him."

As I leave the room I hear Joey and Cree quitting their game to say hello. Mr. Davis compliments them on their nutritious rider selections and asks if he can have some raw broccoli. After that I can't hear anymore.

The Radials' backstage is up one more flight. The door is closed, and I stand on the landing for a full minute before I knock. I try to gauge what is happening inside but the English accent leaves me confounded. Finally, I knock, loudly, as if I am the police, and a crew person comes to the door.

"Can I help you?" he says, blocking much of the room from my sight.

I am still devising my comeback when Brant says, "I know who he is. Let him in."

"Hello everybody," I say to the room. There's Tim, Brant, the crew guy, and then Gemma and the mystery girl sitting on the couch. I get an assortment of waves and nods. I turn to Tim, who is playing with the wrapper to a bite-sized Snickers bar that is now obviously in his mouth. "Your parents are here," I say. "They're right downstairs, waiting to see you."

"Ah ha ha ha," Brant laughs, unnaturally. He's smoking and wearing a shirt that says "Fight Racism." Before he goes onstage he'll change, as is his custom, into something silk. "So the folks are in town," he says to Tim.

Tim swallows what's in his mouth. He grins at Brant, and laughs, "Ah ha ha ha."

"Ha, ha," Brant says, taking a drag. What's going on?

Gemma decides to stand up then and says "Lou," making it a question, and when I nod, she says, "Lou, I'd like you to meet my old friend Louise. Louise, this is Lou. You already have something to talk about, now don't you?"

Louise laughs, "Ah ha ha ha," the most guttural laugh I have ever heard out of a woman, and when Brant and Tim make the same sound almost simultaneously, I realize they are imitating her. So the joke's not on me.

"I leave you to do with that information what you will," I say to Tim. "Louise, it was nice to meet you. Gemma, it was nice to meet Louise through you. Brant, it was nice to be invited into this room by you." I don't know what to say to the crew guy, so I don't say anything. I go trotting down the stairs, all of them, to the ground floor, and then I walk across the concert hall and through the lobby and then out the main doors on to the street. I've forgotten my coat, but that doesn't matter, I should be able to find a drugstore within a couple of blocks. I have a headache, or at least I have something like a headache, something I'm certain aspirin would cure.

I spot a CVS across the street and go in. Less than two blocks from the club, this is the punk rock drugstore of my dreams. I can't walk down an aisle without encountering multiple members of the alternative nation. A girl with upwards of twenty metal rings in her face stands in front of a rack of rubbing alcohols, comparing the CVS brand to a product made by Johnson and Johnson. Two handsome young men with short hair pass me carrying loads of Huggies stuffed under each arm. My head hurts so bad I pop open the bottle right there. The twin fluffs of cotton fall about my feet. I tip my head back to swallow the pills and see that someone at the register is watching me via the tilted mirrors on the back wall. I don't look away. I observe this teenage person as he alerts his co-worker, pointing with a long, skinny arm. He and the co-worker watch me through the mirror. I watch them. I try to establish eye contact, but their expressions don't change. Do they not understand the concept of "mirror"? I saunter up to the register, like a gunslinger at high noon, the uncapped bottle in full view. My adversary is also prepared.

"You're not supposed to open that until you've paid for it," he says in his best nasal voice.

"Fuck you," I say. I lay down a five spot. "Keep the change."

I stroll over to the door. "Excuse me, sir," says the clerk. "But with tax that comes to five-oh-eight." The way he says it I know it's going to go down as one of the classic lines of his young life. Unless . . .

I sprint out of there. I bang off the automatic door as it opens much too slowly. On the other side of the block I stop running. It is darker here; instead of storefronts, there are store backs and Dumpsters. A few streets down is the alley behind the club where we parked the van. I know I'm not going to get arrested over eight cents, but I feel paranoid just the same. My heart pumps blood into my head at a faster rate. My headache is now beyond the reach of mere aspirin. I'd like to take a nap. I'd like to do a light jog over to the van, get in—Joey gave me my own set of keys— and lie down in the back seat. I'd pull the sleeping bags and duffel bags around me and make a nest. And when the night was over, Tim, Joey, and Cree would come back to the van, unlock the door, pull away all the bags and say in quiet tones, "What happened, man?" They would spend the rest of the tour protecting my fragile mental state. It would bring them together in a way no one could have thought possible.

But a lot of T-shirts wouldn't get sold. Not just tonight, but for many nights. There would be that many less teenagers garbed in the word and image of the Day Action Band. The process of infiltrating a nation would be corrupted. Is this how I want to be remembered, as the man who crumbled an infant dynasty?

On the way back to the club I recognize someone, John, a childhood acquaintance of Tim's. He's lurking across the street from the ticket office, with a tall ratty winter hat atop his head. I say lurking because there's no other way to describe it, the hunched posture, the hands in the pockets, the wary looks from side to side. He went to middle school and high school with Tim and believed that this forecasted instant friendship in college. I don't know the guy well, I just know that Tim used to like him and now he feels uncomfortable around him. I try to make it into the club before he sees me, but of course that doesn't happen.

"Hey, I know you!" John shouts over the cars.

"Yes," I say, not shouting, so all he sees is me opening and closing my mouth in unenthusiastic affirmation.

He comes across the street. "It's Lou, right? What are you doing here, man? Up to see the show?"

"I thought they could use my support, yes," I say. I don't want to lie, but I don't want him to know I'm touring with them either.

"Yeah, man, I've come here with the same intentions. Alas, I have no ticket."

I nod to commiserate.

"Man, this is fantastic. This is a big deal! You know?" He looks up to the marquis at the entrance to the club, where it says RADIALS in capital letters and DAY ACTION BAND in lowercase. "I remember when Timmy got his first guitar. He used to play 'Smoke on the Water.' I remember that."

"John," I say, "I'd love to catch up, but I have to meet some people." I put my hand on his shoulder. Intuitively, I know it's the sort of gesture he appreciates. "See if you can get a ticket, maybe I'll see you inside."

"Sure, you gotta go," he says, retreating. This seems like it's going to work, until Tim's parents come out of the club with their friends, on the way to dinner.

"Hey, Mr. and Mrs. Davis!" John says. I realize he's drunk. He says to me, loud enough for them to hear, "I've known these people my whole life."

The Davises say hello to John and receive several rounds of congratulations from him. They check their watches and say they're late for their reservation. As they walk away, Mr. Davis says, "Lou, Tim was looking for you. He said he needed your help with something." Shit.

An increased look of intelligence passes over John's face. "You're helping out the band?" he says.

"I'm their tour manager," I say. "Not permanently, just for this tour."

"Cool, yeah, what does that involve?" he says.

"Mostly I sell T-shirts and CDs," I say. "I do my share of the driving—you know, carry equipment, whatever they need."

"Do you change the strings on Tim's guitar?" he says, grinning.

"No," I say. "He likes to do that himself." I had forgotten about my headache, but it sure hasn't forgotten about me.

"Well, hey man," he says. He throws his hand out in a wide arc. "Congratulations. You're some kind of hot shit now. I'm not sure what kind, but hey."

"Thanks," I say, as we shake. Shaking the hand of an asshole always makes me feel like a sellout. John doesn't let go right away.

"Speaking of strings, do you think you could pull some and get me inside tonight?" he says.

"No," I say. I rescue my hand with noticeable force. "I'm afraid that's not something I have any control over."

"Well you take it easy, man," John says. "Tell Timmy I said hello."

As it turns out Tim didn't need my help. He just wondered where I went.

"We have some aspirin right here," he says, holding up a minuscule bottle of Bayer. "The club gave it to us. We didn't even ask for it."

"I needed a breath of fresh air," I say. "It was time to step outside." I almost add a sentence or two on the subject of John, but I decide it's not something he needs to hear about.

"You and Brant are buddies now," I say instead.

"He's a strange guy," Tim says. "Not that I know him very well. He just doesn't seem like the same guy who gets up there and jumps around and lets the girls touch his fingertips. It's like he gets in character before he goes on."

My vantage from the T-shirt table hasn't so far been the best, but I have been able to get a decent sense of how Brant works the crowd. The character he gets into is polished but familiar. He's every prancing Mick Jagger wannabe that ever graced the stage of a high school talent show, only a thousand times more intense. If it's a ballad he pulls his arms against his chest so the microphone rests under his chin and paces slowly about, as if in shackles, eyes fixed on a distant part of the ceiling, perhaps the place God would sit if he were in attendance. If it's a rocker he seems to fly around the stage on a string like the lead in one of those old productions of *Peter Pan*. To the audience he says things like, "I wish I could make each one of you feel the way I feel right now." Last night, Tim tells me, as the Radials waited to come down the stairs to the stage, Brant hid behind a curtain from the vibrating masses. Ever so slowly, he kicked out a foreleg. Violent, multilateral screaming ensued. Then Brant sent Edward halfway down the steps. Silence upon silence. After Edward scurried back up, Brant said, "You've left the ladies speechless, Ed." Tim reports that Edward then said, "As usual," and bowed modestly, leading Tim to believe that this had been done before. "Otherwise," Tim says, "that would have been a pretty low thing to do."

Tim's basic strategy is to be himself. It doesn't make him uncomfortable to be on stage. That's not to say that the moment he has an audience, his inner pilot light catches fire and he becomes an inferno of entertainment. Rather, he proceeds as usual, as if it were three people watching him play guitar and sing instead of nine hundred. He smiles, makes wide and easy eye contact, strolls around as much as his guitar cord will let him, and if the music calls for a period of seriousness and attention, he responds with what's appropriate. He said to me once, "My job as a performer is not only to make people want to be me, but to make them feel like it's possible." It made me feel very strange to hear him say this, and I thought about it for a long time afterwards. At first it seemed like something a person might say during a fit of high egotism. But to think that would be to ignore the real compassion in the second part of the statement. Here is what I think. There are times when I sit in a room full of other people, my friends even, and begin to take note of the frequency with which I readjust the position of my hands. I look around at the crossing and uncrossing of ankles, the constant wiping of noses, the breaking off of speech when a move to conversation is ignored or overridden by a louder voice. I think then that there would be nothing better than to feel complete ease in the presence of other human beings. Why is Tim a performer? I can't say for sure, but maybe it's because he feels that complete ease and that's what makes *him* uncomfortable. He is the one person that everyone wants to have as part of their group, and the one person that can never be part of any group because he lacks the insecurity with which all people construct their relationships. The music he plays is pop music. The words, the melodies, the rhythms, the harmonies, and the sounds are all chosen to make the listener feel good. The ease is externalized and amplified and projected out to the very people who believe they have come for music but are actually there for something else. See, Tim is saying, this thing that you have heard so much about is real. I am a person and I have it; therefore you can have it, too. It's not magic. It just feels like magic. And when the show is over and the music is gone, you may accuse Tim of making false promises, you may say that he has given the crowd nothing, but if you have ever been a part of that crowd, then you know you have been given something and that is hope, and really, what more could you expect the guy to give you?

Cree's mother is beautiful. Seeing her walk into the club on the arm of her white-haired, slightly befuddled husband, I realize in a very profound way that Cree's own beauty is no temporary fiction. She's going to look good at thirty, forty, fifty, right on up until she dies. There's not much I can do with this new knowledge, however, and so when Mrs. Wakefield asks to see a medium-sized T-shirt, I hand her one. She asks who I am in a moderately heavy accent, and I tell her, and then she asks if I know Cree and I tell her that too. Finally she asks me if I think the T-shirt fits her—she's got it draped across her chest—and although it looks like it's going to be a little tight, I tell her it fits fine. Mr. Wakefield comes over and tells her it's unfair to put me on the spot like that. I say that's what we in the customer service industry are supposed to do, but Mrs. Wakefield doesn't respond. She steps away from her husband into the middle of the lobby and takes a deep breath. Then, slowly, she rotates. She's taking in the whole sordid scene, from the dirty, cheesy, faux red velvet, old-time theater surroundings to the ambisexual, vulgarian, partially nude teen predator occupants. Her reaction? A pleased exhalation and a big smile. Cree has nothing to worry about.

Pretty soon more Indian people come into the lobby display-

ing varying levels of American cultural awareness. These are either relatives of Cree's mother or friends of the family in general,
and there are quite a few of them. Cree likes to say that all Indian
people know each other, and more than once have I seen her
shoot down the unsuspecting social liberal who tried to dispute
this claim. Two suave young women in the midst of high school
glide up and compare the Day Action Band merchandise favora-
bly to the stuff sold by Bob. Bob doesn't appear to take this cri-
tique personally. An overweight, bespectacled man in his
twenties with buck teeth stands in the corner, visibly self-
conscious, trying to tuck in the other half of his shirt. Children
less than ten years old trail closely behind their parents, who,
after a few minutes of aimless wandering, decide to comport
themselves like the middle-aged tourists they are. I sell a great
many T-shirts of all sizes during this time. I only sell a few
CDs; most of Cree's relatives are in the market for something
on tape. "You can buy the CD and then have a friend tape it for
you!" I suggest, but they are too savvy for that. Then the lights
dim in the main room, and the lobby empties, leaving Bob and
me to discuss how some people are slow to pick up on new tech-
nologies.

They play a good set. At least my ears tell me they do. I have
an image of the youth of the Cree nation, fanning out once inside
the theater to occupy key points of a carefully wrought crowd
enthusiasm network. The voices I hear tonight are high and young
and unjaded. Except for the voice of Mr. Davis, who keeps his
pitched at a mid-ranged bellow for much of the forty-five minutes
his son is on stage. The most touching aural moment belongs to
Cree's mother, who, in the millisecond of silence after her daughter finishes singing "The Only Way to Talk to Her," calls out,
"You do a great job, honey! You keep singing another one!"

Afterwards the lobby fills again. The Davises and Wakefields
exchange congratulations. "This is the first time I've ever seen
your daughter in a dress!" exclaims Mr. Davis. Mrs. Wakefield

laughs and says, "Tim was great too!" Tim's mother wears an expression of religious epiphany. "My son's an entertainer now," is all she can say. Well-wishers from all walks of life complete page after page of the mailing list, many pausing to add little notes with exciting marks of punctuation. I meet Tim's former babysitter, his street hockey buddies from the seventh grade, even a favorite customer from one of his old paper routes. The atmosphere reminds me of those days in Boston when there is a big snowfall and the city shuts down, and the people are out walking in the streets and shoveling out their cars and you actually want to talk to them.

When all the respects are paid, almost everybody associated with Tim and Cree leaves. It's late, and, with the exception of a few college friends, these people don't know who the Radials are. Bob watches this exodus with bewilderment. "I never heard of your band before tonight," he says. "I didn't know they were so popular."

"It was a hometown crowd," I say, and Bob nods and says, "I've seen a few of those."

An hour later, the Radials are at the point in their set where they play three consecutive ballads. I am starting to think of this sequence as the beginning of the end of the night. Somnambulant reverb sounds hold the very air molecules in stasis. My band, as Bob put it, is backstage entertaining guests; except for when Cree ran out to bring me a Coke, I haven't seen any of them for a while. Bob himself is nodding off in his chair. In the land of the fully conscious, it's just me and one of the bouncers, and we don't have much to say to each other.

John comes out of the men's room. One way or another, he made it inside. He's drunker and wiser now; on his way across the lobby, he pauses to give me a scornful appraising look. I can take it because my own head is full of speculation about his future, speculation that I am withholding due to my maturity and upbringing.

John goes over to the bouncer and asks first for a cigarette, then for a light. The bouncer points to a sign and says there's no smoking in here. John acts as though he's cool with that and settles in against the wall. "What'd you think of that first band?" he says. "Did you like them?"

The bouncer says, "I liked that drummer. She's got some talent. Just give her a couple of years, she'll be pretty good."

"Hell!" John says, misunderstanding, "She's old enough now!"

"Get your mind out of the gutter," the bouncer laughs.

"Why doesn't your mind get down in the gutter with my mind?" John says. He thinks this is witty.

The bouncer sighs. "My mind's been there, and now that I have it back, I'm going to keep my eye on it, thank you."

"Suit yourself," John says. He straightens his collar and buttons several of the lower buttons on his coat. "Take it easy man," he says to the bouncer, and pushes through the door to the street.

A few minutes later the Radials break before their encore. When Brant returns I listen carefully for the response to the opening chords of "Glorious." I had assumed that it was an old favorite being given the acoustic treatment, but now I hear the clapping and screaming as a welcome for a new hit. The song is much better than anything else the Radials play, and Brant sings it as if he knows this.

TIM, JOEY, AND I spend the night at the Davises. Joey sleeps in the guest room and I sleep on a futon in the attic. At breakfast, Mrs. Davis tells a story about a funny thing that happened in the night.

"As Michael will tell you," she says, "I'm not a very heavy sleeper."

Mr. Davis nods his head gravely.

"Last night, oh, I don't know what time it was," Mrs. Davis continues, "I was awakened by the sound of something rustling in the hall. I thought, well, it's just one of the boys on his way to the bathroom, so I lay there for a minute, I was trying to go back to sleep, but this thing kept rustling! Then I thought maybe some squirrels had chewed through the insulation and gotten trapped in the walls—that happened once in our old house—so I debated about whether I should wake up Michael—"

"You made the right decision dear," Mr. Davis says, patting his wife on the arm.

"—and when that didn't seem like a good idea, I thought I would go out in the hall and investigate myself."

"So what was out there?" Mr. Davis says, in a way that indicates he has already heard the story. I notice Joey has put his fork down.

"At first I couldn't see anything," Mrs. Davis says. "I didn't want to turn the light on, because—I wasn't thinking clearly, you know—if it was squirrels, I didn't want them to run back into the walls. But it wasn't squirrels. It was this slowly . . . whirling . . . thing—and it was very tall! I came closer and I realized it was Joey. Turning round and round and round. I didn't want to disturb him, he seemed so intent on what he was doing."

"What was I doing?" Joey says, as if he truly wants to know.

"Well I don't know," Mrs. Davis says. "I was going to ask you that. But you spoke to me!"

"No!" Joey says, laughing but nervous.

"Do you know what you said? You said, 'Are you Susan?' and I said, 'No, Joey, I'm Tim's mother,' and you said, 'Oh, it was something in the way you moved,' and then you lowered your head and walked straight back into your room, and when I looked in on you, you were fast asleep. So my question is, who is this Susan?"

"Yeah, who is this Susan?" Tim says.

"She must be quite a dish," says Mr. Davis.

"I don't know," Joey says. "I don't know anyone named Susan."

Susan receives a fair amount of airplay during the drive to D.C. Cree draws upon resources from a dream analysis class she took as a sophomore, but the best she can do is come up with the anagrams "Nussa" and "San-su," neither of whom is anyone Joey knows. Already there are signs that "something in the way you moved" is going to become a catchphrase for this tour, as in "Tim, something in the way you moved makes me think it's your turn to check the oil."

It's cold and raining again, and pretty soon I fall asleep to the ambient sounds of National Public Radio. When I awaken we are in the heart of D.C.'s warehouse district, which previously I did not know existed. I feel as though the last scenes of many action movies were filmed here. We drive around until we find the warehouse with the marquis and then we unload. Joey has parked the van directly over a giant puddle; by the time I set foot in the club, my shoes are making a squishing sound I haven't heard since my middle school years.

The discomfort fades when I realize we have come to the Taj Mahal of clubs. The stage is distant, the ceiling is cathedralesque. The floor area could host a whole battery of Olympic gymnastic events. For the thirsty there are bars and mini-bars at regulated close distances, the massed liquor bottles glinting softly in the indoor night. Above, a balcony, yes, a balcony, stretches, curving, wide, like nothing so much as a beach with black sand. Backing up toward the stage, I begin to see the largest bar of all, as it rises, terraced and spectacular, from the center of the balcony. I turn to Joey and say, "This place is dark in a really cool way."

"Yes," he says. "And listen to this. Think of the balcony as a horseshoe. As we face the stage, our backstage is at the right tip, the Radials' at the left. Both backstages contain a shower. Furthermore, this venue contains its own restaurant, from which we are permitted to order at will. I have this menu. I have my eye on the black bean nachos."

Half an hour later we eat. Tim tries his first ever veggie burger and pronounces it disgusting. I am only partially satisfied by my mushy pita concoction, but the nachos are good, maybe too good. Respecting them, I choose to take a preemptive walk around the upstairs of the club.

On the other side of the giant bar I find Bob sitting with his hands on his knees, a half-eaten veggie burger at his side. Not knowing what other kind of small talk to make, I ask him what percentage of merchandise sales the club is taking tonight.

"The bad news is," Bob says, "they're taking twenty-five percent. The good news is, they sell it for us."

"What does that mean?" I say.

"It means you take your stuff to the guy downstairs, and tell him how much you want to sell it for, and then he sells it and you're free to do whatever you want."

It takes Bob close to a minute to say this sentence. When he's finished, he just sits there, looking from side to side, perhaps for a trash basket to vomit into once I'm gone.

For the first time I get to see how they conduct themselves before they play. Most of the forty-five minutes between doors and showtime pass quietly. Tim reads a magazine and drinks a Corona. Joey paces through the room and hall, occasionally wandering out as far as the balcony, where he checks on the status of the crowd and then reports it back to us. Cree gets up to go to the bathroom again and again, complaining of her small bladder yet continuing to nurse a bottle of spring water. No one seems interested in conversation, so I don't try to make any. At five minutes past eight a club orderly shows up and tells them that they've got ten minutes until they go on. Tim puts the magazine down and says, "All right, let's change quickly. I think tonight we should have a band moment."

Joey and Cree react to this hilarious statement with surprising solemnity. Cree grabs her backpack and takes it into the bathroom. Joey changes right there in the room. He takes off the shirt he's wearing and puts on what he calls his "rock shirt." The shirt is white with mild yellow polka dots the size of nickels. It's made of a very thin fabric, and it's long, even for Joey.

Cree comes out of the bathroom in a purple felt dress that stops at mid-thigh and a string of fake but tasteful pearls. It's a good thing she's going to have the bass drum in front of her when she plays; otherwise those closest to the stage might be able to see up her dress.

Tim is already wearing what he's going to wear: jeans, a light blue short-sleeved oxford, and a brown vest. The vest is the only real concession to performance; each night, he puts it on over whatever shirt he's wearing at the time.

"Let's try a harmony," Tim says.

"Which one?" Joey says.

"How about the chorus to 'Somebody Lose,' " Tim says. Interesting choice. This one they play mid-set, when the crowd's beginning to warm up to them. It has a bit of a sing-along quality, that, Tim has remarked, occasionally induces members of the audience to sing along. It's not the song I'd pick if I were having a band moment, but I'm getting ahead of myself. Tim opens his arms and draws his bandmates into a close group. He nods his head in a silent count-off, and, on three, they all sing, "Everybody choose / Go to bed in twos / Somebody lose."

"How'd that sound?" Tim says to Joey and Cree when they're finished.

"Good!" Joey says.

"Great!" says Cree.

"Is that how loud you normally sing?" I say.

They look at each other. "Yeah, I think so," Cree says, and Tim and Joey make noise in support. "Why?"

"It sounded kind of quiet," I say. "You know, after hearing it through the speakers . . . It sounded about as loud as you guys talking, if you talked in notes, that is."

This last part is a joke they don't get. I almost add some parenthetical ha ha ha's, but the mood isn't right, and the joke isn't worth rescuing. They look confused and sad, as if I've asked for directions they don't know how to give. Finally Tim says, "I guess we really need the speakers." He pauses for a moment and then says, "We need a couple of minutes alone. I hate to kick you out . . ."

"Sorry," I say. "I thought that was the band moment. I'll just step into the bathroom here . . ."

I go in the bathroom. There's a shower, as advertised, but it doesn't have a curtain. Some rock-and-roller from a time long past has left a sliver of what looks to be Irish Spring in one of the soap holders. I take a seat on the closed hopper and press my fingers to my temples. What happens in the band moment? Do they place hand on hand on hand, chant "Day Action Band!"

three times, and throw their arms in the air, hooting and screaming like some fifth-grade soccer team? Do they light candles, burn
incense, and practice their melismas? Do they somehow arrange
for lightning-quick, stain-free group sex? Whatever it is they do,
I know I can never ask about it. The asking alone would betray
too great a trust.

A minute later Tim knocks on the door, to convey that the
band moment is over and that he would like to use the bathroom.
When he comes out all four of us go down the stairs together.
Each step brings us closer to the crowd and the noise. A fluid
energy passes through me that I know I am not meant to feel. I
picture adrenaline boiling in the vein. At the bottom we diverge.
They go into a tunnel that leads to the stage; I move past the
security person and into the crowd.

They play. I stand in multiple places, a look of dazed concentration on my face, as I seek out and identify sonic irregular-
ities. The audience is not yet thick enough to prevent me from
moving from region to region without difficulty. The left front
side of the room is submerged in throbbing bass frequencies; toward the back and center I hear too much of Joey's voice in the
mix. I conduct internal debates over whether these observations
would be useful to the soundman. Finally I reach the place in
front of the sound booth and stop. The mix here is good, as I
expected it would be.

A group of emissaries from a local Greek organization con-
gregates a few feet away, the men in hats, belts, and shirts tucked
into jeans, the women all with hair of identical length, color, and
cut. The Top 40 stylings of "Glorious" must be what brought
these people out here tonight; even at this late date, a few of
them might not be able to produce the name of the band that
sings the song.

I notice them because one member of the group is making fun
of the Day Action Band. He's bopping along in time to the "na na
na's" of "Lottery," half facing the stage, half facing the women

he's trying to impress. The women laugh, rock back on their heels, and let their pelvises push forward in subtle encouragement. Soon all the guys are involved in the act; one mimics the little dance Tim does when he steps away from the mic to play a solo, another holds his hands up around his head to indicate the size and shape of Joey's hair.

I've seen this behavior before. Two years ago my inclination would have been to march into the middle of the group and say, "You stupid assholes, what do you know about music? Why are you so impressed by loud guitars? What do you mean when you say 'that drummer rocks'?" I would have then begun a mass ridicule of bands that like to jam, starting with the Grateful Dead and moving right up on through Blues Traveler, leaving out Phish because once a hippie got me stoned and I thought they were geniuses. But I am wiser now. Mellowed by time and experience, I know that, given fifteen minutes, these disrespectful socialites will be getting down to the Day Action Band in a manner both reverent and satisfactory. I need only watch the transformation take place.

In fact, tonight it doesn't take fifteen minutes, it only takes five. The derision persists in full force through Joey's rendition of "Going Country." The opening lyric of that song—"Think my body's going country / Hope you'll help me save it / It remembers all the girls / And all the love they gave it"—prompts questions about Joey's sexuality and more discussion of his hair. But the gentle swells of "The Only Way to Talk to Her" have a hypnotic quieting effect. By the time Cree sings in a downward stepwise melody, "The only way to talk to her / Is not to talk at all," these young men and women are ready to listen. They stop their talking and face the stage and those in couples sweetly hold hands.

And soon it happens to me too. I stop thinking about whether the song is being played at the right tempo. I stop thinking about the tastefulness of Tim's fills. I stop thinking about how years ago Cree would drop one of her sticks and look up with an expression I can't hope to describe except to say that it was without embarrassment or self-consciousness. I stop thinking. And though my eyes see the forms moving on the stage and my feet feel the floor beneath my shoes, these senses are in the service of my hearing, which is for this extended moment complete. I have one thought in the final twenty minutes of their set, and that is that I could choose to feel betrayed, that they have done this to me at the same time that they have done it to so many others. But that is a choice I don't think a feeling person could make.

"Outside Tokyo" ends and I push up to the stage to help them break the gear down. Cree, struggling under the bulk of the floor tom, says, "Oh, good, you're here," and then says, "Could you take this? I have to go meet my cousin."

The lights have come up, and the drama is gone, but the audience is still there. I sneak a few looks out there as I carry objects off the stage. A few people look back at me, but their faces are difficult to read. What are they thinking? It probably varies from individual to individual. I fight off the urge to grab the mic and say, "Testing, one, two, three, testing." I concentrate instead on not falling down or walking funny. Joey pulls the van up and we load out through a side door.

Backstage, Cree and a pretty Indian woman are in the midst of a greeting. This must be her cousin Siri, our hostess tonight and tomorrow night. Two women who appear to be with Siri have opened beers and are drinking them quietly on the couch. Tim and Joey go straight for the towels, wiping away sweat that has already nearly dried.

A flamboyant young radio DJ arrives to interview them, his mute blond photographer girlfriend in tow. He swoops down in a dashing bow, and on his way back up says to Tim, "Excuse me, are you Tim Davis, the author of all these incredibly great songs?" With the aplomb of an amateur magician he produces a copy of *That One Five Jive* from behind his back. He turns to me in a very public aside and says, "The soundtrack to my life these past fourteen months." He corners Tim, who is removing and folding his vest, and begins to fire away with preliminary questions. The girlfriend eschews the expensive camera around her neck in favor of a Polaroid and pads around the room taking pictures of everything, whether it be animal, vegetable, or mineral. The finished photographs pop out the front of the camera and float to the floor.

The chaos achieves a new dimension upon the entrance of Sarah Renshaw, the nineteen-year-old sister of Sunday Driver president Will. She knew Tim back when he was just someone her brother got fucked up with in high school. "Ohmigod!" she screams. "That was incredible!" She rushes across the small crowded room and throws her arms around Tim's neck. She gives him a big wet sisterly kiss on the cheek. In a postmodern twist the DJ decides to interview Tim and Sarah simultaneously. He pulls out his microphone and presses RECORD on the tape player at his hip while they get reacquainted. For someone who says "like" with such frequency, Sarah manages to sound remarkably intelligent. Cree doesn't think so; I look over at her and she points her eyes at Sarah and makes a face.

I sit down on the couch next to the beer drinking girls. My presence intimidates them. One has finished her beer but pretends to drink from it anyway. I start to gather the photographs that have fallen nearest my feet.

From my pile I pick out three solo portraits of Tim, Joey, and Cree. I fan them out in one hand and hold them at arm's length. It would be obvious to any observer that these are not ordinary citizens. They can only be rock stars, and not just rock stars, but rock stars in cahoots. I hold out a picture of myself in my other hand. I don't look like a rock star, but I don't look like an ordinary citizen either. I look from one hand to the other, trying to think of what the third category might be.

Joey leans against the armrest of the couch. "What are you doing?" he says.

"In this hand," I say, "I have the inside jacket for your next album." I turn around the hand that has their pictures in it. "And in this hand, I have the cover." I turn around the hand that has my picture in it. Joey laughs. The interviewing DJ is alerted.

"And who are you?" he says, coming up beside us to get a look at the Polaroids.

"I'm a joker," I say. "I'm a smoker. I'm a midnight toker. I play my music in the sun."

"No he's not!" Tim says in the voice of a playful whining degenerate. "He's the roadie!"

"Yeah!" Joey says. "Interview the roadie!" He steps back and points his long arm at me in judgment.

Cree and Siri stop their conversation. The girls on the couch turn in my direction, their fear at being noticed overcome by their curiosity. Sarah looks on from her place at Tim's side.

"Interview the roadie?" the DJ says, thoughtfully scratching his goatee. "I think I will." He flips a switch on the recorder and speaks into the microphone, low and mock serious: "And with me now, is"—he pauses while I say my name—"Lou Farren, roadie extraordinaire, man about town, and, from the looks of him, a sartorial force to be reckoned with. Lou, you've been with the band how long?"

"Four days."

"And what insights have you gleaned in that time?"

"Regarding what?"

"Regarding the state of our nation's youth."

"There are more of them than ever."

"It's like an infestation, isn't it?"

"You said it, not me."

"Do you know what they want, Lou?"

"Sometimes I feel like I do."

"I'll tell you what they want, Lou. I'll tell you what they want." He leans in close, pokes me in the chest, and says in the loudest stage whisper I have ever heard, "They want you."

"They do?"

"Oh, yeah. They're out there screaming for you right now, boys and girls, men and women, dogs and cats, steak and eggs. They all want you, they just don't know it yet. You're a lucky man, Lou Farren. I envy you." He stands up then and snaps off his recorder with a loud click. He grins and says in his real voice, "Thanks for playing along man, that was really cool. You're going to be on the radio."

"When will it broadcast?" I say.

"I'm not sure," he says. He shrugs his shoulders to indicate powerlessness. "It all depends on my music director, blah, blah, blah, et cetera, et cetera."

The DJ's girlfriend comes up and plucks the picture of me out of my hand. She looks at the picture, looks back at me and frowns. She speaks for the first time since entering the room: "You really look much better than this. I'm going to take a new one." And she does.

The room where I sleep is devoid of all amenities. It belongs to Siri's brother, away at medical school, and he has left no remnant of his occupancy, save for a short stack of anatomy textbooks, which, for some reason, he believes he no longer needs. The bed is flat and hard, a thin sheet covering several layers of plywood. The extra blanket Siri brings me I wrap around myself to form a primitive human roll-up. During the night, I wake up every fifteen minutes to maintain the integrity of the roll-up, and so when daylight comes I am ready for an excuse to unwrap and say hello to the world.

The world is covered with about two inches of wet snow, already morphing into slush and running drain water. The temperature must have dipped below freezing sometime after one o'clock. No one is awake. I dress and go immediately to the front doormat, but the paper isn't there. I decide to go get one. I put on shoes and a jacket and close the front door very quietly behind me. The light reflecting off the snow is unpleasantly bright, and I wish for sunglasses I don't have. I walk through and out of the neighborhood, taking note of street names and landmarks. Next I walk along a major road for fifteen minutes, passing a church, a softball complex, and an on-ramp to the beltway before I come to a convenience store.

By the time I get back it is nearly nine. Joey, Cree, and Siri are all awake and talking excitedly about what museums to go to. This is Joey's first time in D.C. as a tourist, and the two women want to make sure it's special. Cree is pushing for the National Gallery of Art and the Air and Space Museum. Siri, the hipster insider, names some museums I've never heard of. Joey says over and over that the only thing he absolutely has to see is the Hope diamond.

Although it's not a Saturday, it feels like one to me. I have been working four days straight and now I have a day off. I'm considering undressing and spending the day in boxers and a T-shirt, watching Siri's television, investigating the contents of her pantry. But then Tim comes up from the basement where he has been sleeping and informs the room that he has made lunch plans with Sarah and her friend Terry. Anyone is free to join them. A longtime critic of museum patronage, I throw my hat in with the lunch people. "Do we know what we're eating?" I say, and Tim says "Ethiopian food."

We pick the girls up in the van and go straight to the restaurant, which Sarah has never been to but has heard good things about. A waitress with a wicked smile exerts a strong influence over our menu selections. "Delicious!" she says when she brings us our plates. My food is a large piece of porous bread onto which colored piles have been placed at strategic points. I imagine a tiny Ethiopian army manning its outposts to defend a sacred burial ground from Nazi archaeologists. I would be frightened and dismayed by my meal if it didn't provide such a rare chance to flirt with these younger women. Soon we are all trying each other's food. Sarah keeps going back to a reddish pile on my plate. When the waitress comes by Sarah asks what the stuff is. "Raw beef," says the waitress. "Delicious!"

"Aaahhhh," Sarah wails, "I'm a vegetarian." I am surprised to learn this this late in the meal. Most vegetarians I know talk about it constantly. Sarah drinks all the water at the table trying to wash the taste of meat out of her mouth. Tim, Terry, and I are not thrilled about the raw meat either, and we leave the restaurant feeling unsatisfied and on the verge of possible illness. The upside of the affair is that we all endured it together; the rest of the afternoon is spent in coffee shops and record stores with the kind of camaraderie known only to those who have nearly died in each other's arms.

Night falls and we are not ready to say goodbye. Tim suggests we grab some beer and head back to Siri's for a little MTV. He'll be happy to give Sarah and Terry a ride home when the evening is over. We stop for the beer and the girls have to wait in the van. I keep wondering if Tim has designs on Sarah, but I truly have no idea what'll he say if I ask. He might say with sincerity and confidence, "Yes, I do." He might say, "Who's askin'?" and act squirrely. He might say, "My God, man, she's my best friend's younger sister, what do you take me for?"

We come through Siri's front door with beer, women, and an attitude that says, "party." Joey, exhausted after a day of marble and granite majesty, is already asleep for the night. Cree is in the shower. Siri has put on her glasses and nightgown but attempts to play the gracious host. "We have a big television in the basement," she says, "and I'll prepare some snacks." She bustles off to the kitchen muttering about miniature bagel pizzas.

Several videos in, Cree appears at the top of the stairs. She is wearing a long bathrobe and a towel is wrapped high around her hair. "What's going on, Tim," she says in a very stern tone. She doesn't acknowledge Sarah or Terry in any way.

"We're just hanging out," Tim says. "Drinking a few beers."

Cree looks at him for a second. "Okay," she says, and turns to head back up the stairs.

"Hi, Cree, how are you?" Sarah says, intending to sound pleasant.

"Oh, I'm just fine, Sarah," Cree says. "I'm going to bed. Tomorrow, wake me up whenever you have to. I don't need to take a shower." She shuts the basement door with medium force.

There is some low-voiced discussion about what Cree's problem might be. "I've never seen this side of her," Sarah says. "Maybe we should leave."

"No, no," Tim says, "this is something she has to deal with."

We hear the basement door open again. People whisper in disagreement at the top of the stairs. The acoustics of the stairwell allow us to get the gist of what they're saying. Siri has actually made the miniature bagel pizzas and is trying to bring them down to us. Cree is forbidding her to do so, on the grounds that we did not have permission to invite Sarah and Terry into her home. Siri is saying she doesn't mind. Cree is now saying she's going to tell Tim to take the girls home, "because we have to get on the road early. He doesn't need to be getting drunk with teenagers." She seems to place all the blame on Tim.

"Tim," she says, coming into view. "We've all got to get up early tomorrow. I think it's time to call it a night." She says each word deliberately, stressing what she believes are the important syllables and underscoring them with nods. She looks at Tim as if he were the only person in the room. When she turns to go up the stairs a final time her eyes meet mine and there is no recognition in them.

"Well, you heard the boss," Tim says. He stands up and collects the half-empty beers from Sarah and Terry. I can sense

Sarah's desire to make a bitchy comment, but an air of uncertainty about what just happened prevents her. Tim and the girls put their coats on in silence. I am reaching for mine when Tim asks if I would mind staying here to make sure things are okay with Cree. I tell him I wouldn't mind.

"We had a good day today," he says with strange formality. Sarah and Terry agree in tones of dawning awe. I say goodnight to them and listen as they troop up the basement steps and then quickly out the front door. I hear Siri call out after them, "It was nice having you."

After a few minutes of pacing in front of the TV, I steel myself and head up into the kitchen. The untouched bagel pizzas are arranged in concentric circles on a plate on the stove. Siri attempts to justify Tim's actions to Cree, who stands with her arms crossed, staring fixedly at the lower half of the refrigerator. She shakes her head independent of Siri's arguments and soon goes off to sulk over a crossword puzzle in the dining room.

To pass the time Siri tells me of growing up in India and the day the death cloud descended on her hometown of Bhopal. A sikh in a turban woke them at 3:00 A.M. and told them their lives were in danger. Siri's father was suspicious until he looked up and down the street and saw others leaving their houses. The family packed themselves into their car and drove away. When they returned, they drove slowly through streets strewn with bodies. Siri remembers asking her mother why these people slept on the pavement. Her mother covered her eyes with her hands and stroked her hair and told her she was dreaming.

Then Siri says the words, "Union Carbide," and I realize I have heard of this disaster. "Wow," I say. "You were there?"

I am reduced to this idiocy in part because during the course of the story Siri has been moving closer and closer to me, until her breasts are less than an inch from my chest. I look down into her large passionate eyes and think about how this situation might merit a kiss. I think of those who died choking in Bhopal, and then I consider Cree fuming half a room away. I can't afford to make a misjudgment here. I say to Siri, "What do you think is the best way to reheat these pizzas?"

It is a good thing I do, because seconds later Cree charges into the room raving about the amount of time Tim's been gone. "This is fucking ridiculous," she says. "He's been gone an hour."

"Maybe he got lost," I say.

"Give me the phone!" Cree says, even though it's closer to her than to me.

She calls. I hear a female voice pick up. "Sarah, this is Cree," Cree says. "Let me talk to Tim." There is a pause, and then the ranting begins.

"We have to fucking get up in seven hours and drive to fucking North Carolina tomorrow. I don't care what the fuck you're doing, stop doing it, get in the car, and drive back here now . . . Why don't we just go to bed? Because someone has to let you in the fucking front door, Tim. This is Washington, D.C. You don't leave the fucking front door unlocked. Just come home now."

"Can I talk to him?" I say.

"He's your friend," Cree says, and hands me the phone. I take it into the dining room.

"Yo, hoss," Tim says. "What's she so fired up about?"

"Several related issues," I say. "You probably know what they are."

"We've been talking to Will," Tim says. He seems pleased to be able to say this and have it be the truth. "He wanted me to call and tell him how the interview went, and Sarah hadn't talked to him in a while, so . . . I didn't know about locking the front door."

"You should get back here as soon as you can," I say. "My efforts at peacekeeping have failed." I am glad Cree and Siri are not in the room as I say this, because they might somehow indicate to Tim that I haven't made any efforts.

Tim sighs. "Thanks for trying," he says. "Tell Cree I'm on my way."

FOR THE FIRST HALF of the four-hour drive I am the only one awake in the van. There are several moments when even that is an issue; the soft gray cloudy light, the deep rumbling engine, and the warm air from the vents seem the perfect representation of what sleep could be in the waking world. I remember driving to the Cape with Kaitlyn after our senior prom, and how she fell asleep shortly outside of Boston. I began to develop theories, mad theories, about how to sleep as I drove. By alternating five-second naps with five-second periods of wakefulness, I could sleep thirty seconds out of every minute. Testing this theory, I woke to see a SOFT SHOULDER highway sign as it disappeared under my front bumper. We drove the rest of the way with the windows down and the air-conditioner on full blast, shivering cold but awake.

My younger brother Jamie is the person I am driving to see. He lives in Chapel Hill, where he has been a student for the past three and a half years. During this time I have turned down many invitations to visit, citing technicalities, a lack of transportation, an obligation to work. Every year I see him twice, once at Christmas and once at the beach in Rhode Island. That has always been enough for me. As I have often told those who've asked, it's not that I don't like him, it's just that I don't *like* him. It's all in the inflection, I have been heard to say.

But when I woke this morning after another fitful night on Siri's brother's board-bed, it was with an image of Jamie in my mind and a sense of guilt above my head. I roamed frantically through the house, forcing everyone to get up early so that I might have an afternoon with my brother before the show. "Fine," they said in emotional unison, "as long as you drive." What I look forward to most isn't seeing him, but seeing where and how he lives and how this reality differs from the life I've imagined for him. I picture him walking through a neighborhood of student apartments with his backpack over one shoulder. I see trees blooming and upperclassmen sitting on porch swings. They've turned up the stereo so it can be heard through the screens on their open windows. The second side of *Fables of the Reconstruction* is playing. A sweet breeze blows. Somewhere a dog barks once. My brother inhales deeply and thinks that this is a great time and place to be alive. Immediately after, his heart fills with melancholy. He goes home and turns on the television and watches it until the four o'clock sun heats his forehead and puts him to sleep. Later, maybe he orders a pizza. I don't know. I haven't thought about what he does at night.

This morning, Tim, Joey, and Cree shuffled out of the house, Cree still in pajamas and slippers. I watched Tim and Cree for signs of tension but they both seemed preoccupied with getting settled in the van before they became more fully awake. Joey missed last night's conflict altogether, and part of my mind looks forward to the time later today when Tim and I will fill him in. For now, I try to drive as quietly as possible. I keep the wheel steady, and when I feel the transmission about to downshift, I ease up on the gas.

The van comes over the top of a large rise. Huge banks of mist lend the valley on the other side an infinite quality, and I look down at my watch to time how long it takes to drive through it. Joey opens his eyes in such a way that it's obvious he's been awake behind them for a while. He's been biding his time, waiting for the appropriate scenery.

"How far do you think that is?" he says.

"I'll tell you in a minute," I say. I raise the arm with the watch on it, and he nods. We don't talk as the van moves down into the mist, and then back up and out of it.

"Five minutes," I say.

"Five miles," Joey says. "When we used to go on trips my dad would pick some distant object and ask how far it was. I'd say 'fifty feet,' and he would say 'try again, Joey.' "

"I think my dad did that once or twice," I say.

"By the time I was in my teens I was pretty good at it," Joey says. "But then I didn't want to play anymore."

He asks me if there's any bottled water in the van, and I tell him I don't know. From the constraints of his seatbelt he conducts the most thorough search possible. His physical behavior, and his speech, for that matter, lack their usual goofy syntax. This early in the morning, he is still minutes away from assuming his social persona. I feel that this is as close as I will ever get to seeing how he behaves when he's alone. We chat about the cities we grew up in, and Joey reveals an enhanced interest in metropolitan areas, especially when viewed from a distance. As a youngster he hated Philadelphia because at the time it was the fourth most populous city in the United States, one spot ahead of Houston.

Soon Cree awakens with the words, "Anytime you want to stop for breakfast . . ." Tim, also waking, attempts to start a dialogue about places we might eat, but Cree says that she wants to stop at "the first place we see." Tim doesn't argue. Joey tells Cree that that kind of attitude is less prudent once you enter the South, and she says, "Maybe."

Fortunately the first place we see is a Waffle House. This information means little to me, but to Tim, Joey, and Cree it is a symbol of comfort and good fortune, an old friend from earlier trips through the region. This particular Waffle House has been defaced, either by nature or by local vandals, so that the sign visible from the freeway reads WAFFLE HO.

"Are you the Waffle Ho, Cree?" Joey asks.

Cree laughs for a long time. When she's finished, she says, "Do you see any other hos around here, honey child?," and laughs for another extended period.

The "Waffle Ho" banter continues down the exit ramp and into the parking lot. Tentative at first, Tim gets in on some of the action during the short walk from the van to the restaurant.

"What are you going to order for your breakfast, Waffle Ho?" he says.

"Grits," says Cree, "The Waffle Ho is going to have me some grits."

She seems to have no recollection of her recent anger. It's not like she's decided the adult thing to do is put the incident behind her, it's like she's forgotten it ever happened. Tim's cautious behavior of a few minutes ago is all over now. He's joshing Cree left and right, making humorous comments about the strange food pictures on the Waffle House menu. He is clearly familiar with her powers of instantaneous forgiveness.

After breakfast Joey says it's time for the first hack of the tour. He instructs us to stand on the grass next to the parking lot and runs back to the van to get the hackey sack. I've been waiting for this moment with some apprehension. From what I've heard, these three people have been honing their hacking skills on the road for over four years now. Whatever apparent lack of athleticism they ordinarily possess will be dispelled in a frenzy of kicking legs and bobbing heads. They will individually keep the sack aloft for thirty minutes at a stretch before sending it over in my direction, where it will bounce comically off my hip and fall to the earth. We will drive away in the van and never speak of it again.

Joey returns. He stands on one leg, then the other, stretching his quads. When Cree laughs, he says sternly, "I'd advise you to do the same." Tim, looking uncertain, reaches down to touch his toes.

We form a loose square. Joey tosses the hackey sack at Tim's knees. Tim's foot comes up and punts the little bag thirty feet in the air, far over Cree's head. "Sorry," Tim says.

"A little excited there, Tim?" says Cree. She retrieves the sack and tosses it to Joey. Joey catches it on the inside of his left ankle, juggles it once, twice, three times, and passes it to me. Lunging with my forehead, I drive the sack across the square to Cree. She knocks it over to Tim with her knee, and Tim hits a hard line drive in the vague direction of Joey. The sack nicks the tip of Joey's fully extended leg and dies in the grass several feet later. I have the physical sensation of euphoria departing my body, but the rest of the group is in good spirits.

"That was a hack!" Joey says.

"Barely," says Cree, looking pointedly but affectionately at Tim.

"On only our second attempt," Tim says. "Good job, everyone!"

"Should we do another one?" Joey says.

"No," Tim says. "We should quit while we're ahead."

"What's a hack?" I say.

"Everybody has to touch the sack at least once," Cree says, "and then one person has to touch it after that."

"We hack until we get a hack," Joey says. "Then we get back in the van. Usually it takes a lot longer than this."

"Good headwork," Cree says to me, one competitor to another. I have no problem giving her my most natural smile.

Tim and Joey make several lame jokes about "using your head" and "headwork," and then, sure enough, we get back in the van.

My brother lives in a small, decrepit apartment complex at the bottom of a long hill. The picturesque campus area is at the top of the hill, so his residence has a humble, subservient feel. My revised mental image still includes my brother and his backpack, but now there is sweat on his face as he struggles up the steep incline, leaning forward into each slow step.

The complex consists of several long rows of connected two-story units. We pull into a parking space in front of my brother's and he opens the door and stands there grinning. I half expect a young woman to appear in the space behind him, and pretty soon one does. She puts her arms loosely around his neck and presses into the back of his shoulder, working to make her expression of greeting match his. My brother's grin increases, as if to say, "Look at what a ladies' man I've become."

We get out of the van and everyone shakes hands. My brother impresses me with his grip. He introduces himself to the band as "James," though for as long as I have known him he has gone by Jamie. I don't call attention to this because he doesn't. The girlfriend's name is Erin. She is bursting with unnatural confidence, and when Cree compliments her on her interesting regional accent, she seems momentarily confused.

Inside, the apartment has been freshly cleaned. The glass coffee table is polished and bare, except for a casually elegant hors d'oeuvre arrangement, featuring cheese, two kinds of crackers, and a bowl of colorless paste. Joey exclaims as if this is the very thing he has been waiting for and digs into the crackers and paste. Cree heads over to the cheese. Erin asks what everyone wants to drink, listing water, orange juice, Coke, and beer as options. Tim bends down on one knee to examine my brother's CD collection.

With everyone else occupied, Jamie turns to me and speaks.

"How was the drive?" he says.

"A little bit wetter than I would have liked," I say. We are going to cover the topics of driving and weather within four sentences. My mind scans a dictionary list of further subjects and comes up with nothing. I see Jamie's lips moving and I know I'm not going to be able to respond. I decide to blow him away with a non sequitur.

"Does Erin live here?" I say.

"Technically, no," he says. "Technically she lives four apartments down. She goes there about once a week to get new clothes. She doesn't get along with her roommates. Which is fine with me."

He lowers his voice and says, "Any women in your life?"

"Only the one you see in this room," I say, indicating Cree, absorbed by cheese.

"Really?" Jamie says. He takes a step back as if to pay me some sort of homage.

"No," I say. "Technically." I say the word with obnoxious overtones, and Jamie hears them. He laughs, choosing to pretend I was making a joke. Maybe I was.

"Well, that's one technicality that might get you off," he says. "With this judge anyway." This is not a perfectly phrased witticism, but somehow it restores his balance.

Erin reenters the room, bearing drinks. She sets them on the coffee table and we all gather around, in chairs and on our knees. We divide into two camps, guest and host, and exchange backgrounds. Cree is the spokesperson for our camp, with occasional insights added by Joey. Jamie and Erin split their conversational duties equally. I listen to both parties throw around the phrases "your brother" and "my brother." I nod and smile in recognition when they are spoken. I don't feel worthy of these titles, however, and after a while I start to feel mocked by them. Then I feel that this kind of paranoia has no place in a rational human being. I decide what I really am is tired.

"I got up too early today," I say. "I've got to take a nap." Everyone seems slightly shocked by this announcement.

"You can sleep in our bed," Jamie says. "It's made, but don't worry about that, just get right in. Up the stairs and first door on the left."

"Thanks," I say. I go upstairs and into the room and lie down on top of the quilt. Rainwater moves loudly through a gutter outside one of the windows. Downstairs I can still hear them talking and sometimes laughing. After a few minutes of trying to fall asleep, I get up and close the door.

When Tim wakes me it's dark outside. "It's time to go to the club," he says.

"How long did I sleep?" I say.

He looks at the clock beside the bed. "Five hours."

I say the words, "I didn't mean to sleep that long," although not in the correct order. Tim smiles and leaves the room, respectful of my disorientation and my need to recover from it. Once he's gone I allow myself a single shocking spasm of regret over the wasted afternoon. Then I rise, straighten my twisted clothing, and prepare for the assortment of nap-related comments I am certain to hear. But when I get downstairs, no one says anything, except for Cree. "Are you feeling better?" she asks, and I tell her I'm feeling much better.

We walk into the club and witness the entire Radials entourage gathered around Edward at the foot of the stage. There are about a dozen people altogether; I knew the number was about that high, but it's impressive to see them all in one place. Edward is making some kind of announcement, and he's attempting to do it in style, with dramatic pauses and sweeping arm gestures, neither of which come naturally to him. He leads up to a final statement, after which there is hollering, hugging, and chest bumping, particularly among members of the crew.

"What's up with that?" Cree says.

"Edward just announced that they're all going to get free tote bags emblazoned with Brant's face," Joey says. "It's something he's been promising them for years."

"I wouldn't mind having one of those," Cree murmurs.

"Neither would I," says Tim. "Wouldn't be able to tote much after I got through with it, though."

When the equipment is loaded in, I disembark immediately for the merchandising area. Just before we left for the club, Erin revealed a craving for a special brand of sandwich, and Jamie offered to take her to get one. For some reason it seems imperative to get the T-shirts hung and the CDs arranged before they return. I work feverishly, cursing every time a piece of duct tape gets stuck to itself. I tear off a new piece with my teeth, aware that this is not standard human procedure.

I have long since finished by the time they come back. The doors have opened and a sizable mass of individuals has already filled most of the available space. Jamie and Erin must have gotten the sandwich and then sat down somewhere to eat it, perhaps using that time, as all couples do, to reflect on the obtrusion of others into their lives. They walk up, giggling and poking each other, their legs bumping with each step. A few feet away, Bob sits on a stool reading a comic book. Tonight the scraggly ends of his white hair have been tamed by a rubber band. I observe as Erin looks at Bob, whispers in Jamie's ear, and then laughs.

"I think we'll watch from back here," Jamie says. "Things look like they're going to get a little bit crazy up front."

"So far these crowds have been pretty sedate," I say. "You might see some people shake their hips, but so far, no one's gotten hurt."

"I'm more worried about my ears," Erin says.

"Your tender little ears?" Jamie says, lightly pinching one of her earlobes. She swats away his hand.

"I'm serious," she says. She tells a very sad story about her first concert experience, Debbie Gibson, at a community college auditorium. Some fiendish configuration of speakers and audio dynamics left permanent hearing loss at her uppermost frequencies. My observation that those frequencies are not good for much does not get the laugh it deserves. Jamie segues into his own first rock and roll show, Richard Marx at the Paradise.

"You gave me so much shit about that," he says, grinning.

"But eight years later, my ridicule is revealed to have been wisdom," I say, winking at Erin. She waits until Jamie laughs before she does.

The club's sound system, which up until now has played nothing but obscure European girl groups, shuts off, signaling the beginning of tonight's festivities.

"You should get in there," I say to Jamie and Erin. "Later, when you have become official adults, you will look back and be sorry that you missed this. Go on, get in there." Behind my cheerful exhortation is a real need to remove Erin from this scene. I have only known her a few hours, but I have already determined that she is not as intelligent or as interesting as she purports to be. If I have to talk to her much longer I am going to start making faces and retard noises instead of responding to what she says. Then Jamie will have to take me out back and kick my ass, something that he is probably now able to do thanks to the university's nationally ranked fitness center.

"Why don't you go ahead," Jamie says to Erin. "I'll be in in a minute. I want to talk to my brother. Just stand someplace I'll be able to find you."

"I don't know if that place exists," I say, ambiguous about my own intentions. Erin looks worried.

"You'll be okay," Jamie says. "The room isn't that big."

Reluctantly, Erin departs. We watch her walk over to the edge of the crowd. She stops behind a group of denim-embossed women and spends a minute on her tiptoes trying to peer around their bobbing heads. Then she looks back at us, sees us looking at her, and pretends to be involved in a circuit of rigorous neck motions.

"What do you think?" Jamie says.

I hadn't expected him to be this direct, but I have an answer. "She's pretty and she seems like a nice person," I say. "It was very thoughtful the way she brought us drinks when we arrived."

"No," he says. "I mean, what do you think of her body?"

I squint in the direction of her backside, fifty feet distant. First I say she has nice hips, but this sounds too prurient. Next I ask if she spends a lot of time at the gym. Jamie nods, grinning, and then I say forcefully, "Do you really want to encourage me to have sexual thoughts about your girlfriend?"

The grin disappears, and along with it, Jamie's entire facade of simulated maturity. The person I see now is insecure and uncertain, capable of being destroyed by a single word from his older brother. He is a computer-enhanced version of the sweet, ridiculous thirteen-year-old I left behind when I went to college. I feel generous toward him and completely in control. I decide to impart a life lesson, and then, just as quickly, I decide that only the pompous impart life lessons.

I say, "Jamie, it's a good thing I'm your brother, 'cause . . . damn!" I shake my head to indicate the rest is obvious. Then I soften my tone and say, "Not that she'd have me, of course."

His face is still crossed with confusion, but the hurt look is gone. I smile, and then he smiles.

"I guess I should go keep an eye on her," he says awkwardly.

"You probably should," I say. He walks into the main room. I watch as he comes up behind her and presses his pointer fingers into her sides. She jumps and turns around and hugs him.

The Day Action Band makes a very strong impression on both Jamie and Erin.

"You said they were good," Jamie says, "but I thought you were just saying that because they were your friends. That Tim plays the guitar like a motherfucker."

"They're going to be stars," Erin says, implying that it would be futile to argue otherwise. "Do you think it would be tacky to get them to sign this?" she says, holding up the "Wrestling" seven-inch I just sold her.

"If my friends were in a bad band, I would have told you so," I say. "I don't think anybody should be subjected to a bad band." To Erin I say, "They're still in the stage where they get a kick out of signing autographs." This is true where Joey and Cree are concerned; Tim can't help but wonder what makes a person want to have an autograph.

The club darkens as the Radials begin to play. The loose eddies of atmosphere draw themselves into a taut swirling intensity. I can see a good part of the room from where I sit. There is an active sense of bodies yearning forward, toward the music, toward the stage, toward Brant, farther into the darkness. It is always a little disorienting when people choose to come out of that room into the place where I am, which is moderately well-lit, quiet enough that you can talk without having to raise your voice too much, and sparsely inhabited by the less glamorous. They come through the arch that divides the two regions and the magic surrounding them evaporates instantly under the dim overhead bulbs. I am the sentinel at the gate and a voice in my head calls out, "Hark, what business have ye here!" Usually that business is to attend the restrooms. Still, I feel a spirit of resolution when I see the person walk back into the room. Now Tim, Joey, and Cree come out of the pulsing shadows, distinguished from the rest of the mortals in that they are able to maintain their magic look. They glide up and receive praise. Joey and Cree sign autographs for Erin with a marker borrowed from me. Tim fields questions from Jamie about the gauge of string he uses, favorite soloists, whether Led Zeppelin will ever get their due from the critics. I could add to this discussion, but I don't; to do so would be to inject an element of the mundane into the transcendent. Whether or not Jamie knows it, he will consider this conversation sacred and think back on it warmly in private moments. Or maybe he will get drunk and blab to his friends that Tim is a nice guy, really easy to talk to. I don't know him well enough to say.

A third of the way through the Radials' set, Brant says, "This next song is called 'Everywhere I Want to Be.' We wanted you to be the first to know that it's the second single off our new album, and hopefully"—he looks significantly at each of his bandmates—"and hopefully, our second number one!"

Most of the audience regards this news as cryptic. The faction that does understand responds with such vocal enthusiasm that soon the whole crowd is cheering along anyway.

Reaction among my party is more subdued but no less elated. Joey says, "I had no idea it had cracked the Top Ten."

Cree says, " 'Glorious' is number one?"

Tim puts his arm around her and says, "Pretty cool to be touring with the band that has the number one song in the country."

Erin says, "Do I know that one?" and Jamie sings her a few bars until she nods.

Bob looks up from his magazine and says, "Seven thousand plays on commercial radio last week. That's amazing. A thousand times a day you could hear that song, if you lived everywhere in America at once." He giggles and says, "I'm going to sell a lot of T-shirts tonight. I'd better get ready."

Bob does a spectacular amount of business. A compress of bodies six deep in places waves cash and calls out requests. I can see Bob's brain evolving under the duress. There is no gimmick, no jive patter, no from-the-hip aerial T-shirt distribution, just constant assured motion, the exchange of product for payment. Bob would be a calming presence on the floor of the New York Stock Exchange. When the last indecisive youth has been shooed away by the bouncers ready to go home, Bob turns to me, grins, and holds up a stack of bills three inches thick. I hold up my own wad, which consists of two twenties, three tens, a five, and eight ones. Bob says, "Wanna trade?" and doubles over laughing.

We pack our boxes in silence. The open spaces of the club are nearly empty now; what people that remain are concentrated in the fifteen-by-twenty-foot area that is the Radials' dressing room. Those that cannot fit flow out the door into the lobby. Some of these on the outside appear to be there by choice, a desire for audible conversation or the chance to consume an entire beverage without spilling. Others are constantly peeking around the door-frame, looking for an opportunity to approach one of their heroes, now more drunk and accessible than ever before. They may get their wish. There will be no closed door tonight. A number one single is not just the accomplishment of a person or a band but of a nation. This after-show party is more populist than any concert could ever be. Not only are Tim, Joey, and Cree inside, but also Erin and my brother.

After I finish packing my box I help Bob with several of his. He doesn't plan to attend the party—"Every night on the bus is a party," he says—he plans to get in his bunk and go to sleep. I tell him I'm not in the mood to get down either, and he says, "After a while, it gets kind of old." But soon I have no choice. I can't drive the van back to Jamie's apartment; the others wouldn't have a ride home. I can't stand here at the defunct merchandise table; the adjective that best describes my demeanor at the moment is "lurking," and any minute now, someone's going to ask me what the hell I'm doing and be perfectly justified in doing so.

Eventually, the broad hand of fate pushes me through that door. Once inside, I realize I can exist here with nothing expected of me. Ever-flowing waves of alcohol have obliterated the concept of "outsider." I am merely another life force strengthening the aura of the collective.

My associates occupy key posts in this landscape. Joey stands with Edward next to a giant basin of canned beer as both of them look down at something in Joey's hands. Edward's shoulder moves to the right, and I see that the object is a jar of olives, very tightly lidded judging from the strain showing on Joey's face. Crammed into the end of a couch by four larger people, Cree nonetheless displays typical animation in an exchange with Gemma and Louise, who sit crosslegged and expectant on the floor in front of her. The female shouting I hear I attribute to them, and every so often Louise punctures the room noise with a few of her strident "Ah ha ha ha's." In a more somber scene I discover Tim and Peter sitting side by side against a wall, a couple of feet below the general plane of activity. Peter has quaffed a majority of a bottle of bourbon; the wasted smile he bestows on Tim contains thousands of years of contemplative self-pity. Or maybe not; when Peter puts his palm beside his mouth and hollers, "F-sharp minor!" I understand that they are talking about music, not life, one songwriter to another.

The greatest surprise is Brant. On this night of triumph he has chosen his companions strangely. There are beautiful women in this room, and yet he is not with them. There are colleagues and professional admirers here, and yet he eschews their company in favor of my twenty-one-year-old brother and his winsome girlfriend, neither of whom has paid more than passing attention to the Radials before tonight. When I first see this trio together, I assume I have caught them in a moment of temporary congratulations. But they don't move apart. I watch people walk up to Brant and shake his hand, clap him on the back, and then proceed onward. Always he turns back to Jamie and Erin and speaks to them with enthusiasm, even intimacy. At one point he excuses himself only to return bearing freshly opened beers. The conversation continues. I can't guess at the substance of it. I see only the ease and confidence with which Jamie conducts himself, the lack of deference, the lack of self-consciousness. It's as if he has no idea who he's talking to. I approach the vegetable plate and remain there for the next twenty-five minutes, subsisting on celery and carrots, occasionally looking up to see who is still conversing with whom. Finally I catch Joey's eye and we begin the slow process of rounding the others up to leave. The fondest goodbye of all comes from Brant. He says to Jamie and Erin, with real feeling, "It was nice talking to you." Jamie says, "Take it easy, man," and Brant says, "I will."

Our own farewell the next morning seems staged by comparison. The sun is out, and the temperature is in the mid-fifties, but the sidewalk in front of the apartment is still wet. Jamie and I shake hands and hug. Erin kisses me on the cheek. Jamie says, "We'll have to do this again," but it's unclear whether he means the tour, the visit, the concert, or the experience in total. I agree with him anyway.

Before we get in the van I decide I have to ask.

"Hey," I say, trying to conceal the interest in my voice. "What did you talk about with Brant for so long last night?"

Jamie laughs. "Sports," he says. "That dude loves American sports. He said he likes baseball better than soccer. Well, he calls it football. If you want to get him talking, ask him about the '93 Phillies."

"The '93 Phillies?" Cree says, showing some southeast Pennsylvania loyalty.

"Their first American tour was during the '93 playoffs," Jamie says. "Brant got into the Phillies. He said he went into a funk when they lost the Series. You should ask him about it."

"Maybe I will," I say, knowing I never will.

"Maybe I will," Cree says suggestively.

"Whoa!" Jamie says.

"The girl is on a mission!" Joey shouts, taking a step back.

"I wouldn't call it a mission . . . ," Cree says. She adjusts her pullover, pleased to have her romantic prowess publicly acknowledged. She looks over to where Tim was standing, but he is gone, already walking toward the van. We drive away and Jamie and Erin wave until we pull out of the complex and onto the main road.

IN SOME WAYS THIS feels like the first day of the tour. The shackles of visitation have been broken and thrown off; from here on out, it's just me, the band, and wide-open America. The weather, with its emerging sun and imminent heat, underscores this feeling. I drive with the visor down and the window cracked so that I might touch, taste, and smell the breeze of liberation.

The chatter in the van is as vibrant as I have ever heard it. All members of the band, but Cree especially, consider last night's aftershow a raging social success.

"I'd been going through withdrawal and I didn't even know it," Cree says. She waits for someone to question this statement, and when no one does, she adds, "I'd forgotten what it was like to hang out with girls."

"Ah Siri," Tim says in a funny voice, "so quickly are ye forgotten." Abruptly, he shuts up, perhaps to avoid further mention of that tumultuous night. Cree doesn't seem to notice.

"It's different when it's a relative," she says. "Gemma and Louise are just women, you know?"

"I think Louise used to be a man," Joey says. "Ah ha ha ha."

"Ah ha ha ha," says Tim.

"This is why I don't like to spend all my time with boys," Cree says, although she doesn't sound as if she minds at all.

The talk turns next to Philadelphia area sports teams. Both Tim and Cree went to see the Phillies play at the Vet growing up, but neither harbored a day-to-day interest in the club. Cree says she could probably fake it if she had to, especially in front of a foreigner. Joey says he has some old baseball almanacs from the early–mid eighties at his parents' house in Houston. She can use them to brush up on Mike Schmidt, Steve Carlton, and others, and blame her recent indifference on college and rock and roll. As the son of a man who has for twenty years owned season tickets to the Boston Red Sox, I know a thing or two about baseball, but when I volunteer my tutelage, Cree says, "Thanks," and follows it with, "Is anybody getting hungry?"

We stop for lunch at a Burger King in South Carolina. The King sits in the middle of an enormous empty parking lot that seems to have been built for the Wal-Mart yonder. Tim comes through the door and decides what he really needs is something refried. Squinting, he spots a Taco Bell on the horizon. "I'll be back," he says, and strides off.

The three of us that remain move into the line. We have never been in this combination before, and no one seems to know exactly what to do. Joey reaches out with his arms and grips both of the railings that form the line. Then he lifts himself up and lets his feet swing back and forth. I fear that his tall hair may touch the ceiling, but a glance upward tells me he still has a good eighteen inches of clearance. This cavalier physical behavior is made possible by the fact that the restaurant, like the parking lot, is empty, except for the neutral-gendered obese person now ordering at the register. It is this transaction that Cree fixates upon. The person requests a Whopper, a fish sandwich, a box of chicken strips, and one, two, three orders of onion rings. With each successive order of rings, Cree's eyes grow wider. This is not done for effect; this is a reaction of pure amazement. I view her eyes almost in profile and the muscles of her craning neck and the perfect signature of her jawline. What a short film this would make: Beauty, in Absorption, Witnesses Gluttony. Suddenly I see it, the chance to say something funny, something empathetic, something to show her that I know the ways in which she is strange and that I approve of them. But the words that come into my mind are complicated and unwieldy, and what I need to say is so simple. My brother could probably produce an effective comment without even thinking about it. The register chings shut, the person moves away to fill their soda, and the moment is gone.

At the table I learn she was captivated not by the customer but by the employee, a much older man of grudging temperament.

"It's so sad," she says. "His whole life, and now he works here. I wonder what he wanted to be."

"He probably wanted to be a garbageman," Joey says. He suspects that this is a terrible thing to say and laughs nervously.

"How old do you think he is?" Cree says.

"I'd say he's an octogenarian," I say. This table has a more natural order than the line; I can feel my wit rising to the surface.

"A what?" Cree says, on the verge of laughing outrage.

"An octogenarian," I say again. "A human between the ages of eighty and ninety. Once you turn ninety, you're a nonagenarian. It goes right on up the scale. Somewhere in this world right now, a dodecagenarian takes another breath."

Cree makes a loud cawing sound, the laughing outrage achieved. Joey joins her with some full-throated ha-ha-ha's, and I realize that I have done it, cracked the wisecrack of my recent dreams. There are actual tears in Cree's eyes. Now when I look across the table at them, I see a willing audience for my comedy. I think about how if Joey laughs too, that only makes me look better.

It is not long before Joey accidentally dips his elbow in the pile of ketchup he's made for his fries. He runs off to the bathroom, keeping the elbow bent and perpendicular to his body as I've instructed. When the laughter dies down Cree and I are left facing each other across the table, our trays piled high with leftover wrapper, sauce, and bun. The dynamic has changed again, and, once again, I can't think of anything to say. I think back to middle school cafeteria, the way at the end of lunch I would combine all the foodstuffs that remained on my tray into a distinguishable object, a volcano, a nonlinear pyramid, once, even, the Colosseum. I remember the praise I received for this, the concealed admiration from the young women who pretended to be grossed out. Cree is not so unlike these women, the girls with whom I first fell in love. I wish the same rules applied now. With my adult sophistication I could fashion a still image from *Back to the Future,* Biff plowing headlong into the truckload of manure as Marty skates off an object of feminine lust, albeit his mother's. Would she see it? Would she say, with scorn, "What are you doing?" Or worse, would she behave as if she didn't notice at all?

The perfect gentleman, I say, "May I take this for you?" and then I carry her tray and my own over to the trash. I assume the position for the tilt and scrape, but the seventh grader who lives inside me takes control of my nervous system. He does not look into the kitchen to see if the coast is clear. He does not look back at the table to see if he has an audience. He jams both trays, one after the other, into the trash. He turns and walks quietly back to the table. He observes that his actions have escaped notice. Then he relinquishes control, the young master, as if to say, "This is how it's done. You used to remember."

As I stand there in secretive temporal flux, Tim and Joey converge on the table from opposite directions. Joey's elbow region is soaked to transparency, the dim red spot over the bone like the flag that flies over the Japanese nation. Tim's hands are stuffed with still-wrapped and uneaten delicacies from South of the Border.

"I've been making some calls," Tim says. "I've got some exciting news."

His first call went to the person in Arizona mastering the new album. Tim read to the man a list of how many seconds should separate each song. The man played him back the mastered version of "Outside Tokyo" over the phone. Tim says, "It sounds great, it has that extra level of presence." I say, "You should be a pitchman for Bell Atlantic."

The second call was to the London West offices in Los Angeles. Tim spoke to Alithia, one of Colin's assistants. She has booked the band two new shows, one at a small club in San Diego during an off night next week, another in San Francisco following the last Radials show in L.A. Cree looks pained until Tim good-naturedly reminds her of the quality of burritos in San Diego. I have been hearing Alithia's name in association with Day Action Band affairs for several days now. I imagine her power-broking and raven-haired, staring down a middle-aged executive as she crosses her arms confidently on his desk. I asked Joey about her once, and he said, "She works really hard for us. She has a nose ring."

The third call was to Sunday Driver in New Orleans. Tim asked to speak with Will and was told he was unavailable. He heard a sequence of muffled mutterings, and then the voice came back on the phone and said, "Will wanted it to be a surprise, but he's going to meet you in Atlanta. He took a bus out last night." This is the exciting news.

"What does that mean?" Cree says, frowning.

"Will's meeting us in Atlanta tonight," Tim says. "He's going to ride with us in the van back to New Orleans."

"Doesn't he have a baby?" Cree says, stressing the word *baby*.

"Maybe the baby cries," Joey says.

"Of course it cries," Cree says. "That doesn't mean he has to abandon it."

"It wouldn't surprise me at all if the baby had a mother. Does it?" I say, directing the question to Tim.

"Fortunately, it does," Tim says gravely. "It will be well taken care of."

Cree groans and admits that the thought of Will in the van agitates her. "You guys will just encourage each other," she says, shaking her head.

"We're going to rock out tonight!" Joey says for the thirtieth time. "It's a mathematical identity. Will equals party. Party equals Will. If you had an equation with 'Will' in it, you could substitute the variable 'party' and nothing would change."

"Is that so," Cree says.

"That is so," Joey says. The downtown area of Atlanta has drawn nigh; we drive in the shadow of some of the taller buildings. A few minutes ago Joey observed that there seemed to be two downtowns, distinct skyscraping clusters separated by a mile of low-rise territory. "I bet the mayor thinks every day about how to bring this city together," he said.

"George Michael," Tim says. He has not spoken for about an hour. The words float in the tepid air of the van.

After a moment Cree takes up the challenge. "Yeah?" she says.

"George Michael," Tim says again. "Let's see where we can go with that."

Eyes squint and veins in temples pulse. Joey rocks in his seat. Cree emits noises that are repressions of the question she would like to ask. I bring the van into the slow lane and pump the gas at uneven intervals.

The setting sun flashes between skyscrapers. Joey lifts his head.

"George Michael Jackson," he says. Tim nods. Cree says "What?" and takes an internal vow to concentrate harder.

"George Michael Jackson Browne," I say. Tim claps his hands. Joey gives me the thumbs up. Cree says, "Give me a minute. Nobody talk, okay?"

Nobody talks. According to the digital clock in the dashboard, between two and three minutes pass. Joey warns that we're getting close to our exit.

Cree says, "Okay, okay, I got it, I got it." She smiles and says, "Boy George Michael Jackson Browne."

Joey says, "Congratulations, Cree. You're on the inside, baby."

We all turn back to look at Tim. "You're up, bucko," Cree says.

Tim feigns innocence. "What," he says, "you think this is some kind of game?"

Cree says, "We had to do it, now you have to do it." She is struggling to keep her tone playful.

"All right," Tim says. "This might take a few seconds." He looks thoughtfully around the van, as if the correct addition to the name is written somewhere on the blue felt. Cree makes noises similar to the noises of a few minutes ago. The new noises, however, indicate triumph.

Then Tim says, "Got it."

"Let's hear it," Cree says. She prepares herself for bullshit, as do we all.

Tim says, "Boy George Michael Jackson Browne versus the Board of Education."

We all laugh. Cree describes it as a "breakthrough." Joey's laugh decomposes into actual chuckling, which stops, starts, and then stops and starts again in time with his continuing ruminations. I wonder if I am the only one to see the link between this incidence of cleverness and Tim's creative powers in general. When Cree adds "My Little Pony" to the front of the phrase and gives herself equal congratulations, I decide that I probably am.

The van comes out from under an overpass and a beam of sunlight hits my eye. I think of Will and his coming introduction into this environment. I first met him late in our freshman year, when he flew up from Tulane for spring break and spent the week camped out in Tim's dorm room. One night we all got stoned and listened to *Red Headed Stranger,* and I remember feeling impressed by Will's devotion to the beauty of Willie Nelson's voice. At some point during that hazy evening I decided he was well worthy of Tim's friendship and therefore worthy of my own. But today I can't help but see him as a disruptive force. I like

being in the van with Tim, Joey, and Cree. I have become used
to the mingling of these voices, the arrangement of these bodies
in the seats. I was looking forward to it just being the four of us
for a while.

The club is in the Little Five Points area of Atlanta, the local
Mecca for deviant youth culture. This is probably where many
Atlantans purchase their bongs. We pass a shop with a large Gra-
phix sign in the window. Bong use is in evidence everywhere I
look.

The Radials' tour bus is parked against the side of a brick
building. I make a move to pull in next to it, and a young man
darts from the sidewalk and motions for me to roll down the
window.

"You have to back in," he says, shouting despite his close
proximity and the relative quiet of the street.

"Why?" I say, but he is already walking away toward the
driveway, waving me on with his right hand. While this is not a
central business district, it is five-thirty and there is some traffic.
Carefully considering the van's greater dimensions, I execute a
seven-point turn to a chorus of honks and shouts of "Move it,
buddy!" The van in place, I regard the young man, now flanked
by his friends in outlandish hats.

"Why did I have to do that?" I say through the still open
window.

The guy goes into a half crouch and slaps his knee. His face
breaks into silent laughter. The friends mimic the silent laughter and point at me in rhythm with their receding footsteps.
Now the leader sings, "Fuck you," in an otherwise pleasant
tenor. The two friends, still slinking back, chime in with a blue
chord "Fuck you" in perfect harmony. They repeat this twice and
then complete a choreographed turn and swagger away up the
street.

"Professional mockery!" Joey exclaims. "I have to applaud it."

"That was crazy," Cree says. She mutes her admiration of the trio with a dash of contempt, a token to satisfy her inner moralist. Tim is quiet, knowing that any comment will only increase my embarrassment. There is a moment where the three of them are waiting for my judgment.

"I should kick their ass," I say, finally, "but I don't want to." This, I know, is the mature way to respond.

"Something's going on," Tim says, turning our attention back to the club. He points over to the Radials' bus, where the crew appears to be loading equipment back into the lower compartments. A few feet away, Edward stands rigid and nodding while a shorter, fatter man waves his arms in explanation. Joey jumps out of the van. We see him conversing with a dour-faced crew member. Then he walks toward us, smiling and shaking his head.

"The show's canceled," he says. "Something about a building code violation."

"Are you sure?" Tim says.

"Crystal sure," Joey says. "That's why they're loading out again."

"What are we going do?" Cree says. There is a complex note in her voice, one that suggests she hopes Tim doesn't have some alternative work detail planned.

Tim shrugs. "I don't know," he says. "I guess we should find out if we're going to get paid. We still have to wait for Will."

I feel as though I should investigate the money issue, but Joey, strangely motivated, leaps back out of the van and heads over to where Edward and the other man are standing.

We watch the new transaction unfold. Joey stands to one side, his shoulders drawn in, an expression of extreme concern on his face. The two older men move their appendages rapidly, a sure sign of disagreement.

"No one's getting paid," Joey says when he comes back. His

face is sweaty and excited. "Edward's pissed. I didn't know he got pissed. He said the Radials would never play here again."

"That seems dramatic," Tim says. "What did the manager say?"

"He just kept saying that in two hours he was going to have eight hundred angry kids on his hands," Joey says. He tries to do an impression of the manager: "They're gonna fuckin' tear this place to pieces."

"I'm getting out," Cree says. "It's warm here."

No one can find a reason to object to this, and the rest of us follow suit. Tim and Joey spot Peter smoking near the Dumpsters in back and go over to talk to him. Cree says she's going to look for a bookstore she saw on the way in. I walk over to the head shop next door. Incense burns behind dark curtains, threatening headache. I am the only customer in the store. The man and woman behind the counter halt their discussion and move away from each other when I come in. They seem to fear that I am a man of the law. Signs on all four walls declare that anyone heard referencing marijuana will be evicted from the store. I bend down to look into a display case stocked with implements made of finely blown glass. Who are the people that can safeguard these pipes? I prefer something made of metal or plastic or wood, something that can be dropped, stepped on, or kicked under the couch.

Though I would never say so to Tim, I'm glad the show's canceled. Every day now, a small dread grows in me after four o'clock. By five it is large enough to crowd away my sense of humor, by six, my last remaining vestiges of poise. I become incapable of looking past the show. Does anything so terrible happen inside those concert walls? No and yes. I meet people. I establish short-term business ties with them. They give me instructions I am willing to follow. I set up my table and I wait. I wonder if tonight will be the night that Edward takes my picture for the crew pass. I joke around with the band. I watch them depart to go onstage. I listen to them play. I joke around with

them when they come back. I sell their merchandise. I field questions from people who enjoyed their set. Some of these people
clearly envy me. But others with demented joy place themselves
between me and the band on a social scale that I want to scream
at them only exists in this moment. "Are they your *friends*?" one
girl asked me last night, as the rest of her clique strained to du-
plicate her perfect mode of skepticism. "Yes," I said, trying for
unaffected honesty. In that vein I could have continued: They
are my friends. If I had a party, I would invite them and they
would come. And not out of obligation, but out of a desire to
revel in me and the companionship that I provide. Could you
say the same about your friends? What motivates their friendship? Jealousy? Opportunity? Fear? Something unnatural, I'm
sure. I could have said something else to that girl. I could have
lied: "No, they're not my friends. I work for the club. I'm here
every night. Sorry." I have a feeling it would have felt better and
maybe that's why I didn't do it. "Thanks for your time," I say to
the bong shop employees and, much to their relief, I return to the
street.

For all its fame, Little Five Points only stretches a couple of
blocks. I traverse them with utmost slowness, consciously short-
ening my stride and reducing the frequency of my footsteps. My
new gait is a genuine shuffle and I fancy the locals approve of it,
slacking as they do in a number of creative ways. If my jeans were
a little looser and my hair a little funkier and my belt a little
more studded, I might be considered to be wearing camouflage.

I seek to delay my return as long as possible. I have found
that fraternizing with rock stars makes me feel an unpleasant
combination of awe and disrespect, as fraternizing with royalty
might have done in a different place and time. I go into a
shop that sells crystals and observe iridescence with real de-
light. But beads and products made entirely of recyclables leave
me cold, and soon I return to the club to see what progress has
been made.

In my absence Will Renshaw has arrived. He stands with Tim, Joey, Peter, and Brant behind the Dumpsters, talking about "Glorious" and its status as the number one song in the land. Will says he knew the song would be a hit the first time he heard it, and Peter says, "Well, you could have given us a call." Brant smiles and takes an affirmative drag on his cigarette. The conversation pauses as Tim reintroduces Will to me. Will says nothing to distinguish himself, but, watching him, I make a complete assessment nonetheless. Of the six people in this circle, Will is the only man. The rest of us are boys, toying with adulthood but somehow refusing to make the transition official. In a few years, Brant and Peter will begin to seem grotesque, and a few years after that, so will Joey and I. Tim could go in either direction. Someday, we will each buy a house, with a down payment, mortgage, and equity, but we will never buy a house in the way Will already has, with hopes and dreams and plans for upkeep and additions. We will never have a wife and child and not feel as though they are the mere components of fulfillment, rather than fulfillment itself. What problem does Will have that cannot be solved with good intentions and hard work? He has created his own universe and now he dwells in it happily, emerging only for more raw materials, two-by-fours, a gallon of milk. Joey asks to see a picture of the baby, and Will pulls a wallet-sized family shot out of his breast pocket, smoothing a diagonal crease as he hands it over. The picture moves around the circle. Brant says, "You've got a beautiful family," and Will nods and says, "I know." When it gets to me I feel disappointed. I expect the love to be tangible over the surface of the photograph, but there is nothing, only a lightly frictive gloss. I see three people, two large and one small, each trying to smile in their own way. I see this kind of thing everywhere. I hand the picture back to Will without comment, and he puts it back in his pocket where it belongs.

Now that he's here, I wonder why we aren't leaving. Our options for tonight are endless. We could get a head start on the drive to New Orleans. We could have a nice dinner out and put it on the Sunday Driver tab. We could go to a movie. Or we could check in early at a motel room and spend the evening flipping back and forth between HBO, ESPN, and the Weather Channel.

My guess is that we stay out of courtesy to our English friends. Despite the Dumpsters, this is a peaceful scene, what with the Georgia breezes and the last dimming light of the magic hour. The crew seems to have disappeared; unless they're all on the bus having a bridge tournament, they've probably gone to dinner or to a bar. The six of us could stand here talking about the music industry for hours. Or rather I could stand here and listen to the five of them. "I've got to shake it," I say. "I'm going to see if they'll let me go inside the club." I raise my hand in farewell, and Brant and Peter nod, even though they don't understand what it means to "shake it."

I knock on one of the pairs of front doors, and shortly it opens, revealing the agitated visage of the club manager. The hairs at the front of his head have been pinched into dark, menacing clumps; the blotched cheeks seem to have been pulled, taffylike, by the same mechanisms. I expect dismissal but instead find recognition and penitence. The man lets me in and escorts me to not just the restroom, but the employee restroom, tucked away in a small area of offices. When I come out he is waiting with boundless apologies. It occurs to me that he thinks I'm in the band.

"I didn't mean to take the hard line with your buddy back there," he explains, referring to Joey and the denial of compensation. "Just that English prick got me riled up."

I don't react, unwilling to defend Edward, unwilling to condemn him.

"Look, I know you guys count on this money for gas and expenses," he says. "We've got some beer and Coke upstairs, we've got fruit, stuff for sandwiches, candy, mixed nuts—it's all ready to go, you've just got to go up there and bring it down. I'm really sorry about this."

"It's all right," I say. "The building inspector was here. There's nothing you can do about that."

The manager detects more compassion than I intended. "Thanks, buddy," he says.

I make two trips out to the van, carrying first food, then drink. I have the warm feeling that results from an interaction successful on several levels. I provide sustenance, I provide reassurance, I am doing my job. On my second trip out, I see Cree in the van, bent over her duffel bag and searching aggressively through it.

"What's going on," I say, setting the box of drinks on the seat above her head.

"Just getting a few things," she says. She locates a lone tube sock and sets it in a pile on the seat next to her. Already in the pile are a sweater, a purple silk bra, and a copy of *Women in Love.* I feel a jolt as I realize what she's doing.

"That book should be called *Men in Love,*" I say. "Why are you getting a few things?"

"Huh?" she says. She decides not to be coy. "I'm riding with the Radials tonight. I figured I'd give you boys a chance to be alone."

My chest constricts. I feel I have been fatally outwitted. This possibility is something I never considered, but now it seems obvious. She is taking her rightful place among the famous. I have the thought, "Why didn't you stop this when you had the chance?" but of course I never had the chance.

"How did this come about?" I say.

"I told Gemma about my predicament—you know, Will, the van, all you boys—and she said there was an extra bunk on their bus. Right underneath Walter." She makes a face.

"It's not like there are no boys on that bus," I say. It comes out as an accusation and perhaps I mean it to. Part of the allure has to be the chance to spend the night so close to Brant. Why doesn't she just admit this? I wait for her response, but she seems not to have heard me. I decide to say something else.

"Did you tell Tim?"

This time she hears me. She turns around, head cocked, hands on hips.

"Why does that matter to you?" she says. "I mean, really, Lou?" She stares at me.

I shake my head. I say, "I don't know." It's true. I don't know why it should matter to me. She turns back once more and I am dismissed.

"It was my idea," Tim says. "I thought it might be good for her to have some time away from us." We are standing outside the van, waiting for someone in the Radials' camp to signal that it's time to leave. We have never waited for the bus before, but the transferal of Cree seems to have created a bond between the two groups. Edward is reputed to be inside the club, negotiating some kind of cash settlement. Already we have seen several groups of teenagers approach the doors, read the hastily photocopied signs, and retreat in unmistakable swearing disappointment.

"I just wonder if we're sending her the wrong message," Joey says.

"Do you think she feels like we kicked her out?" Tim says.

"That's not what I mean—," Joey says.

"No," I say, cutting him off. "I don't think she feels like we kicked her out. I think this is a dream come true for her. She gets to hang out with the famous in plush surroundings. She gets to stay up all night with her new friends. She gets to escape from the familiar and the boring. This is the adult equivalent of a slumber party."

"There's a reason you've never heard of a soap opera called *The Familiar and the Boring*," Will says.

"I guess so," Tim says. He seems reassured but still interested in considering the matter later on his own.

"I don't know if it's such a—," Joey says.

"Shhh," Will says, looking up and gesturing. "She's coming over here." We adjust our positions so that we form a miniature receiving line.

"I just came over to say goodbye," Cree says. Behind her I can see Edward boarding the bus. Strange pneumatic puffing sounds indicate the vehicle is about to depart. "I'll see you all tomorrow in the Big Easy."

"Have fun," I say.

"Don't have too much fun," Tim says.

"You know why they call it the Big Easy don't you," Will says.

"I can guess," Cree says, smiling. The way she says this makes me feel slightly sick. "Goodnight." She waves to the four of us, even Joey, who has not said anything, and trots over to the bus. We wait until she disappears, and then we slide open the side door of the van and climb inside. Joey fires up the engine and screams out of the parking lot, offering the explanation that he doesn't want to get stuck behind the bus. His driving is uncharacteristically manic until we are on the highway and well clear of Atlanta.

"Now that Cree's gone, we can rock out," Joey says. "I'm putting on The Who."

"Now that Cree's gone, we can get stoned," Tim says. "Lou, I think it's time to break out that bag."

"If you'll hand me my backpack . . . ," I say to Tim.

Since the beginning of the tour, the weed has been residing in my toilet kit, rolled up inside an empty glasses case. There really hasn't been a reasonable opportunity to smoke it before now. Any prior attempt would have been wasted, as we would have had to spend the entire high pretending not to be high for the benefit of Cree.

"Women," Will says, whistling. He pulls a tin of rolling papers from his own backpack and begins to roll joints, commenting on the unevenness of the highway from time to time. I watch his nimble fingers twist the papers into tight, smokable objects, something that I have never been able to do, and consider that those same fingers now have a similar facility with diapers. If I ever have a baby, I will have to give up smoking pot forever. I won't be able to contend with the dimensions upon dimensions of paranoia that my own offspring will inspire.

After The Who and several joints Will says, "How about some bluegrass?" He pulls out a tape of classic Bill Monroe recordings. If we get tired of that, he says, we can flip over to Thelonious Monk on the other side. I sit back and prepare to be culturally enriched. I am thinking that the dark night and the warm van will merge well with the high lonesome sound of the mandolin. The yodels begin, but they don't sound lonesome to me. They sound a hundred feet away on a porch lit by two lanterns, a half-circle of listeners haunting the shadows in the yard below. Hill-billies are out there, sitting on overturned buckets, polishing their Bowie knives with their thumbs. This is promising imagery, and I look forward to forty-five minutes of dwelling on it, but Joey says, "This is making me feel kind of manic. I'm putting on the Monk." As he is the driver his wishes must be complied with.

John Coltrane also plays on this recording, a detail that Will is embarrassed to have forgotten. The songs are ballads, luxurious and delicate. The passing chords describe the particulate nature of emotion. The saxophone is a voice heard not by the ear but by the soul. I imagine Brant seducing Cree to this music. My mind wants to turn away from this thought, but I command it not to. If you can stand this, I tell myself, you can stand anything. The thoughts multiply, and many mutations occur. Somehow I arrive at the understanding that Brant's seduction would fail were it to be accompanied by his own music. Bombast and melodrama will win a girl's affection but not her heart. This realization gives me enormous satisfaction, and soon I am able to lift my head and rejoin the general conversation. When Joey says that he is falling asleep after less than ninety minutes at the wheel, I am right there with Tim and Will to diagnose his narcolepsy.

The motel parking lot is full and vast. Joey estimates there are four hundred rooms in this sprawling complex. Tim, the new driver, glides us through the lot at less than three miles an hour as a solo piano piece plays. The velocity and the music are so well matched that no one questions Tim's ambition to park. We turn left and come up behind a man carrying a fistful of tennis rackets out to his car. We move at the same speed as the man, and even though we cannot see his face, we can all sense him fighting the urge to look back over his shoulder. Finally he stops at his car and puts the rackets in the trunk. He wears an expression of triumph as he walks back to his room, having deprived us, he believes, of what we wanted from him.

We drive on. In the last wing of the complex, we see a space between two Ford Aerostars. The space is narrow, barely wide enough to fit the van. Tim moves in for his first attempt. The piano song trinkles to an end, followed by silence. He has come in too close to one side; the pursuit of this angle threatens to scrape both exterior vehicles. Tim exhales and put the van in reverse. The tape clicks over to the other side. Tim rolls down his window and leans his head out. As he depresses the accelerator the lightning fast finger-picking of Bill Monroe jumps out of the speakers. The van jerks. Tim's driving, once smooth and mellow and cool, is now comical. Soon it has its own laugh track. Tim backs out and tries again. This time, he's too close to the other side. On the third attempt he gets it right.

It takes several trips to bring everything into the motel room, which is about a quarter mile from where we parked. In addition to our bags, we also bring in both guitars, Joey's bass, and one of the boxes of food that we rescued from the club. Tim says it's not good for the guitars to stay overnight in the van, and when I say, "Because they might get stolen?" he says, "No, because the cold warps the neck. I've just been forgetting to bring them in."

Once inside we sit on the beds and smoke more pot. A noise comes from the bed where Will is sitting, and Joey says, "Did you fart, or is that a woman talking in a low voice in another room?" There is a silence as we listen for the woman with the low voice, and when none is heard, Will fesses up. This brings on another silence, this one reflective, and I break it by saying, "What do you think Cree's doing at this moment?"

"I think the real question is who," Joey says.

"Look out!" Will says, grabbing a pillow and propping himself up with it.

"Hmm," Tim says. He picks up the remote and turns on the television. The fourth *Rocky* movie is playing on HBO. Sylvester Stallone runs through Siberia, first chopping wood, then hauling it. I wait for Tim to comment further, but when he doesn't, the discourse ends. I don't sense a lack of interest in the speculation, I sense a rearing up of principle. I don't pursue it. Instead, I reach for a pillow of my own and wait for the inevitable: the petering out of the television, followed by the ravenous and uninhibited eating of candy bars and nuts, followed by restless and dreamful sleep.

IN THE MORNING I wake to the sensation of Joey poking me in the shoulder.

"If only they made an alarm clock that does that . . . ," I say. Joey puts a finger to his lips. He gestures at the other bed, where Tim and Will are sleeping. I sit up to get a look.

What we have here is a Kodak moment. They're both lying on their sides, facing in the same direction, away from us. Tim has fit himself into the S-curve of Will's larger body. Will's right arm is thrown over Tim. They show no signs of waking.

"They're making spoons," I whisper.

Joey starts to laugh. He puts his hand over his mouth and loud sounds come out of his nose. He jumps up and runs light-footed to the bathroom, where he stays for the next two minutes, chortling and then coughing as if in some porcelain echo chamber. When he comes back he asks me if I think we should wake them.

"No," I say. "That would be cruel. Will thinks Tim's his wife."

"Who does Tim think Will is?" Joey says.

"I don't know," I say. I look over at the clock. It's seven-thirty. "Why did you get up?" I say.

"I had to pee," he says.

———

When I next wake up, Will and Tim have abandoned their compromising position. In fact everyone is up and engaged in constructive activity. Will shaves at the sink, Tim sits on the bed and restrings his second guitar, and Joey searches on his hands and knees for a bottle of lens rewetting drops. After I shower Joey tells the story of Will and Tim's morning rendezvous, provoking a spirited homoerotic back and forth between the two principals. I recall that I didn't think of Cree at all during that brief earlier waking. We conduct a final room check, and then we cart our belongings, the depleted food box included, back out to the van.

In southern Mississippi, we stop for lunch at a restaurant called "Restaurant."

"This is where it all began," Will says. The building is a study in rectangles and browns, with dirty white block letters four feet high spelling out the unique moniker. A banner reading BUFFET! BUFFET! hangs limply under the name.

Over an appetizer of fried pickles Will explains that as much as he would like to be able to put us all up, he and his family only have room for one. The room is the guest room, furnished, plush, with freshly washed pillows and a window overlooking the backyard. It has already been earmarked for Cree, assuming she does not receive an invitation to spend another night on the Radials' bus. Will offers this last comment in jest, but Joey responds with concern.

"I don't think she needs an invitation," he says. "Gemma basically told her she could sleep there whenever she wants." He pauses for a dramatic inhalation. "She may never ride with us again."

"Don't you think Gemma was just being polite?" Tim says.

"It's not an ordinary situation," Joey says. He looks down at his empty plate, unable to elaborate.

"I don't think it's something we need to worry about," Tim says. "I think Cree understands that this was a one-time only thing, while Will's here."

"Blame it on the A&R man," Will says. "Everybody else does." Tim laughs; the tension is broken, although without Joey's consent.

"I just don't think it was a good idea," Joey says. Tim begins a low, sustained, "Hmm," but then the waitress circles near with her pitcher of water, and we drop into a monastic silence.

"And as for all of you, you'll be staying with Kittredge!" Will practically shouts when she is gone. "I've spoken to him, and he says he's made the necessary preparations."

"Kittredge!" Joey says, sitting up straight in his chair.

"What does he mean by preparations?" Tim says. "Is he going to get us some whores?"

"I don't know," Will says. "It wouldn't surprise me. I'm sure he's going to get you something."

Much of the remainder of the drive is occupied by discussion of this Kittredge and his proximity to the various vices. As I have never met the man, I cannot listen with more than partial interest. We come to the Big Easy. There in the heart of it all is the Superdome. Somewhere nearby is the Gulf of Mexico. Exit signs advertise famous streets. What does it take to sustain a tradition of public drunkenness through multiple generations? Perhaps an understanding that there is no such thing as a generation, just a succession of overlapping multitudes with similar concerns. "This city runs on beer," Will says.

I think of murders and beatings committed by people drunk on beer. I think of petty thefts as well. Tim has been in trouble with the law in this town. On a previous tour he was in a supermarket late at night, out to get some staples for the next morning. He picked out a lollipop to eat while he shopped, intending to pay for it once he got to the register, but it tasted bad and he disposed of it in the pasta aisle. The store manager insisted on his arrest, even though the cops themselves said it was a waste of their time and space. Tim spent the night in jail, where he carved the legend "The Day Action Band wuz here" into the tan brick wall of the drunk tank with a metal guitar pick. In the morning he went before a judge, paid a hundred-dollar fine, and was told never to go into that supermarket again. Recalling the event, Will says, "I still go there sometimes, if I'm working late, and I need to pick something up on the way home."

The reunion with Cree at the club is uneventful and truncated by the advent of the soundcheck. All she will say is "the bus was fun," and that we'll hear more about it later. Tim and Joey are disappointed by this reticence but manage to remain respectful, Joey taking his cue from Tim. I discover I am relieved not to have to hear her talk about it. On Will's behalf Tim asks Cree where she plans to sleep tonight, and she shrugs her shoulders as if to say, "not on the bus." Tim goes on to explain what accommodations Will is ready to provide, and when Cree reacts with satisfaction, a feeling of calmness settles over my body. I can see Joey relaxing slightly as well. Tonight will be a night free of paranoia for everybody.

During the show I sit back and regard a crowd like many other crowds. There is no Cajun variation on the standard modes of rock and roll worship. The only difference is people here wear less clothes, but that has more to do with climate than culture. If I lived near a bayou, you might even catch me in a tank top.

After their set the members of the Day Action Band wander out from backstage and eventually unite with Will near the main bar. They form a loose coterie of handshakers that moves from region to region within the club, bracing key lieutenants in the college radio mafia. They complete the circuit by coming back to my table, one of the fresh-faced mafioso in tow.

"This is Kittredge," Will says, as if introducing a shameful deity. He takes a step back. "You all can get acquainted and reacquainted. As for me, there are still a few assholes I haven't talked to yet."

"I'll go with you," Cree says. I can sense in her an indeterminate need to escape. She and Will walk off, only to be stopped fifteen feet away by a thin girl with a clipboard and a ponytail.

Kittredge pats me on the arm and grins, providing me with a more permanent definition of the word "unctuous" than any dictionary ever could. This guy can't be out of college yet, but I can see why Tim thought he might be able to produce some hookers. Only five and a half feet tall, he wears a gold necklace.

"So, this is your first time in New Orleans?" Kittredge says. He gives a rich laugh that I associate with people in show business management. "Well, I'll be your host, and I mean that in the best possible sense."

"What sense is that?" Joey says, fucking with him.

"The best possible," Kittredge repeats, this time in a borrowed New York "Whaddya mean" accent. He pats Tim and Joey on the back simultaneously, and I can feel him wishing for a cigar to complete the ensemble. For the next hour he issues forth a stream of commentary unrivaled in the potency of its bullshit. He makes ludicrous statements about popular music past and present. He makes lewd and strangely inaccurate comments about passing women. He punches the three of us playfully in the shoulder several times apiece. I begin to understand why Cree chose to absent herself.

Tim and Joey, however, seem to be enjoying this routine. They speak to Kittredge with an affectionate condescension that he is not only aware of but seems to expect. The guys are giving him shit, and he loves it. Only Brant's solemn performance of "Glorious" during the encore is capable of muting this joke festival. Shortly after the lights come up, Will and Cree return to say goodnight. We make plans to meet at the Sunday Driver offices at nine tomorrow morning, for purposes unknown to me.

Back at his large but extremely filthy apartment, Kittredge gives notice that he plans to spend an extended period sitting on his toilet. As soon as the bathroom lock is heard to click, Joey goes to the food box left over from Atlanta to find something to eat. Instead he finds distress.

"Do you think it's okay to eat this?" he says, holding up a thin deli slice of ham.

"It's been in the van," Tim says. "It's been pretty cool in there. Not refrigerator cool, but pretty cool."

"Hmm," Joey says. He brings the meat near his face and smells it. "It smells kind of funky." He slides his pinching fingers around. "It feels kind of funky too. Slimy."

Whimsy seizes him. He flings the ham slice across the room, where it adheres midway up the wall with a slapping sound. "I'm never that coordinated," he says, admiring the handiwork.

I look to Tim for signs of disapproval, but he seems delighted. I can't imagine another household where this scene could play out. I say, "We might want to take that down before Kittredge finishes making his deposit. He could consider it an abuse of his hospitality." I don't feel very strongly about this, but it has to be said.

"Let's see if he notices," Tim says. He settles down on the couch directly under the ham, turns on the TV, and begins flipping channels. He comes across a rebroadcast of a talk show from the seventies, on which tonight's guests are Sly Stone, Muhammad Ali, and a white Republican senator. The show has just begun, so we get to see each guest make his entrance.

First comes the senator. He's in his sixties but personable; before he sits, he gives the audience the cheerful wave of a much younger man. He seems to feel right at home on television. Next is Muhammad. Dressed in a dark suit, he appears to harbor a greater anger than the situation warrants. He sits, crosses his legs, and proceeds to faintly menace the audience from this position, frowning at particularly explosive outbursts of applause. Last comes Sly, wearing the bell-bottomed opulence of hippie royalty. When he walks, his pants flap behind him. He smiles the smile of the stoned, wide and increasing. He smiles at everyone, the host, the audience, the senator, the pieces of furniture that compose the set, even Muhammad, who only glowers in response. After some difficulty, he takes the seat to the right of the great boxer, and the debate begins.

They are gathered here to discuss issues of race. The senator is conciliatory but firm. The boxer is hostile but rational. Neither party says anything that goes beyond the pedestrian. The real conflict exists between Muhammad and Sly. Every time Muhammad makes a point, he turns to Sly for confirmation and support. But Sly was not born to be a debate partner. Eventually Muhammad becomes disgusted with what he perceives is a lack of focus and seriousness. He starts to ignore the musician altogether. This goes on for several minutes. Then Sly decides he has something to say. He begins to talk, but Muhammad talks him down without even a glance in his direction. He says "Hey! Hey!" in his strange voice, but no one listens. Finally he puts his hand on Muhammad's arm. The boxer says, "Don't touch me!" and violently jerks away, recovering to resume his speech in mid-sentence. Sly turns to face the fixating camera. He looks into it so deeply that I feel he has entered the room. The look conveys sadness and humor and understanding, and all the other component pieces of personality that I'm forgetting to mention, but most of all, it conveys a moral sophistication beyond the gods. The only way I can think of to articulate this is to say, "What a loss that that man never got to be president," and Tim and Joey nod at my attempt. Then the toilet flushes, and I know what I have to do. I reach up over Tim's head and pull down the ham. I ball it up in my fist and take it into the kitchen to throw it away. When I get back to the couch I receive a dual thumbs up from my compadres. A second later the bathroom door opens and Kittredge enters, waving the air behind him, none the wiser.

At 2:00 A.M., a bout of pot smoking inspires a quest for food. Kittredge, the man with all the answers, says he knows about "a place across town" that's still open. This being New Orleans, it seems like plenty of places would still be open, but who am I to cause my host embarrassment? Kittredge even says, "I'll take you there," and winks at the three of us.

We insert ourselves into his Volkswagen Rabbit. He drives with the window down so he can smoke, and after several chilly minutes, Tim asks him to please roll it up. The shifting is erratic, too, only taking place at the higher RPMs and after excessive clutch depression. Nonetheless, there's something infinitely gratifying about being driven through this city while in a state of stoned incompetence. A mere shell of an automobile protects me from the ravening darkness, now animated by a combination of metaphor and THC. I could be driven around like this for hours, down the same nightswept thoroughfare, each time sensing new demons in the foliage beyond. Pretty soon I realize that this is exactly what is happening. Although Kittredge doesn't say so, it becomes apparent that he has forgotten the precise location of the restaurant. We traverse the same sequence of streets multiple times. After our third silent pass by a small grocery store called Oma's, Tim says, "Yo Kittredge, are we lost?"

"No, man, we're right here," Kittredge says. He pulls into the lot of a diner-type establishment. We've been driving past this place too, but the little guy's tension is palpable and our collective tact has reached an all-time high. "Looks good," I say, and Kittredge extends his gratitude by holding the door open for me.

Inside it could be midday. Waitresses carrying laden trays move in swift patterns among the tables. Consumers belch and clink their silverware against their teeth. Generic New Orleans music plays on a hidden jukebox. We step down into a lower region where there's a bar with stools, a cash register, and a girl behind it waiting to take our order.

"We'll be having the 'take out,' " Kittredge says, leaning way into the counter in some uncertain attempt at flirtation. A brief scenario plays in my head, in which Kittredge follows that sentence with, "And I'd like to take you out," but no, he just stands there, impervious to my telepathy. The girl, however, hears my mental call, and gives me the classic raised eyebrow. Kittredge orders a burger and turns the floor over to me.

I go for the muffuletta, a meat sandwich topped with a dressing of salty olives. The first time I try to say the word, I say, "Muffalo." The second time, I say, "Mo-flo." The third time I point at the upside-down laminated menu on the counter and say, "I want that." The girl finds no humor in this.

Joey has similar troubles with this woman. He steps up to the plate muttering something about "sides." He says, "Let's see," and touches his mouth repeatedly. Then he asks what substitutions can be made, onion rings for french fries, mashed potatoes for cole slaw and the like. Every time, the girl says, "There are no substitutions." In extremis, Joey orders a thirteen-dollar ribeye special. He moves away from the counter saying, "Oh shit, oh shit," under his breath.

Tim mocks us with his efficiency. In a loud, clear, confident voice, he says, "I'll have the soup of the day and a garden salad." The girl shows him no favor either, but at least he has the gumption to call out after her retreating figure, "Thank you, miss."

With this we take a seat on the stools four across. We face away from the kitchen, looking out a big window into the parking lot, where Kittredge's car resides under a short, leafy tree. Each person turns his thoughts inward. I can only speak for myself, of course. I focus on the conversations coming from the dining area, or rather, the collective conversation. I think of a topological map, full of swirling peaks and viscous valleys, sometimes punctured by a jabbing fingertip of altitude. Then I think of the table the map rests upon, a rectangle circumscribing another rectangle. A giant appears, crumpling the map and hurling it into a corner. "But what are the people saying?" he demands to know.

I hear Russians, their accents, their passions, their sorrows. I know how to say three things in Russian: "beer," "thank you," and "my key, please," from a trip I took in the eighth grade. These

Russians use none of these words. They bellow and cheer and stumble over curses. I become convinced that they are playing cards and that someone has always just won a hand.

I hear a couple. The man has recently bought a ring and would like to propose. He knows this isn't the place, and yet he also knows he will never feel this confident again. He says he wishes the waitress would come refill his water, but in his mind he is thinking of the jewelry store and its fourteen-day return policy.

I hear a man eating alone. He is very hungry and his food looks delicious to him, but he knows he must eat slowly. The fork rises to the mouth, the mouth chews, the throat swallows, and then a half-minute of silence is observed. This meal is scheduled to last until 4:00 A.M., at which time he will go home to bed. His shift begins at noon. By expanding all activities to two to three times their normal size, he can fill the twenty-four hours in a day quite comfortably. Weekends he relies on the local interstate. Predictably, the paranoid voice of my subconscious begins a chant of "This could be you, this could be you." There is no wisdom in it, though, just the boorish repetition of a drunk at a sporting event.

One by one our dishes appear on the counter behind us, enclosed by steaming Styrofoam. We peek inside, but that is all we do; an unspoken decree states we will consume this bounty within the walls of Chez Kittredge. My muffuletta is an exodus of olives from a stratified plateau of Italian meats. After fifteen minutes, all the food has arrived except for Tim's garden salad.

The passing of more minutes has no bearing on the situation. The stool sitting gives way to mass pacing. Every now and then Joey places his hands on the Styrofoam that contains his ribeye, as if to cradle one last time the departing warmth. Kittredge says he has never known this place to be so slow, which is technically true. Tim says we can go ahead and eat if we like, but no one does. Soon his feelings of responsibility couple with his own hunger. Standing at the register, he raps three times on the counter with a nearby pen. Out of the kitchen comes the girl, looking perturbed.

"Yes?" she says.

"I ordered a salad about half an hour ago," Tim says.

"Yes," the girl says. "The kitchen has your order. They're making your salad."

"Well," Tim says. He puts his hands on the counter. He makes a visible decision to pursue justice. "The last of the food that you see here came out a long time ago. There are some sandwiches here, some soup, and even a steak that's cooked well done. The only thing that isn't here is my salad. How long does it take to make a salad?"

"I don't know," the girl says. "I'll check on it."

"It's just lettuce and tomatoes," Tim says. "I'll put the dressing on myself."

"Yes," the girl says. She goes back into the kitchen. Tim turns to us and says, "How long does it take to make a salad?"

"I don't know, man," Joey says.

"It doesn't take this long," Kittredge says. Neither of them look Tim in the eye when they say these things.

I can't offer any superior consolation, so I don't try to. Tim is in the interesting position of having lost his sense of irony. Therefore he suffers the emotional consequences of this failed human interaction while the rest of us look on with a mixture of detachment and boredom. Kittredge tries to empathize, but the best he can do is displace his agitation over his cooling hamburger, which is not really the same thing. When the girl comes back seconds later, holding a container bursting with lettuce, Tim thanks her and apologizes for his earlier tone. The smile he attempts, though, looks suspiciously like a wince. During the ride home to Kittredge's, he is talkative to the point of chattering, making bright announcements about subjects too uninteresting to re-

count. Only after he gets some food in him does his masterful
persona return.

We get up at eight after less than five hours of sleep. On the way
to Sunday Driver, Tim explains that he and Will thought it would
be a good idea for everybody to listen to a sequenced and mixed
version of the new album together. We have to be on the road by
noon to reach Houston in time for a six o'clock soundcheck.

To get to the office we drive through a neighborhood that
seems to consist entirely of cemeteries. Weeds sprout up higher
than the mausoleums they surround. Rusty gates crawl with spiders. My sun-bedazzled eyes fail to pick out a single complete
headstone in the bunch.

Joey parks the van beneath a train bridge at the end of a block
of storefronts. The Sunday Driver storefront is covered with posters of the bands the label represents. Including the Day Action
Band, the label's roster is only four deep, so some posters appear
many, many times. The Walking Sticks, who have just put out a
new album, are particularly well-represented on this fine November morning.

Will and Cree are waiting inside, having coffee at a table next
to a modern kitchen facility. The space is one large room, organized by dividers. There are two desks with computers, each
spilling over with telephones, papers, and cassettes. There is a
reception area, with a couch, some nice leather chairs, and a gratuitously large television set. A white board covered with erasable
pen jottings hangs at a central location on the wall. Beyond this
board is a completely distinct cubicle, which I sense is the do-
main of Will. Everywhere, small, unopened boxes are piled in
twisting towers.

Will apologizes for the mess and assures the band that their
affairs are not being run with similar disorder. He also apologizes
for not bringing down his wife and child, referencing an episode
of pre-dawn screaming. Apparently Tim was an important player

in the wedding and was up for serious godfather consideration. Best wishes are sent in both directions. Cree talks briefly about how spending time with the young Renshaw kindled her own womanly feelings. "I think I want one," she says, although some of this may be intended as a compliment.

Soon Will says, "How about it?" We move as a group into his cubicle. Will offers the only chair to Cree. Kittredge, Joey, and I take a seat on the floor while Tim leans gingerly against one wall of the enclosure. Will hunches down and removes a tape marked "you think you hear—final mix" from a cassette rack to my right. He puts the tape into his high-end stereo system, and before the music begins, I note that the speakers are the same ones that Tim has in the control room of his barn.

The album begins with "Back in the Eighties." Most of the sequencing discussions were based around where to put this song. Cree thought it made a good ending track. Joey thought it should fall somewhere near the middle, "because you want to be sitting down when it comes on." Tim held to the simple view that you ought to lead with your strongest work. His only worry was that the intensity of the experience might make the rest of the album seem like a letdown.

Hearing these opening bars, the concern seems justified. The organ is there flashing eighth notes just as I remember it from earlier listens this summer, but something inside the organ is shading those notes blue, pushing them until one seems like it might topple over the next. The bass drops in rich in the very lowest frequencies and receives immediate augmentation from a guitar figure that would fairly blaze were it not so dry in tone and quiet in the mix. A second, rounder organ begins the countermelody that means Tim is about to sing, and then he does: "Back in the eighties I had many fine things to say / I used to dream about love but it always seemed far away."

The melody is at the top of Tim's range, and to sing it properly he must involve the part of his voice with which he shouts. The tone is defiant; it will not be mocked for the sentimentality it invokes. The first time I heard this song I felt that Tim was singing to all those waiting to become lovers, to tell them, "Hold on, your time will come." Now I hear the speaker singing to a younger version of himself, demanding to be heard and under- stood but angry knowing that youth will never learn from any- thing but experience. I don't remember myself at fifteen very well, but I know I would have loved this song. I might not have heard it and truly believed that someday I, yes, I, Lou Farren, would fall in love, but I would have been gratified and thrilled at the attempt. I'm thrilled now, washed over with a power that I know has nothing to do with me.

The powerful feeling fades to silence after three minutes and five seconds. Kittredge notes that the length is perfect for radio, but Will ignores him, saying quietly, "That one gets me every time."

"A one, a two, a one two three four," Tim's voice says on the tape as Cree's drumsticks click behind him. Although this is the final mix, the countoffs will not be edited out until the mastering stage. A three-note major arpeggio played on a guitar, fast, with the two higher notes ringing, moves up and down a whole step. "Potential energy," Tim once described this interval. Four dusty snare hits come and go in an oscillating pattern. Every eighth beat there is a crack as if two pieces of wood have collided. This tune, known tentatively as "You Can't Stop Me," is sung entirely in falsetto, and owes its melody, Tim has said, to the genre of the Christmas carol. The lyrics, however, pertain to Halloween and the first year he was not permitted to go trick or treating. I had thought this information might ruin the song for me, but the opening lines—"I'm going out on a Saturday night / And the wind is cold and the streets are bright"—are devoid of spooky under- tones. In some ways, I find myself thinking, this song is more brilliant than the one that preceded it.

As the album plays, the aura of respectful silence erodes. By track five the tiny cubicle is a hotbed of commentary. Cree says she finds the countoffs endearing and asks if there's ever been a record where they've all been left in place. Joey says, "I don't know, but that would be cool," at the same time Tim says, "I hope not." Kittredge has risen and now stands next to one of the speakers, poised to indicate upcoming favorite moments. Will attempts to guess the techniques that Tim has used to achieve various sounds. "Did you put that vocal through a guitar amp first?" he says, and Tim nods and talks about the microphone he used, how far away from the amplifier he positioned it, and what part of the room the recording took place in.

I don't feel like joining any of these discussion groups, and so I duck my head and step out of the little area. I pace around the office, noting how the tenor of the record changes with my location. I imagine myself walking down a city street and coming to an intersection with a red light. An automobile, a white '77 Monte Carlo, pulls up with its windows down. The final mix of *You Think You Hear* by the Day Action Band plays loud on its stereo. What do I think? Is this the music of the future, priming itself for classic rock radio twenty years down the road? No matter how much I pace, I cannot acquire the correct perspective.

I rejoin the ensemble in time for "Outside Tokyo," tentatively, the closing cut. Everyone seems exhausted but cheerful; the wooded path up the mountain has opened upon a majestic vista clearing, and it's time to break out the refreshments. As the last chorus repeats out into a fade, "You left me outside-a Tokyo / There's not a lot that I could do," Will shakes his head and says, "Damn. That's how you end an album. Damn." For the first time I detect a hint of jealousy in his admiration. When there is silence he says to Kittredge, "I think we have a top-five record on our hands." Kittredge gives him the thumbs up.

"That was the plan," Tim says. He leans against the wall, ankles crossed. His chest seems to have swelled slightly inside his shirt, as if the praise from Will was of a premium grade. Kittredge says, "Top-five, I guarantee," imitating the Cajun chef. Joey and Cree affirm this projection with confident body language.

A cloud of paranoia engulfs my head. I have never heard of anything so diabolical. This tiny band with career record sales of ten thousand is sitting in an office plotting with cool certainty the takeover of the pop nation. They make it seem as though *Rolling Stone* has already taken the cover photo. How many weeks before I catch myself saying to a stranger, "I knew them way back when"?

This is no place for a skeptic, but I have to ask: "How can you be so sure it's going to go top-five?"

"The last one did," Will says. "We like to set realistic goals here at Sunday Driver Records."

I continue to look confused until Joey says, "He's talking about college radio."

"Oh," I say.

"I wish he wasn't," Tim says.

"We all wish he wasn't," Cree says. Will laughs warmly at this and my inappropriate question is forgotten.

Brunch occurs at a place with washable napkins. Joey and I share tension because we feel the cost of this food could exceed the per diem, which today is ten dollars. Although I have built up a small surplus over the past nine days, I can tell Joey is thinking hard about last night's steak. It's a relief to see Will lay down a Sunday Driver Visa on top of the eighty-five-dollar bill.

As soon as we are away from Will and Kittredge and on the interstate heading west, Tim says, "Cree, the time has come. To tell us about your night on the bus."

"We want details," Joey says. "Omit nothing." He seems to have gotten over his apprehensions about the sleepover.

Cree laughs the laugh of protestation. "I can't tell you everything," she says.

"Oooohhh," Joey says, unbuckling his seatbelt and turning around to face her. Tim's reaction is different. "Really?" he says, the question genuine.

"No," Cree says. She puts her hand on his arm. "It was fun. It was really interesting."

"Start by describing the intoxicants," Joey says, pounding his fist.

"There was a lot of alcohol," Cree says. "Everyone was drunk, except for Edward, who was asleep in his bunk. At least he was trying to sleep."

"You're a poet, Cree," Joey says. "Who coked up?"

"Huh?" Cree says. Then she says, "Just Brant. It was pretty mellow." This seems to be all she wants to say on the subject.

"Just Brant?" Joey says. "Did he do it in front of everyone, or did he go off by himself?"

"He went off by himself," Cree says.

"Then how do you know he did it?" Joey says. "Were you hiding in the toilet?"

Cree laughs through the question. "I could just tell, okay?"

Before Joey can ask her for clarification Tim says, "What was the dynamic like? Do you get the sense that they're all friends?"

With this Cree enters the more relaxed storytelling mode that she had planned at the outset.

"Brant and Peter are definitely friends," she says. "It's harder to say with Gemma because of the kind of person she is. She's really funny. She gets along with everyone. Walter is a little bit standoffish. Everyone just kind of waits for him to go away. I think he reads a lot, so I guess that's cool."

"Does the band interact with the crew?" Tim asks.

"Yes!" Cree says. She smiles. "In fact, I have proof." She rummages through the outer pocket of her bulging backpack and pulls out a wad of Polaroids. "After everyone was intoxicated," she says, "we went a little crazy with Gemma's makeup." She passes the pictures around.

The results are typical. The women have all taken the route

of excess, their faces luminous and bruised. Louise in particular now resembles a transvestite, and the thought of her "Ah ha ha ha's" filling the bus only increases the effect. Brant and Peter each appear with concentric black circles around their eyes. Arms linked and solemn, they look as though they're about to waltz right through the picture-taker. My public comment: "Gemma's going to have to get some new makeup."

The crew are the recipients of the more delicate work. In one photo, Cree sits on the lap of a long-haired guitar tech done up to look like Pippi Longstocking. In another, the soundman gazes out the bus window into the empty night, caught as if unawares, his face the archetype of androgynous beauty. I reach to hand the pictures back to Joey, and I notice an ink smudge on my thumb. I discover the source is a poem written on the back of the picture of Peter and Brant.

"What's this poem here, Cree?" I say.

"Oh my God," she says. "I forgot about the poem. Brant wrote it. Let me see it."

"I'll give it to you when I'm done," I say.

"Read it aloud!" Joey shouts.

"You can read it when Cree's done," I say. It's a very strange little verse, and it would make me uncomfortable to read it aloud:

> *Pieces of sentiment hung from the work.*
> *He reached up his hand and wiped them away.*
> *A janitor came by and swept the debris into a dustbin.*
> *"Now that is something to behold."*
> *Lou, in silk bandanna flowing,*
> *Lou, he was, he flowed.*

"It's nuts," I say, passing it over to Cree. "Why is my name in it?"

"He asked what your name was, and I told him," she says. "Is it funny? I remember it being really weird."

"It is weird," I say. I listen to her giggle as she reads the poem. So I am now known by name to international rock stars. I feel a rising pompousness, but I allow uncertainty to punch it down. That verse could easily be read to be mocking me. After all, I am not someone who would wear a silk bandanna. I begin to think that Brant might be some kind of asshole. Cree giggles again, and I see that she is giving the poem a second reading. She seems to find it very charming.

CREE AND I DRIVE IN SILENCE. Shortly after Tim and Joey fell asleep I related to her to the saga of the tardy salad. That was the last time we traded words. Having stayed up all night, she ought to be asleep by now. But she stares flatly and grimly over the oncoming highway, thinking about the thing that's keeping her awake. At least I think that's what she's doing. I only look at her out of the corner of my eye.

The road crests a hill and begins a long, gradual decline. A half mile before us is a bridge. The twin sides of the highway split, bow out several hundred feet, and then rejoin on the other side. Tall furry trees grow along the outer edges of the bow. The imagery is undeniable.

"Do you know what that looks like to me?" I say.

"A vagina," Cree says. There is no surprise or question in her voice.

"That's right," I say.

"Somebody's feeling a little bit horny," she says.

"I cannot deny it," I say.

"I know what you're talking about," she says.

"Yeah?" I say.

"Yeah," she says. And so we drive on.

We change drivers at the last rest area before Houston. Joey would like to be at the helm when we enter the city limits. "It just seems kind of fitting," he says, as we pass each other walking around the front of the van.

His first act as captain is to select new music. Out go the Modern Lovers; in come the Rolling Stones, specifically, "Street Fighting Man." Tonight's agenda undergoes a subtle shift to the right: we are no longer going to just rock Houston, we are now going to kick its ass. When the song ends, Joey's fingers touch the tape deck. We hear the sounds of rapid cassette movement. There's a click, and then . . . it's "Street Fighting Man," back again for one more round. Houston is going to burn baby burn, the fire so deep and red that helicopter news teams will mistake it for blood.

The song ends for a second time. We still have yet to reach the city limit marker. Joey's fingers twitch. He knows he can't enter his hometown to the strains of "Prodigal Son."

"Give me the cassette box!" he commands. I hand it to him, and the van veers wildly in its lane as he attempts to decipher the tiny handwriting on the tape labels.

"I can do that for you . . . ," I say.

"No!" he shouts. "I've got it!" He pulls out a tape and thrusts his hand up into the ceiling. The van veers. Cars honk and move away. In the distance I spy a small green sign. "You'd better hurry," I tell him.

He holds the tape up to the setting sunlight. "It's rewound," he says. He pops it in. Five knucklebending seconds tick off the meter. Then, as we pass the marker that signals the beginning of Houston proper, it hits us, a synthesizer sound so badass that Satan himself would kneel to kiss its ring.

"Yes!" Tim shouts. Even though I cannot see it, I know his fist is pumping in the air. I feel like pumping mine too, for we are now listening to "Tom Sawyer" by Rush, the ultimate anthem of male adolescence. *What you say about his company is what you say about society!* These words take me back to the days when I walked the halls of my local high school, shielded from the bandits and cheerleaders by nothing more than the guitar of

Alex Lifeson, the drums and lyrics of Neil Peart, and the bass and vocals of Geddy Lee, who also sometimes played keyboards with his feet. That voice like a thousand banshees held captive in a bottle of Molson Golden! That fabulously overstated instrumental interplay! Those lyrics always reaching, always reaching . . . vanquishing my enemies to the land of the dust simply by describing them. Oh! But then I turned fifteen. I discovered the Replacements. And although I became much cooler, I lost something forever.

That Joey carried this passion for Rush into his collegiate years only makes this moment all the more poignant. And we let him have it, even Cree, who cannot possibly understand. The album plays through, "Red Barchetta," "YYZ," for which the trio received a Grammy nomination, "Limelight" and then even the bizarre and fanciful second side. It has been seven years since I last voluntarily listened to Rush, and this dose will probably fulfill my needs for the next seven. When Joey removes the key from the ignition, cutting "Vital Signs" mercifully short, I exhale the breath that I have been holding for over thirty minutes.

The Sundown Corral was named with an irony long since deceased. I have never seen a club so rustic. Had Davy Crockett wandered past a century ago, he might have chosen this very place to found his coonskin cap empire. The coons would have grazed in this field now used to host the Summer Concert Series Spectacular. The stage would have been occupied by a brass band playing the soothing sounds of Stephen Foster, designed and test-proven to enhance grooming habits. The actual cap production would have taken place inside the central log edifice toward which we are now headed. Crockett could have been the inventor of the assembly line.

"You don't think we're going to play outside?" Tim says.

"No," Joey says. "That ends the first week in October. There's another stage inside. It's just as big." He relates this information with burgeoning authority. I sense that he wants to be asked more questions.

"Have you ever been here before?" I say.

"No." He shakes his head bitterly. He says that growing up, he thought of the Sundown Corral as a place of decadence, where "bad things happened after the sun went down."

"Now I see that it's nothing but a big wheel of brie," he says.

"What does that mean?" Cree says.

"It means it's cheesy," he says. "And I was a fool to let it intimidate me."

The inside of the club is low-ceilinged and dark as if lit by torches. Great running knots are visible in the wood. We pass underneath a stuffed deer's head into the main concert area. Peter and Gemma stand on the stage, basking in the freshness of the new soundcheck. When they see us, they break into a punk rock version of "Wrestling." They smile and raise their eyebrows every time they change chords. Tim and Cree wave back, instigating an awkward but good-hearted fiesta of waving, nodding, and smiling that ends when Joey calls out, "Is this food for us?"

He stands in the back of the room before a gleaming silver buffet arrangement at least thirty-five feet in length. Lifting the lid off one of the tins, he makes a cutthroat gesture to indicate nothing's inside. Peter leans into his mic and says, "We don't know who that's for." Gemma says, "It's a mystery," into hers.

Cree nudges me and whispers that she loves their accents. "That's the way English was meant to be spoken," I tell her. "Now if you'll pardon me, I must take your leave. My wares grow cold in the carriage."

When I get back I discover that Bob, for the first time, has exercised the full power of his seniority. The area set aside for merchandise is a small enclosed bar fifty feet from the stage. The entire long wall of this region is plastered with Radials' paraphernalia, which now includes pins, patches, and bumper stickers. I'm left with about two square feet of space to the right of the doorway.

"Sorry," Bob apologizes. "But you probably weren't going to sell that much." I am supposed to be disarmed by the frankness and sincerity with which he delivers this phrase. Suddenly the dopey old man routine seems to have been contrived for this purpose. I look up to the ceiling to see if any of the lights can be turned away from his product to focus on mine. But each one is held in place by an angry and inflexible order of bolts. I am glad the band is not nearby, for I fear Bob and I are about to have words. When he turns around, I'm going to tell him what's what about what.

Bob turns around. He holds a pair of Radials T-shirts in each hand. He sees that I am about to speak. He offers me the shirts. "Here," he says. "I feel bad. These aren't much, and someone in the band probably gave them to you already, but here."

"Thank you," I say. I take the shirts, roll them together, and drop them on top of my merch box. Residual emotion left over from the Rush experience has swarmed to the surface of my consciousness. If the light were better Bob would be able to see the beginnings of tears in my eyes. I look down at the T-shirt wad and wish there were some way to express my gratitude. I would put one of the T-shirts on, but that could be construed as sarcasm. Instead I begin the repetitive tasks of taping and hanging and wait for the tears to subside.

All the people who are part of tonight's performance move about the room, walking at varying speeds, carrying a diverse array of objects. It is a fusion of different camps, the Radials, the Day Action Band, the Sundown Corral, and looking at them is like looking out at a carnival through a rainy window. I cannot distinguish the individual faces, but that only enhances the impressions of energy, momentum, and life. Do my own motions make me a part of this scene? There I am, behind the bar, reaching up to smooth away the folds in a sleeve. It may be imagined that I sometimes converse with the white-haired man beside me. The PA crackles, and Gemma twangs her bass with her thumb. Everyone in the room hears it. I tape the last of the CDs to the counter. My eyes no longer water, but there is the sense of pressure and ache in my throat.

A wave of hollering surges up through the entry corridor, and I know that the Amontes have arrived. For Tim, the hometown show was merely a prophecy come to pass, the return of the conquering hero. For Cree, it was simply a chance to show a few Indian people a real down-home American rock-and-roll club. For Joey, however, there is real triumph, the see what I've become all you doubters, the birth of the cool. His parents, sensing this, have turned it into a coming-out party, inviting not just friends and relatives, but rivals and other dissenters, children and parents of children who used to terrorize him during playgroup.

This first influx is an amalgam of cousins, aunts, and uncles. Soon only Joey's hair is visible above their hugging arms and loose-fitting shirts. Young twins with pigtails are lifted one at a time by their father to say hello. Teen boys step in and shake his hand with careful reserve.

Off to the side stand Joey's mother and father. I've never met them or seen their picture, yet there can be no doubting who they are. Mrs. Amonte is small and stylish, her closed mouth belying not only a scrupulous attention to detail but also a rhyming tendency toward the frantic. She holds her arms tightly to her chest as if they might fly open and start embracing passersby indiscriminately.

Mr. Amonte cuts a more relaxed pose, overlooking the scene like a man who understands the principles of delayed gratification. When the other relatives are finished with their hellos, he puts his hand on his wife's waist and leads her forward. He watches, smiling, while she stands on her tiptoes to put a kiss on Joey's cheek. She moves to one side, and then the moment is truly his, as it has been from the beginning. With both hands resting on Joey's shoulders, he is nearly able to look his son in the eye. "It's so good to see you, Joey," he says. Joey can only nod and smile in return. These words are almost always empty of real feeling, but coming from a father with such loving, friendly eyes, they contain the simplest eloquence. I see now that Joey's own formal approach to greeting has its origin here.

Within fifteen minutes I am sold out of T-shirts. The Amontes seem to want to outfit the better part of Houston. Sales records are falling left and right. One particularly well-coifed teenaged gentleman hands me a hundred dollar bill, and I do not flinch, for he requires less than ten dollars of change. The supply dwindles, but the demand only grows more fervent. And they all chant his name, "Joey, Joey, Joey," muttered, whispered, sung, by aunts, uncles, cousins large and small, in-laws, friends, converted enemies, skeptics and their partners. "Can you cover for me?" I ask Bob, and he nods, even though there is nothing left for him to cover.

I duck out the back door, expecting to be alone in the cooling night. Instead I find a thick and rowdy line stretching alongside the club and halfway up the next block. I must cross the line to reach the van; as I make my attempt, someone in a cowboy hat notices that I have come from inside the club.

"Hey, what's the deal!" he says. "I've got my ticket. What's this wait all about?"

"I don't know," I say. "I don't work here." This denial has worked for me before.

"Yeah, you don't work here," he says. To his girlfriend I hear him say, "Fuckin' punk."

I open the side door of the van, and keeping my feet planted on the pavement, I rummage through the auxiliary T-shirt box. It feels dangerous to have my back turned at this juncture, and I work quickly to make sure that all three shirt sizes are represented. I wedge the shirts under my armpit and then grab two twenty-count CD boxes. That should hold them.

I turn back around and a woman in her mid-thirties says, "Hey sugar, it's cold out here."

Being from the Northeast, I have to scoff at this claim. It's not a degree less than fifty-five.

"Look at me, I'm freezing," she says. This may be a reference to her nipples, which currently seek refuge from the restrictions imposed by her blouse. I take a moment to size her up. Her breasts are large, but her stomach may have the last word yet.

"I'm sorry, ma'am, I can't help you," I say.

"If you let us follow you back inside, my boyfriend will give you a hundred dollars," she says. "And I'll give you a kiss."

"That's a great offer," I say. "But as much as I'd like to take you up on it, there's really nothing I can do."

"My kisses are pretty worthwhile," she says. "Aren't they, honey?" She nudges a different man in a cowboy hat. He tips the hat at me and says, "Believe me, son, you don't want to miss out on this."

I'm not going to be able to make them understand. I secure the shirts and boxes, put my head down, and charge back through the line. "Don't you like girls?" the woman calls out after me.

The club is beginning to fill with non-Amontes. Instead of pressing up near the stage, they mill around the buffet area. Tim sees me watching them and says, "What do you think is up with that?"

"I guess they're more into food than they are into rock," I say. "Must be a Texas thing."

"No," Tim says. "They're all adults. What do you think is up with *that.*"

I look out at the faces beneath the ten-gallon hats and aerosol hairdos. I see vanishing youth and impending middle age. Sex is no longer an end unto itself but a mere pawn in the chess game of procreation and lifetime companionship.

"It's a radio station benefit, or a contest, or something, I don't know," Bob blurts out. A fleck of spittle lands in Tim's hair and I observe how it refracts the dim light. "They bought all the tickets and then they gave them away. Half the people probably won't even show."

A line is forming at one end of the buffet. Men and women wearing aprons have moved into place behind the silver tins and now stand poised with ladles and gigantic forks.

"So this is basically a party for the radio station," Tim says. "They get to invite all their friends, impress their dates, eat and drink for free, talk as loud as they want, turn their backs when we play, go home if they're bored." He raises his voice with each new phrase, as if wants everyone in the club to hear. "Boy, that's terrific. And I guess all the kids who actually wanted to see the show are just going to have to wait until next time. Gee, how often do you think the Radials make it to America? Gee, you think we'll ever play a place this big again?"

He pounds his fist on the bar, cracking the case of the *That One Five Jive* CD I've taped there. I peel it up and quickly replace it with another.

"I didn't mean to do that," Tim says. "It's just . . ."

"Don't worry," I tell him. "I'll sell it at a discount." But he is already walking away, cutting a straight path through the crowd, bumping shoulders with those who refuse to step aside.

The next time I see Tim he is onstage. A curtain draws away to reveal the Day Action Band already in their positions, ready to rock. But tonight there is a special addition. A man wearing sunglasses and a bow tie stands at Tim's microphone. He holds up a sheet of paper and begins to read.

"Hi, everybody, I'm Carl Santiago, from the Morning Madhouse on 96.4 WHOS, Houston's House of Rock. I'd like to welcome y'all to the WHOS House Party '97. Have we got a treat for you this evening. I can barely wait myself. From all the way across the Atlantic, here to entertain only you, ladies and gentlemen, we have the Radials! Let's give them a good old Texas howdy-do, how about it folks?"

He lowers the microphone while the audience delivers a moderate amount of nonspecific applause. A lone rebel lets loose with a mighty "Yee-ha!" and follows it with another.

"People, I've been backstage with the Radials, and let me tell you, they're ready to come out and show you folks a good time. Now just to make sure that y'all are in the same time zone, we've got a little warm-up for you, a nifty little three-piece all the way from Newark, Delaware. Folks, I'd just like to ask the band one question, if you'll bear with me."

He gives the crowd a serious look to make sure he has their consent.

"My question is, what is Delaware exactly? Where is it, what does it do, what is it known for? Is it even a state? Can you tell me? These people would like to know."

He tilts the microphone toward the band.

"It's on the East Coast," Cree says in her flattest voice.

"The state bird is the Fighting Blue Hen," Joey says. "It's also the mascot of the University of Delaware athletic program."

Tim takes the microphone from Carl Santiago, who willingly gives it up.

"Actually, Delaware was the first state admitted to the Union," Tim says. "On December seventh, 1787, Caesar Rodney rode his horse all the way from Dover, which is Delaware's capital, to Philadelphia, which was then the nation's capital, to ratify the Constitution. So on our license plates, it says that Delaware is 'The First State.' It's also known as the Diamond State. We have a big city, small towns, farms, beaches, and even a speedway on the NASCAR circuit, the Dover Downs. You may have heard of it. My question for you, Carl, is when did Texas become a state? It was pretty recently, wasn't it? What does it say on your license plates? 'Texas, the Thirty-third State'?"

Parts of the audience make a low oohing sound. Tim hands the microphone back, looking out of breath and a little bit shocked.

"Actually," Carl says, "on our license plates it says 'The Lone

Star State.' But we understand your confusion and we thank you for the thoroughness of your response. Folks, you may be riled up enough already, but I'm going to give 'em to you anyways. Ladies and gentlemen, the Day Action Band!"

In the split second of silence that follows, I wonder if this is going to be it, the meltdown. Carl takes a few steps backwards, clapping, and then turns and walks quickly off the stage. The crowd rumbles, somewhat interested now. Joey and Cree wait at their instruments, watching Tim's hands because "Lottery" begins with a solo guitar lick. From where I stand I can see he has the first chord fretted. He moves up to the microphone, as if to speak, and then backs away. He looks over to Joey, then Cree, and then out into the room. I have never seen a performer make a face onstage quite like the one Tim's making now. It's an intimate face, the kind one person makes for another. The eyes are calm, the mouth shows the beginnings of a smile. He seems to be saying, very matter-of-factly, "You've asked for it, and now you're going to get it." He looks down at his guitar, mouths a count-off to himself, and hits that opening chord.

The set is the best they've ever played. The audience will remember this night for many, many years, as a night when non-existent expectations were met with the most incandescent joy. The difference between a poor show and a great show is never easy to quantify; one is almost always forced to resort to words such as *energy, atmosphere,* and *connection* The same is true of this performance, but I might add the fourth word *motivation.*

There is everything that makes the Day Action Band good: the music, the singing, the chemistry, the band members themselves and their obvious affection for one another. But for the first time the idea of three charismatic kids losing themselves in their hearts and talents seems quaint to me; this is monolithic, a moment made physical, a piece of the earth. I look at them and I know that someday soon, they are going to be famous.

Tim is conscious of it all, of what he is doing not only to the audience but to Joey and Cree, who play as if they are having the best time of their lives. I think to myself, "Why doesn't he do this every night?" and my first answer is, "Because it would be exhausting." My second answer is the correct one, however: "Because it would be unfair." Not to the people who came down to the Sundown Corral on a Friday night, but to the people who are up there with him now.

The break between sets is the most frantic I have yet endured. All the Amontes who didn't buy something from me before the show are here now. Some are back for seconds and thirds, including Mr. Hundred Dollar Bill, who still has a pair of fifties left in his arsenal. I am on my feet and selling for a full ten minutes, the longest such stint of my young career.

"Hey," Bob says to me, "Look what's going on over there."

I turn my head and discover nothing less than a modern-day recasting of the Holy Trinity. On the left, in profile, is the large breasted woman who spoke to me out at the van. On the right, in profile, is Tim. And in the center, facing me, ever presiding, is Joey.

The woman has pulled down one side of her blouse to expose her breast up to the nipple. Tim leans gently over the area in question, an uncapped Magic Marker in his right hand. As he begins to write, he reaches up with his left hand to support the breast. He apologizes for having to do this, and the woman says, "Don't you worry, honey. A man needs a steady surface to sign his name."

Joey's eyes have expanded to their maximum circumference. His smile has stretched his mouth so wide that tomorrow he may contend with soreness. There is nothing natural about these facial contortions, but then again there is nothing natural about public voyeurism either, particularly when conducted in such close proximity to one's parents and extended family.

Tim's last penstrokes run over into the cleavage. "All done," he says, and puts the cap back on the marker. After inspecting, the woman carefully readjusts her blouse so as not to smear the ink. She gives Tim a hearty kiss on the cheek and says loudly, "I'll see you later, darling." She moves off into the crowd and Tim and Joey come over to the bar.

"Did you see that?" Tim says.

"Yeah," I say. "All I have to say is, I hope you signed your full name."

"All that and more," Tim says.

"He signed 'esquire'!" Joey shouts, slapping his thigh with amazing force. He seems in danger of falling over.

"Isn't esquire what lawyers sign?" I say.

"My dad's a lawyer," Tim says.

"It's too bad Cree wasn't here," Joey says. As soon as he stops speaking he looks uncertain. Tim laughs and says, "Yeah," but I can tell that he knows that Joey is wrong, that if Cree had been here, she wouldn't have found it funny, she would have shaken her head, turned her back, and gone glowering off to a distant part of the club. If she had been here, Tim would have offered to sign a napkin instead.

After the show I wait on the curb with the merch boxes. Joey is using the van to shuttle relatives to a distant parking lot. Tim and Cree are missing. I asked Joey before he drove off if I should be looking for them, and he said, "Don't worry about it. They can take care of themselves."

Farther down the street the Radials' tour bus sits in its perpetually idling state. The bus's lower compartments are open to the world; the crew still has a good half hour of packing up to do. The Radials themselves are through for the evening, and I imagine they sit now around a table in the front cabin, drinking and playing cards, as someone, Peter perhaps, strums an acoustic guitar.

As I watch, a light in the very back of the bus turns off, on, and then off again. Figures pass by the large window that looks into the front compartment. The door opens and a person steps down onto the pavement.

It's Cree. She looks up and down the block, and when she sees me she breaks into a little run, wrapping her arms around herself to prevent her unbuttoned cardigan from billowing out behind her.

"It's crazy," she says when she is close enough to be heard. She is both out of breath and incoherent. "I can't explain it."

"What?" I say.

"I can't explain right now," she says. "I'll tell you later. It's happening really fast. Just tell Tim and Joey that I'll see you guys in Austin and not to worry. I just can't explain this to anyone right now."

"Okay," I say. I wish there were something I could say to keep her here, but there isn't. She says, "Thanks, Lou," turns, and, hugging herself, runs back to the bus.

A few minutes later the van glides into view. Someone has forgotten to close the side door, and through the opening I can see the silhouette of Joey's hair, rising above the headrest against a backdrop of windshield and moonlight beyond.

Inside the van, I tell him that Cree will be spending another night in the company of the English. He counters with the information that Tim was last seen chatting up the woman who now bears his signature across her bosom.

"You know," he says, "I think it's fine that they want to go out and get laid. When you're on tour, you're disconnected from reality. Sometimes it's nice to just be mellow for a little while. But when it starts to interfere with the band, that's where I draw the line. I mean, it's just you and me tonight. We don't know where Tim is. We know where Cree is, but we don't have any way of getting in touch with her." He pauses before issuing his summation: "I just don't feel like I'm in a band right now."

"Mmmm," I say. My mind is moving too quickly to offer more

of a response. Who is Cree with? I want to ask Joey what he thinks, but I don't feel like I would have any control over my tone.

Joey doesn't speak again until we reach the strip mall nearest his own neighborhood. He points out the convenience store where he bought baseball cards, the record store where he bought his first tape, and later, his first compact disc, and the all-night Wendy's that served him well when he was up late writing a paper. In all of these recollections, there is never any mention of any person but himself. I have always suspected it, but in this moment, I see it confirmed: growing up, Joey was a loner. I think about how the band must have changed his life. Perhaps it was nothing more than the simple miracle of hearing his own voice on record. Now some of his dreams have come true, enough for him to believe the rest will follow. I suspect it to be the feeling of living in a good mood. He slows the van sharply as we turn into the driveway that must be his, and I wonder if he had a moment where he could not remember which of these very similar houses he used to live in. I am no longer confused by his response to Cree's defection. He does not want to return to his life before the band.

I sleep in the bedroom that used to belong to Joey's sister. The room has since been sanitized to remove all traces of her presence. Before I turn out the light, I open the drawer in the bedside table to check for a Bible. All I find, however, is a little package of unopened stationery.

As I lie there in the dark, I think about the romantic possibilities. There is someone new in Cree's life and that someone rides on the Radials' bus. Who is it? I feel certain that I can rule out Edward and Bob. It could be one of the roadies, the guitar tech or the lighting tech or the soundman who looked so pretty in Gemma's makeup. It could be Peter or even Walter, two oth-

erwise unremarkable gentlemen made attractive by their mem-
bership in a successful rock and roll band. Or it could be Brant.
This is the possibility that I dread. I don't know why he should
be worse than any of the rest of them, but he is. I lie there, trying
to fall asleep, and I hope and hope and hope.

In the morning I wake with the desperate sensation of having
slept too long and missed a life-changing opportunity. I am already in a sitting position by the time my eyes open. Through the
closed door I can hear the faraway sounds of *You Think You
Hear,* taking its first walk through the Amonte family stereo.

I dress and wander out to the living room. Joey and Mr.
Amonte sit in similar robes before the hi-fi apparatus. Joey cues
up "Going Country," the song he sings, and leans back on his
hands to listen. As the song plays, he tells his father about the
various ideas he, Tim, and Cree had for the sound concept.

"We decided it should be a period piece," he says. "That's
why the tambourine is so prominent."

He goes on to describe his overall role in the percussion sche-
matic, how it was his suggestion that the stomping bass drum
pause during the verse and go into double-time for the chorus.
Mr. Amonte says, "That has a really interesting effect. If you'd
done it the other way, it'd be a completely different song."

Joey smiles, and then says, "Yeah, yeah," looking around the
room for no reason except to casually downplay his accomplishment.

"Have you heard from Tim?" I ask.

Joey's father chuckles. "He knocked on the door at seven-
thirty this morning. I didn't know who it was. When I opened the
door I probably looked like I was going to kill him."

"He's sleeping now," Joey says.

"As well he should be," Mr. Amonte says with a wink.

For lunch we eat fried chicken, tamales, twice-baked potatoes, and a salad hearty enough to be a meal in its own right. If I
had to guess I would say that these are Joey's favorite childhood

foods and that his mother could not pick just one. The salad alone contains more fruit and nuts than several famous breakfast cereals combined.

As I unwrap the genuine piece of corn husk from my third tamale, I regard Tim in his half-wakened dishevelment at the other end of the table. There is an air of dehydration about him; seconds after he sat down, his orange juice and water were completely consumed. Nonetheless, he manages to comport himself with his usual charm, fielding the Amontes' references to the rock and roll lifestyle with sincerity and grace. It has probably been many years since Joey's parents last had the opportunity to insinuate.

While Joey helps his mother clean up after the meal, Tim and I carry the guitars and backpacks out to the van. It's a cool, sunny morning and I am glad to be wearing short sleeves. Trees at irregular but close distances provide enough shade that I am struck by the contrast between the winking places of light and dark on the road. This neighborhood is not unlike the one I grew up in, though its unfamiliarity dooms it to feel generic.

Joey's garage door opens, and Joey's voice shouts "Exercise!" from somewhere inside. A half-inflated soccer ball shoots out into the street. Tim runs up to kick it, but the ball spins off the side of his foot and rolls under the van, where it is trapped by pipes and other gadgets. I lay down on my side and poke at the ball with my leg. The sun heats one side of my face while the road cools the other. I feel like I could lie here for at least fifteen minutes before this process becomes boring.

Above my head, Joey says to Tim, "What are you doin wakin' up my daddy at seven-thirty on a Saturday?"

"Tell him I'm really sorry about that," Tim says. "But I had no choice. I just had to get out of there."

"What happened?" I ask, getting up from the asphalt.

"Quite a bit," Tim says.

After Joey and I left, Tim went backstage with the breast

woman, Arlene, and her friend, Karen. Their boyfriends, he was told, were both associates of the radio station that gave away the tickets and wanted to schmooze for just a few more minutes. Pretty soon Tim and Arlene were making out. But then Karen said, "I want to kiss him too." Tim worried that this was some kind of setup and that he was going to be beaten up shortly thereafter, but he couldn't pass up the opportunity to fool around with two women.

The boyfriends returned during a break in the kissing and all five of them went back to Arlene's expensive house for cocktails. Both of the men were interested in how things worked on Tim's side of the music industry, and they and Tim dominated the conversation. The women poured drinks, talked to each other mostly, and occasionally made comments about how late it was getting. Tim had never been so aware of possible subtext. It was after three o'clock, and he still no idea what was going to happen.

Abruptly, the two boyfriends and Karen stood up and said it was time to go. Arlene's boyfriend said he would see her on Monday. They left the house, and Tim listened until he heard three car doors shut and an engine start. He and Arlene went to bed. In the morning, she dropped him off at the Amonte residence on her way to coach a Little League girls' softball team.

"It was either that or wait until she got back," Tim says. "I was feeling kind of creeped out. She said she doesn't usually do this kind of thing, but . . ."

"She made an exception for you," I say.

"You're a very special man," Joey says.

"I should rush the both of you right now," Tim says. He dances back a step, mimicking the light movements of a boxer. His foot catches the sagging soccer ball, and he stumbles over it, hopping up onto the curb to avoid falling down completely.

Joey laughs and laughs. I say, "You're a very special man indeed."

Tim smiles dutifully through the ridicule. When the last dying chuckle has vanished from the air, he says, very seriously, "If we could not mention this to Cree . . . ," and lets his voice trail off. It takes me a moment to realize that he's not talking about his encounter with the soccer ball.

"No problem," I tell him.

"My lips are sealed," Joey says.

"Thanks," Tim says. He places his hands at his waist and nods several times without making eye contact. This unpleasant business behind us, he seems to be saying, we are now ready to begin our day.

THE DRIVE TO AUSTIN is brief, a mere three hours, but it is only the second we have made without Cree. The first was a novelty, a chance to smoke pot, listen to loud music, and say the word *bitch.* But this time her absence implies the death of all that is feminine. All around us there is nothing but big sky, dry grass, and hot sun.

We do the only thing we know how to do in this situation, and that is talk about women as they relate to drugs and rock and roll.

"I have trouble when I get stoned with a girl and she gets silly," Tim says. "It really changes how I think about her. Ana and I used to get high and it used to make me crazy. I was really into Cheap Trick then, it didn't matter which record it was, I would put it on, and she would pick up the album jacket and for the rest of the night it was Bun E. Carlos. Look at Bun E. Carlos. Look at the hat he's wearing. Isn't that a funny name. What do you think it's short for—"

"Bunnilingus," Joey says.

"Yeah, right," Tim says. "I just found it very distracting." I wonder if he's going to talk about what it was like to be high with Cree, but he seems to be finished.

"I hear you," Joey says. "I went out with this girl one summer and every time we got baked, all she wanted to do was fool around."

"That's rough, Joey," Tim says. His tone is more sarcastic than he intended it to be, and he shuts up.

"When I'm high, I have trouble with people in general," I say. "People who say typical stoner things, you know, 'Listen to the music, man' or 'Those colors are amazing' or 'This cereal tastes incredible.' I just find it difficult to be around people who are trying too hard."

As I utter these sentences, I realize the mistake I'm making.

"What do you mean?" Joey says immediately, attempting to sound both amused and conversational. "Do you think people who say those things are just trying to be cool?"

"Not exactly," I say. "It's just . . ."

"Maybe their sense of how to talk about music isn't very evolved," Joey says. "Or maybe this is the first time music has ever sounded that way to them. There's really no way to know."

"I didn't say it was rational," I say. "It's just something that gets on my nerves."

"I'll remember that the next time we get high," he says. He grins and looks back at Tim. I can sense that he would like to use this quirk to open a full-blown investigation into my psyche.

"Who do you think Cree is with?" I blurt out. This is a desperate attempt for a number of reasons, but once I say it I feel relief.

"Brant," Joey says, disapproving.

"Brant," Tim says. He sounds certain.

"Why do you think that?" I say.

"I know that," Tim says. "Peter told me before the show last night. He said it happened the night we left Atlanta. He said they had to turn the music up, if you know what I'm saying."

I have an image of myself driving my fist not just at Tim's face but through it. For this one moment it seems like the most natural thing in the world to do. Joey is asking him now why he didn't volunteer the Cree information earlier, and Tim is saying he would have felt like a gossip. How noble of him. I would like to fall deeply asleep and wake up in a place far removed from this van and this continent, a white beach eclipsed by a rising blue ocean as a volcano steams placidly several miles inland. I settle instead for what's out the window, hoping that the rhythm of the engine and the road will be enough to nod me off, but of course it isn't.

In the past few years Austin has become the national home for creative youth. One such youth is Clay, the younger brother of my ex-girlfriend Kaitlyn. According to reports I've heard, he is a rising star on the University of Texas fraternity scene. Tonight, he will be my host.

I remember him a scrawny lad, prone to tears. Even as a high school senior Kaitlyn would work to produce these hysterics, accusing him of molesting the family cat, Pucker. She was healthy then and had yet to develop the gravity that seems to govern her behavior now.

"You should see him," she would say to me, as the thirteen-year-old Clay stood there red-faced. "He lifts Pucker over his head and then he looks up his butt." And Clay would shout, "That's not what I'm doing!" These incidents made me feel uncomfortable on behalf of all three involved. I hope that when I see Clay tonight, he will remember that I never once laughed.

We arrive at the club and search the compound. The Radials' crew is midway through the unloading process, but neither Cree nor the band seems to be on the premises. Tim gets a tip from the lighting tech that Cree may be on the tour bus and asks if I would mind being the one to retrieve her. I would mind, but it seems unreasonable to say so. "I'll have her out here in two shakes of a lamb's tail," I say.

I approach the bus from the far end and take a long slow walk underneath the major windows, in the hopes that I'll be recognized before I reach the door. But the door is still closed by the time I get there, and I'm forced to knock. It is a demeaning thing to have to knock on the door of a bus and even more demeaning to wait at that door for a full minute while those inside the tinted glass determine by conference if it is safe to let you in.

Eventually, access is granted. I step into the cabin and discover a full-blown tea party only moments underway, the little tea bags still floating belly-up in their mugs. Louise removes a croissant from a white wicker bowl and passes the bowl over to Walter. Peter turns his mug round and round on the booth table.

"I take it you're here for Cree?" Gemma says, rising to meet the social challenge when no one else will. "She's . . ."

"I'm right here," Cree says from the darkness of the long hallway. There's something wrong with her voice. She steps into the light, and I am relieved to see that she is alone. "We're having some tea in my honor."

"She's come down with a terrible cold," Gemma says. "We're hoping to clear her sinuses. Would you like to join us?"

"No," I say. "Actually, I'm having the opposite problem, and I'm afraid the tea would only make it worse." To Cree I say, "I just wanted to let you know that we're here. I hope your condition improves." I wave goodbye and walk off the bus.

"Where is she?" Joey asks when I return.

"She's having some tea," I say. "She'll be out in a minute. She has a cold."

"How bad?" Tim says.

"Her voice has that nasal quality," I say. "But her spirits are good."

"All the more reason—," Tim says.

"We've made some decisions," Joey interrupts. "And we need you to be the messenger."

Both Tim and Joey want Cree to ride with us for the rest of the tour. I have no doubt that it was Joey who proposed the idea, although it probably didn't take much to get Tim to accept. On the surface their logic is pure. The next show is two days away in Phoenix, and it will take two full days of driving to get there—

having Cree absent for that much time would violate fundamental principles of band unity. But after Phoenix, the bands will diverge, the Radials moving on to Los Angeles for media engagements while the Day Action Band bides its time in the burrito mecca of San Diego, two hours to the south. Though we will rejoin them for one final show in L.A., the effect of this sanction will be to severely reduce Cree's remaining time with Brant.

"And something may come up, you never know," Joey is saying. "We might actually need her to do something."

"If we all contracted a case of desert blindness," I say, "we would need her to drive us to a local hospital."

"Are you being some kind of smartass?" Tim says, only partly kidding.

"No," I say. "The sun is brighter in the desert. As you know, sand is made of glass, and when the light reflects off the sand, it can cause a person to go blind. If this happened to all three of us at once, we would perish. We would wander into a canyon or a butte."

Tim punches me lightly in the shoulder. "Seriously," he says. "Don't be like that when you tell her. I know I should tell her myself, but given our history . . ."

"It's all about band unity," Joey says to me. "Just remember that and you'll be fine."

I think about this task as I set up my table. The sense of foreboding I feel is balanced by a sense of impending calm. I don't want Cree to ride the bus either. I want her in the van, and I don't care whether she sleeps or reads or listens to her headphones. As long as I can see the top of her head when I look back through the rearview mirror, I'll be happy. I won't have to think about what she's doing or who she's doing it with.

The bonus is that I get to bear this unpopular news without being held responsible for it. Cree won't say, "Did Tim put you up to this?" but she will know that he did. She will nod and frown and say "Mm-hmm" tersely through closed lips, knowing that she has no good argument to the contrary, and that even if she did, I wouldn't be the one to hear it. And I will resist the urge to sympathize, because that would increase the very tension that I'm supposed to deflate.

I can see her standing now with Tim and Joey in front of the stage, having a conversation about something besides the bus issue. She is bent forward, laughing, and when she straightens she puts one hand on her stomach and moves the other up to her throat. Her mouth opens wide and a faint off-key falsetto reaches me all the way at the back of the room. She bends over laughing again, and Joey pokes her in the forehead with his finger.

I have never associated Tim's actions with duplicity before, and I'm not saying that I do now. Almost everything that Tim has done, he has done in the best interests of the band. But carrying this temporary secret has revealed to me something that probably should have been obvious by now: that the best interests of the band are not always the same as the best interests of the people in the band.

Clay and his brother Whitey show up at the end of the Day Action Band soundcheck. It has been several years since Clay and I last met, and in that time he has become muscular. His neck has widened to the point that it seems not just to support his head but to serve as a pedestal for it. His arms have nearly doubled in circumference, creating the illusion that they have also been shortened. His face is still overseen by a single dark eyebrow, but this feature, once amusing, now gives him an unrelenting pensive look. Whitey is not really Clay's brother, but that's how Clay introduces him.

"Yes, sir, it's my real name," Whitey tells me. "It's a family name on my mother's side. It dates back to the Civil War."

Soon I see that this relationship, like most, has a dominant partner. Whitey functions as a scout, scanning the growing crowd for women of varying physique and attire. When he spots a winner, he nudges Clay. If Clay doesn't see her right away, Whitey provides crude coordinates—"thirty feet straight ahead, red sun-dress"—and then the two share a moment. Sometimes Clay does not wholeheartedly approve of Whitey's selection, and then Whitey, bearing the criticism in mind, returns to his post with a new resolve, determined not to disappoint a second time. Joey has described fraternities as "the last great bastions of repressed homosexuality" and notes that this phenomenon is particularly striking in the latitudes below the Mason-Dixon line: "Where else in the South do you find large crowds of fit, shirtless men enjoy-ing each other's company on a sunny Sunday afternoon? Buggery, I tell you! Buggery!"

A half hour passes. The music begins and Whitey wanders off to be closer to it. Clay stays with me, however, and peppers me with a number of polite questions about plans and residences, past, present, and future. The pleasure he derives from this in-teraction seems to have less to do with the substance of it and more to do with that fact that it's taking place at all. He is a man now and part of being a man means going out to pay your respects to the man who once dated your sister. The transformation is so complete, the code of maleness so forthrightly present, that it is all I can do not to whisper the name "Pucker" into his awaiting ear. But then he surprises me.

"How was my sister?" he says. "I mean, did she seem healthy to you?"

I hesitate before I answer. In addition to concern, Clay's tone also indicates curiosity. What is the protocol here? I don't want to tell him about the paleness and the crutches and the dark places under the eyes, and then have him tell his parents, who will descend upon the Upper West Side with an army of doctors and emotional disorders specialists. Kaitlyn might never speak to me again. But I don't want to lie to him either. I don't know how sick she really is. I don't know the meaning of that tube insertion device in the back of her hand. What if I were to say, "Oh, she's doing great," and then next week she died?

"She's on crutches, Clay," I tell him. "She walks very, very slowly." I do a respectful impression of Kaitlyn taking ten steps. "She says she has good days and bad days. I don't know exactly what that means. I think she goes to the doctor quite a bit—her work insurance pays for it—and since she works at home, they're really none the wiser. What else do you want to know?"

"Nothing," he says. "Thank you." He puts his hands in his pockets and stands there looking thoughtful but unemotional. At one point he turns to the stage and shakes his head, as if disgusted by what he sees there. When he turns back I say to him, "Please talk to her yourself, if you're going to talk to her. She really doesn't want your parents to be involved."

"I know," he says. Then he says, "I've got to take a piss." He walks proudly off toward the restrooms, maybe not to cry, but definitely to be alone.

After their set the Day Action Band migrates out to my section of the room. Joey leans against a far wall conversing with a pair of his cousins, both of whom are students at the university. Tim dances with a curvaceous blond whose wire-rimmed spectacles allude to a hidden intellectual precocity. Cree, for a reason I can't discern, comes over to talk to me and Clay.

"You hit the high notes," I say.

"My throat is killing me," she says. "It's starting to fill up with phlegm and shit."

"I thought you sang very well," Clay says, deploying the polite diction that forms a central part of his charm.

"Oh, thank you," Cree says. She becomes very flirtatious over the next few minutes. There are smiles and laughs and hands on the hips galore. She's not coming on to him though. She's playing the role of the best friend's older sister, sexy and wise but ultimately unattainable.

"I have to tell you something, Cree," I say. I put my hand around the top of her arm and lead her a few feet away. "It concerns your accommodations for the next few nights."

I tell her. Her reaction is less muted than I thought it would be. Her tone sharpens, her swearing increases, and she starts a number of sentences that she does not complete. "I don't want to stay with Joey's fucking asshole cousins!" she hisses at one point. The angry words are not necessarily directed at me, but I feel them nonetheless. There are forces in this world that conspire to deny her happiness, and I am aligned with them by default. The vocalizations wind down and finally she simply stands and watches Tim dance with the blonde.

"I don't mean to butt in," Clay says, coming forth, "but if you need a place to stay, I've got extra room. You can have my bed."

"No, no, I can't do that," Cree says. "I can't kick you out of your own bed."

"You seem pretty upset with those guys," Clay says. "I just thought you might like a break from them. Don't worry about me." He waves his hand in my direction. "Me and Lou are just going to smoke pot until the sun comes up anyway. It won't matter where I go to sleep."

I wince when he mentions smoking pot, but Cree doesn't seem to notice. She considers and then she says. "If you don't mind. That would be great. I could really use a real bed to sleep in. I have this cold—oh!—but don't worry, you won't get it."

The bed procured, her angry countenance returns. "I'll be on the bus," she says. "Come and get me when you want to go." She storms into the crowd, passing close by both Tim and Joey but not speaking to them.

"Whoa, dude," Clay says, watching her go. "How can you stand to be around that every day?"

"She's not usually like this," I say. "She's in a bad mood because she's not getting her way."

"That's not what I meant," Clay says. "She's beautiful, man. It's going to be hard, thinking about her asleep in my bed. Her hair on my pillow. Her body wrapped in my sheets. When you leave tomorrow, I'm just going to lie in my bed and smell my pillow."

A flash of hostility prevents me from joining him in this rhapsody. Fortunately, he is interrupted by the arrival of Tim and Joey, who witnessed the storming off and have suspicions about the cause.

"Did you tell her?" Joey says.

"Yes," I say. "She wasn't happy."

Tim and Joey look at each other and shrug. I continue with, "She's going to spend the night with me at Clay's." I feel a secret, inappropriate thrill as I say this. "So we ought to make some kind of plan to meet tomorrow."

"You can probably count on me to complicate the plan," Tim says. He turns to where his dance partner is waiting, about fifty feet away, and raises his arm to indicate that he'll be right there.

After calling over one of Joey's cousins for consultation, we agree to meet for breakfast at a diner on the edge of town. Once again the band is going to be split into three parts, but tonight Joey doesn't seem to mind, the puritan in his heart half satisfied.

When the show ends, Tim and Joey depart almost immediately for their respective destinations. I take Clay and Whitey backstage and outfit them with expensive beers, which will otherwise go unused. Tonight's backstage is one large room with food tables in opposing corners. The Radials' side is a bustling mecca of consumption and conversation, the hint of high culture wafting across the room on a modified Cockney accent. The Day Action Band side consists solely of Clay and Whitey, reading the labels on their imported beers and pretending familiarity with the hops listed there. I expect to see some cross-pollination when I return.

The Radials' bus has changed since the last time I boarded it. It is darker now, populated only by Gemma, Louise, and the silent driver, and the tables are empty of the tea and croissants of this afternoon. Once again Gemma is aware of my mission, but this time she seems to regard me as an interloper. Without a word she rises and disappears down the dark hall. Louise shuffles through a deck of tarot cards, occasionally dropping one and using that as an excuse to throw me a wary uplooking glance. How quickly this has become Cree's territory. I can't imagine that I would ever feel comfortable here.

The Cree that follows Gemma out of the shadows is ravaged by sniffles. Her face is sleepy and confused, her footsteps uncertain and arrhythmic. She does not carry a soft, fluffy blanket, but it would not seem strange if she did. Gemma and Louise stare at me with such accusation that I say, "I'll take good care of her," as if it were an involuntary reflex.

I lead Cree out to Clay's urban assault vehicle, intending to put her in the back seat, but the doors are locked. Guilt runs me inside to the backstage area, where Clay and Whitey have indeed engaged some of the roadies in a tribute to the excesses of rugby. Taking a few beers for posterity, and dropping Whitey off at "the house," we finally arrive at Clay's surprisingly modern and well-kept apartment.

While Cree is in the bathroom, Clay astutely removes his bedding for the evening. He piles one of his two beanbag chairs on top of the other and begins to unfold the down comforter that will serve as his mattress. I hear the sound of Cree brushing her teeth as the faucet runs. The water stops, and she blows her nose for a long time. Then the toilet flushes, the bathroom door clicks shut and a lamp switches off. I listen for the rustle of the sheets but I don't hear them. A voice calls out a faint "Goodnight," and Clay and I say it back.

Lowering the volume on the stereo, Clay puts on a CD by a popular contemporary hard rock band. He sits down on the beanbag tower and leans back as if it were some sort of recliner. The move is tinted with defiance; he knows I can't think much of this music but purports not to care. We listen to two entire songs before he leans over and snags a plastic bag. A pipe made of dark-grained wood comes out next. We smoke and he tells me of his trip to New Orleans for Mardi Gras the previous spring. By the end of the celebration, he says, "drunkenness and sobriety were interchangeable." He shows me several photographs of himself with girls lifting their shirts up. These girls are neither wearing nor holding bras of any sort, leading us into a discussion of various forms of premeditation. Clay concludes that the same forces operate at a baseball park, where a single person can start the stadium doing the wave. He amends this by saying, "You know what? The same forces operate everywhere. There's nothing interesting about it at all. So why does it seem interesting?"

"Because they're breasts?" I offer. I don't know what he's trying to say. I do appreciate the effort, however.

"No," he says. "For people to do what they want to do, there always has to be something else." He seems first excited, then disappointed by this conclusion. I feel responsible for seeing him through the point.

"Some external construct—?" I begin to say.

"Let's call my sister," Clay says. "Let's wake her up and see what she says."

This does not sound like a good idea to me, but to voice practical dissent—"Don't you think it's kind of late to call?"— would be to dishonor all of the relationships at hand.

"Do you know her number?" I say. He shakes his head, mildly devastated, and gets up to find his address book.

Clay takes the phone into the kitchen and sits on the floor behind the counter, where I can no longer see him. Sometimes his whisper modulates into his actual speaking voice, and I hear words and phrases that mean nothing to me. I watch the seconds move on the CD readout and think about the relative lengths of verses and choruses.

At some point Clay pokes me and says, "You're up, dude." I realize I've been dozing. He holds the phone out, and my first instinct is to recoil from it.

Clay tries again. "She wants to talk to you," he says.

"Where is he?" Kaitlyn's voice says from somewhere inside the phone.

I take the phone from Clay and say, "I'm here," into it. Clay returns to his spot on the floor in the kitchen.

"Who wanted to call?" Kaitlyn says.

"We both did," I say. She doesn't say anything as she ponders this. The sounds of New York are so dim over the connection that I feel I might be imagining them.

"What did you do today?" I say finally into the silence.

"Let's see," she says. "What did I do today? I woke up. I threw up for half an hour. I took a shower. I rode the subway to the doctor's. I rode it back. I threw up for another half hour, but this time it really hurt because there was nothing in my stomach to throw up. Then I took a nap. Then . . ."

She gasps quietly and for a moment all I hear is shivered breathing.

'Are you okay?" I say.

"Oh yes," she says, unnaturally bright, the sarcasm of seconds ago replaced by something far worse. "I'm fine. Why wouldn't I be? How was your day?"

I say, "I'm really high right now."

"Oh. That's nice," she says. "Listen. I have to get up really early tomorrow, so I'm going to go back to sleep. Tell my brother I said goodnight, please. I'll talk to you sometime, okay? Goodbye."

I smooth my sleeping bag so it covers the scratchy areas of the couch. Clay doesn't seem to have made it back from the kitchen; I can hear loud consistent breathing coming from the other side of the counter. Every couple of minutes Cree coughs sharply from the bedroom, and I imagine that she is half awake and wishing that the night would come to an end. I think about what I would do if I went in there and climbed in bed with her. I would stroke her hair until she fell asleep. I would blow the beads of sweat from her forehead. In the morning, I would curl her up to protect her from the sunlight. The CD player begins its ungainly changing of discs, and I wait to see what the new music will be. The voice of John Fogerty, something I can fall asleep to. Kaitlyn is two thousand miles away, and Cree is twenty feet away, and I am equally distant from both of them.

The diner of the following morning is not really a diner at all, but a trendy brunch spot that has been misclassified due to its location on the beginning edge of a strip mall highway. Clay had been intending to drop us off, but Cree felt that he ought to be rewarded for his hospitality. Since she made no mention of buying his breakfast during her closing arguments, I can only assume that the reward is a few more minutes of her grateful company.

When we pull up, Joey and the cousins are standing outside the entrance of the restaurant, as are several other groups of people. Tim bends on one knee before a rack of *USA Today*s, gleaning the two-day-old news on the front page within. "There's a wait," Joey confides, "but from what I've seen, things are moving fast."

Conversation is kept to a minimum during this wait. At first Joey remains in the vicinity of his cousins, while Clay, Cree, and I adhere to our own subgroup a few feet down the line. But after Tim finishes reading the captive front page, Clay goes over to have a look. Then after he's done, one of Joey's cousins, and then finally Joey himself. And all of them down on one knee. This amusing spectacle takes place without the ironic commentary that would normally accompany it. I feel this rarity ought to be savored in and of itself. But soon the urge to know the news of several yesterdays overcomes me as well, and I forfeit my encompassing perspective.

Some time later we are seated at a large round table out in the center of the restaurant. Using a complex system of initiatives and pauses, Cree determines the placement of every person at the table relative to herself. Clay and I sit on either side of her, and the two cousins sit directly across, the end result being that she doesn't have to associate visually or verbally with either Tim or Joey. When the menus are distributed, Cree opens hers up as if it were a roadmap. Only her tiny fingers curling around the edges give proof to her existence behind it.

This freeze exerts a subtle but meaningful force on the breakfast. People attend to their menus with new devotion. An obvious silence falls. It is broken when Clay and Joey's eldest cousin each discover that the other is a fraternity member and that they often frequent the same bars. They talk enthusiastically of a road called Sixth Street and exchange escalating accounts of debauchery and intrigue perpetrated there. Clay shows a faint scar just below his hairline from when he was kicked in the head by a bouncer wearing steel-toed boots. Moments earlier, he had vomited on those boots, and he says now that if he had been that bouncer, "I would have kicked me in the head too."

"I don't think I can top that one," the cousin says. He leans back in his chair and thoughtfully sips his orange juice.

"Tell about the time you thought you broke your neck," Joey says.

"Ah," the cousin says, looking at his brother. "The tale of Hotman and Coldman."

"Yeah!" Joey says, getting excited.

"It was a day of neutral temperatures . . . ," the younger cousin begins.

". . . and it was also a day of new responsibilities," the older one finishes. They apply this tag-team approach to the whole story. By the time it is over, Cree's dark fog has been burned away by the hot sun of real-life comedy.

Joey's cousins were admittedly children of privilege. Their house was so large it had two thermostats. At the time of this incident they were eleven and thirteen years old, and their parents, out to attend the symphony, had decided that they were old enough to be left home alone for the first time.

They were playing a crude variant of hide and go seek. When the elder cousin could not be found, the younger had the idea to flush him out with heat. He turned up the thermostat in that section of the house to ninety-five degrees. He waited at the periphery of this region for thirty minutes and was beginning to sweat himself, when he heard his brother moaning. He felt that this might be a ruse, but when the moaning persisted, he thought he had to act. He rushed into his parents' bedroom and found atop the bed his brother, clad in what had to be in excess of six sweaters, a winter hat, two scarves, and multiple pairs of wool socks. "I am Hotman, ha ha ha!" screamed the brother, jumping and waving his arms so that sweat flew off him in traceable arcs. The younger cousin sensed that the competition had deepened several levels beyond hide and go seek. He turned and ran full tilt back into the other section of the house. He found the thermostat for *his* area and made it go as low as it would go, an estimated forty degrees. He stripped down to his tighty-whities. He removed crescent-shaped ice cubes from the refrigerator and held them in his fists. Then he returned to the border between the two regions, faced his reddening brother and shouted, "I am Coldman! I am going to make you cold! Ha ha ha!"

Seconds after this historic summit, the parents came home, their evening truncated by stomach distress. The sound of their key in the lock produced instant panic. The thermostats were the first to be readjusted. The superheroes themselves were next. Coldman, in a moment of inspiration, grabbed his father's bathrobe and wrapped himself in it. He hadn't done this in years, and he thought his parents might find it both touching and cute. But Hotman could not conceive of putting on another garment. Heat stroke was far less than a bathrobe away. His only option was to remove. And so he tried to take off all the sweaters at once. He had his head through the collars when he felt something up near his neck pull hard. After that was darkness. They took him in the car to the emergency room, his mother trying to hold the sweaters away from his face so he could breathe.

Cree laughs so hard that she sloshes the top off her second extra large glass of grapefruit juice. Tim volunteers his napkin with great earnestness, and she accepts it with a forgiving smile. I notice that this reconciliation, unlike the others, seems to have required something resembling an apology.

After breakfast, Clay and I part with a manly handshake.

"That dude was intense," Joey says, as Clay's car squeals out into traffic. "I thought he was going to come around the table and kick my ass."

"Why did you think that?" I say.

"I've just never known anyone who had a firsthand experience with violence," he says, touching his forehead in the place that corresponds roughly to Clay's boot scar. "Sometimes you forget that that stuff goes on." He looks back and forth along the highway before fixating on a car dealership on the other side of the road. A shining row of pickup trucks points in our direction, and I imagine Joey is thinking that Clay belongs behind the wheel of one of those. If the Day Action Band ever does make it big, it wouldn't surprise me if Joey counters with a pickup truck of his own.

Today's drive is the most crucial of the tour. We must cover a thousand miles by 6:00 P.M. tomorrow. Accounting for convenience stops and the van's inability to capitalize on the generous speed limits of the Southwest, Joey and I estimate a total driving time of twenty hours.

"We should do at least twelve of those today," he says. "Otherwise, we're fucked."

"That's six hundred miles," I say. "If we leave now, that'll put us in El Paso at one-thirty in the morning. As my father likes to say, daylight's burning."

"Hit it," Joey says.

Moments after I get the van on the highway, I know I'm going to be able to take us all the way. I have that good driving feeling and a completely unambivalent sense of duty. Each exit passed feels like an accomplishment. The band is quiet, tired by their late nights and bored by the empty terrain. Cree reads and sleeps stretched out across the back seat, her cold reduced to the occasional clearing of her throat. We stop for dinner at a truck stop, the lone exit over a fifty-mile span. As all four of us move silently through the salad bar, "Glorious" comes on the radio. Brant's voice, plaintive and distinct, is the loudest single sound in the dining room. Tim and Joey stop serving themselves, their faces softening in wonder, for this is the first time we've heard "Glorious" on the radio since it went to number one. The scattered truckers, some sitting alone, some inexplicably sitting at tables together, continue as they were, their ears detecting only a minor shift in the background noise. But at the first syllable out of Brant's mouth, Cree shudders. Tim reaches out to touch her arm, and she pulls away. She struggles to reaffix her blank expression of this afternoon and this evening, but she can't do it. Frowning, she repeats what Joey has just said: "Wow. This is really strange." She says it again, and this time Tim looks at her as if he expects her to elaborate. An openness comes into her eyes, and she seems about to speak. But then she looks down at her salad and begins to ladle on the dressing. Tim and I return to the table, where Joey has already begun to apply rigorous shakings of salt and pepper. By the time Cree joins us, the song is over.

After dinner the band sleeps. The Ray Charles tape that had been Tim's selection ends, and I put on *Nebraska* by Bruce Springsteen. Tim wakes up briefly and says, "Are you sure that's not going to put you to sleep?" and when I say no, he says, "Well wake me up if you're having trouble staying awake." I tell him I will. There are no lights here except for those that run along the edges of the highway. Sometimes there is a glowing place at the bottom of the sky, and this means a town is forty or fifty miles

distant. It may appear at first to be to the left or to the right of
the highway but I know eventually the road will bend to go
through it. As the van closes the distance the glow becomes a bed
of jewels, spreading and spreading until finally it clarifies again
into a mass of gas stations, all-night eateries, and yellow flashing
traffic signals. A town of hundreds, the last shapes of trailers and
bungalows less than a half mile from the road. El Paso, when it
comes into sight at just after 2:00 A.M., runs the length of the
horizon and seems capable of harboring its own sun. To the left
is Mexico, conveying a vast and mythic sense of its own. I pull
into the first motel I see.

IN THE MORNING, JOEY runs out onto the balcony in his bare feet to see if he can see Mexico. "What a fucking dork," Tim says good-naturedly. He bends to one knee and begins to roll up his sleeping bag. A few feet away, in the space in front of the sink, Cree does the same. The two of them shared a queen-sized bed last night; when I woke up around three to relieve myself, I saw that Tim lay sprawled and out of his bag, palms outstretched, occupying over two-thirds of the available surface area. Cree held rigid to one edge, facing away, a papoose on a precipice. Joey and I did not use our sleeping bags and instead slept together maturely under the covers. Feeling a small sense of solidarity, I join him on the balcony. "Do you see it?" I say.

He gestures at some hills beyond the city to the south. "Obviously, it's all Mexico after a point," he says. "I'm looking for the line of demarcation, in this case, the Rio Grande. I think that might be it there, where the pattern of the buildings changes."

Joey waits in the driver's seat while the rest of us load up the van. His duffel bag is secure under the backseat, but he has forgotten to bring out his bass. When he sees me carrying it, he apologizes and says that his mind is "on other things."

We drive into El Paso. It seems to be a city-sized housing development of one-story square buildings, each surrounded by a low but uniform concrete wall. Streets barely wider than alleys run between the walls, intersect other streets, and move on. Children who aspire to major league greatness must learn to keep their pitches down, lest they break a window or pelt the family pet. Idly, I ask Joey when we'll be able to get some more T-shirts, because these past two shows in Texas have nearly cleaned me out. "I'll tell you later," he says. "I don't want to miss Mexico."

The rebuke angers me but also increases my anticipation, which doubles back and washes over the anger. The road curves to the left, and now, suddenly, we are riding along the banks above the Rio Grande. The murky waters and middling span hardly seem to support the body of legend attributed to the river, but I have never made the crossing myself under cover of darkness and with my entire future at stake. The houses on the other side are wooden boxes built into the hills at odd angles and locations. Twisting dirt roads connect them, leading up to front doors flanked by lightless windows. Every tenth house is painted a pastel pink or blue, and these are what the eyes tend to land upon. I don't see people or animals or even vehicles. There is no wind to raise the dust.

An hour past town we stop at a Mexican restaurant whose unadorned exterior speaks to our desire for authentic cuisine. I buy a tall styrofoam cup of beans and drink it down. Joey drives us farther into the desert and the land they call "New Mexico."

Patsy Cline sings of willows and pillows on the stereo, just as Bruce Springsteen will three decades from now. I am sleepy from the beans; the empty cup lies discarded at my feet. I think of the other word that rhymes with pillow, "billow," and then some words that nearly rhyme, such as "stiletto" and "kilo." This last, vague as it may be, counts as the only premonitory moment that I have ever had.

"Oh shit!" Joey says, applying the brakes. The van slows into place as the temporary last car in a traffic jam. The line of automobiles stretches nearly a mile before detouring off to the right and underneath a large, curved structure. Beyond this strange monument, single cars resume their passage westward, accelerating rapidly to make up for the lost time.

"It must be a fruit check," Joey says.

"What!" Cree shouts, waking up, her voice much too loud in the van. "What's going on?"

"It's a fruit check," Joey says. "They don't want people to bring new kinds of pests into California and ruin the crops. We don't have any fruit in here, do we?"

"No," Tim says. "I threw it out. It was starting to go bad."

"That's good," Joey says. Tim remarks that there is still another state between us and California, but the comment dies unconsidered.

Twenty minutes pass. Heat accumulates inside the cabin, the vents rendered useless by the lack of speed. Shade provided by the large, arcing structure gives the illusion of coolness. A young man in sunglasses and a dark uniform knocks on Joey's window.

"Where are you headed?" he says after Joey rolls it down. He rests one arm on the mirror and leans in close to Joey's face.

"Phoenix," Joey says.

"What are you going to do in Phoenix?" the officer says.

"We're a rock band," Joey says. "We're going to play a show."

"Oh yeah?" the officer says. "What are you called?"

"The Day Action Band," Joey says with pride.

"Never heard of you," the officer says. "Would you please pull the van over there and turn your engine off." He points to a curb next to the building part of the structure.

Joey drives the van over and parks by the curb. "I guess they're doing random searches today," he says. "One car in every ten or twenty. I guess we're the unlucky ones. I hope this doesn't take too long."

"He didn't say anything about fruit," Tim says. "Huh?" Cree says, before rolling over and pulling her pillow against her head.

The officer returns and asks Joey to step out of the van. While he is gone Tim and I wait in silent speculation. Cree sleeps. Twice Tim pulls the curtain open with his finger and peers out. Both times he says, "They're still talking." Finally the door opens again and Joey's upper body comes through it. He smiles but the rest of his face contains elements of fear.

"He says that if we have any drugs, we have to give them to him now," Joey says. "Otherwise, he's going to bring out the dogs. If they find anything, we're going to jail." He extends his arms and places his palms on the seat. "Do we have anything to give him?" he says.

Joey knows damn well we have something to give him. "It's in my toilet kit," I say. "Tim, would you hand me my duffel bag please." Tim struggles to dislodge the bag from beneath the backseat. Cree's eyes open suddenly and this time she is fully awake. "What's happening?" she says.

"We're getting busted," Joey says, speaking grimly to distort the unseemly note of excitement in his voice.

"For what?" Cree says.

"Drugs," Joey says.

"Who the fuck brought drugs?" Cree says.

"I did," I say, accepting the toilet kit from Tim. I unzip the kit and locate my glasses case inside. I pull it out and hold it in my fist.

"That's so fucking stupid," Cree says to me. "You fucking put us all in danger." She is looking right at me. "We let you fucking come on tour with us and you get us arrested."

Tim looks at me but doesn't speak. "No one's going to get arrested," I say. "If anyone does, it'll be me."

"Fuck you, Lou," Cree says. "Just fuck you." There is no sympathy in her eyes. I look away.

"You'd better give it to him," Joey says.

I get out of the van and walk around the long end. The cop is standing about fifteen feet away, polishing his sunglasses with a piece of tissue. Joey walks up from the other direction. I am grateful for the support.

I hand over the case. The cop opens it and pulls out the bag of weed, which we have smoked down to an eighth.

"Is this all you have?" he says.

"Yes," I say.

"If we find any with the dog, you'll go to jail," he says.

"I understand," I say.

The cop pokes at the bag with his thumb. He reaches in and removes the largest remaining bud.

"How have you been smoking this?" he says, twirling the bud in his fingers. "Any pipes?"

"No, joints," I say.

"Do you have any Zig-Zags?" he says. I don't know what these are, so I say, ambiguously, "We've been rolling them in the cities we've been in."

He asks to see my driver's license. "Massachusetts," he says. "I bet you drive like an asshole."

"No sir," I say, and he laughs. He speaks seriously for a few moments about the quality of the break he's going to give us, and then he relates several stories of rock bands who have had their drugs confiscated at this very checkpoint. "You're the least famous band I've ever busted," he says and laughs again.

"We're going to prove you wrong," Joey says. "You'll be able to tell your grandkids about the time you almost arrested the Day Action Band."

"I hope so," the cop says. "Drive carefully and stay away from illegal substances." He turns and walks into the building. I expect to see him slip the Ziploc bag into his pocket, but he doesn't. "We got lucky," Joey says. "That guy was cool."

Back in the van Tim and Joey talk about what caused the cop to pull us aside. Cree looks out her window, either not listening or pretending not to, a book closed on the pillow on her lap.

"He said he smelled weed," Joey says, "but we haven't smoked in here since before New Orleans."

"Maybe it was the Mexican food," Tim says. "All those crazy spices lingering in the air."

I listen to their theories about the half-life of smell, and then I say, "Maybe he took a look at Joey and made an educated guess."

"Huh," Joey says.

"Could be," says Tim, nodding his head.

"I think it has to do with the hair," I say. "You're like the character on the Harlem Globetrotters cartoon. Whenever they get in a jam, he pulls whatever they need out of his Afro, whether it be a flashlight, a frying pan, or a trampoline. It's the same way with you, Joey. Who knows what's in your hair. For all the authorities know, you could be growing pot plants in there."

I combine aggression and humor in my speech in a manner not seen since adolescence. The individual words, sentences, and sub-themes are incidental; the weapon is my voice, loud, confident, and, I am certain, maddening to Cree. I speak with stupidity and irreverence. I allude to the confiscated marijuana with open regret. I make jokes about the circumstances of the avoided arrest. Throughout this speaking I pause in places where she might deliver a withering rejoinder, but one never comes. I blather on until I believe the point has been made, that what she said to me meant nothing to me. Then I stop talking, and when I do, there is quiet in the van.

Inside my head, the noise goes on. Why were Tim and Joey not criticized? Just minutes ago, participating in the conversation led by me, they acknowledged their own complicity. Tim said, "At least we smoked most of it." Joey asked me what I paid for it and then proceeded to compute the dollar value of what was lost. What did Cree think, that I had been stealing off into the woods to smoke my pipe alone under the oaks and pines? And what of Tim and Joey, feigning confusion at the moment of disclosure? I had felt certain that Tim would say quietly and simply, "It was all of us, Cree," thus redirecting the assault into a harmless impersonal context. After a guilty downbeat, Joey would have confirmed the truth of this, and we would have faced her together. But neither of them spoke up when they had the chance. I went to the gallows a solitary man and some say my corpse swings there still.

We stop for gas. Joey and Cree walk off toward the convenience store, mumbling happily about beef jerky and Coca-Cola. Tim waits until they have entered the building and then says, "Look, if it comes up again, I'll take some of the heat."

"Thanks," I say.

"You shouldn't worry about it," he says, attending to the pump. "I can't tell you how many times she's flipped out on me. It's all little stuff. She just gets tired of being on tour, and then one day she goes boom, you know?"

"Yes," I say.

"I know how it feels," he says. "It feels like she hates you with all of her being. The trick is to wait an hour or so. Her moods never last."

"I'll remember that," I say. Tim turns back to the pump, his wisdom dispensed. I shout things at him from inside my head: *I do not accept your half apology. I did not come on this tour to absorb your conflict. You sold me out for five minutes of band unity.* When I do speak, it is to ask him if he wants a bottle of water. He doesn't, but my offer requires me to get something from the store for myself. I enter the small building and the supersonic air conditioning changes the very nature of my skin. Joey and Cree stand near the cured meat display, laughing and waving some of the thicker sausages at each other. They don't see me as I glide into the beverage zone at the back. I wait there, holding my elbows mere centimeters from the refrigerated glass, imagining the tiny hairs on my arms extending to meet the cold. The bending hinge at the top of the door tells me they have left the store and only then do I make my own move toward the cash register.

The new dynamic in the van is fun and carefree. Perhaps I am even meant to be a part of it. Joey and Cree sit in the front two seats, eating jerky and exchanging meat and fart jokes. Cree unwraps a two foot Slim Jim, snaps it in half, and turns around to give the pieces to me and Tim. Her face is lit with unpenitent sweetness and generosity. I stare into the depth of it, searching for hidden clefts of agitation, but there is nothing but smooth dark skin, pink lips, and brown eyes. "No thank you," I say, "I'm not hungry right now." I turn away so as not to see her give my half to Tim. In ten days we will cross the Maryland border into Delaware and my obligation will desist. I will live in town and run into Tim and Joey occasionally at record stores and late night eateries. I might see Cree at the mall at Christmas. I will ask them how the rock and roll business is going. If it is going well I will have heard about it already from independent sources, and my query will be a gesture of politeness and congratulation. If it is not going well I will conceal a warm glow of triumph with sympathetic expressions and appropriate second rank platitudes. I will say: Keep trying. If you keep working hard, things are bound to work out for you. I will think: There is no way to fail honorably at this profession.

Joey dominates the approach into Phoenix.

"You're going to see a stop sign eight feet wide," he says to me. "The traffic lights dangle fifteen feet down. Everything's huge. It's insane!"

He explains that the large traffic signals are in place for the benefit of the elderly. He also notes that the city is a grid in perfect alignment with global magnetism.

"People don't speak in terms of left or right," he says. "There's no need for that. Instead, they say north, south, east, or west. The last time we were here, when we got lost, we just whipped out a compass."

This time, the van is in a lesser state of preparedness. Compass-free, we roam the darkening strips in search of the venue, pausing at intersections for entire minutes to sit in awe of the giant signs. When we round a bend to be confronted by a billboard-sized YIELD, it's as if God has unleashed the final, cumulative commandment. Cree demands that we pull over to ask for directions. Joey parks in front of a Polish deli and I jump out even before the vehicle has stopped moving, every inch the tour manager. Within seconds I am back in the van, furnishing our driver with a concise set of norths and wests. "Turn west at the fourth light," I say, "and keep to the north of the cul-de-sac. The club itself faces east." These movements completed, I jump out yet again to secure the locations of the load-in and permanent parking. I can feel myself sweating inside my clothes. I imagine no one knows what to make of the dynamo I've become.

For the first time the soundcheck doesn't meet my specifications. The drums are louder than drums should ever be and so echoey that they ring well into the next beat. The vocals are too quiet and strangely off-center, giving the impression that they are being sung from somewhere outside the building and to the left. I walk right up to the sound booth and ask the character within if he would mind altering his mix.

To my surprise, the man is amenable. "Hi, I'm Gene," he says, lifting his hands from the board to greet me. "They're your band. Just tell me what to do." He invites me to stand with him in the space behind the equipment, and I marvel that he never once instructs me not to touch anything. In appearance he is a hairful gnome, born to ghost the fringes of rock and roll culture. He moves with diaphanous ease through crowds of roadies, soundmen, guitar techs, and T-shirt salesmen. He plays every instrument a little bit. Many years ago his instinct persuaded him to forgo bitterness, and so he is a friendly man, helpful and desperate. We spend some time together removing the echo from the drums; I assure him that his attachment to the effect is justified in all cases but this one.

"You're welcome to hang out here during the show," Gene says. "I could use the company."

"I have T-shirts to sell," I say, flooding my voice with regret. "But I'll catch up with you later."

These last two statements are technically not lies. I will see him later—the soundman is always a cagey post-show presence, on hand to make sure none of his equipment is damaged during the loadout. And I do have T-shirts to sell, two of them, mediums both. One will hang on the wall behind me while the other rests in the merchandise box, empty except for a roll of duct tape and a loose rolling Magic Marker. The CDs ran dry midway through the Austin date; Joey has informed me that all will be replenished once we reach Los Angeles.

Thanks to temperatures that persist in the seventies, Bob and I will be selling outside tonight. Young girls wear outfits that weigh in at under a pound, their flip-flopped feet clapping lightly as they move about the tiled pavilion. A garishly painted radio station minivan blares its own modern rock from a discreet vantage on the cul-de-sac, somehow invoking the Doppler effect in spite of its motionless state.

Bob has posted a sign that reads BABY T'S—ONE SIZE FITS ALL. I smile in appreciation and he says, "It's my joke on society." This setting has animated him in a way I associate with indoor animals that have been permitted to step out onto a porch or into a yard. His hair fluffs, his skin twitches, and he seems on the verge of lifting his head and sniffing the air. A song by U2 comes on the radio and he says, suddenly, "I saw them once."

"When?" I ask.

"Oh, years ago, in a bar in Dublin," he says. "There was chicken wire in front of the stage so they wouldn't get hit by bottles."

"Were they good?" I ask.

He thinks. "I guess so," he says. "They were just little punks. They didn't know what they were doing."

He tilts back in his metal folding chair and has a sip of Coke, the only beverage I have ever known him to consume. This is less an invitation to further questions than a resignation that they are now inevitable. I don't want to disappoint him, so I ask him if he ever saw the Band. "At Woodstock," he says, and we are off. It turns out that Bob has seen live over three quarters of the current members of the Rock and Roll Hall of Fame. He has ridden in an elevator with Mick Jagger and dined at the home of Lou Reed. For a brief period in the mid-seventies he was part owner of the first New York record store to cater to the punk market. "So you must have encountered Lester Bangs . . . ," I begin to say.

"I would like to buy a T-shirt," a girl says to Bob. She is very young and very cute, and judging from the T-shirt that she is already wearing—light blue, short-sleeved with a cartoon image of Minnie Mouse coquettishly blowing the fuzzies off a dandelion—aware of both assets. "Do you have anything small?" she says.

"I have some baby T's," Bob says, reaching down to get one.

"Those are too tight," the girl says. She crosses her arms. "Do you have a small?" Bob rummages through his boxes, picking up shirts, looking at the tags inside the collars, and then discarding them. Finally he produces a keeper. "This is the last one," he says.

"Would you mind holding on to it for me?" the girl says as she hands over the cash. "I'm afraid if I bring it inside, I'll lose it. I'll come back and get it when I leave."

"How will I know it's you?" Bob says, triumphant.

"I'll tell you my name," the girl says.

"I'll never remember that," Bob says. "We'll have to think of a code word."

"Okay, what?" the girl says, hips cocked.

"I know," Bob says, after a minute of consideration. He leans forward conspiratorially, inducing her to do the same. "Dog," he says in a loud whisper. The girl nods, looking him in the eye, thanks him, and strides off.

"Dog," Bob repeats. "You have to help me remember that."

I promise to help him remember. With this, the period of

divulgence ends, and we return to our side by side contemplation of the night. Sitting there, I begin to juxtapose Bob's past and present. I consider how his various and distinctive deeds have accumulated to this moment, placing the chair under his body and the nearly empty Coke in his hand. I decide that he has had an interesting life but not one I would want for myself. It occurs to me that Tim would still be talking now, moving beyond fact into understanding, and, finally, empathy. He would in Bob's mind restore these lost histories to their full glory, as if they had happened only minutes ago. He would make Bob feel as though he had made a friend forever. But he wouldn't be doing these things now. He would have done them that night in Philadelphia when Bob first joined the tour.

Soon Tim himself comes out the front door of the club, looking somewhat frantically for Cree. Showtime is in fifteen minutes and he has to put new strings on his guitar. "If you could round her up," he says, "I'd really appreciate it."

He knows she is somewhere with Brant and doesn't want to be the one to separate them. "Yeah, I'll do it," I say. This time I don't disguise my tone. Only ten more days, I think, only ten more days. I instruct Bob to watch over my two shirts and depart immediately for the Radials' dressing room. Tim is still standing there when I leave.

I rap on the door frame and lean my head around. The unlikely trio of Walter, Edward, and Louise sits together on a single couch even though there is other seating available. Edward gets to his feet nervously, gripping a wallet in one hand, and says, "You've come for your photograph, eh?"

"No," I say. "I'm looking for Cree. Have you seen her?"

"No, I haven't seen her," he says. He half turns to Walter and Louise on the couch. "She's probably on a moonlit walk with Brant." He laughs with his mouth closed. Louise laughs too, one of her traditional "Ah ha ha ha's," but a dryness in her throat turns the laugh into a cough midway through. Walter regards the ceiling above his head with the boredom it deserves. I leave this strange gathering and head outside to the bus.

The back of the club is a dark nexus of three alleys beyond which glimpses of moving traffic are visible. The bus is parked tight against the wall of one of the alleys. I am standing at the door about to knock when Cree and Brant round the corner of the farthest street. I know it is them the second I see them, but I keep watching, wondering if they will emerge from the shadows two other people. They're walking slowly, looking at each other's faces. Cree carries a bundle of long-stemmed roses across her chest. Their hands are not clasped but held so they brush against each other in the natural rhythm of their walk. Twice Brant reaches up and presses gently against her side with his fingers. His arms are as pale and as skinny as my own.

When they close to within twenty feet, I decide I have to say something. What comes out is a spirited "Yo!" Brant says, "Yo!", imitating me, and Cree says, "Oh, it's you. What are you doing here?"

"Looking for you," I say. "It's time for you to go play the drums." I intend this to have the effect of a mock command. Brant frowns.

"We're going that way," Cree says, aiming her roses at the Dumpsters directly behind the club.

"So long," Brant says. Turning back to Cree, he puts his left hand on the very lowest part of her back and massages her hip with his thumb. They resume their slow walk. His hand moves lower to stroke her bottom, up and down, and I see her hand come down and brush it away. A few steps later and he puts it back, and this time she permits him to keep it there, thinking perhaps, that I am no longer around to see.

Midway through the Day Action Band set, I sense that Gene is beginning to reapply the reverb. "Do those drums sound okay to you?" I say to Bob, and he says, "Oh they sound all right," but I am unconvinced. Seeking a better aural perspective, I walk over to the entrance of the club, flash my stamped hand at one of the bouncers, and step inside.

What I discover disturbs me. Gene has fashioned a sound-scape for the deranged. Every snare hit releases a boxcar of empty oscillation. A band of whining tom feedback hides out at the upper-mid-level frequencies, tucked into the overtones of Joey's too-trebly bass. The vocals, all of them, drown quietly in this sonic furnace. I look up at Gene, laboring in his booth. He sees me and hangs his head. As I approach, he restores the knobs to their agreed-upon pre-show settings. The specter of insanity re-treats to the far end of the hall, where it waits, engulfed in a dark cloak. "Just trying to spice things up," Gene says. "I thought you wouldn't mind."

"Oh, no, it's fine, really," I say. "I was just coming through on my way to the bathroom. Sounds good."

"No, man," Gene says. "I know what you were doing, and I respect that. I really respect the way you look out for your band."

I accept this compliment, unsure if it is deserved. Nonethe-less, I allow its momentum to sustain me for the next two hours, through the end of one set and the entirety of the next. During that time I sell one of the two T-shirts. I go to the adjacent pizza shop to buy Bob and me some Cokes. I make a pencil on paper sketch of the cul-de-sac. Shortly after the crowd lets out, the girl in the Minnie Mouse T-shirt returns. Bob rises, shouting, "Dog!" and the girl, unstartled, says, "Dog" in her own sweet voice, and they make their exchange. I sling the remaining shirt over my shoulder and carry the empty box back through the club and out to the van.

The van is nearly packed, our next destination San Diego. Cree waits in the back, body tensed, eyes wide and humorless. Whatever farewell she made with Brant will have to last her until we meet the Radials again in Los Angeles, two days from now, maybe three. The roses, clearly meant to span the separation, rest darkly across the middle seat. Their future is uncertain. If they find a vase, they will flourish, their petals projecting into the van not so much color as the very impression of life itself. If they find neglect, they will dry and crumble into the navy carpet, their pieces mingling with other pieces, forgotten bits of food, hair, and mud from shoes.

Tim climbs into the driver's seat. We are about to pull away when Joey remembers that the rider sits untouched in the dressing room. "I think there were some drink boxes," he says. "I think we should check it out." I volunteer to go with him. Working quickly, we unearth not only drink boxes but also several tins of mixed nuts. We shake off mutual fits of self-congratulation and head back to the van. But we don't make it there unscathed.

"Hey, guys!" Gene says, stepping out of the shadows. "What's going on?"

"Not much," I say. I can see over his head to the van, less than thirty feet hence. I think I can make out Tim's arms on top of the steering wheel.

"Hey, great show!" he says, more to Joey than to me, but definitely to both of us.

"Thanks," Joey says. I smile but don't say anything. Gene pauses to allow the moment to reach maturity. When it has, he speaks again.

"I don't know what kind of plans you have," he says, "but you're welcome to crash at my place. I'll call up some friends, we'll get some guitars together, play some music, drink some beer, smoke some pot . . ." He nods after each item.

"Ah," Joey says. "That sounds like fun, but we have to get going."

"We had a rough day today," I say, intending it to be a passing comment. But for Gene, there is no such thing.

"Yeah?" he says, interested and concerned. "What happened?"

"We got busted," I say.

"Some people took our pot," Joey says. "Some government people."

"Yeah, I know what that's about," Gene says. He looks around at the various people engaged in their closing down activities. Satisfied, he says, "I think I might be able to help you though." He reaches carefully around to his back pocket and takes out his wallet. Thumbing aside a wad of single-digit bills, he comes to a tight little ball of cellophane. "Take the whole thing," he says. "You earned it."

"No!" Joey shouts. "We can't take all your weed!"

"Go on," Gene says. "Take it. I don't even smoke pot anymore."

We nod at him, not wanting to ask why.

"I stopped smoking it when my girlfriend died," Gene says. "Now I drink."

"Your girlfriend died?" Joey says. "That's terrible."

"I'm sorry," I say.

"It's all right man," Gene says. "It was a few months ago. Yeah, I didn't expect it. She had pneumonia for a week and she went in the hospital, and she took a turn for the worse. Her family flew in—she's Filipino—but I didn't think she was going to die. I came in one day and she was in a coma. The next day she died."

"That's awful," Joey says.

"I don't know what I'm going to do," Gene says. "I was with her four years. I thought she might be the one."

This is a terrible, inappropriate conversation. It is my turn to speak, and I fear I cannot summon the proper gravity. A thousand innocuous phrases come into my head and then disband. Only one thought remains, and it comes from a women's magazine, *Cosmopolitan* or *Glamour,* something that caught my eye as I paged through in search of lingerie ads many years ago. I say it because I have no choice.

"I've heard that an average person has seven chances to marry during his or her lifetime," I say. Taking a bold guess, I continue with, "That means you have six left."

"Is that a fact?" Gene says. "You really heard that?"

"It really stuck with me," I say.

"That's awesome," Joey says.

"Well shit," Gene says. He smiles down into his hand and repeats "seven chances" in a quiet, wondrous voice. The air stills around him, sounds mute, and lights dim respectfully. Gene extends the hand, and we both shake it. He is late for a dream, and we mustn't keep him. "Take care, you guys," he says. "Drive carefully, get rich, fall in love. That's what I say." He waves until I pull shut the van's sliding middle door. Then he walks back inside the club.

"What happened back there?" Tim says, guiding the van through the streets that lead to the freeway. "That looked intense."

"We'll tell you in a little while," Joey says. He rolls his window down and lets his arm dangle out. The cooling wind rushes over me and I shiver. Joey is only waiting for Cree to fall asleep so he can relate the story in full, the accosting, the reluctant drug acceptance, the uncomfortable condolence, and finally, apocalyptically, my moment of grace. He is right to do this, for the story is all of a piece. But this pause for me is more than a simple tactical maneuver, for it allows me to dwell in the satisfaction of having said the perfect thing.

Sleep comes quickly to Cree and soon Tim knows the details of our miraculous encounter. "It was amazing," Joey says. "It was like he knew exactly what that guy needed to hear."

Deflecting the praise, I say that we had better smoke the pot before we cross into California. "Let's not let this gift turn into a curse," I say, less worried about the law than Cree.

"Then we'd better stop soon," Tim says. "We've got a lot of smoking to do."

There are not many towns out here west of Phoenix. The first town we see is called Gila Bend. The first building we pass is a motel, and not just a motel, but a motel having a two for one special. Gene's miracle has more than just local truth.

We rent two rooms. Joey and Cree take one of them, and Joey waits until Cree falls back asleep before he sneaks over. Tim rolls two crisp joints. We smoke the first and decide that nobody needs to be more stoned. Joey says that we should have known that a soundman would be unable to tolerate bad pot.

I lie on one of the queen beds. The television is tuned to an action series from the late seventies, but the volume is turned off. The air conditioner to my left blows out vaguely hostile air. I defend myself against it by thinking about how I said the perfect thing. My period of modesty has passed, and I am ready for the incident to be discussed.

The toilet flushes and Joey returns to his place on the bed.

"Dude," he says, drawing the syllable out. "I can see colors."

"What?" I say.

"Listen to those guitars," Joey says. "I can see the music. The music is making the colors."

"I don't hear any music," I say. Then I realize what's happening. "Hey—"

"The colors are coming over here," Joey says. "I think it's the guitars. Go away guitars! Stop rocking me!"

"Fuck you," I say.

Tim laughs stupidly. "He got you," he says.

Joey unmutes the television and then there really is music, drums crashing, urgent strings, a gong. Tim seems content with this entertainment, and so I resign myself to watching it. After a while the show ends and another one begins. I look over and see that Joey has fallen asleep, the remote still in his hand. During a commercial Tim slips off the bed and removes one of his guitars from its case. He sits in the space between his bed and the bathroom wall and plays. This is not something he usually does and I listen over the television but all I can hear is an occasional *plink-plink*. Then he starts to sing, very softly, in his falsetto. At first it sounds like nothing more than gentle hooting, the sweet owl of Motel 6. But then I catch the phrase "seven chances." I try to listen more, to strain my ears even though it is physically impossible to do so. I imagine sophisticated sonic filters activating in my brain. Always, the strings swell, obscuring. Finally a commercial plays whose gimmick is silence, and I hear Tim's chords and melody complete. The guitar plinks, the voice soars. This song is about seven chances. It is new and beautiful and perfect and I could never have written it myself. "Were you one of mine?" he sings. "Were you one of mine?"

I AM BEGINNING TO understand Joey's obsession with the minor artifacts of Americana. I was able to pick out today's breakfast diner several seconds before he was. I saw it coming up on the left, a tribute to the space age, a swirling saucer design with cockpit windows and rocket engines abutting the parking lot. The name was "Moon Landing" and the four decades that had passed since it was built had rendered it in stark hilarity. It was this aspect that I knew would appeal to Joey, the potential for unreciprocated loving mockery. I had the further thought that he would never be able to love anything he truly respected, and vice versa, but this seemed unnecessarily dire and possibly a remnant of the previous night's stoning. At any rate, when he saw Moon Landing, he said, "We're eating there," and no one argued with him.

Now we sit, waiting for our waitress to clear the plates away. This particular booth is devoted to the first space shuttle launch, but, with the exception of a few stray headlines trapped beneath the plastic, the event is obscured by our mess. Tim and Joey talk across the table about the benefits of hiring someone to engineer their next record. Cree stares off toward the highway, a look of dreamy satisfaction on her face. "What are you thinking about?" I ask her. "Nothing," she says. "Everything." She returns her eyes to the road. I am surprised that she answered me at all. These past few days may have been the most exciting of her life.

I wonder if someday I will count them among the most exciting of mine.

"What do you think, Lou?" Joey says. The talk has turned to the new order of T-shirts—what color should they be? Everyone feels that the dark green of the last batch was a mistake. "We want something people can see in a dark room," Joey says. Cree suggests a pastel, yellow, pink, or mauve. Tim sneers at these selections, and Cree says, "What's your great idea, bucko?" Tim puffs out his chest, tightening his own T-shirt against it, and makes circular motions around his pectorals. "A shirt with these cut out," he says. Cree slaps him lightly on the shoulder and says, "You're so helpful."

Joey's last act before we departed the motel was to leave the leftover joint on the windowsill above the air-conditioning unit. Though he claimed the gesture was intended to "brighten the day" of the cleaning maid, we all knew the real aim was to avoid further persecution. And thus far on this sunny morning, we have been the beneficiaries of a kind of karmic justice. The food has been good, the service has been good, and Cree has been good.

"How about something in cream?" I say.

Tim snorts and Cree slaps him again. "That would totally wash out the lettering and the graphic," Joey says. "Unless—"

"Unless you inverted them," I say. "That might be kind of nice. The off-white background, some colorful lettering, maroon maybe."

"I could get into maroon," Cree says.

"I could get into cream," Tim says.

"Have we made a decision?" Joey says. Tim and Cree nod. I wait until the three of them look at me before I offer my own assent. Cree touches my arm just below the wrist and says, kindly, "You're the one who knows."

Tim gets up and goes outside to the pay phone. He is calling London West, to speak to Alithia about the new shirts and our

Los Angeles accommodations. While he does this, the rest of us make some last minute preparations in the restroom. I am conspicuously the first one to exit the diner, and when I come upon Tim, he is facing away toward the road, whispering unmistakable sweet nothings into the receiver.

"Who're you talking to?" I say.

Tim says something tender into the phone and hangs up. "That was Laura," he says. "The girl from Texas. From Austin, not Houston. You remember her. Glasses, blond hair . . ." He lists attributes until I nod in recognition.

"I just wanted to make sure she still has good feelings about the time we spent together," he says.

"Does she?" I say.

"Seems like it," he says.

When Joey and Cree emerge several minutes later, Tim makes the announcement that he has spoken to Alithia and that the new maroon and cream T-shirts will be ready in time for the Los Angeles show. He also says that Alithia has offered up her own apartment for our use. Cree says she might stay with a friend if the location is convenient to our operations, and Tim says that's fine. We are about to get in the van when he raises his hand and says, "Hey, wait, I'm not finished."

Tomorrow Colin has secured an appointment in the offices of one of America's leading record labels. Two industry legends will be on hand to describe the services their company can offer. "Alithia said not to get our hopes up, but damn!" Tim says. "That's what L.A.'s supposed to be about, right?" The three of them mill around in a general state of excitement. I express my approval by saying, "Wow, that's awesome," and "This could be it for you guys." I think of a fairy tale, Brant, the prince, Cree the lovely peasant girl whose noble lineage is discovered at the last possible moment, allowing them to be wed. These are momentous times and I catch myself wishing I were not going to be around to witness them.

If the desert is an oven, then the van is a toaster. Though the cooling systems are long defunct, we drive with the windows closed. The air outside is too hot to be permitted to enter. The air inside would challenge a thermometer to a third digit.

Boulders descended from mountains loom piled in the distance, like the massed ruddy faces of schoolboys in the Fenway bleachers. Petrified they have become and grotesque, hinting at the unreal possibility that they may disband and begin rolling toward the road. Soon the rocks take angular shape and form a structure. It is a rest area, a little Stonehenge before the ascent into the high hills.

After the water fountains we meet wordlessly in the dust behind the outpost. A chain link fence separates us from parched brush and telephone poles. The poles follow the contour of the highway, a thousand crucifixions to the sunset. Tim picks up a rock and chucks it at the nearest one, missing by a good thirty feet. My own throw sails ten feet wide. Joey grazes a wire and scores a hit on the carom. *Clink!* Cree has struck one of the metal footholds near the base. "You little bitch," Tim says, throwing with even greater force and inaccuracy. "I've proven myself," Cree says. She crosses her arms to show that she will toss no more. Finding his range, Joey connects again and again and again.

I let my own arms drop to my sides. This heat, this landscape . . . I feel the onset of a new perversion. And here it is: What would it be to run shouting into the desert, to coat the inside of my mouth with sand, to prick my eyes on needled vegetation. Would I shiver under the night serenade of the coyote, groove to the rattle of the snake. Would it take a scorpion to bring me down. In the lean-to I call home . . .

Out there I might have a vision. Perhaps this is why they erected the fence.

The Day Action Band has played the Omnivore twice before. The club is situated just off the freeway, one exit from the airport. I have already been told several times that you can sit in a car in front of the venue and watch the landing planes come perilously close to an adjacent parking garage. "Kids used to stand on the roof and throw rocks," Joey is telling me now, "so they put up a screen."

"I can relate to that," I say.

We load in the gear and decide to break for dinner. It is seven o'clock now, Alithia will not arrive until nine, and the band is not scheduled to go on until close to midnight. A vote is taken, and we begin to move in the direction of a known taqueria. Cree, who had been complaining about the late showtimes of tiny clubs, now says she likes to play late because it allows time for food and socializing. "We haven't had the chance to relax and just be," she says.

This taqueria boasts the interior of a fast-food joint, with booth tables, tiled floor, and overhead fluorescence. The lone customer wears a veil and sits contemplating a vast mountain of nachos. Behind the counter, a young man and woman nudge each other in giggling flirtation. Cree whispers, "Something's going on here."

We place our orders and slide into a booth at the front corner of the room. Almost immediately the two teenaged employees duck down, only the tops of their heads visible from where we sit. We are discussing the possibility of sexual misconduct when a flickering red dot appears on the side of Joey's face. When he learns of it, he forces a smile of recognition and waves out the window, to show the operator that he appreciates the technology. The dot tracks him for another minute before whipping across the ceiling and cutting out.

"Your food is ready!" calls the young man, standing briefly to set the trays on the counter. When I go up to get mine, I sneak a look down at the girl and am surprised to find her sitting primly, legs crossed, clothes untampered with.

Three bites into his chimichanga, Tim farts loudly, the noise rippling off the plastic bench seat. "That didn't take long," Joey says, and Cree bursts forth with suppressed laughter. This cascade of sound animates the natural reverb of the restaurant, and soon everyone is laughing, with the exception of the veiled nacho woman. Cree's attempts to hush the proceedings only have a giddying intensifying effect. When all is quiet again, the woman comes by, carrying the nachos.

"I haven't touched these, would you like to have them?" she says. Behind the veil I can see that her face is young and beautiful, but the skin is mottled and her voice is rough.

"I think we're okay," Tim says. "We still have a lot of food here." Cree makes a short barking laugh and then presses her lips together with all her strength.

"Well," says the lady, "I'll put them here if you change your mind." She sets the plate down on a table two booths over and walks out of the restaurant. She stands a little ways up the street and looks back at us through the window. Tim looks speculatively at the nachos. "You're kidding, right?" Cree says, and Tim admits he is kidding.

We all chat happily for the next twenty minutes. The veiled woman returns twice more, just long enough to see that her offering remains untouched. These have been strange proceedings, but I feel pleasantly insulated from them, as if watching them take place on a stage, my three best friends with me in the audience. I haven't felt this purely happy since this trip began, and I'm not sure if that's a simple effect of the laughter, or something deeper and more worth cherishing. As we walk slowly back to the club, I wonder if I should be worried that I can't tell the difference.

Alithia is waiting for us, talking with the club manager whom she has spoken to on the phone many times but never met. She is pretty, in her late twenties, with brown hair and liquid brown deer eyes. She combats a faint nervousness with her advantage in age and her several years of business experience.

The period of catching-up is dramatic but short-lived. Tim notices that something has changed with Alithia's hair. Cree, feeling preempted, compensates by describing in technical terms the nature of the change. Alithia nods through the compliments and then says that several club employees from earlier shows have called to say how much they enjoyed the Day Action Band. "That never happens for an opening band," she says. "Most of those guys don't give a shit."

She does have some new information about tomorrow's meeting, which she has been instructed to characterize as symbolic. According to Colin, a different unsigned band comes in every day, for free drinks and a chance to gab with history. The purpose of the meeting, therefore, is for Tim, Joey, and Cree to become familiar with the process before the stakes rise above nonexistent. I expect this news to create disappointment, but the three of them react as though that was what they expected to hear. "That's a process I don't mind becoming familiar with," Tim says, and they all laugh. I laugh too, but I am thinking about how Brant may have to wait for his princess after all.

There is an awkward moment when Alithia says to Cree, "So how is Brant?" Tim gives Alithia a pained look at the same time that Cree says, "How do you . . . ?" Alithia puts her hand to her mouth in embarrassment, and Cree, understanding, says, "He's okay." Alithia says, "Oh" and gets up to make a sudden phone call. Tim begins to apologize and Cree says, "It's fine, it's fine," waving her hand to stop him from talking.

This is the kind of club that the Day Action Band knows well. It is the hip rock club of this town, the grudging center of the universe for an inbred net of scenesters, musicos, and flanking artistes. A certain subset is out here tonight. In one corner we have a bundle of pop aficionados, lithe, yes, fresh-faced, yes, but willing to stand in prominence because the DAB backs its twee with rock's essential edge. Over near the bar, away from the colored lights, wait those who have decided, based on a calibration of music, hearsay, and press, that the DAB is one month away from becoming the hippest band in America. In their deepest hearts these people would like to be photographed conversing with members of the band, but their policy forbids not only photography but conversation. And then we have the canonists, unassuming yet potent, their passions driving them into academia, through arcania, and finally, to the truth. They will want to talk to Tim, to ask him if he shares their belief that the studio is the ultimate instrument, rock and roll's true legacy to Art. They will not be intimidated by him, debating with another mortal, as it were, the attributes of a higher power.

Joey comes back from the bar area holding a curling ream of drink tickets in one hand. Over his shoulder I can see a sign that says the lawful occupancy will not exceed 125.

"I had forgotten about these," he says, waving the tickets, dropping them, and then picking them up again. "Beer is more exciting when it comes from the bar."

"Who's opening up?" Tim says.

"First," Joey says, "we have Jim Buttmason and the Old Home. I don't know anything about them, but that's a pretty cool handle. Then there's Bass Fishing. They have three bass players."

"What's the point of that?" Cree says.

"What's not the point of it?" Joey says, righteous.

"It feels good to be the last band again," Tim interrupts. He looks with fondness upon Joey and Cree, as if he might draw them together in his arms. The dance floor is empty, save for one couple, a man and a woman. The man leans down and listens while the woman points at the monitors. Music that no one could ever dance to, quiet, ominous, staggering, pipes through various hidden speakers. A whiff from a freshly lit cigarette gusts by before receding into the olfactory landscape. I look calmly around until I spot the glow.

At nine-thirty Jim Buttmason claims the stage. He is a lanky man of indeterminate middle age, with a battered red acoustic guitar and a straw hat with a white band. The Old Home seems to be nothing more than a pile of 45s that he sets on a cardboard box behind him. "Let's have a hand for the Old Home, shall we?" he says, turning and applauding the half-sized records. He sings a cycle of songs, many of them humorous, about attending his mother's funeral in Duluth, Minnesota. During the last, however, he weeps openly, and when he is finished, a young lady from the small audience runs up and gives him a hug.

Bass Fishing is another matter. Augmented by a drummer with two floor toms, the three bass players fragment into fairly traditional roles, bass, rhythm, and lead. One sings while the other two shout harmonies. The subhuman frequencies roil Cree's insides, and she asks me if I would like to wait outside with her in the van. I say yes I would.

The van is parked right in front of the club in a space marked off by two traffic cones. The parking garage is less than fifty feet away, diagonal and to the right. Joey has made sure that those sitting in the front seats will have a view of the descending aircraft. The low rumble of Bass Fishing is tangible even at this distance. I offer to drive us to a different location, but Cree says she wants to see the planes.

A plane comes shrieking in. From our angle it appears that the corner of the garage is going to knock into the closer wing. Cree inhales sharply and clutches my arm, pinching. When the vehicle has safely passed, she lets go.

"That was so close," she says.

"It's probably a game among the pilots," I say, "to see who can come the closest without crashing. You think of an airline pilot as being a responsible person, but it's like any other job. You get bored and you lose respect for it."

"Yeah," she says. She rolls down her window and requests that I do the same. More planes come and go. Bass Fishing rumbles on. Soon Joey sticks his head through Cree's window. "I couldn't take it anymore," he says. "I told Tim to stay inside, to keep up appearances." He gets in the van and sits in the middle seat, leaning forward to improve his view out the windshield. A conversation develops, and, during a lull, Cree makes the surprising statement, "Yeah, so I'm feeling kind of bummed right now." She doesn't seemed bummed though, she seems like someone who wants to talk about something.

"What's wrong?" Joey says.

"Brant's a hundred miles away," she says.

"You and Brant have become close," Joey says.

"Yeah," Cree says, letting the syllable wilt, the very cup of pining.

"Are you doing the hokey-pokey?" Joey says, grinning suddenly.

"No!" Cree says. I had thought this type of question would provoke outrage, but her indignation is false.

"Are you sure?" Joey says, nudging her in the side.

"I'm sure," Cree says. Her smile tells otherwise.

Joey starts saying, "I knew it, I knew it." Cree revises her stance and says, "I'm not denying anything." Their voices rise in bantering connotation. I feel a darkening in my chest. Certainly I knew Cree and Brant were sleeping together. I had even thought about it somewhat. But to hear her talk about it . . .

Unless Cree quits the band and moves to England, her relationship with Brant will be over in three days. During that span it can be reconsummated perhaps five times. That is five times too many, but at least there is a limit to it. Another plane howls down the garage, and I have the thought that she would not be talking about this if Tim were here. I reach for the latch and let myself out of the van.

As the headlining band they play for over an hour. This means the resurrection of a half dozen old hits. It also means an encore,

and for this encore, they play a cover of "These Dreams" by Heart.
They play it without the irony that any other band of their stature
would give it. Cree sings and Tim and Joey join her on the chorus.
I remember this song coming on the radio as my family drove
home from the pool after a cookout. The way everyone quieted,
even Jamie, who was only nine. Tonight people stand in groups
of twos and threes, not moving. Alithia whispers, "I've never
heard them do this one before," and I whisper back, "It's great,
isn't it?" When they finish, there is enough applause to warrant
another encore, but the house lights come up, and the ominous
music comes back on.

We drive two hours along careless roads to Los Angeles, Alithia and Cree leading the way in Alithia's hapless hatchback.
Our route takes us through the downtown area, which, at 3:00
A.M., resembles the very shadowy underworld metropolis that it
often purports to be. Alithia lives on the edge of Hollywood, spit-
ting distance, she has said, from the Walk of Fame. We trundle
into her small apartment, peruse the bathroom and the cat, and
take our bedding on the living room floor.

ALITHIA HAS LEFT US a note on the kitchen table. "There are some shops down the street," it says. "You can buy cereal there. Have fun kiddoes!" Cereal! Milk! And who knows what else? Pineapples, maybe. The concept of groceries has never seemed more appealing. To walk into a store, to buy food, to bring it home and put it in a cabinet or a refrigerator and then to return to that food over a span of multiple days. This is why people choose to live in one place. I plan to get something healthy, Grape Nuts, Wheat Chex, or Puffed Rice.

"I wonder if she has any milk," Joey says. He goes over to the refrigerator and reaches to open it. Then he stops and stares long and hard at a photograph affixed by a magnet.

"Come look at this!" he shouts. "Do you think this is Alithia?" Tim, Cree, and I crowd around. In the picture a nubile young woman has been stripped and bound to a short post. She lies prone, her mouth open wide in posed anguish. Her diminished breasts drift toward her sides. Her stomach glows in the contoured light.

"It could be," I say. "Five years younger, ten pounds lighter. But why is it on her refrigerator?"

"I don't know, man," Cree says. "Are those tattoos?"

"Maybe she's on some kind of diet and she's using it for inspiration," Joey says.

"Yo," Tim says. "Yo." He pounds his fist into his palm. "I think I'm going to have to take it in the bathroom."

"You're not taking that anywhere," Cree says, standing protectively over the photograph. "Have a little respect."

"I just want to get a closer look," Tim says. He takes a mock step forward.

"No!" Cree shouts. She reaches up and jerks the photo from the fridge. There is a tearing sound, and I look up and see that the very top corner is still caught, ragged edged, under the magnet. "Fuck!" Cree says. "Look what you made me do."

Tim backs away, both hands in the air. "I was just playing around," he says. "I didn't know you were going to grab it like that." He tries to smile, but his face will only make a grimace. "We'll just get some tape and tape up the back."

"If we put the magnet a little farther down, she'll never notice," Joey says.

"It'll be fine," I say.

"Jesus," Cree says. She looks at the three of us and shakes her head. "I'm going to take a shower." She turns and stalks out of the kitchen. Tim and Joey exchange astonished glances. From where I am standing, I am able to track her progress down the hall.

"She's in the bedroom now," I say. "She has closed the door."

"What was going on there?" Joey says.

"I don't know," Tim says. He is still grimacing. "Let's try to find some tape."

Cree comes out of the shower to find the photograph repaired and replaced. She asks who did the work, and Tim tells her that Joey did. Satisfied, she opens the refrigerator and reports that Alithia's milk is due to expire today. She passes the jug around for us to smell.

"I don't know," Joey says. "My sinuses . . . "

"I don't smell anything," I say.

"It might be a little off," Tim says. "She could use a new carton anyway." The meeting at the label is not until five o'clock, four hours from now, so time is not an issue. We shamble en masse to the shopping center, complaining of the bright sun, the heat, and the fact that no one packed more than one pair of shorts. This part of town is run-down but unthreatening; a few blocks away, the cylindrical form of the Capitol Records headquarters casts its fourteen-story shadow over low buildings and freeway interchanges.

"Yes," I say, as we walk, "one story for each of the Beatles' thirteen studio LPs. They know who put the butter on their bread."

"That's pretty cool," Joey says, before he counts the ringed floors and realizes that I'm lying. He suggests I compile a book of facts that are almost true, and I nod and say that it's something to consider.

We come to our destination and survey the options. There is a small grocery, a Thai restaurant, a doughnut shop, a flower emporium, and a laundry. Bums roam the small parking lot, bending for bottlecaps and flicking these into the street. We go into the grocery, buy breakfast items and feminine products, and make plans to come back for the laundry. Perhaps Brant's farewell weekend will be less lucrative than I had imagined. Cree holds the rustling package to her chest and hurries on ahead, forgetting that I am the keeper of the keys.

Before we go to clean our clothes, Cree would like to be taken to the home of her friend Betsy, a woman she met at an academic summer camp in high school. Cree puts her hand over the phone and says, "She says it's really close." She returns to the conversation and all three of us hear her say, "You have a washer and dryer? Dig it." When she hangs up she looks at Tim and says that it will only take five minutes to take her there. He consents. I wait for someone to ask if we could do some of our own laundry over there, but no one does.

We sort clothes and prepare to leave. At the moment of embarkation Joey hands me a plastic sack and two frail one-dollar bills. "If you guys could take care of this . . . ," he says. "There's no reason for all of us to go." I accept these gifts and we close the door. On the way to the car Cree talks about how Joey is too lazy to do anything for himself. Tim is silent; I speculate aloud about which cycles and temperatures Joey would like me to use.

Betsy is waiting on a balcony, peering down. Her round glasses seem about to slip off her plump face. "Cree!" she screams. Cree screams herself and runs up the stairs for hugs. Tim returns to the van and brings out Cree's massive duffel bag. He hauls it to the second floor and sets it down next to the girls. We stand there patiently until they separate. "We'll be back to pick you up at four-thirty," Tim says. "Please be ready to go, we really can't be late for this meeting."

"Okay, okay, okay, okay, okay," Cree says. She and Betsy turn and hurry inside the apartment. The door closes. Tim sighs and moves the duffel bag next to the door. He raises his hand to knock and then says, "She'll remember, won't she?" I say yes she will, and we head back down the stairs.

There is no mention of this misbehavior on the return drive. Tim has absorbed countless minor affronts at the hands of Cree and has been a stoic in the face of nearly all of them. In the early days he was sympathetic. "Cree missed band practice today," he would say. "She was at the park, throwing a Frisbee. I can't blame her. It was a beautiful day, a great day to be outside." Later he would state the offense in plainer language: "We can't record this weekend because Cree's going to Cape May with some friends." Now he says nothing. I used to try to commiserate, because something in his manner invited it. But once accepted the invitation was quickly rescinded, and I was left to feel small-hearted and petty, stranded several fathoms below the moral high ground. I don't hold him responsible, however, for I know that morality and self-preservation are the co-governors of conscience, in me as well as in him. It's just disconcerting to see the two elements so well blended, to understand that such a blending is a symptom of purpose, and to reflect that my own conscience is bipolar and distinct. Just once, I would love to hear Tim talk about how much Cree pisses him off.

The laundry is hopping for high noon. Recently pregnant women search in vain for their young. Machines shift and whir, gathering strength for that moment when they will wrench free of their foundations. Taunting bits of fluff float here and there. Tim and I stake out a section near the entrance and set to cleaning.

"Do you think they know Prince?" Tim is saying. He is referring to the aged luminaries we are soon to meet. I tell him I don't know if they know Prince, but that it seems possible. I stuff all of Joey's unsorted clothes into a single washer and push the setting to "heavy, high."

"Do you think they know Randy Newman?" Tim says.

"I think Randy Newman went to UCLA," I say. The only way to parry these questions is with misdirection. Tim says, "Hmm," and plucks at his chin. He wanders off to look at the vending machines, and when he comes back, he asks me if I think they know Chrissie Hynde.

This laundry is a comforting place, the amniotic waves of sound pulsing over me and then rushing back. I lean against the vibrating washer and look across the way, where a single white blouse goes round and round. I did not sleep well last night; in the early dawn the cat came and slept on my legs and I did not move for fear of disturbing it. But I may sleep now, until my balance deserts me or my support switches to "rinse," whichever comes first. My eyelids meet and the whirling blouse disappears.

Tim says, "Is there anything you want me to ask them?"

I pretend not to have heard the question. I ask him to repeat it and he does. His guilt surfaces during the repetition, and he explains that Colin wants the meeting to be as professional as possible. "That means the manager and the band and no one else," Tim says. "Alithia wanted to go, and Colin had to tell her no. You didn't ask, but I figured you had some interest."

"I'm a little curious," I say. "But you'll ask enough of the right questions. I have faith."

If I were to attend this gathering, I would adhere to the strictest protocol. A firm handshake, water to drink, and silence after the introductions. Tim says they will all listen to the new album together "on company speakers." I can hear the elder gentlemen asking me what I think of it, as a commoner, a recent graduate of the target audience. And my response I can hear as well: "Well, I am biased, of course . . ." followed by my boomingest chuckle. Then compliments passing back and forth between the principals, and then finally Tim's much-anticipated Q&A. The truth is I half expected Colin to tote me along for these very purposes. That he has chosen not to is neither a disappointment nor a relief. It would be interesting to meet these people, but Tim will tell me what they have to say. And maybe I could use this break. It has been many days since I spent a significant amount of time alone.

The first thing I discover after they leave is that Alithia's apartment is rich in reading material. Midway through a stack of magazines I hit upon a vein of *Playboy*s. Fourteen consecutive months, yet no markings that would indicate a subscription. At what newsstand does she purchase these, and why?

I lie on my back on the couch. Though the California heat commands respect, the month is still November and the sun goes down early. A sense of melancholy is transported in on the dying beams of light. In five minutes I will have to get up and turn on a lamp.

I think of Kaitlyn enduring these conditions, though where she lives it has long been dark. Her window is open, and the wind has blown a framed picture off her dresser. She worries that her small bottles of perfume are next. The covers are drawn up above her neck. Knocking sounds cannot be verified to have come from outside the apartment. She might like to hear my voice right now.

I call, get the machine, and hang up. What kind of message could I leave? I can't be receiving personal phone calls here. I call again. The beep at the end of her message is over a minute long, as if the machine has not been checked for days. "Where are you!" I shout into the phone, intending to have a humorous effect. But my voice has an angry tone. To compensate I crack several lame jokes about her whereabouts. I am about to ask her if she has up and died when a shiver runs through my body. I jam the phone back into its cradle. A terrible pressure builds around my heart.

The people who access the Austin directory have never heard of Clay. I don't know Whitey's last name. I can't remember what fraternity they belong to. I have an image of the paddle that hangs above Clay's microwave, but the characters that grace the implement are Chinese rather than Greek. Her parents moved to Florida shortly after we left high school. I remember her telling me where in this exact sentence: "You've never heard of it, but it's about twenty minutes outside of Miami."

The last thing I can do is search for an atlas. Alithia doesn't have one. I do come across some more photographs, these of a shirtless woman facing away from the camera. A tattoo of a dragon searing a pony covers her entire back. I return to my place on the couch and rest one of the tiny auxiliary cushions on my face. The cat jumps up onto the bed in the other room. I feel a dampness on my cheek and realize that it must have come from a tear. I press the cushion into my face with my arm, smothering all future tears. I open my eyes upon the false dark and think about regret.

———————

Alithia enters her own apartment with the stealth of a thief. Hearing her key exit the lock, I sit upright on the couch and say, "Who!" I stare at her, unblinking, while she says, "It's me, Alithia," over and over. Several minutes later, we are heading out the door, Alithia clucking over some unknown lateness, me patting down the hair on my unkempt head.

We travel down Sunset Boulevard in her small car. The sun went down several hours ago, but the omnipresence of neon assures that the strip is in a state of constant sunset. I recognize every single intersection from this movie or that. Alithia drives onward, unconcerned.

We are meeting the others at a party hosted by a friend of Colin's. Initially, I am alarmed to learn this, but the warm night air soon transforms my worry to excitement. My expectations are high. The house must be composed of glass. The nine balconies must overlook the Valley. The swimming pool must glow the deepest blue and follow the shape of a letter from a foreign alphabet. The observatory must contain a bar.

The little car turns onto a road that leads up a steep hill. Before we reach the steepest gradient, the car turns again, and we pull into a lot so wooded that the residence might as well be a mound of dirt. Cars are parked in haphazard fashion throughout the yard, a perplexing mix of luxury, hot-rod, and the barely serviceable. A mild segregation seems to be in observance, and so Alithia parks her vehicle between the Day Action Band van and a Geo Prizm with a cardboard license plate. As we walk up to the front door, I notice what must be Colin's Saab, the tiny windshield wipers on the headlights poised, gleaming, and ready for action.

They are waiting in the foyer, having just arrived themselves. Colin comes across the circle of introduction to shake my hand and tell me how good it is to see me. "We missed you today," he says. "The meeting was a smash." Tim, Joey, and Cree stand in shifting excitement, projecting an awareness that big things are about to happen to them. "You guys have to tell me everything," Alithia says, and Colin leans in and whispers something to her.

I am standing between Tim and Joey, about to ask them how they thought the meeting went, when a balding man with a short beard steps forward and identifies himself as the host. "Hi, I'm Gary," he says. "I was about to give the grand tour. Follow me." He leads us through the living room, where various people stoop at bookshelves, their heads cocked at uncomfortable but familiar angles. In the kitchen he mocks his recent purchase of an espresso machine. On the way up the stairs I learn that he makes his living as a sound editor for television specials. The tour is cursory and dispirited until we arrive at the intended destination, Gary's home recording studio.

"This is my baby," Gary says. The studio occupies the entire refurbished attic, and the host leans with satisfaction against the banister that leads up to it. An impressive wall of equalizing equipment looms behind a 24-track mixing board. An object in the shape of a cash register rests with a paisley sheet over it, and as we all watch, Gary pulls off the sheet to reveal the twin-headed tape machine. Next to several tiers of keyboards sits a full electronic drum kit, each drum head octagonal in shape and less than one inch thick. I look for a chair or a stool, but I don't see one. The only thing missing is a place to sit.

I walk to one end of the attic and stand before four large windows. The windows face the lightest part of the night sky and look out over a descending hillside of homes and diligently lit streets. "Is this the Valley?" I ask. Cree shrugs and turns her back to me. The others eavesdrop on the fringe of a technical powwow between Gary and Tim. Colin remarks that Gary's mixing board is identical to the one owned by the Day Action Band. Tim says, "They are the same size . . . ," and scratches his head to avoid completing the comparison.

"You know what?" Gary says. "I do have some hash. I got it

last weekend and I haven't had the chance to smoke it yet. What do you guys say?"

The pause that follows is long enough that Gary begins to regret his offer. Tim's instinct is to reward generosity with acceptance, but Colin's parental presence stays any such motion. Even on the outskirts, I sense the coming awkwardness.

Then Colin says, "I think you'll find some takers here," and everyone animates, more out of relief than any desire to become very stoned. Gary takes the tinfoil-wrapped hash right out of his pocket and displays it for public approval. He then removes a pipe from a cabinet under the tape machine and places a cube of hash in the bowl. Retracting his stained fingers, he passes the pipe to the person immediately to his right. This person happens to be Cree. I watch her to see what she does.

"Is it like smoking ordinary pot?" she says, the ingenue.

"Sure," Gary says. "It's just a little bit harder to keep lit. Here, I'll keep the flame on it for you." He does, and she inhales. When she exhales, a thin but substantial wisp of smoke comes out. She gulps, and then excuses herself to pace around a few feet away, coughing mildly and fanning the air in front of her face. I stare at her with my jaw set, wanting her to look into my eyes and read her own hypocrisy written in them. How does she reconcile this with her earlier righteousness? Is it because, smoking hash here today, she puts no one in danger but herself, whereas I, with my concealed quarter ounce of weed, nearly consigned us all to a life in prison? Somehow I don't think her reasoning is that complex. Somehow I don't think reasoning has anything to do with it. She does what she wants to when it's convenient. "That's fucking bullshit," I think in my head, and for a terrible second I wonder if I said it out loud. But no one seems to have heard anything; Cree herself is particularly nonreactive, her eyelids half open, her smile independent of anything taking place in the general conversation.

Tim smokes, then Joey, then me. If she's going to be stoned,

I might as well be too. I turn to my right. Alithia has backed away and now peruses the instruction manual that came with the electronic drums. I lift the pipe up to Colin, but he raises his hand in a gentle, "No thank you please," directing the device back to its owner, a monument to the resistance of peer pressure if ever there was one.

The pipe orbits the circle three times more. Gary says, "Maybe we should see what's happening downstairs," and when Cree starts laughing, he does too. Joey lifts his head to see what's so funny, takes a step back, and then begins to blink furiously. "That's fucked up," he says. "That's fucked up." He explains that he had been staring at a power cord behind Gary's feet, and when he looked up, his plane of equilibrium remained in a line with the power cord. "I was looking at your face," he says to Gary, "but it was like I was looking up in the air." Gary nods as if he has been living with the same condition for some time now.

This hash has enabled me to remove Gary's beard and regrow the hair on top of his head. I see now that he is a young man no more than five years older than myself. His equipment seems to have been acquired simultaneously, and I wonder what it was that provoked this action. The hair loss? The impending thirtieth birthday? A moment of clarity during a solo hash expedition? I can see Gary sitting on the floor in this very room, the empty pipe on its side in front of him. David Bowie sings his songs on the stereo as Gary leans forward, entranced. He may believe he has fallen asleep, but when the record ends, the silence wakes him from every state of false contentment. Many dark forces come into the room, even Death. Confronting them, Gary makes a series of cold, rational, profound decisions. He goes downstairs, consciously avoiding the kitchen, gets into bed, and goes to sleep for real. The next morning, he doesn't shave. He combs his hair so as to tastefully accentuate his baldness. He goes to the library, spends several hours reading back issues of *Consumer Reports* and *Audiophile,* and then he hits the music stores. It all has to start somewhere, he thinks. It all has to start somewhere.

We trace a single file path back to the living room. As no one is in a hurry to get there, the pace is slow. Tim walks in front of me, half turned around, talking about the meeting. "We got the treatment," he says. He tells me they were led to a conference room with a long black table, where on one side four chairs were already pulled out at even distances. Across the table were two larger chairs, rotated so they faced each other slightly. After several minutes, a young woman came in and asked them what they wanted to drink. Joey spoke first, requesting water, and watched in dismay as Cree followed with a piña colada, Tim with a martini, and Colin with a gin and tonic. "My first martini," Tim says. "How was it?" I say. "Nasty," he says, "but I'll have to try another one."

The legends arrived together, continuing a loud conversation as they entered the room. They hailed Colin upon seeing him and came around the table to shake hands. After adjourning to their seats, they opened an oak cabinet by remote. A freshly mastered tape copy of *You Think You Hear* was cued up in the stereo, ready for exhibition. They listened to the whole album. No one talked, except for when one of the legends paused the tape at the end of "Goodbye Summer" and said, "a perfect place for an intermission."

After, compliments were forthcoming. "Brilliant" and "ingenious" were heard. So was "a modern classic." Cree was told she was "a real timekeeper." Joey received praise for altering the tone of his bass from track to track, and his claim that it was Tim who deserved the credit was perceived as modesty.

"Yeah, it got kind of embarrassing," Tim says, "but at the same time it was really cool. It's nice to have smoke blown up your ass every once in a while, you know?" I nod, pretending I know.

As expected, there was a period of reminiscence. The legends recalled that Prince was "the first guy who could do it all since Stevie Wonder." This is not exactly exclusive information, but Tim repeats it as if it were. We enter the kitchen and suddenly Colin is gathering the band up and saying, "There's someone you need to meet." Alithia follows Gary into the dining room, and within a span of five seconds, I find myself alone, stoned, and three thousand miles from home. The kitchen is the brightest room in the house; I know there is no refuge here.

I cut a diagonal slice through the dining room and make for the darker enclave beyond. Three chairs crowd a coffee table; a fish-shaped ashtray gapes up at me, wanting a butt I cannot deliver. I sit in the inward facing chair, hoping that persons looking into this room will be unable to infer life from what they see. I rest my eyes in a calm and meditative state. I listen to the party move nearby.

Gradually, several voices distinguish themselves. One plaintive and excitable, one dry and deliberate, one tending toward laughter. I estimate that this trio is drifting toward my room at the rate of five feet per minute. In three minutes they will arrive on this spot, deafening me with their conversational jazz. Already their words begin to make sense. I look for a means of escape, but there is only one way out of this room, and they are blocking it. I close my eyes again and will my limbs not to move.

"Well, I can use myself as an example," says the plaintive one. "For many years, the only band I would listen to was R.E.M. To the exclusion of everything else. In my house, in my car—in my Walkman—I couldn't see how anything else could be worthwhile. Eventually one of my friends had to say to me, 'Chris, you're musically stagnant.'

"But I got older and my aesthetic changed. And as my aesthetic changed, I learned that there are many kinds of good. I learned about things like history and technique. I forced myself to adopt different perspectives. Now it doesn't matter whether or not I like something, it matters whether or not I appreciate it. Is it good? Is it good? That's the question I have to ask myself, the question anyone has to ask themselves. I don't know, it just seems very clear to me."

Very deliberately, the deliberate one says, "So you like things that are good?"

"Well, Steve, as I said, *like* isn't exactly the right word—"

"—but it's close enough?"

"Sure."

"So what do you hate?"

"The corollary, I guess. Things that are bad."

"That's interesting," Steve says. "For me it works this way: I can't hate something that's bad. It's the work of incompetent people that have nothing to do with me. To truly hate something you must also truly love it and fear it because it represents a justifiable alternative to your aesthetic. You must either embrace it and willingly reconstruct yourself—when that happens, we say someone is having a life change—or you must reject it, which means you must hate it. I suppose a third option would be to learn to suspend your aesthetic so that you don't feel much involvement. Many people who do this I think turn to television. The best writing today is done on sitcoms, et cetera."

The group is almost on top of me. I wonder if Chris is a closeted sitcom writer and if Steve knows this. I did not expect to hear this type of talk out of L.A., though I must have known I was going to hear the word "sitcom" spoken at least once.

"You are confusing aesthetic with self," says the third member of their group, who has been silently formulating this thought the whole time. This is the most interesting idea yet: music as prominent cultural accessory. For me, the most prominent. I feel a swell of pride for having phrased it so cleverly. When this fades I understand why I will never be a musician myself.

"See," Steve says. He turns to set his glass on the coffee table and notices my inert form. "Whoa!" he says. I see part of his drink splash up onto his arm. "Sorry, buddy," he says. "I didn't see you there." He mumbles something to his friends, and they all stride away toward the kitchen. I overhear the fragment, "sitting there, not moving," and then they are gone.

Some time later I get up to use the bathroom. I remember its location from Gary's preliminary tour. There is a line of one person, so I wait at the end of the hall near the laundry nook. The toilet flushes; the person ahead of me goes in. I can only assume the worst. I step into the lightless nook and scan the shelves. Up near the top, above the hot water heater, three plastic laundry baskets are stacked, each with a crack running down the same corner. Stuffed underneath them is a bra. I reach up for it and pull it down, nearly bringing the baskets down with it. Red lace, size 34C, something that Cree might be able to wear. A dark part of my mind tells me that it belongs to her, but I know this is ridiculous. She is sitting right now in a well-populated room, fully clothed, struggling with her stoned brain to follow what the person across from her is saying. I drape the bra over the top of the washing machine, leaving Gary to wonder about it what he will.

I hear Tim's voice out in the hall. I walk out of the nook and see him and a very tall young lady standing by the bathroom door, their arms around one another. I am about to call out to them when the door opens. The guy coming out jumps slightly when he sees them and hurries away. Tim and the girl try to go through the door at the same time, nearly wedging themselves in the narrow frame, and after, I hear someone locking the door inexpertly from inside. For a moment I think about how comfortable they must be to go to the bathroom in front of each other, but then I realize that's not what they're doing. A few minutes later, Tim comes out, zipping up his pants and grinning. The tall girl tucks a loose flap of blouse into her skirt.

The bathroom shows no evidence of its recent use. In the bidet next to the toilet, a giant clay fist punches the air. I lock the door and stare into the mirror above the sink. My complexion is particularly sallow in this light.

The course of a relationship is determined seconds into the first one-on-one exchange. Or at least it should be. People who grow on each other are destined to become better friends, not lovers. It is sad, I have heard it complained, that the sexual attraction is strong but they just can't seem to get to know each other. This is absurd and emblematic. There are two kinds of knowing and the sexual knowing is far more natural and complete. Suddenly I have an image of myself paddling bravely through the wide sea, then realizing it is really a small lake in a public park, the banks heretofore hidden by a dim industrial fog, now removed by a dim industrial wind, perhaps coming up a grate from the subway. I shut my eyes and will the fog back. People who want to obliterate this sexual knowing have nearly won. Repression has been suspected and discarded as a cause for rising cancer rates, but that is just more repression. Nobody wins, I think sadly, and leave the room, my work there incomplete.

At midnight, Gary stops the party for an appreciation of "I'm Looking Through You." Though I am several rooms away, the cut of his voice rouses first my consciousness, then my curiosity, and, finally, my actual person. "This is the Beatles' most underrated work," he says. "In its way, it's just as good as 'Day Tripper,' and I think you all need to understand that." While the song plays, Gary stamps his foot and claps his hands in time. This sets off a loud sixties reminiscence spearheaded by Tim and Steve of the life-changing aesthetic. My personal contribution is a three song river of soul that runs through the Anglo-pop delta: "These Arms of Mine," "Natural Woman," and "Tracks of My Tears." Some of

those unassociated with the revival shake their booty, and, standing there next to the receiver, I do take a little credit for this. In
the van on the ride home, right before we drop her off at Betsy's,
Cree asks what was the last song I played. Shortly thereafter, I
pass out.

WE WAKE THICK-HEADED but more capable of difficult logic than the day before. A caucus is again held in front of Alithia's refrigerator, but again no conclusion can be reached. Tim, once so certain of Alithia's presence in the photograph, now theorizes that a friend gave her the picture because of her resemblance to the bound girl. Joey, unconvinced, asserts that Alithia "has a past," but Tim argues that if she does have a past, then she seems to want to put it behind her, and so why would she keep this relic on prominent display?

"To remind her of what she doesn't want to be," Joey says. His voice contains the weight of pronouncement, and Tim yields.

We sit down to a light breakfast of cereal, bananas, and unbuttered toast. In less than two hours, we are scheduled to meet Alithia and a reporter from a national magazine for lunch. The Day Action Band is going to be profiled in a special "music of tomorrow" section. They have been promised two hundred fifty words of text and a two-by-three-inch group shot. The magazine does not normally cover rock music and apparently Alithia has been criticized by Colin for not arranging more consequential publicity.

Cree calls as I am rinsing my dishes. Her cold, dormant since we left Austin, has flared up again. She sniffs twice and clears her throat right after she tells me this. Without rest, she says, she may not be able to perform tonight. I relate this information to Tim, and he asks for the phone.

"It'd be really nice if you could make it," he says. After a pause he says, "What are you going to do then?" There is another pause, longer this time, and Tim nods even though he doesn't say anything. "Okay," he says finally, making his voice much more cheerful than it needs to be. "I hope you feel better. See you at the club at six." He hangs up.

"What did she say?" I ask.

"She and Betsy are going to lay low," Tim says. "Rent movies, eat soup, brush each other's hair."

"That's lame," Joey says.

Tim shrugs. "I don't have a problem with it," he says. "If she's sick, she's sick."

I feel certain that this time her sickness is a ruse. "How do you know she's not meeting Brant?" I say.

Tim shakes his head. "She wouldn't do that," he says.

"Nah," Joey says. "That's not her style."

I begin to feel reassured. Then Joey squints at me. "What," he says. "Are you jealous?"

"No," I say.

"Come on," Joey says. "It's okay. Tell the truth."

"You holding out on us, Lou?" Tim says.

"No," I say. "I'm just trying to be a good roadie." To my surprise this satisfies them. They walk out of the kitchen and into the living room, where they each pick up an old issue of *Rolling Stone* and sit down on the couch to read. I watch them suspiciously for the next couple of minutes, to make sure they have desisted their teasing out of boredom, not out of respect for my feelings for Cree. I have worked too hard to keep those feelings hidden to have them revealed in such a pointless interaction. Fortunately, Tim and Joey do not behave as though they have come by any new information, and my suspicion dies as quickly as it was born.

Following precisely scripted directions, we take a freeway known as "the 10" to an oceanside community remarkable for its concentration of restaurants and traffic lights. Today we will dine at La Fuda, described by a review in the front window as "irreverent New Mexican." Alithia and her past are waiting at a round table in the back; the interviewer, she tells us, has called to say he will be a little late.

The small talk soon escalates into gossip. Answering an innocuous question about relations with the Radials, Joey broaches the subject of Brant and Cree. I can feel Tim surging up to stop him, but before he can think of an appropriate distraction, the words are out. "Isn't it crazy?" Alithia says. She looks at Tim, who is blushing, shamefaced. "Sorry I brought it up in San Diego," she says. "I hope I didn't get you into too much trouble." Tim says it's no big deal but then makes a request that she be more circumspect about the information in the future. Alithia says, "Oh, don't worry," as if the best secrets are always the easiest to keep.

"Why don't you tell us something," Joey says.

"Something about what?" Alithia says. She laughs nervously. I wonder if Joey is going to ask about her role in the nude staking. Instead, he says, "Tell us something about Colin."

After a bit of coaxing, Alithia chooses to favor us with some of the terrible fights Colin and his girlfriend have had at work.

"He started bringing Jane to the office a few months ago," she says. "Supposedly, she's 'helping' him, but aside from making a few phone calls, all I've ever seen her do is go out to lunch."

The fights have pertained to the secretive resetting of the office thermostat. Alithia does not deny the right of a couple to argue about such a transgression, only the right to do it in front of subordinate employees in an intimate space.

"They scream at each other, horrible things," she says. "Once Colin said the devil could come up from hell and slit his throat if it was seventy-five degrees. And the crying. It always ends in crying. They go out on the steps for that, but we can still hear them."

Aside from Colin and Jane, Alithia shares the office with two other women, both of whom have considerable seniority. Each is assigned to one of the two famous bands on the London West client roster. They ride in limousines to the Grammys and fly the SST to Europe. I picture Alithia braiding her hair in front of the television, watching as the camera pans quickly across the faces of her boss and co-workers. The hair braided, she knots a final lace on her combat boot before heading out on foot to a desultory rock club, a dusky Cinderella without even a pumpkin to transport her. Jane, if nothing else, has brought her closer to these two women, a bond forged in the crucible of common dislike.

The interviewer glides in, suavely out of breath. He tells Tim and Joey he recognizes them from the *That One Five Jive* album jacket, and Joey expresses mock relief, saying that people are always mistaking him for Cree. The interviewer mutes his disappointment at the absence of Cree: "I think she's great, but my wife is really crazy about her. Sometimes I think I should be worried . . ."

I recede from this table. The interviewer was sent by a glossy magazine, a periodical so sleek, so bulky, and so crisp that other magazines instinctively slide away from it on the rack. The story will be small, but tens of thousands will read it. To think that the piece has its genesis here, in this restaurant, in this man . . . it is no wonder that our culture has the sense of proportion that it does. I listen to Tim recite his spiel about the inextricable relationship between a song and the way it is produced. I remember the spiel in its prenatal stage, when it sounded less like dogma, more like discovery. The interviewer nods, a false sage, and redirects the conversation once again to the perils and pitfalls that await a young band thinking of signing with a major label. "When my band was gonna sign . . . ," he says for the fourth time. Fortunately, another of Tim's talents is the ability to accept unsolicited advice with grace.

When lunch is over, the interviewer gone, and Alithia safely on her way back to the office, we drive down to a guitar store on Sunset Boulevard. I have never heard of this place, but I am willing to believe it is famous; out front, in the concrete, are Brian Wilson's handprints. He has small hands for such a large man, and stubby little fingers. There are other handprints here too, but they might as well belong to a local kindergarten class. I make this remark, and Joey says, "That makes sense in a couple of ways." Tim doesn't respond, comparing his hands to those owned by David Gilmour.

Inside, graduates of professional rock music conservatories police the floors, their manes of hair fluffing slightly when they pass over a vent. I lift a five-string acoustic bass down from the wall and plunk out the riff at the end of "The Chain." Tim comes by wearing a '76 white Telecaster with double humbuckers and says, "All the instruments in this store and you choose that one?" He does, however, condescend to add a high guitar part to the foundation I've laid.

Soon we separate, drifting into the nether zones of the store. I come across a wall devoted to tablature and take a seat there, learning the bass lines to classics such as "Don't Fear the Reaper," "Cinnamon Girl," and "All the Young Dudes." A salesman approaches, smugly appraising my lack of virtuosity, and tells me I've got "a nice axe for an intermediate player." I tell him I've never played any kind of guitar before and keep a straight enough face that his departure, after five minutes of "no shit" and "you should nurture your talent," is marked by disbelief. I look up above my head. A skylight tells me the afternoon is waning. There is something I have wanted to do ever since we arrived in Southern California. If I am going to do it, I had better find the others soon.

They are hiding in the last room I come to. It is not even a room, but a single strip of walkway that inscribes the highest part of the store's atrium. The walls are hung with vintage mandolins and other small folk instruments that I would not care to name.

Tim and Joey lean over the balcony, looking down on the room below, where an epic battle is taking place.

Directly underneath, wielding a red sunburst Heritage—a high-grade Les Paul knockoff, says Tim—stands a businessman, tie loosened, carefully attending to the blues. The notes burble as if from the brook beside the crossroads, bending over blue rock, clearish water, the twang of a rusted bicycle spoke half submerged. His mouth twitches in random time, his pupils tiny behind weightless wire-rimmed spectacles. He does not appear to hear the enormous sound coming from less than twenty feet away.

Its genesis? A Crate amplifier, attached to a nameless power cord, attached to a hot pink Flying-V, abused in the hands of transcendent punk rock obesity. Notes ring a paean to the major scale, distortion gathers at the perimeter, sweat darkens the thin carpet. The alchemization of rage into beauty. "He's got to weigh at least three hundred pounds," Joey says, in a voice of pure admiration.

The playing is simultaneous, the pretense that one is not aware of the other intact. The V is louder, awash in the joy of unconsidered possibility, but the Heritage knows who it is, limits recognized, honored, and celebrated. Suddenly, the businessman makes a daring run up the chromatic scale. He concludes with a diminished seventh that puts him dangerously close to the key inhabited by the fat punk. Is this intentional? Is he going to beat the punk at his own game? No, he isn't. With an overhand downward slash, the punk resolves the chord. The six-voiced choir sings my blood to the extremities. A new day rises in late afternoon. The businessman is the fat punk's bitch.

We can't see Mulholland Drive from the parking lot, but we can see the hills. I take control of the van, confident that I can get us to the famous boulevard. Tom Petty's *Full Moon Fever* waits in the inactive tape player, prepared to send forth "Free Fallin'."

My mission is to glide down over Mulholland just as Mr. Petty sings of doing the same. I want there to be no other cars on the road. I want the van to feel like it could drive forever. The conditions could be perfect. But I have doubts they will be, because Tim and Joey are not wholeheartedly in support of this endeavor. Tim respects Tom Petty for his hit-making abilities, but sees no mystery in the construction of his music; Joey has never taken an official position, but earlier in the tour, on the drive from Atlanta to New Orleans, "Don't Come Around Here No More" came on the radio and he promptly changed the station. And he was stoned when he did that.

I have chosen the road up based on its wideness and general air of promise. It seems that I have chosen wisely. A thin band of sun burns over the top of the rise. The van struggles to achieve the speed limit, downshifting into its lowest gears. Gravity forces my head back into the headrest. I grip the steering wheel with rigid arms and imagine I am piloting the space shuttle into the stratosphere.

Tim speaks. "Lou," he says, "it's getting a little quiet back here. How about some 'Runnin' Down a Dream'?"

That's not part of the plan, but it would be, as Joey sometimes says, unmellow of me to say so. Without a word I press FAST-FORWARD. When I think enough time has elapsed, I press PLAY. Sure enough, it's still "Free Fallin'," just beginning to fade. I let it go, and "Won't Back Down" comes on, groovy enough that it begins to ease my dismay.

"Those aren't real drums," Joey says, after a minute. "They sound totally fake." There is a silence, during which I prepare an elaborate rebuttal. But before I can present it, Tim says, "I wonder if Tom made this whole album on his computer." This is discussed with polite derision, until Tim realizes that he and Joey may be giving offense and says, "Sorry, Lou, we won't talk about it anymore."

"Thank you," I say. The road comes to a T, the crossbar of

which seems to run along a ridge. There's no street sign, but I'm not taking any chances; I hit REWIND and cut "Runnin' Down a Dream" off mid-chorus. I look to the sun, I look to the clock on the dashboard, and then I turn left, in the direction I believe to be southwest.

For several miles, all that is known about this new road is that Bette Midler is responsible for keeping it clean. I keep expecting to round a bend and come up behind a limo moving at five miles an hour, trolling for cigarette butts and empty coffee cups with its right rear door open. Then Joey sees a sign. "This is Mulholland!" he says. I press PLAY.

Everything is as I thought it would be. No cars, no talk, nothing but us and Tom Petty at the top of the Southern California coast, movie stars nestled in the hillside below. I hear the line, "I wanna glide down over Mulholland," but more than that I hear the line that follows, "I want to write her name in the sky." The van crests a rise, and the sky before me is huge, the palette of my dreams.

Oh, Cree. I can see it there, her name, in white, puffy cloud-letters, the airplane looping off into the distance. The real clouds move on behind it, and, after several minutes, the motion of the air begins to break the characters apart. But if this world truly has four dimensions, and I believe it does, her name will be written there for all eternity. She is probably inside right now, watching a rented movie in the Hollywood apartment with Betsy. Go to the window, go out on the porch, walk down to the corner shop for a carton of ice cream. She will go to do one or several of these things, and when she does a feeling will come over her, and she will look up at—no, she will *search*—the sky, and she'll see her name written there, and something will happen inside her heart. But so what if it does? She'll never know that I was the one who wrote it.

———————

I get into a traffic accident on the way to the club. Attempting to squeeze the van past a row of cars and into a turning lane, I brush against a parked hotrod, scraping its front left panel with the van's maladjusted rear bumper. We jump out and survey the scene. No cars behind us, no unusual activity in the gas station across the street. No other humans to witness the mishap and aftermath. The only car on the block, it probably isn't even supposed to be parked here. I look up, and a sign confirms my intuition.

"Do you wanna cruise?" Tim says. We were due at the club ten minutes ago.

"No," I say. "I've got to leave a note. I'd be pissed if someone did that to my car."

Tim nods. "I'll write it," he says. He reaches into the van and rips a page from his tour notebook. "I'm going to leave your number, okay?" he says. "That's fine," I say. No need to burden Alithia with this trouble. In a mechanically precise hand, Tim writes, "Please call 302-555-8431 when you get this. Thanks, Lou." He pins the note facedown under the blade of a windshield wiper. I admire the way it fulfills its moral function despite saying almost nothing; Tim did indeed inherit his father's fine legal mind.

I accept Joey's offer to relieve me of my driving duty. As we pull away, I look back at the car and see that the dent is clearly illuminated by the light from the gas station, a blemish on an otherwise flawless piece of thunder. My work will not escape the notice of the owner; upon my return home, I will look forward to an angry message on my answering machine and the outlay of many hundreds of dollars in compensatory damages. Though I do feel the twin mechanisms of assholery and incompetence, the emotion that prevails, strangely, is relief. Cree will hear of this misadventure, but as the van is unharmed and the problem now squarely mine and mine alone, she will receive the news with a minimum of contempt. I can only imagine the hostility had she been present.

Bob and I set up our T-shirts together for the last time. We don't mention this; I'm not even sure he knows this is the last stop on the tour. "This place is amazing," he says. "I've never been in a place this big." I know what he means—that this is the largest rock club he's ever set foot inside—but I choose to hear it differently. This man at the end of his life, provincial, hard-working, takes a trip on which he sees wonder upon wonder, each superseding the last. And here, in the lobby of Wonderland, capacity twenty-three hundred, the journey culminates. Bob can now go home to die. I have a flash of his thin, unetched grave tilting forward into the back of another grave. I was seventeen years old before I first set foot in a club this small.

I step back from the display to see how the new T-shirts look in this light. They look fine—but that is not what strikes my eye. It is Bob's craft, which in every way has surpassed mine. His shirts appear not to be hung but ironed into the wall itself. He has learned to make the duct tape invisible. Three flat strips, folded over—one on each sleeve, one across the shoulders—suspend each garment in all of its unflopping glory. Though I could benefit from this technique, I make no attempt to employ it. This is no museum; one does not dilute the work of the master.

A skinny woman with long straight blond hair and loose jeans walks up and stops about ten feet behind the counter, where Bob now stands with his back turned. She puts her hands deep into her pockets, goes up on her tiptoes, and says in a squeaky voice, "Excuse me, sir, do you know where I could find Bob Rainey?"

Bob whirls around. "Linda!" he shouts. In a move more spry than I could have predicted for him, he swings himself up and over the four-foot counter. He runs to Linda, puts his arms completely around her, and lifts, leaning back until her feet are well above the floor. "You made it!" he says. "I wasn't even sure you still lived here!"

"I still live here," she says.

"I'm so glad," Bob says. His smile reveals new wrinkles. His white hair seems to be trying to extricate itself from his ponytail. He puts Linda down on top of the counter and jumps back over himself, this time more gingerly.

I listen to them reacquaint. From the tone of their banter I guess it has been several years since their last meeting. In that time Linda has divorced, and Bob does not wait for her lead to proclaim that he's happy to hear it. I detect a faint, unconsummated affection between them. Could it be that Bob will not make the trip back East?

"So what about you?" Linda says. "Is someone missing you right now?"

"My landlord," Bob says. "He's missed me for a few months." After the laughing, Bob says, "You know me. I'm doing the same stuff. Knocking around." He looks over at me, as if I'm the one responsible for his vagueness. Then he says, hopefully, "I did just have a birthday."

My interest heightens. How old is he? Sixty? Thirty-five? Ninety-two? Come on, Linda, ask him.

"How did you celebrate?" Linda says. Damn.

"It was great," Bob says, looking off in remembrance. "All my best friends were there—except you. There must have been a hundred of them. They brought photo albums, there was a slide show, there was a big cake. I never knew I had so many friends."

"That sounds really nice," Linda says.

"Yeah," Bob says. "It was."

My faith in my own judgment collapses. Bob's headstone will be proudly marbled, painstakingly engraved, and garlanded with flowers of every color. The hundred best friends will gather at the cemetery for a yearly slide show, the images projected onto the back of a Radials' T-shirt hung on a nearby grave. He will live for some time after his death. To what does he owe this following? A hidden bedrock resolution? A humble nobility? Something pitiable and sweet? Or is it simply the natural accumulation of years? I can think of about fifteen non-family members who would attend my own funeral if it were held locally. Hopefully this number will increase as I age.

The rider is as great a rider as there has ever been. Cold sodas and frosty bottles of beer float in a bin of shaved ice. A fifth of golden bourbon leans manfully against a box of imported butter cookies. Row upon row of vegetables march toward a sullen bowl of dill-flecked dip. Tim and Joey sit nearby, their hands on their knees, staring at the same spot on the floor.

"Why aren't you guys eating?" I say.

"I'm not hungry," Joey says, "but why don't you ask Tim why he's not eating."

Tim gives a look that combines sheepishness with worry. "I think I might be nervous," he says.

"He's nervous," Joey says gleefully, snatching up a celery stalk and snapping it longwise in his mouth.

"I don't know what it is," Tim says. "Tonight it seems like it really matters, like it could go either way. It's giving me the jitters."

"The city is Los Angeles, the crowd is large . . . ," I say. It's hard to sympathize; Joey's reaction, amusement, seems like the best and most natural way to respond.

"I'll get over it," Tim says. "I shouldn't even be talking about it."

"You're a big pussy," Joey says. "Why can't you just get it together?"

Tim treats this as a serious inquiry. "I'm trying. I'm really trying," he says. "We don't go on for half an hour. Maybe it'll be over by then."

"It better be," Joey says, "or me and Cree will throw you over the side."

If there is one man qualified to lecture on living with nervousness, it is Joey. His world is awkward and uncertain, a mine-field of minor rejections and embarrassments. He has learned to tread it well, to employ the devices of hesitance and cynicism with pinpoint precision. Only a fool would pity this existence, with its omnipresence of hope and the frequent lifting of the soul at a mishap avoided. It is something to see Joey in his element and to realize that he most definitely has one.

"Hi," a new voice says. It is Cree, standing in the doorway. Her bearing conveys that she does not mean to enter, only to deliver a message and then retreat.

"How are you doing?" Tim says. He smiles to let her know that she is welcome any time she chooses to return.

"It's been a while," Joey says. He does not smile at all.

She has prepared herself for both responses and moves forward to the substance of her visit.

"Since this is the last show," she says, "the Radials wanted us to come to their dressing room for a little ceremony. We might all go out later, but in case we don't they wanted to do this first."

"Oh, that's really nice," Tim says. He gets up and stands next to Joey until Joey gets up and then they both head toward the door.

Cree says, "Lou, you should come too."

I look at her and I know that she lied to us this morning. She didn't spend the day with Betsy, she spent it with Brant, in his hotel room, the two of them alone for hours. If I accuse her right now she will be unable to deny it. There will be a fight and she and Tim and Joey will scream at each other. The band might even break up over it. I don't know if that will make me feel bad or good or relieved simply to have had some effect on their lives. But when I look at her again I feel too weary to do anything but acquiesce.

"Sure," I say. "I'll come."

I follow the Day Action Band through the passage behind the stage. I have come to accept their tokenism as a product of good intention, blind and otherwise. This event has different magnitudes, however, and as we approach the doorless chamber, I wonder if I should have demurred. I have not spent enough time around the Radials to justify a protracted goodbye with them.

"Hello!" Edward says, clipping off half of the last syllable. He is flanked by Colin and Alithia; the Radials stand back to one side, smiling and looking more formal than usual. In the far corner, Louise sits on a couch and reads a magazine, aware that this is not her occasion. I would consider joining her, but I don't have anything to say to her either.

Colin says, "I want to thank you all on behalf of myself and the band. You have no idea what this means to their career and them personally."

Gemma distinguishes herself and says, "We should be the ones thanking you. This is the best tour of America we've ever done, and the Day Action Band is the best band that's ever opened for us. Isn't that right?" Peter and Walter nod solemnly.

Brant, looking right at Cree, says, "This may be our best tour, period. The next time we play the States . . . there's no doubt. We want you to open for us. That is, if you haven't surpassed us by then."

The members of the Day Action Band are daunted by this praise. Cree seems to have been apprised of it beforehand but still appears affected by the delivery. Joey smiles with all his teeth. Tim, whose nervousness has made him even more susceptible to sentiment, mutters something that sounds like, "That's a great thing to say to a person."

"Some drinks before the show?" Edward says. The formal structure collapses; individual skirmishes commence. I find myself talking with Walter about what he plans to do when he gets back to England. "Martial arts," he says. "I've got a bit out of practice. Next time I think I'd like to bring my trainer with me."

"That makes sense," I say. "The drums are the most martial of instruments."

"What?" he says.

I turn away from him, even though no rule of etiquette permits me to do so. Everyone is talking to somebody. Even Louise, who has left the safety of the couch to stand at the shoulder of Peter, as Colin spins them both the wittiest tale that has ever been told.

Making no effort at concealment, I walk proudly from the enclosure. I pass the backstage security personnel and weave through the burgeoning audience. Perhaps the owner of the dented hot rod is in attendance. If so, my condolences. But next time, he might consider paying for parking closer to the theater.

The lights dim, the lobby empties, and Bob, Linda, and I are alone. "Lottery" begins with chords that sound as though they could go on forever. The rhythm section shakes the wall at my back. Tim's vocal, when it begins, is brash and confident.

At the end of the song I wait for his usual introduction: "Weighing in at one hundred ten pounds and making sure the beat never dies . . ." but tonight it doesn't come. Instead he says, "You know, before this tour we never played in front of more than five hundred people." His voice is unsure, almost intentionally so; in the search for one kind of sincerity he is expressing another. "I mean, I know almost all of you are here to see the Radials," he continues. "And you have great taste. They're a fantastic band. To be honest, I had never listened to them much before the tour—they were always somebody a friend of a friend recommended, you know?" I have to be an eyewitness to this rambling. I jump out of my seat and run to the entrance to the hall.

"But I've gotten to see them play every night. And every night I like them more and more." Tim is right at the microphone; his guitar hangs at his side. Joey listens as if to a lecture, his hand curled underneath his chin. Cree, slightly wild-eyed, reaches to steady a cymbal that is not moving. "Look, I'm not saying they're the Stones, or the Beatles, or the Kinks." A small faction cheers loudly at this last. "And I'm not saying they're not—don't get me wrong. Don't get me wrong." Cree laughs, fortunately, not into her microphone. "It's just been really exciting for me and for all of us to watch these . . . *professionals* . . . rock the fuck out night after night!" The whole audience cheers this time. Tim grins, glad that he was able to get away with saying "professionals." "So what I'm trying to say is, we're the supporting act—we're the Day Action Band, from Newark, Delaware—and there's no one we'd rather be supporting than the Radials. Thanks, guys. This one's called 'Trolley Square.' "

I return to my table. Bob and Linda are now sitting side by side, their legs touching. They lean in and whisper when they talk. The Day Action Band plays on, with no further unorthodoxy from Tim.

With about three songs left in their set, Linda calls my name. Suspicious, I wait to answer until she makes a second attempt.

"I'm so sorry," she says, giving Bob a look. "He told me your name was Lou."

"It is," I say.

"Oh," she says. "Listen, honey, this is your band, they're your friends, this is the last night they're up there. Why don't you go watch them play. Bob and I will keep an eye on your stuff."

Behind the friendly offer I sense a determination grounded in lust. She wants to be alone with Bob. I look over at him and he blinks back in happy resignation. "That's very kind," I say.

The density of the room repels my initial efforts to infiltrate it. Far, far away, the Day Action Band rocks on a dark sea of red and yellow light. The tops of heads suggest a hundred different footpaths to the stage. Detecting a weakness in the left flank, I press inward.

Several times, I reach what I determine to be a stopping point. A massive shoulder, a trio of girls, arms linked, a premonition of tall hats—I tell myself that this spot will do just fine. But once settled, dissatisfaction swells within me, and I move on, elbows prying, apologies flying. By now "Wrestling" is well into its final chorus; Tim sings, "This can't be fake / 'Cause it makes my heart break" while Joey and Cree shout it back. "Back in the Eighties" is coming up next, and I want to be settled when it begins.

Ten feet from the left side of the stage, I break through the edge of the crowd. Before me stands a security person. He doesn't see me right away because he's watching the band, interested in spite of himself. I alter my plan. "Excuse me," I say. "I'm their tour manager. I need to get backstage."

"ID?" he says, turning back to the stage. "Wrestling" is now over; Tim hits the harmonics to make sure his guitar is in tune. I reach into my pocket for the pass and it's not there.

"Look," I say. "I've been on this goddamned tour for three weeks. I don't give a shit about the Radials, I'm not going to harass anyone. My band is about to come off stage. I just want to get them some towels and some water."

He considers. No one has ever taken this approach with him before. He looks over my head to the back of the room, and then he turns and looks at the empty corridor behind him.

"I don't know if you're telling the truth or not," he says, fighting the urge to threaten me further. "But if somebody catches you back there, tell them you came in the other side."

"Back in the Eighties" begins. The staccato riff moves like electric current through the air. I take the stairs three at a time. At the top I make a sharp right and duck into the part of the stage hidden from the audience by the curtain.

I see the band in profile, all three of them looking straight ahead, all three of them singing. The light and heat that pours down upon them they contain and amplify and shoot out into the crowd. Here on the fringe I stand protected from the full force of that power. The heavy fabric of the curtain presses at my side.

Looking down I see a figure sitting on the floor ahead of me, just before the place where the curtain ends. The head turns slightly, and I see that it's Brant. Instead of listening to the music myself, I watch him listen. He rocks his head back and forth and drums his hands on the floor at his sides. When "Back in the Eighties" is over his hands come up to clap, but then he puts them down again, thinking, perhaps, that it might be better to hold all the applause until the end.

I don't watch him during "Outside Tokyo." Tim was right to want to play this song last. The dropped beat felt in the solar plexus, the melody remembered from the crib. I feel that I am no longer hearing music, I am hearing Tim and Joey and Cree themselves, these people I know and have spent so many hours with, transformed into a single, wonderful sound. It is not unlike the feeling of first love, and I am amazed, after all these years, that I am still able to feel it. Toward the end of the song a violent movement catches my eye, and I look to see Brant, no longer on the beat, no longer able to control himself, pounding his hands into the floor, pounding them until they must be bruised and raw. For that one moment I know that he sees what I see and that he hears what I hear and that what separates us is not nearly so large as I have often imagined it to be. It is, in the end, no larger than a girl.

I sit alone in the parked van, just down the street from the entrance to the club. The equipment is loaded out; the band is inside saying their final goodbyes. I will sleep well tonight and wake without the faint apprehension that has accompanied me these past three weeks. I do wonder if it was a mistake to remain aloof from the Radials; those who hear the story of my brush with greatness will certainly listen uncaptivated. But if that opportunity was wasted, at least I can still look forward to spending the last leg of the trip with my friends.

Here they come now, running. However, they number not three but seven. Breathless, they slam into the side of the van before rebounding to pull open the side door. "Drive, drive!" shouts Cree. Though I sit in the driver's seat, I had not intended to drive, afraid the memory of my earlier trouble might diminish my skill. But now I have no choice. I turn and look around the van. Joey, Peter, and Walter sit crammed in the back row. Gemma, Brant, and Cree sit in the middle row, Cree astride both their laps. Tim is the last to arrive; he opens the passenger door and takes his seat there. "What's up?" I say to him, as Cree shouts, "Drive!" another time.

"We're going out for some Hebrew delicacies," Tim says. "We've got to wait for Colin to pull up."

"Why aren't we moving?" Cree demands.

"Be cool," Tim says. Joey and the Radials laugh, and Cree says, "Shit, man, I'm so cool, they call me The Frozen."

"I wouldn't say that's accurate," Brant murmurs. "Oh, really," says Cree, and Gemma makes a noise of disgust and says, "That's it, I want out of this van. There's too much love in here."

Through the window I see a posse of young girls, immersed in conference, but nevertheless edging toward the van. One looks up, catches my eye, and indicates to her friends that she has seen me, whoever I am. Cree glares and clutches at Brant's thigh. Gemma reaches and draws the recalcitrant curtains closer together.

There is a screech of tires and Colin's Saab whips into place before us. Edward, Alithia, and Louise all turn around from inside the car, Alithia and Louise waving as much as the lack of horizontal space will permit. Colin hits the gas and starts to drive. I follow. As the van pulls away, the girl posse makes a halfhearted screaming run into the street.

The road to the deli is strangely quiet. Once every minute, someone makes an unfunny comment and the van chuckles with nervous laughter. But no one has the wherewithal to sustain a conversation for any portion of the trip.

At the deli, Colin whispers something to the waitress about

to seat us, and she trots into the kitchen. An older bald man comes out, the wrinkles surpassing his forehead on their way to the top of the dome. He wears an expensive suit and offers Colin a cigar, which the younger man waves off. We are led to a long table secluded by venetian blinds and told to sit.

As each of us makes their way around the table, it becomes apparent that I am going to be seated across from Brant and Cree. I pause to let Alithia and Joey step past me, but Alithia puts her hand on my back and whispers, "Keep going." I hope then for a miscalculation, but I haven't made one; the chair I pull out to sit in directly opposes theirs.

The young lovers do not attempt to disguise their status. Giggling, Cree removes Brant's napkin from his plate, unfolds it, and places it in his lap. I let my eyes move slowly over the paintings on the wall behind them, seeing nothing, willing the waitress to hurry up with the menus.

The next time I look over at them, Cree is staring at me.

"What's wrong?" she says.

"Nothing," I say.

"You're making a terrible face," she says. "It's kind of like this." She does a wincing, dead-eyed smile that I recognize from certain photographs of myself.

"I didn't realize—," I say.

"Jesus, Cree!" Brant exclaims. "Must this man always be at your service?" Then, to me, "Lou, I apologize for her behavior. She's very young and she hasn't quite mastered the social graces." Cree socks him on the arm, then pats him to show that she's not serious.

"I'm very sorry, Lou," she says. "That was a nice face." She turns to Brant. "Okay, mister," she says. I don't hear what she says next. A warm feeling of mollification spreads over me and I am almost able to believe that Brant and Cree are not a couple but two ordinary people who just happen to be on the other side of the table. Colin orders a round of matzo ball soup, and when the bowls arrive, I make a crack about the bulls that gave the best parts of their lives for this meal. Everybody who hears it laughs.

"Ah," Brant says, breathing deeply. "There's nothing like castration, really, is there?"

"No there isn't," I say, and we clink our glasses in a toast. This inspires a toasting duel between Colin and Edward that ends when Colin announces that he plans to pick up the check.

"Then we'd better order some wine," Edward says, to a roar of approval. He waits for the nod from Colin, calls over the waitress, and orders a half dozen bottles of red wine. We stay in the deli until nearly four o'clock. I can never quite manage to become drunk, but I am the only one who has this problem. Drinks are spilled and cigarettes are smoked. Some grow silent as others become sentimental. Peter vows that the Day Action Band will one day be the most famous in the world. He declares that he is humbled in Tim's presence, that all the songs he writes from this day forward will bear the mark of Tim's influence. Tim blushes and says that he doesn't know what to say. Colin says, "We really have something special, don't we?" and Alithia leans across me to kiss Joey on the cheek. Later, the owner of the deli returns and begins to sing a song in a foreign language whose melody I have never heard. Walter, perhaps the drunkest person in the room, rises to stand beside him and delivers a remarkable phonetic approximation of the tune. "Maybe he should be our singer!" Gemma shouts. "Ah ha ha ha," Louise laughs. "Ah ha ha ha." At the end of the song the owner hugs Walter and claps him on the back. The applause goes on for so long that my hands begin to feel sore. I drop them to my sides and cup my knees under the table. Across from me, Cree moves closer and closer to Brant. I don't know if it is the wine, or the wearing off of my temporary good mood, or something else altogether, but gradually I come to understand that I have never seen her so happy and that I could never hope to make her that happy myself. The impulsive smile, the unthinking certainty of her movements, the eyes barely able

to contain the energy racing through her brain—I want desper-
ately to believe that somehow, indirectly, by my very presence, I
am the one that has produced this joy. But with every little kiss,
every murmur, every light touch on the arm or back that passes
between them, I see that I am not.

Across the street from the Radials' hotel sits their tour bus, dark
under large tropical leaves, idling no more. The group stands on
the pavement, not quite ready to disband. Cree and Brant spend
a moment in discussion and then turn and walk quickly toward
the lobby. Joey is the first to report their defection, and when he
does, Gemma says, "Looks like we're going to be here awhile."

"Not if I know Brant," Peter says slyly. "Should just be a
minute, two tops."

Louise shouts an "Ah ha ha ha" that seems to reverberate
among invisible skyscrapers. Someone makes a motion to get the
hugging out of the way, and so we each traverse the circuit, two
semicircles convening, overlapping, and then moving apart. The
handshakes from Edward, Peter, and Walter are firm and respect-
able; the hugs from Gemma and Louise are warm and indicative
of greater intimacy.

Ten minutes pass. Colin makes the comment that he and Alithia have to be at work by nine tomorrow. He offers to drop her
off at her apartment and she accepts, knowing perhaps, that we
still have a good wait ahead of us. Before he shuts his door Colin
calls out, "Remember the lyrics." This seems a strange parting
wish, and when I ask, Tim tells me that we have to go by the
office tomorrow to transcribe the lyrics of *You Think You Hear*
for the Japanese release.

Soon the Radials grow tired as well. Edward leaves first with
an upward nod and a strangled, " 'Til we meet again." Walter,
Gemma, and Louise are next—Gemma and Louise won't be flying
home right away, but our own departure tomorrow precludes the

possibility of another meeting. Peter lingers long enough to trade addresses with Tim, but then he too is gone.

A warm wind blows down the street, turning Joey's hair into a living entity, a sea anemone high up in the Gulf Stream. He reaches into his pocket and pulls out the hackey sack. "Wanna hack?" he says. Tim and I shake our heads and he puts it away. I look up at the broad flat side of the hotel. Only a few rooms are still lit. I wonder whether Brant's is one of them. "Maybe we should go in there and look for her," I say.

"She'll come out when she's ready," Tim says.

"That's what I'm afraid of," Joey says. "This is getting ridiculous. We have stuff to do tomorrow."

"It might not hurt to see if she's in some common area . . . ," I say, knowing that such an area probably does not exist.

"Let's go get her," Joey says. "I'm ready for bed."

"I'll be out here," Tim says. He seems faintly disappointed, though whether it's with us, Cree, or the end of the tour, it's difficult to say.

The night clerk observes our entry with casual attentiveness, always alert to the possibility that someone famous might walk through that front door. There are two elevators and one of them is out of service; we stand before the one that works and watch the numeral make its slow descent from the fourteenth floor.

The elevator opens and Cree almost knocks us down coming out of it. Whatever exclamation of greeting I have prepared I kill in my throat. Cree's eyes are swollen with tears and the muscles in her face move in painful, confused spasms. Joey blurts out, "Are you okay?" and she doesn't answer, stepping fast out of the bright lobby and into the concealing night.

When Tim sees her he understands immediately and gets in the van to drive. She sits alone in the back row, making no sound except to clear her throat. We take her through empty streets to Betsy's and Tim tells her gently to be ready by noon. The porch light comes on and then the speculation begins, a somber, hushed, questioning excitement as if over a high school classmate who has met an untimely end. What happened up there? Was it the simple act of saying goodbye? Or did Brant deliver a fatal platitude, it was fun while it lasted, maybe I'll see you the next time we tour the States? These distinctions do not interest me in the way that they might have once, and I press my head against the window until Tim and Joey's words become as meaningless as the deli owner's song. Whatever I am feeling right now, it is nothing like relief.

FIRST I HEAR ALITHIA'S morning noise. The shower, the dresser drawers opening and closing, the soft-voiced dialogue with the cat. Her darkened form passes over me en route to the kitchen and soon I hear the sounds of cereal, the rattling of flakes, the cap coming off the milk, the relentless clank of the spoon. Her handling of the keys is quite quiet however, and I lie on the floor in admiration for several minutes after her exit, forestalling the delicious return to sleep. But then the phone begins to ring. The caller has patience, and by the eighth ring, I am realizing that last night's wine has had an unpleasant residual effect.

The next two calls come at five-minute intervals. After the second, Joey rises in stealth, believing he is the only one awake, and goes to the phone to turn off the ringer. He lies back down and pulls his sleeping bag over his head.

Some time later, Tim shouts, "Fuck! It's quarter to twelve."

"Goddamn!" Joey says, throwing off all his bedding with a single sweep of his left arm. He runs to the window for confirmation. Sure enough, the sun is almost directly overhead. "Goddamn!" he says again.

A flashing red light on the phone attracts my eye. Still prone on the carpet, I grip the device and hold it above my face. "According to this," I say. "Alithia has eight messages. Maybe they're for us."

"Who would call us here?" Joey says.

"When I find out who, I'm going to beat their ass," Tim says, sitting up on the couch. He turns his head toward the sunlit window and cringes back as if slapped.

"Any of the people we know in Los Angeles," I say. "Alithia, Colin." I think for a moment and then I add another name. "Cree."

We listen to the messages, but all that plays back is silence. An examination reveals that the volume on the machine is set to zero. "So that's why we didn't hear it before," I say. "Alithia must require silence as part of her S&M regime!" Raising the volume, we try again. The first message is from Cree: "Hi, guys, it's nine, just wanted to see if you were up. I'm meeting Gemma and Louise at the beach at eleven, I hope you'll be able to take me then. Bye."

"Whoops," Tim says.

"There's no time for her to go the beach," Joey says. "We've got to do the lyrics and then we've got to drive. What is she thinking?"

Message number two is from Cree, as well. The content is similar, although a slight urgency has entered the tone.

Messages three through five continue in this fashion, the urgency increasing in the direction of hysteria. Messages six through eight contain no text; the phone hangs up as soon as the machine is activated.

"What's her problem?" Joey says. Tim has already opened his wallet and removed a slip of paper; looking at it, he dials.

"I'm sorry," he says into the receiver. "The phone didn't ring here. You really wouldn't have had time to do that anyway." He is silent while a loud stream of syllables flows into his ear.

"I'm sorry," he says again, this time not sounding sorry at all. "Whether or not you believe me, we need your help for this. I don't know all the words to the parts you sing. We don't want to have to keep rewinding the tape—it's really a lot easier if you do it."

Abruptly, Tim puts the phone back in its cradle. "She hung up," he says. "Let's go."

At Betsy's, Cree refuses Tim's offer to help her get her duffel bag down the stairs. It bumps behind her from one stair to the next before gaining momentum and nearly overtaking her in its pursuit to reach sea level.

From the back row of the van, she passes up two sheets of notebook paper and tells me to please give them to Tim. On one sheet, hastily scribbled, are the complete lyrics to "The Only Way to Talk to Her." On the other, various single lines have been written out under song titles; these, I have to assume, are her backing parts. Underneath "Goodbye Summer," she has written, "Bye bye bye bye bye, goodbye summer," either interpreting Tim's assignment with extreme literalism or extreme sarcasm. Judging from her well-maintained glower, I would say it is the latter.

Tim looks at the papers briefly while he drives before dropping them into the space between the two seats. His understanding seems to have reached its limit. With the on-ramp to the freeway in sight, he brakes suddenly and pulls into a small decrepit shopping center. Cree doesn't ask why we're stopping. Tim says, "I'll be right back" and runs up the sidewalk to the far end of the row. Five minutes later he comes walking back with a bouquet of wrapped carnations.

He gets in the van and says, "Hold these." Joey takes the flowers, and Tim looks over his shoulder to back the van out of the lot. He looks right past Cree and out the rear window, partially obscured by drums. Once we are back on the road he says quietly, "Those are for Alithia, for letting us stay with her." He says this, I believe, to make sure that Cree doesn't think the flowers are for her.

The London West offices are not as glamorous as Colin's accent would suggest. The white large-windowed building sits adjacent to a pair of railroad tracks. Through the chain-link fence and beyond I can see a home improvement complex and its satellites, McDonald's, Hardee's, and the mighty Papa John's. Next to the space where we park is an abandoned dentist's chair, perhaps left in monument to the former tenant. Stripped of tools, it refuses to gleam. Joey gives it a good long look before deciding it unworthy of his comment.

"I gather those aren't for me!" Colin says when he sees the flowers. He steps aside as Tim, Joey, and I make our way toward Alithia, who is too engrossed with a telephone and a calendar to notice what we have. When she hangs up Tim says, "These are for you. Thank you for all your hospitality." Alithia tears up and says, "That's so sweet, guys, you didn't have to do that. You really didn't have to do that." She continues to repeat this phrase, seemingly bent on forcing some kind of confession. I am about to disclose that Tim acted alone when Cree says, "Didn't we come here for a reason?"

There is an edge in her voice and everyone hears it. Colin says, "The lyrics need to be typed. Probably the best approach is for two of you to write them out while the third types them in. Does anyone here type particularly well?"

Joey says that he does. Alithia gets up from her desk with a pile of papers and relocates to a table out in the middle of the room. "You can use my computer," she says. Tim and Cree move to opposite ends of an unused desk, a mobile hung with miniature gold discs between them. Tim bends and begins to scribble immediately. Cree relaxes in her chair, shifting her weight to move it from side to side. She looks slowly around the room, from the high white ceilings and thick white columns to the two similar dark-haired women working quietly on the far side of the office. The three wide open doors let in distended rectangles of sunlight. Suddenly Cree gets up and walks out the closest of the doors.

Tim lifts his head. "Where is she going?" he says. No one answers. The door to the van slides open. A beat later the door slams shut and we all wait for the rumble of the engine. Instead, Cree comes back into the office, carrying the two pieces of notebook paper on which she has written her lyrics. She gives the sheets to Joey and takes her place in the chair. Her current expression is difficult to quantify but there seems to be the hint of a contemptuous smile on her lips.

Though there are only thirteen songs on *You Think You Hear*, and though no one in the band is especially verbose, it takes a very long time to type out the lyrics. Colin sits on the corner of Alithia's desk and further impedes the process with speculation of the reviews the album is likely to generate. Several times Cree gets up and makes a phone call from the most remote telephone in the office. I never see her speaking, however, and, each time, when she returns to her seat, her eyes seem to glow with hatred. During one of these trips Tim looks up and whispers, "What do you think of the way Cree's behaving?"

"She's not very happy," I say, and he says, "Hmm . . ." and continues to scrawl.

By mid-afternoon the work is complete. "I can take it from here," Colin says, and behind him Alithia makes a face to indicate that she will be the one to take it from here. The farewell is neither climax nor anticlimax; band and management expect to be in frequent contact over the next month as the album comes public. Sentiment does revisit Alithia briefly, and as I pat her on the middle of her back, I think of the dragon breathing fire beneath my palm. "I'm glad to know you, Lou," she says. "Next time they come out here, I want you to be with them." Colin is brusque, his capacity for speech exhausted the previous night. "You did a fine job," he says. My reply, the last thing I ever say to him, is "So did you."

The tour is over, yet it is not over. The Radials are gone, but there is still rock and roll to be played. One show remains, a five-band pop blowout at the minuscule Candelabra in San Francisco. When it was first added to the tour, Tim spoke of this last concert as "a chance to cool down, a chance to let some of the air out of our big heads." Now I sense that he regards it as a burden, that he would prefer to turn east and drive the three thousand miles home in one continuous burst. I think Cree would prefer this too, provided she and Tim could spend the trip in total isolation from each other. Their current solution is avoidance by sleep; both were unconscious less than half an hour after we left London West. This leaves Joey and me to address the fundamental question: to take or not to take the Pacific Coast Highway.

The band attempted it once before, Joey tells me. "The wind knocked us about like a playful kitten," he says, his knee bouncing in excitement. "The speedometer didn't crack twenty-five." He describes hairpin turns, potholes the size of bathtubs, and hundred-foot cliffs that began inches beyond the guardrail. They turned back after less than five miles, mostly to pacify Cree.

"We should try it again," I say. "Any objections?"

Tim and Cree of course have no objections. Joey says, "I don't know, I don't know," but I can tell from the jiggling knee and extended syntax that he does know. Looking at the map, I set a course for San Luis Obispo.

At five o'clock, the sun has descended behind black mountains. We race to escape the freeway before shadow becomes night. Beside us glows the neon of the last fast food before the coast. Cree wakes up and says she's hungry. "We want to get a little farther before it gets dark," Joey says. "Don't worry, they'll be plenty more places." The first part is true; the second part is conjecture. The Pacific Coast is no good to us if it can't be seen. But will it have restaurants? In my mind the dueling objectives combine: dining atop the bluffs as the sun paints a shimmering path to the end of the world. By dessert, the candles are lit and the waiter asks if we would like him to close the window.

We turn onto the Pacific Coast Highway and night falls. "Damn!" Joey says. "We were so close."

"Yeah," I say. "Now it's just a bunch of dark."

Somber, Joey puts in a cassette by Love. The eerie, disjointed songs confound my brain. Cree says, "I'm hungry" from somewhere in back and I picture not Cree on the seat but a little tape recorder set to repeat its message every quarter of an hour.

The driving requires my full attention. Straightaways rarely last more than fifty yards and end in turns so sharp they nearly bring the van to a halt. The terrain is unknowable beyond what the headlights reveal, guard rail, pavement, rock. Often I have the sensation of trees a thousand feet tall, bending at their tiptops to form an archway over the road. Talk is rare, save for the occasional dinner call from Cree. Whenever the van jars over a pothole or an unfinished section of road, she disapproves with a sharp intake of breath.

Green signs promise towns ahead, towns with names like "Silky Perch" and "Lovers' Lull." The mileage traveled, however, these places are revealed to be honeymoon resorts, abandoned in the off-season. At the first Tim, Joey, and I disembark the van and wander about, peering in windows, straining to perceive the words *duck confit* on the unlit room service menu posted outside the office. "Maybe there's an entrance around back," I say, not because I think there is one, but because I wish to convey to Cree my sincere desire for her to eat. She is not fooled, however, and waits in the open vehicle, making the dead-voiced comments "There's nothing here" and "Let's go."

Back in the driver's seat, I sit with my shoulders hunched, my neck tensed. The rebuke is waiting in Cree's mouth; it is only a matter of time before she lets it out. What will it be? "Stop fucking around, Lou"? "Whose idea was it to take this fucking road?" "Why don't you let somebody who knows what they're doing drive?" I can hear all of them with perfect clarity.

Big Sur, twenty miles distant, represents the last hope before Monterey, which, at the present rate, will not be reached until unacceptable midnight. Tim recalls a connection between Big Sur and the Beach Boys and begins to anticipate our arrival. Love comes out of the stereo to make room for *Smiley Smile.* "I think the real thing might be too heavy right now," Tim says, and I agree with him.

At the nineteenth mile we find two resorts nestled in the crook of the same falling hill. Cars pattern the lot of each, and forms move seductively behind pulled blinds. I can feel Cree pushing closer to the edge of her seat. I allow my shoulders to relax to 50 percent tense.

The upslope brings a stand-alone restaurant, the Overlook. A succession of stone-lined terraces culminates with colored fountains and the hint of an enclosure behind them. Cree makes a noise of longing. "I bet it's really awesome," she says, and Joey says, "And really expensive, too."

"Don't worry," I say. "There's something else here. I can feel it."

We pass more romantic getaways, each of diminishing quality and tastefulness. We pass a post office made of logs and a general store. Ahead, the road brims with darkness. We seemed to have reached the end of Big Sur.

"There's nothing else here," I say. "I can feel it."

An argument breaks out between Joey and Cree. Cree wants us to turn around and go back to the Overlook. Furthermore, she thinks the meal should be paid for with band money. Joey counters with the news that we haven't even broken even on the trip. If we go back to the Overlook, he says, he's going to order a bowl of soup and be really pissed to pay nine dollars for it.

"What's the point of being in a band if you can't do anything fun?" Cree says with real feeling.

"What!" Joey shouts. "What are you talking about? Everything we do is fun!"

"Can't we compromise?" Tim says suddenly. "Maybe the band could kick in fifty or sixty bucks. It's true, we never treat ourselves to anything." He seems to have decided not to feel angry with Cree anymore.

Joey looks betrayed but reaches under his seat for his finance folder. "I'll see what we can afford," he says.

A campground appears on the right. There is still the question of tonight's lodging. I swing the van into the lot and ram the curb in my eagerness to park. Cree doesn't comment, already sliding open the door on her way to the office. "You can camp if you want to," the night clerk tells her, "but since you don't have a tent, you might prefer one of our bungalows."

The bungalow is eighty dollars, twice what Joey wants to pay, but circumstances offer him no choice. He asks if we are willing to contribute ten dollars each toward the room, and Cree gives him a look that says that won't be happening. Then Tim pats him on the back and says, "We've gone this far. We might as well go the rest of the way." Joey sighs deeply. "Tonight's meal will be paid for by the band," he announces, "but we should all try to order something light." Tim smiles and Cree claps her hands. Joey continues to look pained. I enjoy watching this democracy unfold, as I can only benefit from the process. Aside from the per diem, I'm not getting paid to do this, and at this point, I feel entitled to one fancy meal and a comfortable bed.

The Overlook, the clerk informs us, doesn't close for another hour and a half, and so we have time to go to our bungalow and make ourselves look nice. Cree sets her hunger aside long enough to hop in the shower, and when she does, Tim breaks out a surprise supply of hash. Looking at the tiny cubes sitting askew on the armrest of his chair, I wonder why we still feel the need to conduct this activity in secret.

"I got it from Gary," Tim says. "I wanted to keep it low-key. It was supposed to be for the ride home, but this is a special occasion."

I can see Tim's mind at work, contriving to make Joey first grateful and then ravenous, knowing that these conditions will loosen the strings of his purse. With no pipe present, we fashion one out of an empty Coke can and some duct tape, using a safety pin to poke the holes. The usual MacGyver joke is made. A window is opened to disperse the accumulated smoke. By the time Cree comes out of the bathroom wet-haired and glistening, we are all very stoned. "Why is it so cold in here?" she asks. "Why are the lights so dim?" Tim responds, "We should get going. We don't know when they stop seating."

The Overlook parking lot is several terraces below the actual restaurant. A black chain separates the walkway from the carefully kept gardens, and Joey leans down to let his hand run over the links. "Excuse me," Tim says, and sprints suddenly up to the fountains. We watch him run from the red to the blue to the green, looking deeply into each, perhaps searching for the source of its color. Cree says, "This is the kind of place you come to with your lover."

"Yeah," Joey says wistfully. I don't say anything.

"But none of us have lovers, do we?" she says.

"Nah," Joey says. He kicks a leaf and it blows up and over my head.

"Yesterday I had one," she says. "And today I don't."

Something lurches in my chest, and I feel completely, coldly sober. Joey tries to kick another leaf and misses, his foot making a loud scuffing sound on the concrete.

"I guess he didn't really love me," she says. "But I guess I didn't really love him either."

We are close to the fountains; pale blue light moves against her hair. "It's just too bad, that's all," she says. She stops and tilts her head toward the sky so that the light now moves over her neck in slow delicate waves. I don't see how it would be possible for her to look more beautiful. I stare at her, hoping to make an imprint of this image, but she steps away to look at the menu. Then Tim walks up nonchalantly and indicates to Joey and me that we might enjoy dipping our hands in the water. I don't, but Joey does. While we are waiting to be seated, he flings droplets from his wrists. "What are you doing?" Cree says.

"My hands are wet but they don't feel wet," Joey says. "They feel like they're covered with a substance."

"Are you high?" she says. "Are all you guys high?"

No one answers, yes or no. Cree says, "Jesus," in a low voice because the maitre'd has arrived. He takes us to a table in the middle of the room, away from the windows and the moonlight vista. A few couples clasp hands at other tables. Champagne tilts in ice beside them. I recognize the music of Gershwin and wonder why I don't own any myself.

The food is ordered, two tenderloins, half a roast turkey, and some french onion soup, Joey's, as promised. As the waiter is about to depart, Joey makes a frantic attempt to split a plate of cheese with someone, anyone, but the rest of us are secure in our selections. "It had better come in a fucking cauldron," he snarls. I picture three hands on a giant ladle, bubbles floating up and popping with atmospheric force. A two-foot slab of Swiss leans against the far wall. "What if it did come in a cauldron?" I say. I describe my vision in detail. Cree normally finds this sort of thing funny, but not tonight. She gets up and goes to look for the bathroom, her second such visit in the last thirty minutes.

"Why is she so adamant that we not be stoned?" I say. "She got stoned the other night, right in front of us! What about Brant and the coke? That seemed to be all right, once she got to know him a little better. Who knows? Maybe they coked it up together!" I realize I have been wanting to say this for days.

"Whoa, hoss," Tim says.

"She's always been like this," Joey says bitterly. "But every now and then she likes to come down off her high horse and have lots of sex and do lots of drugs."

"It's actually a lot of fun when that happens," Tim says. Then he raises his palm and says, "Just kidding, just kidding." He's not kidding, though; he's been there to help her with the dismount, many, many times.

When she comes back from the bathroom we fall into silence.

The menus gone, there is not much to do but straighten the silverware and play with the wax in the candle. I fill my spoon with wax and smooth away the excess so the bowl is transformed into a perfectly flat surface. Cree looks from me to the spoon, expressionless, and I struggle to maintain a neutral countenance of my own. Finally she says, "Lou, that's so mature," but she says it with affection. She has decided that a sweet condescension will handle all of us just fine. At the moment, it seems like the right way to be handled.

The blueness and clearness of the sky the next morning cannot be overstated. "I can see the place where space begins!" Joey says, holding up a hand to block the sun. The air is cool and shorts are discarded in favor of trusty jeans and denim overalls. I tell Cree she looks like she knows how to work the fields, and she smiles at me, not understanding.

The complimentary continental breakfast leaves us famished, and Tim suggests we suppress our appetites with a walk through the forest. Since we will later see the coast from the highway, we opt for an inland trek to a waterfall. The trail is less than half a mile long, but by the time we reach the falls, we are all sweating and out of breath. A pair of fat newlyweds who surged past us on the path now drift around with matching videocameras, filming us as if we are part of the scenery. If the Day Action Band ever conquers the world, those honeymoon flicks will treble in significance.

When we get back, there is fighting between Joey and Cree, this time over who gets to drive. Both front seats are considered prime viewing territory, but Tim has already laid claim to shotgun. As the man who last night guided the van through three hours of unrewarding darkness, I have my own stake in the matter.

"I think it's time to rochambeau," I say, extending my arm.

Joey and Cree don't entirely feel comfortable with this, but they know there is no other hope for resolution. Five seconds later, I drop stone and crush their scissors.

It is beautiful, absolutely beautiful. We drive through a living postcard, the pastures, the cliffs, the beach, and then the water. The sky presides uncontested; no ship comes between it and the horizon. For the first time I am aware of all the dirt and grime on the van's windshield. I crack the window and the compartment fills with an unholy breeze.

At the top of a ridge we stop to admire the view. As we are about to get back in the van, I ask Cree if she would like to drive. "Really?" she says, and when I say yes, she puts her hand on my arm and says, "That's so sweet." Soon we are pulling over again, this time for Joey. Tim offers to give up the passenger seat, but first Cree and then I turn him down, satisfied with what we have seen and what we have done. We sit beside each other in the middle row, and whenever the van rounds a particularly sharp rightward bend, she lets the force of the turn push her body against mine.

JUST SOUTH OF SAN JOSE, the van threatens to run out of gas. Although many businesses line the highway, none of them seems to sell fuel.

"This is really insane," Joey says. "If the band doesn't work out, I'm going to move back here and open a fucking gas station." I can sense that he is composing an angry letter in his mind.

Tim notes that several of the companies are famous for computer manufacture. "So this is Silicone Valley," he says.

"Sili*con* Valley," Cree corrects.

"Ah, that's right," Tim says. "Silicone Valley is what people call L.A." He chuckles like a fool. "If the band doesn't work out, Joey can open a gas station and I'll open a plastic surgery joint. And do you know what I'll call it?"

"I have no idea," Cree says.

"Silicone Valley," Tim says. "Ahhhh." He vibrates his hands in Cree's face and she says, "Yo, man" and pushes them away.

"Finally!" shouts Joey. He points to a towering sign that says DIESEL in the distance. The van does not take diesel, but Joey knows that where there is diesel, there will also be unleaded. He shifts into the right lane and prepares to exit.

In an egregiously offhand tone of voice, Tim says to Cree, "Didn't Ana move to San Francisco recently?"

A paralysis overtakes us all. Joey has left the turn signal on, but no one seems to notice. For a moment the name Ana means nothing to me, and I struggle to remember why it should have such an effect. Then I have it. This is the girl that Tim left Cree for. I am able to picture her standing on the steps of the library, blond, full-thighed, and laughing. She wears a T-shirt that leaves most of her stomach exposed.

"I think that's what I heard," Cree answers finally, her voice unnaturally calm. The terrible silence resumes. I can feel Tim regretting that he asked and Cree regretting that she answered. I can feel Joey divided between righteousness and glee. No one can think of anything to say next.

We pull under the canopy and Tim and Cree volunteer simultaneously to pump the gas. Then they defer simultaneously, so that Cree has to say she would prefer not to get out of the van. When I pass Tim at the pump on the way to the bathroom, he says, "I just fucked up, didn't I?" and I say, "Nah, you're okay. It's all right to mention Ana. Just make sure you don't fuck her."

"I'm not going to," he says. As I walk away he calls after me, "I was never going to."

Tim's aunt comes out of her townhouse to help us back the van into the garage. At least ten years older than Tim's father, she moves with a dignity peculiar to the unmarried and childless. We stand together on the sidewalk, and while she calls out distances and angles of approach to Joey, she extracts from me the most painless biography I have ever given.

The interior of the house is neat and lightly colored, and little bowls of candy are placed on many of the secondary tables. These seem not to be temporary; if they are, then the artifice is complete. I sit on the couch and fill my mouth with red and green M&Ms as Ms. Davis—Ellen—asks the band a number of pointed questions about their status, past, present, and future. Her attitude seems to be one of polite skepticism, and so Tim answers with as much pragmatism as he can muster. While fame and fortune would be nice, he says, his immediate goal is for them to be able to make a reasonable living playing music. "We just want to make what our friends who aren't musicians are making," he says. "You know, twenty-five, thirty thousand a year." He explains that the yearly advance from Sunday Driver is not even that much, that that money is usually gone within six months. "And touring is essentially a nonprofit situation," he says. At this Joey looks at Cree and says, "Sometimes more than others."

Cree appears not to have heard him. She shifts an oval throw rug back and forth on the floor with her bare big toe. She has only spoken once during this conversation, and that was early on, when she said she was looking forward to going home so she could sleep in her own bed again. She smiled after she said this and went back to shifting the rug.

Suppertime is just around the corner, and Ellen says that a good Thai restaurant is too. If we are willing to pick the food up, then she will pay for it. "You probably want to go out and see the town," she says, "but if you feel like having a quiet night in, I belong to the video store next to the restaurant." She will also pay for any videos we rent; evidently the discussion of finances has had some sort of subliminal effect.

After the events of recent weeks, an evening of rentals sounds strange and exotic. Tim speaks reverently of microwave popcorn as we walk through the pedestrian rush hour. Cree says, "Man, I'm psyched. This is gonna be awesome." Her mood has improved radically, and I can only assume it's because Tim seems to have decided to spend the night with us instead of Ana. Joey compares the mass transit system with those of other major cities. I scrutinize every individual we pass for signs of homosexuality.

What happens in the video store is predictable. Cree goes immediately to the independent film section and pulls down one box after another, amassing a stack five deep within a matter of minutes. Joey and I follow Tim to the concert video area and observe as he diligently locates the store's copy of *The Last Waltz*, Martin Scorsese's documentary of the Band's final show.

"I don't know if I can watch that again," Joey says, and I have to sympathize. Though Tim has foisted that film on me half a dozen times during our relationship, for the auxiliary members of the Day Action Band it has been far worse. Both Joey and Cree have told me the stories, about how Tim would repeatedly invite them out to the barn on the pretext of making them dinner, and then, in the peaceful afterglow of the meal, say "Hey, how would you guys feel about *The Last Waltz*?" and slip the tape into the VCR. Often they stayed and watched out of guilt. They knew Tim did it because he wanted *them* to be a band, united in eccentricity against the world. Still, it grew tiresome. Joey was too respectful of the motive to say this outright, but one day Cree let Tim know she found the practice self-indulgent. "All you ever do is act like you have a crush on Rick Danko," she said. "That doesn't make me feel like I'm in a band." Disheartened, Tim resigned himself to watching the movie alone.

Tonight he's hoping for a revival. "Come on," he says. "Remember when he uses those quick cuts to make Garth seem like he's crazy?"

Both Joey and I remember this moment well, and we say so. After being asked to recall several other highlights, we acquiesce to Tim's demand. We join Cree beside the register, where she is shuffling through her stack, deciding which video she wants to bring home. Looking over her shoulder, I see that three of the five films in contention depict the relationship between a young boy and an old woman. Two of the five seem to be road movies, and five of the five feature characters on the cusp of self-discovery.

Thinking of the formless *Waltz*, I urge Cree to pick the one with the most plot. "I hate plot," she says, and chooses the lone young boy–old woman road movie. When she sees our selection she says, "Oh my God. You guys are watching that by yourselves," but part of her seems to find it endearing.

Tim's aunt has set the table with paper plates and plastic forks and chopsticks. The lights are dimmed and chilled mugs await the beer of our preference. Incongruously, the television blares the national news from the otherwise unlit living room. I pull my chair out to sit down and wince as it scrapes over the hardwood floor.

Soon the table is cluttered with the opened white containers of the Far East. Steam floats up as if from a sprawling industrial complex, clouding the surface of the lamp above our heads. I have thought this before, and I think it again: that Asian food is the great chronological equalizer, that initial mechanism by which the old admit they don't want to cook and the young achieve international sophistication. And to think that we have R-rated movies still to watch—now that we have had this dinner, we can ask Ellen to join us.

She demurs, however, citing a backlog of correspondence. "Maybe I'll write your father a letter," she says to Tim, "and make him feel guilty about not writing me back."

"Hey, he's a busy guy," Tim defends, pinching the wire handles of several food cartons and carefully lifting them over to the trash. A clump of rice falls off the bottom of one and dashes itself to bits on a footstool. "He's got two mouths to feed and a roof to keep over his head."

"And a son waiting to join the ranks of the gainfully employed," Ellen finishes with a smile.

"Hey," Tim says. "Are you calling me ungainful?"

Ellen's VCR is not in the living room but in the bedroom that Joey and Cree have already claimed for tonight. There are two twin beds and their future occupants lie lengthwise on each, leaving the narrow backless alley in between for me. The closest to the hi-fi equipment, I am asked to turn on the television, adjust the volume, and get the movie underway.

Cree has actually suggested that we watch *The Last Waltz* first, either because of nostalgia or because she later wants to watch her own film alone. We are already past the FBI warning and the first two previews before Joey wonders aloud where Tim is. He says we might want to pause the movie, and Cree says no way. I say Tim's probably making popcorn and volunteer to retrieve him.

Outside the room, I neither hear the microwave nor smell the artificial butter. All the lights are out except for the one behind the door of Ellen's bedroom. Surely Tim hasn't gone in there. I weave through the house, aware that I am in danger of dislodging a priceless vase or some other Davis family heirloom.

In the far corner of the kitchen, I detect a figure in the shadows. The figure emits a baritone barely above a whisper, and so I know it has to be Tim, talking to a girl that he has either slept with or plans to. When he sees me, he raises a hand. He mutters something lilting into the phone and then hangs up.

"I'm going out," he says. "I'll be back either really late or first thing in the morning. Can you cover for me?"

I'm not sure what it would mean to do that, but I say yes. Then I ask if it's Ana he's going to see.

"Yeah," he says, seeming dismayed by his own weakness. "Look, if Cree asks, don't lie to her. Just try to make it sound okay, okay?"

This is a low-pressure assignment, as it has almost no chance of succeeding. Tim knows that as well as I do; he just doesn't want to have to think about it right now. "Enjoy *The Last Waltz*," he says. "Make sure you tell me what happens." He grabs his rock and roll vest off the back of a chair and heads out the front door, closing it quietly behind him. I linger in the empty kitchen, trying to decide whether or not to make the popcorn myself and thus return to the bedroom partially victorious.

Instead, I slip into the place between the two beds and resume watching as if Tim is about to walk in behind me. It is several minutes before Cree says, "Where's Tim." She says it quickly, giving it an element of suspicion.

"He said he was going out," I say.

"What do you mean, he's going out," Cree says. "We're watching the fucking movie he rented."

"He said he was going out," I repeat. I look at her hoping to engage her sympathy.

"Where was he going, Lou?" she says.

"I think he was going to meet Ana," I say.

Her face blurs and then comes back into focus. She says, "Oh," and looks back over my head to the television. We all stare at the screen, afraid to look elsewhere. The tension in the room gives the movie a more than meaningless quality; the documentary liveliness seems to mock the emotions of real life. Shortly Cree gets up and walks out of the room.

Joey and I have not begun to discuss her reaction when she walks back in.

"I'm really tired," she says. "I think I'm going to go to bed. If you don't mind clearing out . . ." It is not yet ten past eight, but Joey and I depart as if hers is a completely reasonable request. We relocate to the living room and commence the drudgery of Friday night prime-time television. During the first commercial Joey asks me what I think is going on with Cree. "I don't know," I tell him and look away so as to disinvite further questions. But I do know. I know that Brant was nothing more than a substitute, a distraction, and that I was a fool to feel jealous of him. I know that Cree is still in love with Tim and she always has been. I know that she always will be in love with Tim.

Joey retires after the ten o'clock program, and I lie in my sleeping bag on the floor, unable to sleep. This house is full of clocks, imprecisely set, and when one chimes, the others follow in off-time cacophony. Cree is in the room at the end of the long hall, and I become certain that she is awake as I am. I begin to feel that if I went to her and knelt beside her bed, I would be given the words that would free her from Tim's heart and bring her closer to mine. If only I could know them beforehand. I concentrate, but my mind only produces absurdity, and when the clocks finally stagger two, I do not hear them for they have become something else, an unessential part of an unessential dream.

I am the last to get up. I smell the coffee and pick out four distinct voices coming from the kitchen. The remnants of halfhearted bedding drape over the side of the couch; Tim must have made it back before dawn.

Continuing with the theme begun last night, Ellen has planned to take us out for dim sum. As there is only one bathroom, the preparatory showering and dressing stretches for over an hour, and I have time to read the newspaper in its entirety. I am folding the sections back together when Cree sits down next to me. She asks to see the arts section and opens it up to the movie listings.

"How are you doing?" I ask. The question sounded much less poignant when it was still in my mind.

"I'm fine," she says. She turns a giant page in frustration and moves closer to it, peering.

"Did you sleep all right?" I say. This contains a hidden intensity as well.

"I slept fine," she says.

"I didn't," I say. I stand up and step away from the table, aware that I am only a few phrases from revealing the cause of my insomnia. Cree seems not to notice; letting go the sides of the paper, she presses with her finger, a triumphant underlining. Her indifference suddenly infuriates me.

"Aren't you going to ask why?" I say.

"Why what?" she says. She looks up at me but keeps her finger in place on the paper.

"Why I didn't sleep well," I say.

"Why didn't you sleep well?" she says.

"I don't know," I say. "It must have been something I ate."

Without waiting for her reaction I turn and walk out of the room to join Tim and Joey, who are getting ready to leave in the hall. When she comes in thirty seconds later her only distinctive act is to stand so that my body is between hers and Tim's. She does not behave as though I ever said anything strange.

Both on the way to and during brunch, Tim and Cree talk a great deal, but not to each other. The eye contact that is made has been predetermined by quota. This Ana incident, given the public status of their relationship, should be no big deal. But it is. Ellen conspicuously does not interrogate Tim about his evening out; she either senses Cree's discontent or possesses the soul of a discreet puritan. The food provides some distraction. Weird soups, opaque dumplings concealing blue matter—once, a misdelivered plate of duck feet—I observe more than I eat. On the way home, Cree starts talking about why she prefers Los Angeles to San Francisco.

"San Francisco is fine. It's fine," she says. "It's a city. The people do what they do, there are buildings, there's a downtown, there are stores. It's a city. Okay? But an interesting person is going to live in L.A."

On Ellen's behalf I find this immediately offensive. "We haven't really seen that much of San Francisco," I say.

"It's not something that you see," Cree says. "It's more like a feeling you get. In L.A., there's a connection. It's the movies and Hollywood but it's something else. Everyone you meet is going to be interesting, even if you can't tell right away."

"I don't really see how you can say that," I say. Ellen drives on, feigning unawareness.

"I just know," Cree says. "If I ever live in California, it's going to be in L.A. It's cooler. It just is. I can't explain it. If you spent some more time here, you would know."

Raising my finger to her lips, I ask, "Are you talking out of your *mouth*?"

It is the ultimate rhetorical question. Tim explodes in laughter. Joey says, "Ha, ha, someone just got burned." Ellen maintains a silence, but there has to be a smile on her face. Cree does not even bother to respond. She crosses her arms against her chest and looks low out the front window. Tim asks if I invented that particular phrase and gesture combination. Joey says, "That was awesome." With seven words, I seem to have banished Cree from the car. There was a time when I would have felt sorry to have done this, but now all I feel is triumph.

On this afternoon before the final show we fragment. Tim does not attempt to rally the group for one last band activity; his business lies elsewhere, at Ana's probably, although he doesn't say for sure. He takes the van and promises to meet us at the Candelabra at seven-thirty. Cree, mute but self-assured, leaves Ellen's house on foot, bound for the cinema. It's a nice day, and Joey and I decide to walk down to Golden Gate Park to kick the hackey sack around. As two young bachelors in the gayest city in America, it seems almost expected of us.

The hacking takes place near second base of a deserted softball field. Our feet bring up a mist of cool dust. The final hack consists of twenty-seven consecutive touches, and, after, we talk about how much I've improved since the tour began. We move next to a mall filled with barren twisting trees. "Voguing vegetation," Joey says, as we trespass this discotheque.

At the corner of the park Joey points out a crowd of ragged loitering teenagers. He suspects they hail from the suburbs, come cityward for a new kind of companionship. It seems they have found it; most are paired off into couples, body on body, piercing on piercing. A girl tugs on the leg of my blue jeans as I pass by and asks if I have any money for ice cream. "Do you know who I am?" I say to her. "Do you have any idea who I am?" She shrinks back into the arms of her leather-capped boyfriend.

Inspired by the suggestion, we do stop for ice cream. As we wait in line, I notice that we are at the intersection of Haight and

Ashbury Streets. I think briefly of Sly, but beyond that there is nothing. The power conferred on this place has overlooked me. Others of my general age and younger pretend to feel it, but they are only testing the fringes of their own capacities for wonder.

On the way back we stop in a head shop. After years of smoking weed, Joey has decided it's time to buy some paraphernalia of his own. He chooses a pipe with a transparent chamber, so he can see his pot and think about how it resinates further with every puff he takes. The saleswoman asks him several times to please try to say "tobacco." When he is ready to make his purchase she looks at him again and says, "I recognize you." After a moment she remembers from where, a show in Kansas City when the Day Action Band opened up for some of her friends. "I'm not in touch with them anymore," she says. "But you guys were great." She tells Joey that he is free to say the word "pot" in her store whenever he feels like it. "And your friend can say it too." We each say it several times to show her that we are grateful. She has to work tonight and will be unable to make it to the show but promises to buy *You Think You Hear* the day it comes out. When we leave the store there is a glow to Joey that wasn't there before; it comes, no doubt, from the simple joy of making someone else's day.

The trolley lets us off less than two blocks from the Candelabra. This proximity is fortunate, as the street ahead of us narrows sharply up a steep hill. The flanking streets do the same, and I imagine they all converge upon some roundabout, a Maypole whirling colored flags at its center.

Women are not necessary here. Bands of men roam the sidewalks, armed with primitive weapons, slingshots, clubs, and crudely fashioned metalware. Actually this is not the case, but I do wonder if this society has more in common with the prehistoric than the one that prevails.

Tonight's lineup is written on a chalkboard outside the club: the Guido Snatchers, Just Try Harder, Crown Vic, Timekiller, and the Day Action Band. "Fuck!" Joey says. "We weren't supposed to headline!" The show begins at nine-thirty; Joey calculates that he, Tim, and Cree might not take the stage until well after one.

We find Cree inside, sitting at the bar drinking an iceless glass of water. The room is less than fifty feet deep and no more than twenty wide. The soundboard is a pitiful affair, a small box mounted on a plank next to the cash register. I look underneath for the compressor and reverb unit, but there are none to be seen. The soundman, a skinny lad too young for college, spiders about the stage, bending mic stands and re-angling the lone monitor. As there are no instruments yet in place, I assume that he starts from a generic setup and makes adjustments as needed.

A few minutes later Tim wanders in. "Let's unload," he says. His bearing is unapologetic, creating the impression that he has something to apologize for. Outside, he wraps his arms around Joey's bass amp, and I notice he is wearing the rock vest again. Ana must have told him he looked cute in it. Cree notices too; receiving the snare at the back of the van, she pauses to let her eyes follow him all the way into the club.

We are instructed to bring the gear to the basement. A spiral staircase leads down to a pentagon-shaped room mostly occupied by stacked chairs and barstools. A Ping-Pong table with a drooping net is at the center, enticing, although the accumulated amplifiers and percussives would seem to limit the mobility of one of the players. Cree balances the snare on its rim and goes to the table, toying with the net, pulling it taut, and then releasing it to see if it will hold. She has challenged Joey to a match, offering to play the short side, when the club manager comes down to talk about how the show has changed since it was first scheduled.

It has become a benefit, to raise money for an uninsured scenester who broke her jaw in a motorcycle accident. The four other bands, all local, have forgone any fee. The manager does not expect the Day Action Band to do the same; he just wants them to know that tonight will be a night of community and spirit and giving and to play accordingly. The implication, subtly tendered, is that they will be regarded as outsiders, indifferent to the tragedy and perhaps even slightly opportunistic.

When he is gone, Tim says, "Why the fuck did we even bother coming here?"

"So you could get laid?" Cree says. Her mouth stays open after she says this. Her eyes look directly at a dartboard about two feet to Tim's left.

Tim starts to say "That's not fair," but, thinking better of it, cuts himself off with a wave of his hand, and turns and runs up the stairs. It occurs to me that he may be going to intercept Ana to tell her to go home. Cree says to Joey, "Let's play," and takes her stance as if the preceding turmoil were manufactured only to put her in the right competitive mood.

The three of us stay in the basement for nearly four hours, only going upstairs for free beer and to use the decrepit unisex john. There is no soundcheck. The other bands intrude periodically to say hello and shuffle their equipment to or from the stage. They don't linger, though; they are here to support their injured friend, as several of them remind us in tones that verge on the righteous. Coming back from the restroom, Joey reports that the friend is in attendance, swathed in bandages, constricted by wires, and encircled with bottles of beer that cannot be safely drunk. He also reports that he has seen Tim, sitting alone at a table by the door. "He looks really unhappy," Joey says, and Cree says, "Good."

It is hard to say if she truly means this, however, for her temperament has been altered considerably by all the Ping-Pong she has played since Tim left. Until recently, Joey and I had taken turns being her victim, losing games in which our only points came on balls she hit long or into the net. After one such contest,

Joey sat down and said, "That's it, my self-esteem can't take any more," to which Cree actually responded, "You can never stop learning how to lose."

I play on, not, as I first thought, because I am intimidated, but because I am slowly being consumed by the desire to beat her. I am bothered less by the taunting than by the self-satisfaction. "You're good at Ping-Pong," I want to say. "So what?" But in this universe she has created, Ping-Pong is of paramount importance. If I want to earn her respect, I must improve my game.

When Crown Vic goes on, Joey goes upstairs to watch. Then Cree and I are alone in the basement, standing facing each other fifteen feet apart. Her body moves with compact certainty; her hair whirls around her face. After she wins a point she wipes her brow and breathes deeply, hands resting on her sides, most of her weight on one hip. Recovered, she steps back and serves again. Our eyes meet many times and there is more intensity in them than there has ever been. But all that grows between us is anger.

As midnight approaches, I am beginning to learn her game. I forget about my own backspin and concentrate on predicting hers. I let her put me away with violent slams, thinking, zen-like, that a point is just a point, no matter how it's won. My poise injects doubt into her glee and her mistakes begin to multiply. The scores get closer. Joey returns and stands beside my half of the table, saying things like "You've got her" and "Take the bitch down." I am leading the latest game 19–15 when Tim, making a dramatic reappearance, interrupts to say that Timekiller never showed up.

"We've got to go on," he says, "and we've got to play a long set."

"Fuck!" Joey says. "What happened to supporting their friend?"

"The manager said they were junkies," Tim says. He shrugs. "He could have been lying."

Cree has stepped away from the table and wordlessly begins to pull equipment into her arms.

"You're a very lucky young lady," I say to her, and she gives me a look that tells me we are no longer in the universe of Ping-Pong. My right to gloat withdrawn, I grab the tom in one hand and the high-hat in the other and follow her up the stairs.

The audience is dense and lively but not expectant. Even as the Day Action Band makes its final onstage preparations, people are turned around in conversation or struggling toward the bar. The bandaged girl slouches in a cushioned chair at the back of the room, either in need of more painkillers or incapacitated by them. What I can see of her face tells me she wishes the night were over.

Tim begins the set by making a brief speech in her honor. In substance it doesn't amount to much more than "get well soon," but the delivery is sincere enough that it provokes the crowd into all kinds of noise. "Lottery" lurches into being with suitable energy behind it. When Joey and Cree are about to sing their "na na na's," Tim slings his guitar over his shoulder by the strap and catches it in time to hit the next chord. The move is perfect; the bandmates smile in amazement, the audience bellows, and I marvel that the old chemistry remains untouched.

The call to an encore cannot be resisted. They play a stirring "These Dreams" and even whip out "Be My Little Baby" at the request of the bartender. After, Cree answers the catcalls with a tired "Thank you very much" and "You've been great," but Tim still wants to play. He begins to medley, something that I haven't seen him do since their earliest days. He jumps from "Let's Go Crazy" to "Tainted Love," from "867–5309" to "Just What I Needed," pausing to explain just why Prince gave "Manic Monday" to the Bangles. Wisely, he keeps it all in the

same key, but Joey doesn't hear that, wincing and frowning in
search of the right notes. Cree, a more natural musician, manages to stay on the beat but begins to look annoyed every time
Tim demands a new tempo. In the middle of an abbreviated
"My Sharona," she stands suddenly, sets down her sticks, and
walks off the stage.

To everyone else in the audience, the move seems scripted,
I'm sure. The cheers double in volume and deepen in pitch. Tim
himself barely acknowledges her departure, looking back out of
the corner of his eye as he sings a round of "my my my whoo!"
This could be interpreted as suaveness and probably is by most.
Joey's demeanor does undergo a shift, but as it is a shift in con-
sternation, no one notices but me. Half a minute later, Tim brings
the escapade to a tumultuous rock-and-roll halt. Joey twangs the
final note and wipes his brow in unmistakable relief. They lean
their guitars against their amps and step off to the side, just as
Cree did moments before.

The equipment stays on stage, as it will be loaded out later, when
the club is empty. There are still fifteen minutes until last call
and I have to push through the undispersed to reach the basement
door. I bound down the stairs and the soles of my feet clap hard
on the uneven planks. When I reach the bottom I know immediately that something is wrong.

I have entered Joey and Cree's field of vision, but they don't
look at me, focused on Tim as if locked into a tractor beam. The
space between the three of them seems to have acquired a physical presence, and I instinctively reach for the railing to prevent
myself from tumbling into it.

"Don't leave me like that," Tim is saying. His voice is high
and shaking and on the verge of crying. For a horrible second I
have to work to suppress an outburst of laughter. "Don't leave me
up there, please."

"Don't you fucking switch songs without telling us!" Cree shouts.

"I thought you liked it when we did that," Tim says. He seems heartbrokenly disappointed. "I thought that was okay."

"I don't know what fucking song you're going to play next," she says. "I don't know when you're going to fucking switch. It's one-thirty in the fucking morning, Tim. I don't want to jam." She says this last with a mixture of pain and scorn.

"You have to trust me," Tim says. "I'm never going to make you look stupid up there." His voice catches and the light shows moisture on his cheeks. "I'm always going to support you. I'm always going to be there for you."

"That's fucking bullshit," Cree says. Now she is looking at me but not seeing me. She looks back at Tim.

"When have I not been there for you?" Tim says. He tries to gesture conversationally but only ends up wringing his hand around. "I try so hard to make this special. I try to make it something that we all look forward to. I never want it to be a burden. I just want us to be three people who like to play music together, that's all."

"It's not about that!" Cree screams. She is crying now too. "It's not about that! Don't you fucking get it?"

"What don't I get?" Tim says, his voice soft. "What don't I get? Just tell me, please."

In that moment I lose a little respect for him.

Cree is shaking her head and looking at the floor in front of her. Tim doesn't take his eyes off her face. Joey, who had been standing withdrawn a few feet to the side, now steps forward, one hand weakly outstretched. "Sometimes," he says to Tim, "when you change songs so quickly, sometimes it's hard for me to keep up."

Tim says, "Why don't you fucking practice your instrument then?" His eyes return to Cree's face.

"Look," Joey says, louder, "I'm trying to tell—"

"YOU'RE TRYING TO TELL ME WHAT!" Tim screams. He grabs Joey by both shoulders and pushes as hard as he can. Joey crumples backwards, one skinny leg kicking up in imbalance. He lands in the middle of the Crown Vic drum kit and the cymbals crash around him.

Cree says, "Oh my God" and puts her hand over her mouth and runs up the stairs. Tim, momentarily frozen in the act of pushing, reaches toward Joey and says, "Let me help you." Joey waves him off. "Don't, don't," he says. Tim says, "Okay, forget it then. Just forget the whole fucking thing. Just forget about everything." There is a light wind as he passes me on the way to the staircase.

Joey picks himself up and attempts to reassemble the drum kit. He does so with only one hand; the other he clutches against his rock shirt. I can see a dark patch spreading on the thin material. "You should get someone to look at that," I say, and he says, "No, it'll be all right." He looks at me with reddened eyes. "I need to take a walk," he says. Then he leaves too, and I am alone in the basement.

They are not upstairs. I stand for a gratuitously long time outside the bathroom, wondering if a reconciliation is taking place inside. The manager sees me and says, "They ran out of here about ten minutes ago. First the girl and then other two. Something happen down there?"

I tell him no. I step out the door and push it shut behind me. The noise reduces to a hum, felt rather than heard. This is not an otherwise commercial section of town, and the sidewalks are empty in both directions. I walk down to the van, now parked between two other vans. The one behind is so close we won't be able to open the back doors to load the equipment.

I knock. No one answers. I key open the passenger door and swing my legs inside, prepared to sit for hours if need be. Without thinking, I start to murmur the chorus to "Outside Tokyo." In her normal speaking voice, Cree says, "I'm here."

I turn around and she says, "I'm sorry I didn't answer, I thought you were Tim." She is sitting in the back row, almost invisible in the dark, a shadow with a pillow pulled against her chest. From her breathing I can tell that she has halted the crying, although it has taken some effort. I move to the middle row and, surprising myself, reach out to touch her arm near the shoulder. It seems to soothe her.

"He's not even a person," she says. "He doesn't even know what it's like to be one. How can you make someone like that understand?"

"I don't know," I say. Out on the street an enormous rattling truck lumbers by, and she waits for it to be quiet before she speaks again.

"I can't do this anymore," she says. She leans into my hand and sighs with her whole body. "I can't do this anymore. Otherwise it's going to be my whole life. I don't want it to be."

I don't say any of the things I could. Instead I lean over the seat, and I kiss her. She raises her arms and puts them around my neck and kisses me back.

We are not interrupted for some time, fifteen minutes, twenty minutes, half an hour. I don't know how long. All I do know is that the world has changed into something I never thought it could be. It is one thing to hear but it is everything to feel, her mouth, her breasts, her hands on my back, my shoulders, my legs. . . . Then I say her name and she pulls away, her eyes closed, and I know with terrible certainty that she has decided this was a mistake. I try to prepare an apology even though my heart is beating so fast I can barely think.

But when she opens her eyes she takes my face in her hands and smiles in a way that I have never seen her smile before. I realize that this, more than anything, is what I have always wanted from her. There is such innocence, such a desire to be loved. She kisses me again, and I think, over and over, "This is joy" and with every cell in my brain command myself to remember how it feels.

Instead of passing and then receding as others have before, these footsteps stop outside the van. Keys come jangling from the pocket, and I say in a loud voice, "We're in here." We move to opposite ends of the backseat. The door slides open and Joey's face enters. Cree says, "It's just us."

Joey looks startled but acts as though he has not interrupted anything. He reports that Tim will not be riding home in the van. "He said he wants to walk around for a while. He said he wants to think about what to do next."

When Cree does not respond, Joey says, "I think this might be it." I move past him to the driver's seat and put the key in the ignition. The future of the band now seems unimportant to me, as does the future in general. What is it but a vague concept clung to by people helpless in the present? The future is determined by decisions, not vice versa. It is an afterthought and nothing more.

I get us lost, deeply, deeply lost. Traffic lights govern the intersections of five, six, seven streets, but my turns are bold and my accelerations firm. I take us past row houses with tiny gardens, past chain-linked basketball courts, past supermarkets with multiple stories. I take us through the financial district at forty-five miles per hour, disrupting the peace of the nightly holocaust. I take us up an endless hill with a slanted sidewalk and I can feel the bay yawning at my back.

Much later, when we are standing in Ellen's foyer, Joey remembers that we forgot to load out the equipment. He runs to the living room to make the call, and I step close to Cree and kiss her again. She kisses back, but distractedly. When the receiver is heard to meet the cradle, she whispers, "There's something I have to do." She rummages in the kitchen for a phone book and then, carrying it, passes Joey coming out of the living room. "Who is she calling?" he says, and we listen until we hear her say, "I need to fly from San Francisco to Philadelphia tomorrow. Is that going to be really expensive?"

Joey says he has made arrangements to meet someone at the club in the morning. He has been assured the gear will be kept safe. While he talks about these things, Cree goes on making flight reservations in the background. Joey does not comment on this betrayal, perhaps because there is nothing left for Cree to betray. I look down at his damaged hand and see that he has wrapped it crudely in a brown paper towel. He says, "I'm going to bed," and shuts the door to his room behind him. Almost immediately the light goes out.

I go into the living room and sit on the couch while Cree completes the airline transaction. She repeats a six character series of letters and numbers back into the telephone. When she is finished, she stands and says, "I'm so tired. I'll talk to you in the morning." She bends and kisses me lightly on the lips and then follows Joey into the darkened bedroom.

I know I won't be able to fall asleep tonight. I think about Cree and I sweat in my sleeping bag. I listen to all the sounds. After an hour someone gets up to go to the bathroom, and I lie there, not able to breathe, wondering who it is. The water shuts off and the person coughs and I realize it is only Joey.

Just after five Tim comes home. He does not bother to be quiet climbing the stairs. He goes straight into Joey and Cree's bedroom and wakes them up. One of them turns on a bedside lamp and they begin to talk. At first it is mostly Tim, but then the other two join him. I can't hear their exact words, but I can hear their voices and the passions that quietly dwell within each. The longer they talk, the calmer the voices become. I know they are making up.

By this time it is beginning to be light out. I place a call to

New York City. Kaitlyn answers, neither dead nor surprised to be thought so. "I need to see you," I say to her, and she says, "When you get back. Come see me as soon as you get back." I tell her I will because it seems like all there is left to do.

THE NEXT MORNING TIM took Cree to the airport while Joey and I went back to the club to retrieve the equipment. When Cree said goodbye to me she told me that I had been a good roadie and that I ought to consider coming on the next tour. There was nothing in her behavior to indicate that we had ever kissed. Later, Tim, Joey, and I had a nice lunch with Tim's aunt. We spent an hour at a nearby gas station while the van's front left turn signal was repaired.

That night we drove well into Wyoming. We had planned to stop at a motel on the eastern side of Salt Lake City, but there were none to be stopped at. We went up into the mountains instead, and I will always remember the places of blue and shadow where the mountains ended and the darkness began.

The next night we made it to Omaha and the next to Youngstown, Ohio. We ate in many countrified restaurants and truck stops. At Toby's in Rock Springs Tim left the table to make a succession of phone calls, and I wondered if one of them was to Cree. I called Kaitlyn several times myself, but each time she wasn't home.

There was much hilarity on this drive. I so consistently out-rochambeau'd Joey that he abandoned the technique in favor of taking turns. Tim ate all the remaining pot in the van when we were pulled over for speeding in Illinois and then attempted to regurgitate a joint or two with some seriousness. When we felt like we might fall asleep, we listened to *Exile on Main Street* and the greater hits of Bobby Bland. We lamented our ignorance of reggae and vowed to soon correct it.

It was early evening when we pulled up in front of my apartment complex in Newark. I distributed my various bags around my shoulders and got out of the van. "Thanks for coming along," Tim said, his hand ready to slide shut the door. I told him I would give him a call in a couple of days. As they drove away I could see Joey waving frantically from the front seat, sorry that he had forgotten to thank me too.

Among the messages on my answering machine was this one: "Hey, Lou. My name is Daryl. I got your note. If you're calling about the car, it's not for sale. If you want to give me a call, that's fine, but I'm not going to sell it." He left his number but I didn't write it down. There was also a message from Kaitlyn that seemed to confirm her interest in me and my upcoming visit.

I have a college degree, and a hometown I can go back to. I have parents, a brother, and an ex-girlfriend who may want me back. I have three friends who might become deservedly famous. The one thing I don't have is an answer to this question: What more could a person want for their life?